Praise for ***The Lyme Regis M***

"Dead bodies, suffering childı
everyone hiding skeletons in their cupboards; it's a heady mix and leads to an appropriately tortuous investigation. A 'multi-lingual English, Spanish and French-speaking Politics Philosophy and Economics, Oxford graduate with a postgrad MBA, and more than just a smattering of Hebrew' is hired to investigate, but she has other cases to work on, and an unravelling plait of relationships to distract her. Still, she's good at her job, whether that be self-defense or rescuing secret missions. The mystery grows ever deeper as the story progresses, its threads, like its relationships, staying stubbornly apart until the ending. An interesting mystery, blending dramatic characters, complex background stories, convoluted action-adventure, and a pleasing sense of time and place, *The Lyme Regis Murders* is not cozy or sweet, but it's the sort of read that becomes hard to put down because you want to see the ending."

— Sheila Deeth, US reviewer

"I liked the in depth descriptors of characters, places and attention to detail. This book will please those who enjoy language as it's first rate. Damn good read."

— Gail Pearson, UK reviewer

"*The Lyme Regis Murders* was a really great read. A riveting murder mystery with a modern feel. It was fast paced with lots of twists and turns even to the end. The author is a superb writer and I shall be buying more of his books."

— Mrs. H. Bate, UK reviewer

"I thought this was a great read. Found the book very addictive and kept me on the edge of my seat in every chapter. Very well written and would highly recommend."

— Richard W. Knight, UK reviewer

"Read this book! This book is fantastic. Great character development - lots of twists and turns - a Page turner!"

— Kelly, UK reviewer

"Great read! I thoroughly enjoyed the book. I would definitely recommend and have already bought his next book *The Black Candle Killings*.

— J. Walsh, UK reviewer

Praise for ***The Black Candle Killings***:

"Spooky goings on in this fun detective series. Great pace and tension. Well done!"

— Anonymous, US reviewer

"Great P.I. character! First book I've read by Andrew Segal. It was obvious from the first page that I've been missing out."

— Our Town Books, US reviewer

"Great read, thoroughly recommend! What a great second novel in this series. We reconnect with feisty private detective Tammy Pierre in a very original, dark and intricate plot interwoven with suspense and voodoo. Spanning London, the Caribbean and even the violent streets of Aleppo, this clever, fast paced novel with intriguing characters is tied together with richly embroidered detail. I thoroughly enjoyed it. Can't wait to read the third in the series, *The Politician's Wife*."

— RT, UK reviewer

"Really had me hooked from beginning to end."

— Vera Barber, UK reviewer

"Intriguing from the outset, one feels ensconced in the mystery. Highly recommended to all murder mystery fans."

— Darren H., UK reviewer

Praise for ***The Politician's Wife***:

"What a book! If you like James Bond and Sherlock Holmes, you must read this. 'Unputdownable' entertainment that tickles the intellect, too. Beautifully dark characters and surprise plot twists, all thoroughly grounded in a knowledge of the inner workings of politics and underlife. Andrew Segal is a master storyteller – in real life and on paper! When is the movie coming out? And the next book please!"

– Zsuzsanna Pataki, artist, uni lecturer,
choosy thriller addict and Segal fan

"*The Politician's Wife* is a real page-turner and the twist at the end was really unexpected. It was an intriguing tale and well plotted; I became invested in the characters and what was driving them. I don't normally read crime fiction but Tammy Pierre is a credible hero and I am keen to follow her further Runyonesque escapades and Jilly Cooper had best look to her laurels if she wants to stay ahead of the game."

– Lynne Brooke (Mr), Solicitor,
The Brooke Law Group LLP

"Another chapter in the Tammy Pierre saga. Always intriguing, involving, and hard to put down. Can't wait for the next one. Gives Richard Osman a run for his money!!!

– Charles Shiplee, avid Crime Thriller reader

"I have read most of Andrew Segal's books and I have very much enjoyed them all. Once I started reading *The Politician's Wife*, I found it hard to put down. I have no idea where Andrew gets his ideas from, but they make an intriguing story with fascinating characters and twists that you're not expecting. I'm definitely a fan and would suggest that if you like a captivating plot, you should read his books."

– Mike Wylie, Trustee, MidasPlus

"Gripping latest edition to the Tammy Pierre series. I was immediately sucked in by the complex female protagonist and found myself flying through the pages, eager to learn how this 'who-dun-it' tale would unfold."

— Shana Sexton, Luxury Travel Consultant

"Andrew Segal's *The Politician's Wife* is a masterclass in weaving intrigue, emotion, and raw human experience. Every page pulls you deeper into the intricate lives of its characters and leaves you both pondering and eagerly turning to the next chapter. A truly gripping read that resonates long after the final page is turned."

— Kenneth Kufeji, B.Sc. Computer Science & Accounting; MBA

"A gripping, witty tale that kept me on the edge of my seat throughout. Interesting and challenging — indeed at times disturbing — the characters are fascinating. Particularly Andrew Segal's heroine, Tammy, is brought to life, as are all the characters that interact to deliver an exciting plot. Takes the reader on a journey through the complexity of extremism, relationships, and human emotions — with a number of surprises along the way. A great read!"

— Jasper de Q Adams, Retired Army Officer / Security Consultant

THE LYME REGIS MURDERS

Author's Edition

ANDREW SEGAL

Chagal
Publishing Ltd

ISBN: 978-1-917626-02-6 (paperback)
978-1-917626-03-3 (ebook)

This ***Author's Edition*** published in 2025
by Chagal Publishing, Ltd.

First Published in 2019 by Happy London Press

Cover design: Mike Dewey
Interior layout & design: Tom Collins

This is a work of fiction. Names, characters, businesses, places, events, locales, and incidents are either the products of the author's imagination or used in a fictitious manner. Any resemblance to actual persons, living or dead, or actual events is purely coincidental.

THE TAMMY PIERRE SERIES

Book One: ***The Lyme Regis Murders***
Author's Edition - Spring 2025

Book Two: ***The Black Candle Killings***
Author's Edition (coming in Summer 2025)

Book Three: ***The Politician's Wife***
January 2025

Book Four: ***The Clubhouse Slaughters***
(coming in Fall 2025)

DEDICATION

For my Best Beloved
Roberta

Senior medic's observation:
"There will never be another like her."

THE LYME REGIS MURDERS

Three little piggies going to market each,
Changed their minds, went down to the beach.
A lumpen rock then cracked each head,
And, left the three of them, all stone dead.

R.A.

PROLOGUE

THE SHORELINE WAS DESERTED apart from the four individuals cavorting close to the water's edge.

A single gull wheeled overhead screaming out what might have been a warning, had anyone understood, or been prepared to listen. Offshore the swell rose and fell ominously, a restless movement like the bulk of a heaving whale, as it too whispered a plea for mercy.

Set back from the beach, high above it and unsighted, the town went about its usual Saturday morning routine. Barely audible, the muted hum of lazy traffic, a car horn, the trill of a bicycle bell.

Lyme Regis, an English coastal town, where nothing untoward ever happened to disturb the peaceful existence of its residents.

Close to the salt waves came the sound of laughter, a sense of abandonment in the air. A game of tag? A race? They appeared totally absorbed in themselves and their random pastime. How could they know what was about to follow? Which one of them would fall victim?

The wind now whipped up the spume fanning the shore with spray before the plane of seawater receded in a hissing rush.

Mid-morning humidity, high white clouds like shredded lace, gradually dissipating, and the promise of a hot day ahead. But the weather was ever unpredictable. As was life. As was death.

The boulder was large, but not so large it couldn't be palmed, and when it swiftly descended the sound it made on impact was like the cracking of a nut. Except that this was no nut being smashed, but the cranium of one of the four.

An arbitrary choice? Three survived. But only for the barest instant.

A moment later, the stone struck again.

And then once more.

The screams had been muffled by the speed of the assault and the crash of the waves.

Now three lay dead, their crushed skulls oozing grey matter and pulsing blood which quickly spread, staining the shingle red.

Overhead, the gull shrieked its message a final time, swooping low as if to survey the carnage before swiftly wheeling away, climbing toward the morning sun.

Barely pausing to admire the handiwork, the fourth calmly sauntered away, a look of peace on the individual's face. Job done. Overdue. Long overdue.

CHAPTER 1 DAY 1

LATE SUMMER, a sultry, shimmering afternoon, the sun's blaze casting a lucid sheen over everything it touched, burnishing surfaces, scorching lawns, searing exposed flesh. A peaceful Saturday, when lovers walked the parks and families downed iced drinks, or perhaps tea and cakes in back gardens. When small children hooted and screamed as they got up to all varieties of mischief.

A cyclist's bell tinkled rousing a tortoiseshell cat that chased across the front lawn. A flock of Canada geese soared overhead in a wide-ranging V-formation, swerving off in a sudden unexpected change of direction. A bee hummed nearby the front door. Beds of phlox and goldenrod swayed in the gentle breeze.

It was a time of stillness and tranquillity.

The woman's howl was like that of a wounded animal. Something feline. A high keening scream, which turned into a raw cry of rage as she pummelled the female officer at her door on the chest.

"NOOOOOOO! NOOOOOOO! Not my babies. It can't be. Please no, it can't be," she sobbed. "They're someone else's children. They're not mine. They can't be mine."

In her middle thirties, the woman appeared as fragile as if she might break apart in a light gust. As if the news just imparted would shred her like tissue paper. Petite and trim as a ballet dancer, with wavy shoulder-length mid-brown hair, full rouged lips and retroussé nose, she had the sort of gamine good looks that seemed to cry out for the protection of someone bigger than she, someone physically stronger.

"Shall we sit down Mrs Goldcrest?" The uniformed officer, an older woman, tall and deploying a fair expanse of flesh, together with a budding moustache on her upper lip, led the smaller woman by the arm into the house.

Eleanor Goldcrest let herself be helped indoors where she sat at the black marble kitchen bar holding her head in her hands, weeping uncontrollably. Detective Inspector Margaret Copeland, accompanied by Detective Sergeant Susan Trevelyan, stood by saying nothing until Mrs Goldcrest's crying began to abate.

For all of their experience in handling these sorts of situations, the two women looked ill at ease. They kept glancing at each other as though one of them should say something. But not knowing what to say they both remained silent.

The house was a modern five-bed, redbrick detached, with a one hundred and fifty-foot garden, integral double garage and carriage drive. Situated in Pine Ridge, on the outskirts of Lyme Regis, it boasted glorious views of the surrounding countryside.

"Was it all three?" the young woman whispered. "Tell me it wasn't all three."

"I am so very sorry, Mrs Goldcrest."

"All dead?"

Copeland nodded, but said nothing. The DI regarded the younger woman, observed the agony of her twisted features, the wringing of her hands, and wished there were some way she could make things different, make them easier, make it all disappear. "I'm afraid so, Mrs Goldcrest," she put in again, uselessly. And once more, as though it might make a difference, "I am so very sorry."

Eleanor Goldcrest howled again, banged her bunched fists on the surface of the breakfast bar, making crockery jump, then rubbed her eyes savagely so that mascara ran down her face transforming the pretty features into those of a spectral clown.

"Mrs Goldcrest," Copeland enquired softly, "do you have a doctor you can call? I think you should have some kind of support here."

Eleanor Goldcrest stared away at nothing, her eyes half closed, mucus dribbling down her cheeks and chin.

"I think we need to call someone. Sergeant, call Doctor Jackson. Explain the situation. Mrs Goldcrest is going to need to be supervised and probably sedated." She turned once again to Eleanor Goldcrest. "Mrs Goldcrest, is your husband here?"

Eleanor shrugged but didn't reply.

"Do you know where he is?"

The young woman reached for a tissue from the box on the counter and, pulling it free, blew her nose. Extracting another, she started wiping her face and trying to dry her eyes before she was overcome by another flood of tears. "How do you know?"

"I beg your pardon?" The DI looked puzzled.

"How do you know it was them?" she murmured. "How can you be sure it was my babies?"

"They were discovered on the beach by your newsagent, Mr Patel. He was walking his dog when he came across the bodies. He informed us and gave us your address. He recognised the girls right away by what they were wearing. The triplets. It has to be them."

"I can't believe it. I can't believe they've gone. And recognised by their clothes? Their clothes? What the hell does that mean? Didn't he recognise their faces? God in heaven!"

She paused and turned her wrecked face to the DI. "What do I mean, God? There is no God, is there? No God could let this happen...how did it happen? They drowned, did they? They fell from the cliffs?"

"I'm afraid there is no easy way to say this, Mrs Goldcrest," Copeland paused, drew breath, tried to focus her own mind on how best to proceed. Then accepted that there was no 'best way'. She stood with her hands behind her back like a recalcitrant schoolgirl, gazing at the black marble-tiled kitchen wall, avoiding Eleanor Goldcrest's eyes. "But I have to advise you that your three daughters' deaths were not just accidental." Copeland now studied the younger woman's face, as though waiting for the right moment to carry on. But again, there wasn't going to be any right moment. So she continued quietly, "Mrs Goldcrest, I have to tell you, your daughters were all murdered."

At that, the young woman ran from the kitchen. The two policewomen heard a door down the hallway being dragged open followed by the sound of vomiting.

Copeland sighed and brushed the hair out of her eyes. This was not going to be an easy afternoon. How could it be? Any murder was horrifying. The murder of defenceless young children, almost unbearable, even to a seasoned senior police officer like Copeland. She thought about her husband, going down with flu, her daughter was complaining of bullying at school, and this woman was having to face the loss, no not just the loss, the murder of her three little girls. Triplets, aged just six years old. Copeland had nothing to worry about in comparison.

She glanced over at her sergeant, but Trevelyan simply looked down at the floor, hands self-consciously shoved in her pockets. She'd not been involved in advising next of kin as frequently as Copeland. But she'd learn. In the end they all did.

Eleanor dragged back into the kitchen. Her hair was unkempt and she'd made no attempt to clean up. "What happens now?" she said, staring vacantly ahead. "What are you going to do?" She went and stood with her hands on her hips looking out of the front living room window at the empty street beyond, as though doing so might somehow bring the girls back.

"Mrs Goldcrest, we'll be assigning a family liaison officer to you. PC Deyton. She'll be there for you at all times. You'll be able to call her, talk to her, and look to her for support whenever you need it."

If Eleanor heard any of what Copeland was saying, she showed no sign of it.

"We need to speak with your husband, Mrs Goldcrest. Do you know where he is right now?"

"Yes," she murmured. "Eric's out walking with the girls on the shingle at the bottom of the cliff." Then she spun round, as though she'd been slapped around the face. "Where's Eric?" her voice rising in pitch. "Where is he? If he's not with the girls, where is he?"

"That's what we were hoping you'd tell us, Mrs Goldcrest," said Copeland.

CHAPTER 2 DAY 1

THE WINE EARLIER in the evening meant the woman was caught unawares for a mere instant before recovering, but not before the kick, aimed at her stomach, had glanced off her body, the hobnailed boot leaving her blouse ripped open, her ribs bruised and bleeding.

She cursed under her breath, before spinning round, kicking off her six-inch heels and facing her assailant, a shaven-headed giant of around six foot six who must have weighed at least two hundred and eighty pounds against her not inconsiderable six-foot and one hundred and sixty-pound frame. Despite boasting an advanced rating earned through nearly ten years of practising Krav Maga, the Israeli system of unarmed self-defence, the woman felt a flush of real fear. Her scalp prickled and a line of perspiration ran down her back. She'd handled a number of not dissimilar situations, but not with a man of these proportions and seldom with so little notice. The bloodied, broken body of a young woman flickered into vision, a decomposing corpse lying hidden and undiscovered. Her corpse. There'd be no escape from this situation. Everybody had their time. This was to be hers.

The alley was dark, a single street light gloomily reflected in the puddles of recent rain. There was no-one in sight. No-one to call to for help. She was utterly alone. Her pulse thrummed like a drumbeat in her ears, her chest hurt under its pressure. She was sufficiently pragmatic to accept she wouldn't survive. She thumbed the twin triangle, gold amulet at her neck, a gift from her father, its Hebrew inscription designed to protect, providing scant comfort. She'd never believed in the power of Obeah. The occult was no more than children's games played out by the weak or the impressionable. Right now though, she was ready to put her faith in anything.

He came towards her again, coal black eyes boring into hers, a glint of steel in his left hand. Her mouth was dry, breathing almost impossible against the terrified constriction of her throat.

Her years of training mightn't save her, but if she was going to die, he'd know he'd been in a fight. Dragging her tight skirt, frantically, unselfconsciously to her hips, she eyed the man, unkempt, unshaven and broken-toothed, as he leered at the tiny white knickers showing between bare legs, spread wide as she adopted a crouching position. "Alright my beauty," she muttered, with a confidence she didn't feel. "Ready when you are." Except, that she wasn't.

The knife arced towards her head; the man was unpredictably swift, despite his bulk. The steel flashed this way and that as he swung the blade back and forth, seeking a fix, aiming to rip the woman to shreds. She maintained her distance, and swerved, dodged, parried, her breath coming in sobs, the years of regulation and self-control a fading fantasy. Then she had him, or thought she had; he'd lost his footing, slipped on the wet surface, looked as though he might fall, but still the point of the blade connected with the side of her head, slicing through the mat of caramel frizz with a sound like ripping cloth, leaving a tapestry of red flooding down the side of her face and over one ear.

"Merde," she spat, as she felt the warmth of her own blood, smelled its metallic fragrance. Again, the vision of her own demise presented itself. No-one even knows I'm here, she thought. To die undiscovered? Poor dad, she thought, pointlessly, he'll never know.

This time the heel of her bare foot connected in a hook kick. She felt broken teeth impale themselves in her sole and grunted at the stab of pain. Discipline and a determination to persist produced an attack with the other foot, a windmill high, axe kick, connecting with the man's face, breaking his nose and cheekbone. But he was strong, too strong. His fist connected with her stomach in a loud thump. She screamed as the breath was knocked out of her, realised she was weakening. Her legs were like jelly. The shock of an attack for which she was totally unprepared, was leaving her shaking. He was punching her again and again, in the chest and stomach, the knife flailing about trying for another connection. She was out of fuel, running on empty.

"Dieu," she gasped, as she sensed darkness closing in on her, aware that, though he was shaken, it was the end. A final axe kick from her, and he dropped to one knee. A splinter of time, and with the dregs of her energy she spun round, her bent elbow smashing into his face again as he fell back on the wet pavement with a muted thud. Her breath coming in gasps, she stood over him, gazed down at his unconscious frame as he stared unseeing at the night sky.

Grabbing the blade from where it had clattered to the ground, she threw it well away.

It was beginning to rain again, a rumble of thunder in the distance. Her bloodied hair was becoming plastered to her scalp. She was next to his still form, kneeling on all fours now, panting with exhaustion and shock, grasped by an almost overwhelming desire to simply cry. She remained like that, unmoving for several minutes, her clothes gradually becoming saturated with the rain. She pondered foolishly on the irreparable damage to her Yves Saint Laurent outfit. Touching the side of her face she became aware of the extent of her injury. She'd need stitches quickly. Her hired car was close by. Sitting back on her heels she pulled the sheath skirt down over her thighs as the man began to stir. He rolled over onto his back, looked sideways at her.

"Who the fuck are you?" he mumbled through the smashed enamel stumps, the sour milk of his breath apparent.

"More to the point," she responded, some of her composure returning, "who are you? Who's paid you to do this?"

"I don't know lady," he said hoarsely. "I get cash in brown envelopes and I do a job. I was s'posed to rough you up, good and proper, the note said. Not to kill you, if possible." The man leaned up on one elbow, looked down and coughed up a gob of clotted blood.

She knew she wasn't popular. She'd rubbed a lot of people up the wrong way. But this? She was paid to organise personal security, usually for visiting dignitaries, and worked mainly as a private investigator. Attempted or prospective murder didn't normally fall within her scope of potential threats. She noted, he'd not been specifically told to kill her. He'd tell his principals he'd carried out the assignment, and they'd not know otherwise. But how long, she wondered, before there was a repeat? Perhaps next time it would be a gun, not a knife.

*****

On a weekend break, away from everyone, including her long-term partner, Ginny, and occasional boyfriend, Dov, her onetime self-defence instructor whom she'd met and imported to the UK after a spell on an Israeli kibbutz, Tammy Pierre examined the belt of shaven hair at the side of her head and the tramline of black stitches holding her flesh together. She favoured a tight crop capping her head, but for now she'd let the natural curls grow out to give some cover. What a bloody mess, she thought. And how did 'they', whoever 'they' were, know she was holidaying in this area anyway? The hotel, in Sidmouth, Devon, overlooked the sea whose soft murmur she could hear at night through the open bedroom windows.

She'd had a scalding hot shower, taking care not to disturb the plasters the nurse had laid over the ugly black and purple sutured gash to her ribs. She was cold. Blanketed in ice. Shivering with shock, despite the shower.

The doctor, bespectacled, harassed, greying, had wanted to notify the police, but Tammy had persuaded him to be discreet, at least for the time being. She knew it would eventually be put on to the back burner and then forgotten. She was a private eye, she told him; she would handle things herself. He shrugged, was doubtful, but agreed to let it go.

The attack had taken place at nearby Lyme Regis. An evening on her own at a well-known, upmarket local, a delicious meal and a couple of glasses of merlot, followed by a Henri Wintermans slim panatella as she left the restaurant. Perhaps she'd been followed there? The only explanation. She'd told no-one where she was going, and not booked anywhere in advance. If 'they' checked with hospitals in the area they'd find she'd been admitted, injured, to A&E. If the beating was to be a warning. But of what? And 'roughed up'? With an eight-inch blade? She'd be left alone for now. Their man would have to account to 'them' for an explanation of his own condition.

She started dialling a number on her mobile. Dov? No, maybe not. He'd remonstrate with her, telling her to be strong. Not what she needed right now. She put the phone down for a moment. Then, Ginny? Again, no. The young girl would just start panicking. She loved Ginny, but couldn't look to her for that sort of support.

She gazed out at the full moon, partially obscured by pillowed landscapes of clouds drifting by; then she dialled guiltily.

A sleepy voice answered, "Who's dere?"

"Daddy?"

"Tamsin? Dahlin'?"

"It's me, Daddy."

"You okay love? Y'all soundin' bite up. What happen dere?"

"Nothing Daddy. Just a tough day. Wanted to hear your voice, that's all. I'm turning in now."

"Y'all go to sleep now, you hear? You soundin' real tired."

"Going to sleep now Daddy. Love you."

"Love you too dahlin'. Y'all take care of yourself, you hear?"

The accommodation at The Royal was five-star. The bed, invitingly soft; she lay back under the duck-down duvet, caressed by her new black silk baby-doll, and started to doze. She'd still got a couple of days away. Time to unwind a bit. Sleep. Glorious sleep.

The fire bell crashed into her subconscious jolting her awake. She shuddered with shock, returned to the scene of the attack. He was big. Towered over her. She'd not prevail this time. He was here now. In her room.

What the hell? Not the fire bell. The bedside phone.

Rolling over, she reached out and grabbed the receiver. "Who the Devil?" she remonstrated. "Who is this? It's 2.00 am."

The voice was practically screaming, "Help! For God's sake help me!"

"Dov?" she said. "Is that you?"

CHAPTER 3 DAYS 1 & 2

"MUMMY, MUMMY," cried the little girl. "Jimmy kicked me and made my leg bleed and Bella punched me in the tummy. I hate it there. I hate it, hate it, hate it!"

DI Copeland had just arrived home, having parked her Ford Focus on their tiny drive, after one of the longest days she could remember. The debate at the police station had gone on interminably, but no-one was any nearer suggesting a motive for such a despicable crime. Her Detective Chief Inspector, Downey, was bellowing for results, results she was in no position to give.

Meanwhile, her little girl's leg was running with blood. Where the hell was Jessica's bloody father?

Copeland's home was an Edwardian semi-detached, shared with her husband Reg, in a street not far from the centre of Lyme Regis, a town that could trace its roots back to William the Conqueror, even gaining a mention in the Doomsday Book.

Both peaceful and picturesque, its mixed sandy, boulder and shingled beaches are famous for their fossilised sea creatures, mainly located in the local blue lias clay and dating back to the Jurassic period, 180 million years ago. It was twelve-year-old Mary Anning, who lived and died in the area from 1799 to 1847, that discovered the first complete ichthyosaur. Despite a lack of any formal education, she went on to become a celebrated palaeontologist, working with such luminaries as Buckland, Conybeare and Henry De la Beche.

At low tide on Monmouth Beach, to the west of Lyme Regis, may be found fools' gold (iron pyrites), ammonites and bullet shaped belemnites in the large boulders.

It was among boulders such as these the bodies of the babes had been found with their heads smashed in. Odd that no-one had reported seeing them on the way between Sandy Beach, at the back of the hotel area they'd been taken to by their father, and Monmouth Beach, several minutes' walk away. Perhaps someone other than Mr Patel would come forward in time to add to the paucity of information currently available.

Copeland, barely into the narrow hallway, kicked off her shoes, slipped out of her too tight jacket and unbuttoned her blouse at the neck. She'd been looking forward to a large sherry, a takeaway Indian, and a couple of hours with the boxed set of *Breaking Bad*. The day, she realised, was far from over.

"Come, Jess. Tell me what's been going on at school," she said, kneeling down in front of the agitated little girl and taking the child's hands in her own.

Her husband, Reg, wandered into the hall from the living room in slippers, suit trousers creased and tie askew. He was carrying a glass of what looked like lager and seemed somewhat vacant, as though he'd addressed the problem presented by his daughter without success. Deputy head of accounts at the local Council, he'd never qualified, but hard work and long hours had seen him advance as far as he was ever likely to go.

A small man with receding brown hair, slightly pockmarked skin, timid, withdrawn and wearing a permanent frown above shoelace eyebrows, Meg Copeland had thought, when they'd first met, she'd perceived a quietly ambitious man who would make something of himself. Instead, nerves and self-doubt had contributed to his having repeatedly failed his final professional exams, and eventually gaining his present status of deputy, rather than head of accounts.

Meg's hopes and ambitions for them both had, over the years, degenerated into her own snappish short temper with her husband's perceived shortcomings. To her own shame, she now bullied him, remorselessly.

"Have you seen your daughter's leg, Reg?"

"What's that, love?"

"For God's sake, Reg. Look at it. Couldn't you at least have mopped it up?"

"Sorry. I didn't...I didn't. Feeling a bit under the weather you know."

At times she despaired of her husband. Nonetheless, their three-bedroom home was comfortable, with its somewhat dated chintz in the living room, favoured by Meg, and its simple IKEA kitchen in whites and greys, which they'd both managed to agree on. The walls were mostly adorned with framed prints of well-known Constable landscapes, French impressionists, and a number of pictures by the renowned 1950s' and 1960s' painter, Vladimir Tretchikoff, including the popular, blue-faced, Chinese Girl.

By mostly restricting themselves in terms of holidays, clothes, entertainment and the modest second-hand cars they both drove, the Copelands had been able to scrape together the cash to fund their daughter at The Meadow School, a mixed private school in Yeovil some twenty-five miles from their home, taking pupils from ages three to eighteen, either on a day basis or as boarders. It was proving to be a costly error.

The school, one of the finest in the area, had every facility one could hope for, with an ambitious and committed staff achieving admirable academic results. The problem was Jessica, who seemed to have inherited her father's timidity, resulting in her being picked on relentlessly at school. A pretty fair-haired child of eleven, with freckles and an elfin face she simply would not defend herself.

Her father, unsurprisingly, continually counselled a strategy of walking away from trouble. Meg, while not advocating violence, encouraged her daughter to stand up for herself. Neither policy was listened to nor followed. As might have been expected, she frequently emerged from school on Friday's weekend exeat with abrasions on her legs from the kickings she'd received.

It wasn't as though the child was physically weak, far from it. A strong swimmer, her favourite school activity was gym. She could climb a rope using just her arms, something few of the others of her age could manage. Her great hero was Nicola Adams, the young British Olympic boxing gold medallist. The family had a DVD of the 2012 Olympics with footage of the boxer, which Jess had watched time and again.

"Don't you never try nothing like that, Jess," her father had insisted.

"Don't be ridiculous, Reg. As if she would. Still, Jess," she'd said, turning to her daughter, "you need to say something when they start getting stroppy. You know, stand up and tell them to leave you alone. Don't be a doormat. Like your father," she'd muttered under her breath.

Jessica had said nothing in response, merely hanging her head, looking resigned, hands clasped behind her back.

A second issue impacting on them was the family's apparent lack of social status. They were clearly not wealthy when one compared the household's Ford Focus, driven by Meg, and her husband's battered VW Polo with the type of vehicles driven by most of the other pupils' parents. Again, Jessica had come in for some abuse on that front too.

The headmistress had been wonderful. An attractive fair-haired woman in her early forties, she'd explained there was only so much she could do. If Jessica could only brave it out for now, the chances were that the incidents of bullying would lessen in time. The kids would get bored eventually and turn to other things with which to occupy themselves. She'd seemed eager and positive. The parents felt reassured.

The incidents of bullying did stop. Eventually. But not in a way Meg Copeland could have ever envisaged.

Meanwhile, she had a new case to concentrate on, one without a single lead, comment, witness or piece of tangible evidence upon which the police could begin any sort of enquiry. She'd not been impressed with Eleanor Goldcrest's husband, Eric. He'd been located through a call to his mobile and had a brief chat with Meg Copeland in one of the station's interview rooms, subject to the usual cautions and a reminder of his rights to be legally represented. The meeting was entirely voluntary and informal. The man had been as distressed as his wife, more so if anything. He'd claimed he'd been searching for the children himself. He'd turned away for a moment while they played a sort of hide and seek in an area behind a hotel overlooking the beach. He'd been about to call the police when Copeland called him.

She didn't like him. He was aggressive and had decided the police were jumping to all sorts of conclusions that she'd given him no reason to believe. He wanted to know how his wife had reacted. Decided that Copeland's attempt at an impartial and discreet report on Eleanor's attitude was enough for him to avoid going home. He'd clearly decided they all thought he was involved. The man was unfathomable, but agreed to be available if and when required.

For now, Meg Copeland packed her daughter off for an early night with a hot drink and a promise to talk things over when they were fresh in the morning.

Then she looked at her husband, and sighed. "Well for God's sake man, don't just stand there. Make yourself useful for once in your life. Pour me a bloody sherry." As she said it, she felt familiar pangs of guilt. Judging by the perspiration on his forehead, he clearly was suffering from flu.

Reg, looking utterly crestfallen, went obediently to the reproduction antique drinks cabinet and extracted a glass and a bottle of Harvey's Bristol Cream. *One day*, he thought. *One day.*

CHAPTER 4 DAYS 1 & 2

"DOV? WHO'S DOV? What're you talking about? My name's Eric. Eric Goldcrest." The voice was high pitched, frenetic. "I'm calling because the local police are suggesting I murdered my three little girls. They were found bludgeoned to death yesterday morning on the beach. My wife was told by the police yesterday, early afternoon; by evening the police had all but convicted me of the bloody crime. My little babes."

His voice was becoming ragged, irregular, practically hysterical. Tammy waited, she could hear him sobbing at the other end of the line.

"Calm down Mr Goldcrest." Tammy drew her legs from under the duvet and sat sideways on the bed, her feet touching the carpeted floor. "First off, where and how did you get my number? Nobody knows I'm here."

"I called your office, someone called Ginny, your PA? Said you were away for a few days' break; she didn't know where. But if it was really urgent, she said, I might try some of the better hotels in Lyme Regis or Sidmouth. You're the fifteenth hotel I've called."

"Alright, Mr Goldcrest, let's take this one step at a time. Are you under arrest? Are you in custody? Presumably not if you're making all these calls."

"No." His voice was slow now and sounded weary. "I was hauled in for questioning yesterday afternoon. They seem to be treating this whole thing as a foregone conclusion. My wife won't talk to me. She's hysterical. I told her I was going to contact you. Told her she should speak to you as well. Texted her your number. Said if anyone could sort out this crap, from what I've heard of you, you can. I'm not at home, I'm in a guest house outside Lyme Regis. Always look to the father, they say. But you see, I have to tell you..."

"Mr Goldcrest, excuse me," she interrupted. "Apart from the police's apparent presumption of your guilt, do they have any evidence of any wrongdoing on your part? I mean, how was this murder supposedly carried out? How have they concluded it was a murder and not an accident? Have they found any weapons of any sort?"

"The girls were clubbed to death with a large round stone on the beach." The man's voice was hard now, angry. "It was left by the bodies, not even thrown away. Can you believe it?"

"Do you know if there were any fingerprints found on the stone?"

"No, none."

"In that case the murder was clearly premeditated."

"What? How can you say that?"

"Because, Mr Goldcrest, it's unlikely that a random murder, committed without malice aforethought, would involve a perpetrator readily equipped with gloves."

"I hadn't thought of that."

"Come to my office tomorrow. Can you get to London for 11.00 am? If I can't meet you at your home, London will be easier for me. If I need to speak to your wife at a later time, I'll come back down here."

"Okay. I don't suppose I could see you now, could I? I'm desperate."

"No, Mr Goldcrest. I need some sleep. I'll text you the address; it's in Bruton Street, off Bond Street."

There was a long pause, then, quietly, "With that address you sound as if you might be expensive, Ms Pierre."

"You get what you pay for, Mr Goldcrest. Now goodnight."

She flopped back against the cotton sheets. She was seeing white flashes. Exhaustion, she realised. Her head throbbed and her ribs ached. She'd taken all the analgesics allowed by the hospital, but was now fully awake. Picking up the phone again, she dialled Ginny's number. Her fearful voice came on almost immediately.

"Tams? Is that you? What time is it? What's wrong?"

"Nothing, darling. Really, nothing. Only, I've got a possible client. A man whose daughters were murdered not far from where I'm staying. Police are suggesting he's involved. He sounded pretty desperate. Police are drawing lots of the usual conclusions. You know, adopted children, stepfather involved. Can you put any other urgent matters on my desk?"

"Okay, love. You sound really tired. Is this break not helping?"

"Listen to me, Ginny. I had a bit of a dust up with some idiot"

"What?" Fear in the voice again.

"Ginny, I said, listen to me. I scratched my head and bruised my ribs, so I look a bit of a fright. Hospital says…"

"Hospital?"

"Oh Ginny, let me finish. I'm absolutely fine. No broken bones. All put together again. Looks a bit ugly. Stitches and so on. Now hush," she said before the other could protest further. "If I'm okay to work, then I'm okay for anything. Now let's both get a bit of sleep."

Tammy lay awake, fretful and tense, thrashing about. Unable to rest, she climbed out of bed and spent time aimlessly tidying the bedroom. The activity usually helped her relax. Refolding clothing in the wardrobe, lining up combs and brushes on the dressing table and dusting imaginary bits of lint from the curtains, all to little effect.

Finally, she gave up, and popping in her ear buds she selected a Bach cello concerto on her iPod. It worked to calm her nerves and eventually saw her off to sleep, but not until around 3.00 am. Her wake-up call came at 5.00 am and then she was showered, breakfasted and on a crowded train, in first class, aiming to be at Waterloo station in good time to be at her desk before Mr Goldcrest's arrival.

As the countryside flashed by Tammy asked herself, for the umpteenth time, what a multi-lingual English, Spanish and French-speaking Politics Philosophy and Economics, Oxford graduate with a postgrad MBA, and more than just a smattering of Hebrew, was doing risking her life in this profession. Why, when she'd had the makings of a successful career in the police force, had she abandoned the job to be a private investigator?

She gave herself the same answer each time. Nothing and no-one gave her the intellectual stimulus and the adrenalin rush like the risks involved in running this business, her business.

She drank black coffee during the journey, but was still feeling the after-effects of yesterday's events, and her subsequent lack of sleep. She idled her way through the *Daily Telegraph*, but found herself unable to focus, so turned instead to her Kindle and Anthony Trollope's *Doctor Thorne*, which provided a satisfying diversion. She noticed several passengers looking at her sympathetically, then realised why. She knew it looked pretty ghastly. She'd wear a bandanna to cover the shaven area of her head until the hair started to grow back.

The traditional architecture of the frontage of the building that housed the offices of Pierre Search & Security, and in smaller letters below, 'Discreet investigations, forensic accounting, personal security', beckoned her. Tammy felt her tiredness drain away as the slight rush of a new day at the office, with the uncertainties it promised, loomed. The building's modern interior, with its bold art deco themes in black and white, was carried through to the elevator and out on to her landing on the fourth floor.

She was greeted by her PA, Ginny Jones, all copper curls and bright red owl spectacles perched precariously on a tiny nose. "My God, Tammy! What's happened to you, your beautiful face? You look as if...as if..."

"Ginny, I don't have time for this. Paperwork? Correspondence? Up-to-date files on everything?"

"On your desk."

"Okay," she said, excusing herself and going to the ladies.

Like the rest of the office, the décor was taupe and brown with flashes of fawn. There were two cubicles and Tammy entered one, locking the door softly behind her, as if it mattered that no-one should hear. Reaching into her Louis Vuitton handbag, she extracted a small transparent plastic bag of white powder, a quantity of which she deposited on the top of the lowered lid of the loo. With her credit card she separated the powder into two lines which she inhaled deeply through a plastic straw. Then she sat back on the lid of the toilet and closed her eyes as the powder did its work.

Both calm and energised, she went back into the office, to the hostile gaze of Ginny. "Tammy, no!" she hissed. "You haven't. You promised."

"Not now Ginny. I said. Not. Now."

Eric Goldcrest arrived at 10.30 am. Tammy surveyed him through the venetian blinds of the double-glazed glass partition of her office. Wearing an expensive-looking light blue woven sports jacket and jeans, he was drawn, had a haunted look. Aged about forty-five, bull-necked and middle-height, his hair was uncombed, prematurely grey, veering to white. His eyes were bloodshot and wild. Having been shown in to Tammy's office, he alternately sat and walked around restlessly. "What happened to your head?" he asked Tammy.

Tammy sat behind her curved walnut cantilevered desk, fiddling with a pen and pad, and surveyed her client. She'd dressed in a plain white blouse and short black skirt. A string of pearls about her neck and a pearl bracelet completed the outfit. The side of her head looked raw and angry. "Mr Goldcrest, why don't we discuss your problems? At my charging out rate, you really don't want to waste time discussing mine."

Goldcrest stared at Tammy as though he not seen anything quite like her before. "You know," he said, "I didn't realise."

"Didn't realise what, Mr Goldcrest? That I was this young?"

"Yes. Well no. I mean, you know." Goldcrest shifted about uncomfortably in his seat. "You're sort of black."

"You make it seem like a disease." Tammy tapped her Bic ballpoint impatiently on the notepad on her desk blotter and frowned at her prospective client. "And, sort of black? What's wrong with black? Or more precisely mulatto. My father is a black Trinidadian, my mother, now dead, was French. Does that seem to cover it?"

"Why yes. I meant no offence. And that…those stitches? I mean, what happened to you?"

"And you've scratched your chin, shaving I presume. Again, Mr Goldcrest; shall we focus on you now?"

"Of course." Goldcrest sat back, touching the shaving cut self-consciously with his fingertips, then rested an ankle on the opposite knee and said, "What am I going to do?"

"Let's start off with some basics," Tammy said, reaching for the box of cigars on her desk, and lighting one with her Dunhill lighter; then, she pulled her notepad towards her. "Your full name, address, bank account number, sort code and national insurance number, if you have it. Wife's full name, maiden name, date you were married. I'll want a certified passport picture and recent utility bill." Tammy paused. "I'll also want the date of birth of the triplets," she said quietly. Then looking up from the notepad, she added, "But why don't we start with what you know of yesterday's events?" Again, she paused.

Goldcrest was crying. "I'm sorry," he said. "I'm sorry. I just…I just…"

"Take your time, Mr Goldcrest," said Tammy, her tone and attitude softening. She blew cigar smoke towards the ceiling before flapping fumes away from her eyes, placing the cigar in the ashtray and regarding her prospective client. The man looked crushed and broken. Like a disabled tank. A sinking battleship. She went on quietly, "Then when you're ready, I'd like to know, before anything else, if you'd taken your three little girls for a walk on the beach, or shingle, where were you when this thing happened?"

"I wasn't on the beach. We were walking in the gardens overlooking the sea at the back of one of the hotels. There're winding paths there, and garden shed-type things all over the place. Some are like pergolas with tables and chairs set out, others look as if they're used to store stuff. Maybe deckchairs and tables. The kids could run around, play hide and seek. It's perfectly safe in that part. What am I saying?"

He ran his fingers though his hair, distractedly, stared up at the ceiling as though he might find some answers there. "They ran off to hide somewhere. I couldn't find them. I shouted. I looked. I ran everywhere. I went into the hotel." Goldcrest bent forward, elbows on his knees and put his head in his hands. "They must've thought I was mad. In the hotel, that is. Next thing, Eleanor is screaming down the phone at me, calling me names, saying I've abused the girls. Then I'm at the police station. You know the rest."

"You're not under arrest, Mr Goldcrest. So, whatever you say about the police jumping to conclusions, clearly they've nothing on you. At least nothing at this stage."

Goldcrest sighed, sat back and crossed his arms defensively. "They've got nothing because there is nothing."

Ginny tapped on the door and looked in, the copper curls bouncing. "Tea? Coffee? Anything for anyone?" Then noticing the cigar, she looked down at Tammy and frowned, mouthing, "In the office?"

"Mr Goldcrest?" Tammy enquired, ignoring her. "Can we offer anything?"

"Coffee. Black. No sugar."

Tammy nodded at Ginny. "Strong black for me, Ginny, as usual."

Turning to Goldcrest Tammy asked, "Tell me, do you have any enemies, Mr Goldcrest?"

"A few. I'm a market maker. You need to be pretty ruthless. I've upset a number of other dealers."

"Could you be clear about the function of a market maker?"

The enquiry seemed to concentrate Goldcrest's mind for a moment, taking it off the tragedy he was facing. "Well, we're sort of liquidity providers. What we do is to quote a fixed buy-and-sell price for financial instruments; you know, cash, derivatives, that sort of thing."

"And were your fixed prices always fixed, Mr Goldcrest?"

Goldcrest shrugged and looked down at the carpet. "Not always."

"Not always?"

"Well, you know. All's fair in love and war."

"Is that how you define business?"

"How do you mean?"

"Is business war to you? Is there any room for honesty in dealings? Any room for old-fashioned integrity?"

Goldcrest fixed Tammy with his gaze. "Frankly? No. You do what you can get away with. Bit like the Wild West, but without the guns."

"So, we could be looking at a revenge killing. Or a premeditated murder carried out with the object of implicating you. Or both together."

"You tell me." Goldcrest sat casually sideways to Tammy's desk, resting an elbow on the leading edge of it.

They paused for a moment as Ginny came back in carrying a tray with two bone china cups of black coffee and a plate of biscuits. As she placed it on Tammy's desk, the underside of the tray caught Tammy's Bic ballpoint causing a drop of coffee to overspill. "Oops," she said, smiling. "No damage done."

But Goldcrest jumped back as though he'd been stung. "Mind the bloody jacket," he hissed. "It's a Cucinelli"

"Sorry? A what?" said Tammy, looking bewildered.

"I've just bought it, it's a Brunello Cucinelli, Italian sports jacket. Cost me two grand."

"For heaven's sake, nothing's happened to the jacket, Mr Goldcrest. Don't you think we might get back to the subject at hand?"

"Yeah, yeah. I'm sorry. Sorry. Getting all my priorities wrong. I'm in a helluva state." He leaned forward away from the desk, elbows on his knees, his hands hanging down.

"Very well, then. Let me get one thing out of the way, Mr Goldcrest."

"Well?" Goldcrest stretched his fingers out and concentrated his gaze on the backs of his hands.

"A straight question. I'll only ask it once. Did you kill your daughters, Mr Goldcrest?"

"Don't be bloody ridiculous. I mean, for crying out loud." Goldcrest's voice had risen till he was practically screaming, as he had done on the phone during the night. "If that's really the best you can do."

"Okay, okay. I hear you loud and clear." Tammy had raised her hands palms up as though to forestall the full-on attack of a bull elephant. "But you have enemies, yes?"

"If you like."

"Let's be frank here, Mr Goldcrest, you're not a very nice man."

"What the hell's that got to do with the price of eggs?"

"Think. Is there anyone you know of who might want to get at you by hurting your daughters?"

Goldcrest scratched his head thoughtfully. "Lots of people would give their eye teeth, probably, to see me dead, but the girls? Why them?" He stared down at the floor. He looked utterly lost. "Why them?"

"I want names and addresses, backgrounds, jobs, spouses, children, where they holiday, what golf clubs, health clubs they go to, who they're having affairs with. Anything and everything about your family, friends, business associates, business competitors, business enemies. Think hard. Somewhere in that lot is someone who has set out and succeeded in hurting you and your wife, and is now breaking up your marriage."

"I live in Lyme Regis. You're here in London. That's a bit far, isn't it?"

"I'll come down and stay at Lyme Regis whenever I need to. You work in London anyway. There'll be plenty for me to do here. We can meet up if necessary, wherever convenient to both of us."

Goldcrest pinched the bridge of his nose with his forefinger and thumb. "Am I just wasting my time? No insult intended, you understand. I mean, you're a pretty girl. But can you really produce the goods?"

"Your call, Mr Goldcrest," she snapped. "Just make up your mind." And taking the panatella from the ashtray she drew on it, inhaling deeply. "I'm flattered you find me a pretty girl, though that's hardly relevant here. I might add, I'm also a busy one."

CHAPTER 5 DAY 2

DETECTIVE INSPECTOR COPELAND surveyed the team. Pictures of the three little girls were pinned up on the display board behind her, their heads horrifically crushed. A lunatic attack. The place smelled of sweat and coffee. Desks were festooned with paper. People were restless. Looking for ideas? Leadership? Direction, more likely.

The clouds outside seemed to swaddle those inside with a sense of gloom. Copeland knew she must act as though she was in control, but she felt at a loss. The press conference that morning had not gone well. The newspapers, local and national, were unanimous in their intimations; the father was involved. Must be. And, where was he? Had he disappeared? Was he on the run? Why wasn't he under arrest? What did the police have? What and who else were they looking for?

Copeland assured the press that all lines of enquiry were being pursued. The whole area was being searched for clues, beach and clifftop. Motives were being considered. Timings of death and the possibilities of anyone seeing anything or anyone known or unknown in the area were being looked at. Other than that, they had nothing. It was a genuine mystery.

One reporter brought up the news that a local paedophile convicted of the murder of a nine-year-old girl had recently been released from prison after serving a twenty-year sentence. Could the police elaborate? Copeland repeated the mantra that all lines of enquiry were being followed up.

Copeland's immediate boss, Detective Chief Inspector Downey, a stooped and melancholy-looking man with a short temper, digestive problems and a nagging spouse, had read Copeland the Riot Act. Results and results fast were what was wanted. As though she could magic an arrest out of the air. The public needed to be reassured. A tourist spot involved. Local hotels might lose business. No, they wouldn't, thought Copeland. The ghouls would be touring the area in numbers.

Downey went on. Residential area. Particularly horrifying that it was three innocent little girls. And where the hell was that bloody husband? On a jaunt somewhere? Absconded? Get him back to his home town where you can keep an eye on him. Like, now. Understood? Etc, etc.

His voiced had droned on until Copeland thought she'd scream. Downey had, in his temper, ignored the fact that following Copeland's interview, the husband had agreed to be available as and when needed.

But she'd kept her cool and was now looking for ideas, suggestions, anything that might give a clue to the motive. In the absence of anything convincing so far, she'd started allotting individuals to the task of talking to householders, shopkeepers, hotel staff, anybody who might be able to come up with something. A sighting, a view, an idea about a motive.

People shuffled out of the room, and Copeland went to the ladies' where she took a couple of diazepam prescribed by her doctor. She did not like working with her Chief Inspector, but she'd have to live with it.

* * * * *

In London, Eric Goldcrest's mobile sang out. "Yes," he answered, irritably.

"Mr Goldcrest? It's DI Copeland here."

"Oh you. Are you the one responsible for all that shit I'm reading in the newspapers? I'm being bloody hung out to dry."

"I am not responsible for what the press chooses to print, Mr Goldcrest, but you are wanted back here in Lyme Regis."

"What, so you can keep an eye on me?"

"We'd be happier if you were closer to hand."

"Sorry to leave you unhappy DI Copeland, but I'll be back when it suits me, or when you've a warrant for my arrest. Not before." Goldcrest disconnected the call.

There was no point in staying in London anyway. He'd get that list to Pierre as soon as possible. Then he'd see Pierre if she needed him, but for now he'd get back to his boarding house in the Lyme Regis area. Not that Copeland was aware of just how close he was to the Lyme Regis nick a lot of the time. But best to lay low for the time being. On the other hand, he pondered, being seen out and about close to home might provoke abuse from any of the locals that knew him, or come to think of it, anyone else that recognised him from his portrait in the newspapers.

With that thought he changed his mind. He'd remain in London, close to the action, out of harm's way. Plenty of hotels to choose from.

* * * * *

Tammy was back at the flat. A small modern block in Queen's Park, North West London, an area of mainly Victorian terraced houses, much of it developed by Solomon Barnett between 1895 and 1900 and showing a mix of clean classical lines, with those built post-1900 depicting more Gothic features. The location had largely been converted over the years by ambitious property developers into flats, the single bed variety often commanding as much as a three-bedroom detached house in the suburbs. The trend in central London property prices having been relentlessly upward for decades, a three-bed house in that area would now command well in excess of £1 million.

Queen's Park itself, positioned on the boundary of the London borough of Brent and the City of Westminster and lying between Kilburn and Kensal Green, was first developed in 1875 and named in honour of Queen Victoria. The park, one of London's green lungs, was described in one research paper as intended, 'To brighten the aspect of our streets and increase the health of our city.'

The gardens, covering some thirty acres, are a lovely spot to walk, jog or simply relax, with their tennis courts, pitch and putt, playground, bandstand and café. Tammy would frequently go there of an evening to simply shake off the day, breath in the clean park air and cogitate. She'd taken a brief stroll around the park prior to going back to the flat. Her head and ribs were sore, and eschewing the benefits of the clear, fresh atmosphere, she'd lit up a Henri Wintermans, and gradually begun to unwind.

Stubbing out the cigar with the toe of her shoe, she sat for a while on a park bench and considered her client. Eric Goldcrest was a puzzle. A mixture of arrogance and uncertainty; rudeness and courtesy. A man who could face up and admit with all honesty to his being disliked to the point of hatred by some of his associates.

Could he have murdered the children, she pondered? She had to admit, anything was possible. The common syndrome of the stepfather murdering the children sired by another? But if so, why commission a private investigator who might prove precisely that? In which case, the unanswered questions. Who? And why? She went on pondering as she made the short walk home.

Ginny was cooking the evening meal. Curried goat with plantain, sweet potato, rice and a mixed salad. The smell had Tammy salivating. Ginny had learned how to cook Caribbean from Tammy, and now produced the better food. Tammy sipped an iced Beluga Vodka Gold, neat, from a chilled glass. At more than a hundred pounds a bottle, it needed to be good. It was. She glimpsed a disapproving glance from Ginny and simply shrugged. She felt her muscles relaxing some more, the day finally receding, and standing close behind Ginny, whom she towered over, she nuzzled her lover's neck, running her fingers through the long copper curls.

Her mobile, on silent, vibrated in her back pocket. Excusing herself, Tammy ambled to the loo, shut the door behind her and glanced at the text. It was from Dov.

'I miss you,' it said. 'We can't go on like this. When can we meet?'

CHAPTER 6 DAY 3

SHE READ IN THE NEWSPAPERS that Eric Goldcrest had a history of violence. He had an unpredictable temper that had got him into trouble on more than one occasion. So far there'd been police cautions and nothing more, but it might not be long before someone got seriously hurt.

Otherwise there was nothing to go on. She was drawing a blank. The lists studiously drawn up by Goldcrest revealed nothing. And, judging by the newspaper reports, nothing had been found by the police either. But the public were restless and wanted results.

She was in her father's snug two-bedroomed garden flat in one of those Victorian conversions in Queen's Park, where he would be close to his daughter living nearby. Tammy had organised the decoration in the muted colours both she and her father, a retired architect, favoured. She was wearing navy flared slacks and a white open-necked blouse with high-heeled Jimmy Choos. Sitting back in one of the Jasper Conran pale grey two-seaters, she found herself restlessly uncrossing her legs and walking around the living room. She'd only been there for a few moments.

She wanted to do more for her father. She felt helpless. He never complained. She wished he would. The fact was, he was unwell. A tall stick-thin man with short cropped white hair, a starkly contrasting ebony complexion and long fingered artist's hands, he looked drawn and tired. At sixty-five he'd thought he'd have years of retirement ahead; instead, he was showing early signs of Parkinson's disease. Several falls in the street had made him cautious of being out alone.

The turquoise and navy-blue bandanna she wore to cover the scar had slipped. The black track of stitches showed up, an angry line against the bloodied shaven skin. Her father's eyes opened wide.

"Oh my, Tamsin. What's happen to your head? Chil', what you all gettin' up to? Why can't you stay in the police? You were doin' so well? Detective Inspector, and so quick? And in the Diplomatic Protection Squad too. My, my. So proud of you. Then you up and go? Just like that?"

"I was bored, Daddy."

"Then all that qualification you work so hard for? Degree? MBA? Languages? What wrong with a career in commerce? Or banking like mummy family?"

"Boring, boring, boring. I wanted some real excitement, Daddy. You know," she said quietly, "to live on the edge."

"Way you're goin' Tamsin, look to me like you goin' over the edge. And what it all for?"

"What's it for? I'll tell you; the contacts I made in Diplomatic? They've pretty well set me up. Dangerous, challenging and remunerative. It gives me all I want, and more."

The old man, looking older than his years, swayed back and forth in the ancient rocker Tammy had picked up in the Portobello Road and sipped from a glass of mellow VAT 19 Trinidad rum. He sighed, resignedly. "Vodka's in the freezer dahlin'. Glass is there too. Help yourself."

Pouring herself a full tumbler, neat, she drank half before rejoining her father in the living room. It warmed her, settling in her stomach, spreading its delicious essence throughout her body. "I've got a bit of work on, Daddy. But this one case seems to be offering a vacuum. I can't find a motive, I can't spot a suspect. The father's an obvious candidate, but he just seems too overwrought. He'd have to be a helluva'n actor. The mother's been sedated, so I'm still waiting to see her."

"What shall I say, Tamsin? Y'all have a puzzle. I can do straight arithmetic. Your mother was the one for cryptic crosswords. But she's not here," he whispered, his eyes rheumy with sadness. "I still miss her, you know."

"Me too, Daddy."

They'd met, her parents, when her mother, the dark-haired, effervescent daughter of a sometime wealthy Parisian banker, related to the original banking Hirsch family, had travelled to Trinidad with the object of finding a holiday home. There being nothing suitable, she had been recommended an up-coming young architect, Matthew Pierre. Matthew, a catholic, was five years older than the beautiful Pascale Hirsch, whom he married, despite their respective families' reservations, in a registry office in Port-of-Spain within two months of their meeting. There were French links in his family, and Matthew had more than a rudimentary knowledge of the language, which he found invaluable when he and Pascale set up home in Paris, and she started introducing him to wealthy clients through whom Matthew built a small but successful private practice.

Fifteen years ago, at the age of forty-five, Pascale had contracted an aggressive form of breast cancer. Only at the very end had she lost the fire and energy which had been her life's signature. Matthew and Tamsin had watched her decline with unbelieving dismay. This irrepressible beauty, this outrageous risk-taker, this once scandalously promiscuous alley cat who had remained utterly and faithfully devoted to her calm and loving husband, was gone. The void she left was as wide and as deep as a black hole in space.

Matthew left Paris, and its memories, and set up home in London, where he practised in a desultory manner, but his heart was no longer in his work. There was enough to retire on, what with savings, insurances and the remains of inherited wealth, and so at the age of fifty Matthew began to wind down, devoting most of his time to charities for children and the homeless.

Now, he too was declining with Parkinson's causing occasional forgetfulness, but more frequently falls as his legs refused to respond to his brain's commands.

She'd resumed her seat on the sofa, and watched fondly as her father rocked contentedly back and forth. "What am I to do, Daddy?"

"About the case?"

"About my personal life. Dov knows about Ginny. Ginny knows nothing of Dov."

"You gonna have to choose some time dahlin'. Can't go on playin' both ends against the middle for ever."

"Maybe."

Tammy gulped back the last of her vodka and considered pouring another, but decided to wait for the moment. Her father, in common with many in his own family, could take vast quantities of hard spirits, seemingly without ill effect. Probably because they diluted their drinks and then sipped them slowly.

She got up again and paced restlessly around the room feeling oddly like one of her own clients. The pictures on the walls were all originals. Matthew had always maintained he'd prefer the cheapest original to the most expensive reproduction. There were etchings and lithographs by Renoir, Vollard and Berthe Morisot. He loved the feeling of precision achieved by the artists, despite the apparent randomness of the impressionists' line work. These were expensive, but not entirely out of reach. But Pascale had, in a moment of supreme extravagance, bought Matthew a tiny Canaletto original for their twentieth wedding anniversary. Here, the architect could appreciate the perfection of detail and the depth achieved through the artist's superlative mastery of perspective. Two years later Pascale was dead.

"You know, I love these pictures, Daddy."

"They'll be yours one day, dahlin'"

"Don't, Daddy. Please. I couldn't bear it if anything…"

"Tamsin, forget about me. You thirty-seven, chil'. When you gonna start a family. Y'all gettin' no younger."

Tamsin stopped pacing and faced her father. "I wish I knew. I love Ginny, she means the world to me. I feel I'm in control when I'm with her. She needs me. She loves it when I'm doing diplomatic security and I dress as a man. With my height, I can pass for a man."

Matthew shook his head, puzzled.

"But when I'm with Dov, he makes me feel like a woman. And I love that too. Can you understand that Daddy?"

"I can try Tamsin. Trouble is, you too much like your mother for your own good."

"What I need," said Tamsin, "is to get some idea of what the Lyme Regis nick have found so far. But it's early days. May not be much just yet."

She sat back down on the sofa cradling the vodka in her palms, concentrating on the tiny Canaletto. She said half to herself, "I'll talk to my old Super. He owes me a couple of favours."

Then her mobile juddered into life. Picking it up from the glass surface of the occasional table, she pressed the green button. "Tammy Pierre."

There was a hollow silence.

"Hello? Hello? Anyone there?"

In what seemed like the far distance, Tammy could just discern the soft sound of someone weeping.

"Mrs Goldcrest?" she asked, speculatively.

"I need to talk to someone," came the response. "I can't cope anymore. Please, please. Can you come?"

CHAPTER 7 DAY 3

DOV JORDAN SETTLED DOWN in front of his laptop with a mug of steaming black coffee. In his apartment just off the Edgware Road, he'd spent two hours working out in the gym that morning and was still perspiring, despite the shower.

At forty-four years of age, Dov was at a peak of physical fitness, having the bulk of a gymnast coupled with the athleticism of a sprinter. He'd served in the Israeli army where he'd first learned and then taught Krav Maga, a skill he'd spent time coaching Tammy on her frequent trips to his country.

Dov's mother, an Anglophile and keen reader, had read Dickens to him when he was just nine years old, and the boy had developed a love of English literature, resulting in his studying the subject at the university of Tel Aviv. *Great Expectations* with its allusion to class issues in the relationship between the characters of Pip and the blacksmith, Joe Gargery, was a particular favourite. He loved Joe's simple approach and gentle observations, 'What larks Pip!' Perhaps he saw something of himself in the honest giant.

The flat was a display of his interest in both classics and modern, with bookshelves wall to wall and teetering skyscrapers of books all over the living room and study floors. In counterpoint, there were fresh cut flowers, pot plants, delicate antique furniture, army memorabilia and porcelain of all descriptions occupying every available surface.

Right now, he was attempting to locate a rare, gold Jaeger-LeCoultre watch for a wealthy client who collected antique watches as a hobby.

Dov's grandfather had fought in Israel's War of Independence in 1948. A fiercely independent widower, he was living on his own in Haifa, aged eighty-eight. Dov's father had died at merely twenty-three in the Yom Kippur War of 1973 when Dov was just a baby. Dov's mother, a writer of children's books, also lived alone in Haifa, close to Dov's grandfather. She'd never remarried.

Dov had met Tammy some five years ago when she'd turned up at one of his Krav Maga sessions. Already well advanced in the art, he was struck by her compelling appearance, her height, her strength, her honey complexion and her tenacious commitment to the skill.

Always comfortable in the company of women, Dov had never felt the need to settle down with one person, but with Tammy, for the first time in his life, he felt like a salmon swimming upstream. Indifferent to his overtures, but interested in his choice of reading and his business dealings in acquiring rarities for clients all over the world, she eventually agreed to meet him for a meal one evening on a trip to Tel Aviv.

The restaurant was multi-national with elegant dark furnishings, black tablecloths, starkly contrasting amber napkins and muted lighting. The clientele all looked well heeled. But she was late. Dov found himself constantly glancing at his watch, idly surveying customers as they arrived, trying to guess their professions, for want of something else to pass the time.

A beautiful young man walked in, tall and sporting a wide-brimmed turquoise hat, turquoise slim fitting jacket and slacks, and with the same amazing skin colour as Tammy. Ignoring the maître d', he came right up to Dov's table and said, "Shalom, Dov."

Looking up, fascinated, Dov said, "How do you know my…? Tammy?"

"May I sit down?" she asked.

"Good God, Tammy! You look…you look…"

"How do I look, Dov?"

Dov fidgeted with his napkin. "For a moment there, I thought you were a man."

"Do you still think that?" she said, removing the hat, revealing the stylishly cropped hair, and sat down opposite him.

Opening up for possibly the first time since he'd met her, she explained, over their meal, that she was indiscrimately bisexual, mostly favouring men, but was presently in a relationship with another woman; that she'd served time in the Met police in London, having been fast-tracked to detective inspector, and had recently left to start her own private detective agency. She'd been engaged in diplomatic security, involving visiting dignitaries and personalities such as pop stars and politicians, and been employed in a number of murder investigations. She was the product of a mixed-race marriage and had been brought up as Jewish, her mother's religion. Israel felt like a second home to her.

Fascinated by her, and venturing to ask more as she was being so frank, he enquired, as a bisexual, wasn't she ever hoping to have a family of her own? She sadly confessed that medical checks had suggested abnormally high levels of testosterone in her system. It was unlikely she'd ever conceive. She'd shrugged and smiled as she'd admitted it would have been nice to have had just the one, adding, "*Tant pis.*"

In time, Dov would find that she was obsessively tidy, except, she said, when it came to office paperwork, possessed of a volcanic and unpredictable temper, and was the most sexually demanding woman he'd ever met.

That temper of hers had got her into trouble on more than one occasion, she told Dov. He was in her room in the Crowne Plaza Hotel in Tel Aviv. They'd been an occasional item for a couple of years. From time to time she needed to crash out, she'd long ago explained to Dov, and her partner, Ginny, understood if she took a few days away telling no-one where she was. She was due back in the UK in a couple of days, but had enjoyed her time in Israel, swimming, reading and making love with Dov, about which she felt no trace of guilt. It was just sex after all, albeit with a dear friend. With Ginny it was love, and that was an entirely different matter.

They sat together, naked and propped against pillows on top of the duvet, Dov with a brandy in hand, swirling the liquid around the brandy balloon, Tammy sipping chilled neat vodka. She smiled as she recalled some of the scrapes she'd got herself into.

In one notable incident, she told Dov, she'd been driving in an unmarked police vehicle accompanied by her then superior officer, DI Reynolds, a burly ruddy-faced man with a penchant for needling her. Never alluding to her race or religion, Reynolds concentrated on belittling her gender. Women shouldn't be in the force. It was a man's job. Would she start complaining when she had her period? How would she cope with yobs if she was ever alone? Would a ladder in her tights be a problem? Had she remembered to bring her perfume? As the hours went by, Tammy felt her temper building up until it was simmering at the same heat as the surface of the sun. But with a supreme effort she'd managed to contain it for the time being.

They'd been asked to check out a sink estate in South East London for drug dealers. Some of the locals were becoming alarmed at the increase in gang warfare and its possible spill-over into the lives of the ordinary inhabitants of the area.

They'd driven around the estate a couple of times in one of the police unmarked 5 series BMWs, noting the usual graffiti decorating walls and doors. Litter lay uncollected, and shredded black bags with rotting food were spread on roads and pavements.

The high rises leaned over them, long afternoon shadows casting further gloom. There'd been a few knots of youngsters idling around the place, but nothing unusual to attract the attention of the police.

Reynolds continued to make stupid remarks and Tammy kept her temper on a leash, until it happened.

They'd left the estate, it had appeared peaceful for the time being, and were heading for home. Nosing their car back out into the main road, she was badly cut up by a speeding Ford Mondeo. It'd barely missed her, and when she'd sounded the horn in irritation, she was treated to a one-finger salute from an arm stretched out of the driver's window.

Without a word to Reynolds, who'd muttered obscenities at the other driver, Tammy put her foot down and gave chase. Despite Reynolds' exhortations, she refused to identify by sounding the police car's siren. They swung in and out of the gathering rush hour traffic, keeping the other car in sight. The finger being copiously displayed,

Reynolds appeared increasingly alarmed at what was going on. Tammy could smell his sweat as she dodged oncoming vehicles. Several times it looked as though the other car had given them the slip, but each time, by burning rubber and with grey clouds issuing from the exhaust, she got it back into view. Finally, on a straight stretch of road, with Reynolds, a hand on the dash, now clearly distressed, she floored the accelerator and effectively threw the car in front of the other. Both cars pulled up with tyres screaming, and Reynolds started to say something, but Tammy forestalled him with a restraining hand on his forearm.

Reynolds then watched open mouthed as she calmly climbed out of their car, walked down the side of it, opened the boot and extracted the large steel jack. By now Reynolds was out of the car too, and he stood with arms folded surveying Tammy. "Flat tyre, have we?" he sneered.

The driver of the Mondeo, a squat powerfully built man of around forty in shabby tracksuit bottoms and hoodie, was now out of his car screaming at Tammy, but she ignored him as she walked casually towards the Mondeo where she paused for a moment, as though lost in thought, then without a word, smashed the jack up against the driver's door, watching it buckle.

The sound was a hollow metal explosion, a whump of thunder, followed by several more as she then proceeded to attend to all of the other doors, side screens, bonnet and roof, until the car was a wreck of crumpled tin and smashed glass. Effectively a write-off. A small crowd had gathered and watched with mixed fascination and alarm as Tammy went about things in a seemingly considered and planned manner, displaying no apparent anger. Very much as though her actions were a sort of acceptable routine.

Reynolds simply stood, white-faced, watching the whole thing, not even interfering when Tammy cuffed the man and told him he'd be charged with driving without due care and attention, as well as a raft of other offences.

Driving back to the station, from the corner of her eye, Tammy had seen Reynolds staring at her oddly, frowning slightly, his head tilted, as though trying to fathom what he'd just witnessed. He never again made jokes about her gender or competence as a police officer, at least not in her presence.

Superintendent Bob Walker was not amused. An imposing figure with gingery curls, bushy eyebrows and piercing blue eyes, he surveyed an unrepentant DC Tammy Pierre in his office as she listened to what he had to say. The room was festooned with golfing trophies, a testament to Walker's prowess on the links. He was pretty much a scratch golfer with his two handicap. Interestingly, his academic achievements were not publicised, in particular his PhD certificate for a thesis on the changing social causes of crime in the twentieth century.

Walker made it clear that Tammy's career was on the line, hanging by a thread. How dare she engage in a high-speed chase on busy London streets, putting the lives of other road users at risk simply because she'd been cut up by another driver?

Walker's voice carried into the general office where staff kept their heads down. If Tammy's temper was volcanic,

Bob Walker's was legendary. As for the public display of rage, he added, and the wrecking of the man's vehicle. He paused for breath.

With the exception of her father, Tammy admired Bob Walker as much as, if not more than, any man she'd ever known. But still, she met his stare with her own defiant look. Walker's tone in no way softened. Indeed, in a habit she eventually adopted, he tapped a staccato beat with his pen on the desk blotter. The one saving grace, he added, was that the man was a wanted criminal. Furthermore, a stash of drugs had been discovered in his car, what was left of the vehicle. Without that she'd have been subject to disciplinary procedures that would almost certainly have ended her future in the force.

"You've a promising career before you DC Pierre, why risk it in this way? Regrettably, it will have to go on your record. I've no choice, for God's sake." He sighed. "Do I need to remind you of the definition of assault?"

"No, sir."

"Well? Enlighten me."

"It's the threat of violence, sir." She still sounded unapologetic.

"The threat of violence, DI Pierre. I'd say there was violence threatened here, wouldn't you?"

"He provoked me, sir."

Walker, looked down at the desktop, shook his head slowly. "He provoked you." Then glancing up at Tammy. "You realise he could have sued the force for assault?"

"It won't happen again, sir."

"Still not impossible that he'll institute proceedings, but unlikely, because of the drugs find. My guess? He'll try to use the assault as a bargaining chip. This could have been one unholy mess."

Walker seemed lost in thought for several moments, then continued, "Be warned, Pierre, if anything like this ever happens again..." he paused, cryptically. "For now, you're admonished. Dismissed," he barked, with a flap of the hand, and she turned to leave.

As she reached the door to his office, he called her again, his tone still unmistakeably annoyed, "By the way, Tammy."

"Sir?" she said.

He was frowning, wagged a reproving finger at her, then smiled. "Enough said."

*****

"That's quite a story," said Dov. "And you're in love with Ginny?"

"I am," she responded, sliding her impossibly long legs off the bed and making for the shower. Looking over her shoulder she said, "I like you Dov. I like you very much. But Ginny's my soulmate. I can't imagine life without her."

And so, a couple of years after their occasional affair had begun, Dov had decamped to London, leaving family, friends and a number of contacts behind. He could work from anywhere in the world, so venue wasn't a problem. He would be near to Tammy, and, whether or not she loved him, she'd be there within some sort of reach.

And too, there were times when she needed his assistance in her own business dealings. She frequently called on his expertise gleaned from his time in the Israeli military police to her advantage. Right now, she'd asked him to accompany her to Lyme Regis to meet with and interview Eleanor Goldcrest.

*****

They travelled first class, chatting amiably along the way. She'd outlined the case as far as she'd garnered information from Eric Goldcrest.

"That's all?" said Dov.

"That's all."

"Not much to go on, is it? Are you going to talk to your pal at the Met?"

"Have to," she said, distractedly. She was thinking about Ginny, and the fact that she'd be away from her for at least one, possibly two, or even three nights. She always felt remorseful when she was with Dov, but there was nothing she could do about it. She sighed resignedly.

It was a glaringly bright day, the sun's rays beaming into the carriage. Pushing his breakfast plate away, the remains of a monumental meal still apparent, Dov said, "You hardly talk about your time at the Met, Tammy."

"What's to talk about? I've told you about the run-in I had with my Super, Bob Walker." She felt mildly irritated by the question. Next, he'd be asking whether she'd ever experienced any form of racism.

"I was wondering."

She'd been gazing at the passing countryside. Now she turned to face Dov. "What were you wondering, Dov?"

"Well, you know, race, religion. Was it ever a problem?"

"God, Dov, you're so predictable. Men!" she muttered under her breath.

"What did I say, Tammy? What did I say?"

"Nothing, nothing." She paused. "Look, for what it's worth, all that talk about institutional racism in the Met? Mostly rubbish. I wasn't the only black face in the force, and the prejudice that was rife thirty, forty years ago, is pretty well dead. Of course, there'll always be pockets of stupidity. Maybe I was lucky. Only once, come to think of it. Someone in Diplomatic of all places, middle-aged guy, asked me how I felt about being black and Jewish. No idea how he knew I was Jewish."

"Could be you look it?"

Tammy smiled for the first time that morning. "Funny man."

"So? How did you deal with it?"

"Not difficult with that sort of customer. I told him the American entertainer, Sammy Davis Jr described himself as, 'a one-eyed Jewish negro'."

"And?"

"Then I told this guy that he was talking to a two-eyed Jewish mulatto."

"And that was it?"

"That was it."

"I'd have laid him out."

"Mmmm," said Tammy. "Hardly appropriate for one in Diplomatic. And anyway, the pen and the sword etc."

"Or in your case, both?"

Tammy smiled again.

The train was pulling into Axminster station, the nearest to Lyme Regis. The couple grabbed a cab from there for the four-mile run to the town, and on to the Goldcrest's home.

As they pulled up outside, the front door opened wide and Eleanor Goldcrest came running out. She was in slippers and a housecoat. Her face was grey and she looked frightened, as though she were trying to escape someone, or something. Her mouth was open as if she were screaming.

CHAPTER 8 DAY 3

GINNY WAS MOPING around the flat. Comfortably snuggled in a bright orange leopard-skin onesie, with matching furry Paddington Bear slippers, she was going to be alone again tonight.

It was a lovely flat, furnished by Tammy, of course, with the same style Jasper Conran sofas and armchairs she'd placed in her father's home. These though were all in cream, offset by a lush dark brown carpet. She'd carried the same theme throughout the flat, with more or less emphasis on either one or other of the two colours, depending upon the room. More cream in the two bedrooms, and more of the brown in the kitchen on work-surfaces and cupboard doors.

She should tidy the place, she knew, but couldn't work up any enthusiasm, and, anyway, Tammy did it so much better. Everything neatly in its place, where it could be easily found. She was obsessively tidy. If only her desk at work were that well organised, Ginny thought. Everything there was committed to memory.

Her lover was in Lyme Regis at the behest of Mrs Eric Goldcrest, while she was left to another evening thinking about how to fill the time, wondering whether Tammy would remember, or even find the time to call her.

When they were together, Tammy made all the decisions and made all the running. And it suited Ginny to let Tammy believe she was fully in control, while she, Ginny, was to all intents and purposes, helpless.

In fact, she was anything but helpless. The rape she'd suffered while at university had been horrendous. Her responses had left her feeling not only conscience-stricken, but also debased, demeaned and humiliated. However, she was also aware a weaker person would not have recovered as quickly as she had. Was she a wolf in sheep's clothing? No, perhaps not, she smiled grimly to herself. More likely, an iron fist in a velvet glove.

She wandered into the kitchen, put on the kettle for a cup of tea and helped herself to a couple of chocolate brownies from the fridge. She was eating rather a lot of the little cakes these days. Running a hand across her tummy she noticed she'd put on a bit of weight, could feel a little mountain of softness accumulating.

Tammy wouldn't be best pleased. Tammy like flat tummies. But Tammy wasn't there was she?

Then back in the living room Ginny put on the TV and found a recorded episode she'd been waiting to watch, of *Broadchurch*. The series dealt with rape, not something Tammy would wish to see. For one thing, no-one was likely to attempt any such thing with her, and, for another, she certainly didn't need to watch police dramas any more than those she encountered all the time.

The drama was good. Excellent, in fact. Approaching the subject with insight, it showed care and sympathy for the victim, who for once wasn't depicted as a young beauty crying out for it, but just an ordinary individual left traumatised by the event.

The evening was beginning to drag. An hour spent watching the drama. She glanced across to where Tammy had left her Kindle lying on the adjacent sofa, and reaching out for it, opened the flap to see what she was reading. Tracey Chevalier's *Falling Angels*. A book she'd already bought and read herself. A brilliant read, as with all that author's works.

Wandering restlessly around, she glanced at the shelf over the wide modern fireplace with its ground level flickering gas flame, where there lay a hardback copy of Alison Weir's *Eleanor of Aquitaine*. The history of Henry II's powerful wife, a woman he entrusted to rule over England and large parts of France when he was occupied with war.

A typical Tammy read, she thought. A strong woman, in control of things.

Ginny wanted company, someone to talk to, so starting to look through all the new and old names and addresses on her mobile's contact list, she came across one: Maximus Dieter. German grandfather. Dieter, meaning, warrior of the people. Max, she thought. Anything but a warrior. More a reliable plodder. Both tall and broad, she recalled a good-looking blond lad. A boyfriend of sorts from school; a kiss and a cuddle in the early days, before disappointment with men in general had set in, and one who'd gone on to great success in the world of IT. She'd read somewhere that he employed more than fifty people in his company. He'd be married by now, probably no longer living in South Wales.

Another cup of tea, and two more chocolate brownies, and Ginny sat back on the sofa once more, chewing the cake, and sipping her drink.

She dialled the mobile number without a second thought. It was answered on the second ring.

"Toby?" A deep masculine tone she barely recognised. So very different from the timorous teenager with the breaking voice she recalled from their schooldays.

"Who's Toby?" said Ginny.

There was a long enquiring pause, then, "I know that voice."

"You do?" Ginny smiled.

"That's little Ginny Jones. My Ginny, isn't it?"

"Not so sure about your Ginny, Max, but yes, Ginny Jones."

They chatted for nearly an hour. He was based in London. Owned an apartment at the prestigious 55 Park Lane overlooking Hyde Park. Wasn't married. Had been too involved in building the business to find time to meet anyone. And yes, he said, when she suggested it, they must meet up for coffee and a chat sometime.

The prospect was exciting, but didn't deal with the immediate problem, which was exacerbated by her conversation with Max. She was bored.

The *Black Swan*, a gastro pub near where they lived in Queen's Park, was Tammy's local. Ginny had been there once or twice with Tammy and found the crowd welcoming. It didn't take her long to get changed into black slacks and jumper, with bright red Adidas trainers and a floating red chiffon scarf.

It was 11.00 pm when she got there, and the place was crowded. For a moment, she felt adrift among the heaving throng of strangers, then the barman, Jimmy, spotted her, a shirt-sleeved young man with a pleasing smile.

"Tammy's friend. Yes?" He pointed a knowing finger in her direction. "Let's see now. It was tomato juice with ice and lemon, salt and pepper, Worcester sauce and Angostura bitters. Am I right? Or am I right?" he said, grinning.

"How could you possibly remember?" she laughed. "I've hardly ever been here."

Then, she heard, "Ginny? Thought it was you. Where's 'Her Maj' this evening? Off solving crimes somewhere?"

Standing at the bar, she spun round. "Kurt! Hi."

She was immediately relieved. It wasn't going to be too difficult after all. Kurt Mathis, a regular at the venue, and an acquaintance of Tammy's whom Ginny had met once or twice. She sipped from the seasoned tomato juice that Jimmy had prepared for her. "Tammy's away for a night or two, so I thought I'd get out for a change. The flat can get a bit claustrophobic when I'm there alone."

He was a thick-set, square-jawed young man of middle height with an easy-going manner, hefting what looked like a pint of Guinness in one hand. On the other, she noticed a prominent black oval onyx set in a gold ring. She'd not noticed it on previous occasions they'd met. It struck her as a peculiarly feminine accessory on such a masculine-looking man. It made him seem safe.

The white T-shirt he wore displayed bulging biceps, suggesting a lot of time spent in the gym. She learned that a qualification from the Design School of the London College of Communication had led to Kurt establishing his own business in brand and product design, employing half a dozen people and located, not that far away, in a studio in St John's Wood. By all accounts, he was doing well.

"So, how's my little Ginny getting on?"

She gazed at him menacingly, through half closed eyes, and prodded his chest with an admonishing finger. "Look you, mister, that's the second time this evening I've been someone's little Ginny. Let's get something clear shall we, I'm nobody's little Ginny, isnet?"

"Isnet?" he enquired, with barely suppressed laughter.

"Isn't it!" she corrected herself. "You know what I mean; horrible man," she added, dissolving into hysterical giggles.

They chatted on amiably for a while, bringing each other up to date with their lives. Kurt bought her another tomato juice and topped up his own pint.

Then, out of the blue. "Fancy a spin in my new motor?" he said, the chuckling finally subsiding.

"At this time of night?"

"Why not? I'm game if you are."

She took a sip from her tomato juice, looking at him over the rim. "So, what is this new motor then? Something exotic is it?"

"As a matter of fact, it's an antique Morris Minor. Pretty rusty, I'm afraid, with bald tyres and the soft top rotting, but I'm going to restore it over the next few years. It'll be a labour of love. Engine's okay, though the clutch tends to slip a bit. Brings back memories of what roads were like fifty years ago."

"What would you know about roads fifty years ago?"

"Only what I've seen on old black and white films."

He gulped back half his pint in one, the froth running down the insides of the glass as he replaced it on the bar. "But those roads were pretty empty, compared with today. So then. Are you up for it?"

He looked so earnest she didn't want to disappoint him. But really, bald tyres? Rusting and rotting?

A thought occurred to her. "What happens if we break down?"

"We call the AA. I'm a member. She's only let me down twice since I got her. AA were out to me each time within four hours. Had me up and running in no time at all. Suggested an MOT might be an idea."

"Are you being serious, Kurt? The car sounds like a death trap if you ask me."

"No, she's fine. Little girl's an absolute beaut. Don't make 'em like that anymore."

"I'm not surprised. Probably not allowed to."

"Not exactly one of life's pioneers, are we? Well? Are you game or not?"

"Oh well, alright," she said doubtfully, not wanting to appear too nervous. But the idea frankly appalled her.

"Two breakdowns?" she enquired. "Since you got the car? How long, exactly, have you had this vehicle?"

He glanced off distractedly as something of interest caught his eye. "Mmm?"

She tapped a gentle, but commanding fist on his shoulder. "You heard. Don't 'Mmm' me, mister. How long?"

"How long? Ah, yes. Well actually, I've had Gertrude…"

"Gertrude?" Ginny practically exploded.

"That's her name."

"The car has a name?"

"Of course."

She looked him straight in the eye. He was being serious. "You still haven't told me how long you've had her."

"Ah, yes. I've actually had Gertrude, for a whole..."

"A whole? A whole? Come on man. A whole bleddy what? Month? Year?"

"Week," he said, looking down at the floor, somewhat embarrassed.

"You're telling me you've had two bleddy breakdowns in the week you've had this car? And you want to take me for a spin in this metal coffin?"

"Where's your sense of adventure?" he protested, shrugging.

"I just drank it down with this tomato juice."

"What?"

"Yes, I had the barman put in extra Worcester sauce. I do take risks from time to time. I mean, it's pretty hot you know."

"Alright," he sighed. "Have it your own way. Tell you what," he said, brightening up a bit. "At least, take a look at her. She'll be upset if you don't."

"Why? Are you going to tell her? Couldn't you keep it a secret, like?"

"Come on. The little girl's parked outside. I'll let you sit in her. If you're really good."

"Whatever makes you think I want to be good?" she said, following him out of the pub.

The evening was mild, with the beginnings of a gentle Autumn breeze. The street was comparatively empty, with one or two vehicles on the opposite side of the road.

"So where's Gertrude?" said Ginny, looking around for an ancient Morris Minor, but seeing nothing that remotely resembled the car. "Had an early night has she? Feeling her age, like?"

"There she is," said Kurt, pointing down to a vehicle parked on a double yellow line.

"What's that?"

"That's Gertrude."

"That's Gertrude?"

"That's right."

She bent down to take a closer look. "This is a Morris Minor, is it? It's longer than I thought." Ginny bent down even lower. "Nice colour," she murmured.

"Silver metallic," he offered. "With black circular spokes." Kurt stood back, legs slightly spread, arms folded, a look of absolute bliss on his face.

"What's this little horse on the back for?" She walked around the car, looking it over from one end to the other. "What's a Ferrari, Kurt? Is it a type of Morris then?"

"God help us, Ginny. The car is a Ferrari GTC4 Lusso. It's cost me over two hundred thousand pounds."

"But I thought you said?"

"I know what I said."

"Are you going to start working on it then? I can't see any rust or anything on this. There's no rot on the roof. And at that price…"

"Ginny! For God's sake. Are you being serious?"

"Were you?" She grinned. "Come on then. Let's take a risk. We'll go for a spin. But not too long, mind. I've work tomorrow. And Tammy might call at any time."

No, she won't, thought Ginny. It's already midnight.

The car door clunked shut with a satisfying thromp, and Ginny sat back in the silver-grey bucket seat. "It's beautiful," she breathed. "Utterly, utterly."

"Isn't she just."

"Tammy would love one like this."

"Em! Excuse me, but you're with me tonight, madam. Not Tammy."

"Of course. I was just thinking, that's all. Come on then. Let's go."

On thinly trafficked A roads in the home counties, he took her for a two-hour spin, moving the vehicle up to nearly twice the motorway speed limit when the road was clear of cars and, so far as he could judge, cameras. He drove confidently and expertly.

"Gosh!" she breathed. "When you rev the engine, I can feel the vibrations running up my buttocks, sort of, and down my thighs. It's really very…very…"

"Orgasmic?" he suggested.

"That's not what I had in mind," she said, blushing.

"Only joking. But she is a pretty exciting drive, isn't she?"

"Brilliant. You know, you're as good as Tammy behind the wheel."

"Thank you, kind madam," he said as they drew up outside Ginny's block.

"Tammy did one of these advanced driving courses when she was in the…"

"So did I," he said, smiling.

"I s'pose I should invite you in for a nightcap, or whatever it's called."

"Not necessary. I've just enjoyed your company. You're fun to be with, Ginny."

"Oh, go on then. Just a quick one. You've been a lot of fun too. Brightened up a miserable evening."

They were inside the flat. "So, what'll it be, sir?"

He was seated on one of the sofa's, looking around the room. She'd taken off her trainers and slipped into the Paddington Bear slippers.

"This is nice," he said. "Your ideas?"

"No. All Tammy's. She's clever with colour and design."

"So I see. D'you have a brandy, perhaps?"

"One brandy coming up." Opening the drinks cabinet's twin doors, she extracted bottle and glass.

"Only me? Won't you join me?"

"I don't really drink that often. Oh well, just this once. Can't do any harm."

For a moment, the shock of the burn when she first swallowed made her gag. Kurt laughed and explained that you hold the drink in your mouth, without swallowing, to get the full flavour, then when you take it down, it's that much more mellow.

He was right, and whether because of the quality of the cognac, or her tiredness, she began to feel comfortable and companionable. Kurt was nice, and he was safe. That word again. And there were no unwanted advances, for a change.

"I should be going," he said softly, starting to get up. "Tammy wouldn't be too pleased if she knew there was someone…"

"Oh, blow Tammy," she said, crossly. "Tammy's not here. She hasn't even rung. You just sit down. Sit down here." She pointed imperiously to the cushion next to her.

"I really shouldn't."

"Oh yes, you really should."

"Okay," he sighed, sitting down where she'd indicated, their thighs touching. He turned to her. "Now what?"

"Now I'm going to kiss you." And she took his cheeks between her palms and kissed him full on the mouth.

"Ginny," he mumbled through her kisses. "Think of Tammy."

"I am," she mouthed. "I am."

She felt the tip of his tongue with hers. He seemed as withdrawn and timid as a little boy. She took his hands in hers and placed them on her breasts, and he began to gently knead them and squeeze them, the tips of his fingers finding the hardened nipples.

Kurt looked startled as Ginny suddenly stood up, without a word, and started undoing her blouse, shrugging it off, then letting her slacks fall to the ground, she kicked them away. She was wearing nothing but a red transparent thong and matching bra with round cut-outs for the nipples to show through.

"Christ, Ginny. What's a man to do?"

"D'you really need me to tell you?"

Kneeling down between his spread legs she fumbled with the zip, and he let her without in any way helping. Then, with the waist undone and the flies open, she dragged the jeans down to his ankles. Then off, together with his trainers. Falling forward on her knees again, she took him in her mouth. He was big, so big she could barely get her lips around him without hurting him with her teeth.

It was a long time since she'd had penetrative sex. The rape came to mind. That bastard had been in control. Her responses then had left her feeling profoundly disturbed. Now she was in control, and everything was different. This was Ginny with Kurt, not Ginny with Tammy, nor Ginny being forced.

She could feel Kurt swelling, and she gently pumped a little faster. But no, she didn't want him to finish yet. It was too soon. She wanted more. She wanted everything. So, she slowed down, reached up for him instead. Kissed him again, tasting sweet breath and shared cognac. Then, without removing her bra, she twisted so that one breast was in his face, pushed the nipple towards his mouth, where he took it greedily between his slips, sucking on it, his tongue playing with the tip. She heard herself moan. She was feeding him. He was her baby. Her little one. She repeated the action with the other breast. He was gentle, so very gentle. She could hear his breath getting faster, but she was leading the way. Leading all the way.

He'd slipped to the floor, and she straddled him, her thighs wide open like a rider, hovering over his erection. His T-shirt had rucked up showing rippling tummy muscles and a ballooning chest. He smelled of almond oil, and it was intoxicating.

"Ginny," he croaked.

"Don't fucking Ginny me," she rasped, dragging the crotch of the thong to one side and holding the tip of him in one hand.

Guiding him in, she was aware of how long since, and how seldom ever, she'd been penetrated, particularly by a man this large. It went in slowly. Her eyes were tight shut, so she couldn't see Kurt struggling to contain himself. It seemed to slip in for ever, and the feeling was more than she'd ever dreamed possible. Drawing her knees up she had him in all the way, while she ground round and round. She was moving faster now, a rhythmic back and forth and side to side. Over and over. Building up and building up. It was like sliding down a mountain, into a black abyss. It was heaven. She was going with the speed of a steam engine, and the screaming she could hear was her own. He was pumping into her, she could feel the flickering of his cum as he shot jet after jet into her.

"Oh-oh-oh!" she stuttered. Then she flopped forward, exhausted, against his chest.

She didn't know how long she'd slept in his arms, but it was getting light outside.

Her mobile, lying on the floor within reach, sparked into life. Kurt was immediately awake. "Who's calling at this time of the morning?"

Picking it up, she saw Tammy's name on the screen. "What the hell time is this Tammy? It's five o'clock." she stormed.

"I know, Ginny. I just missed you and wanted to hear your voice."

There was lots could be said, like why hadn't she called last night when none of this… She looked at the discarded clothes and empty glasses.

"Ginny? You there? I said I missed you."

"I know, Tammy," Ginny replied. "I missed you too."

CHAPTER 9 DAY 3

"I'LL DEAL WITH THIS," Tammy said to Dov, straightening her slacks and jacket as she alighted from the cab. "You get the fare."

Eleanor Goldcrest flopped into Tammy's arms, practically toppling her.

"Hey, hey, hey. Come now, my dear. Whatever it is, we can deal with it."

"You can't bring my babies back," she sobbed. "They're gone, they're gone."

Tammy held the frail body tight, felt the woman's heaving chest as her body shuddered with grief.

"No, we can't bring them back. I know that. I wish to God… But for your own safety, Mrs Goldcrest, we need to know who is responsible. We need to know why this happened. Do you not see? We need to find whoever it was and put them away." Tammy gently steered the woman back to the house.

They were seated in the Goldcrests' living room, with views through the French windows of a broad patio and extensive garden given over to trees and shrubs, and beyond that, rolling countryside. Tammy had introduced Dov as her partner, but Mrs Goldcrest hadn't seemed to hear. The daily help, a pale and melancholy-looking girl with a mid-European accent, had made tea and served up shortbread biscuits.

Eleanor Goldcrest sat hunched and shivering over a steaming mug, arms drawn in tight to her sides, knees supporting her elbows. She looked frail and old beyond her years.

"Eric said I should call you. He phoned me and insisted on it. I don't know what he's been up to. I thought it had to be him. You know, the little ones. Violent man, he can be. Never hit me, you understand. But threatened to. Anyway, he texted me your number."

"I know," said Tammy. "He said he would."

"Have you seen the pictures?" Eleanor asked.

"The pictures?" said Tammy.

"Of the babies. The police showed me. I've got them here."

"Why would they ever want to show you the pictures?"

"I couldn't bear to look at the bodies to identify them. Eric's not come back, so they showed me these." Eleanor picked a brown A3 envelope from the coffee table and handed it to Tammy, who reached inside and drew out the photographs. Then she swallowed hard, felt the bile rise in her throat, burning it, tried not to throw up.

She'd handled a number of murder cases, had always acted professionally, dispassionately. People murdered for all sorts of reasons: financial gain, revenge, passion, random thuggery. The list was endless. The act was usually quick with a variety of outcomes. A bullet or a knife left the body comparatively unchanged. Strangulation could leave a body bloated with a necklace of bruising. A heavy blunt instrument might crack a skull.

But in each case, these consequences left a body that was still recognisable as a body.

What Tammy was confronted with was three children's corpses, barely identifiable as human. The heads were completely smashed in, and the bodies were mutilated by blows that left them hardly discernible as human. She felt her eyes well up, and had to clench her jaw to stop herself from crying. She sat looking at the pictures, but trying not to focus on them, breathing slowly, until she'd calmed herself sufficiently to begin questioning Eleanor Goldcrest. Not yet trusting herself to speak, she handed the photographs to Dov, saying simply, "Here. Look."

Dov reached forward from where he was sitting and took the pictures without comment. He glanced at them briefly, shaking his head in disbelief.

Finally, in control of herself, Tammy said, "I have to ask you some questions, Mrs Goldcrest. You understand, I am a private investigator, not the police. As you know, I've been retained by your husband to look into this terrible case. He believes the police have already prejudged the murder and are convinced he is the guilty party, despite their having absolutely no evidence with which to proceed against him."

"If you say so," Eleanor responded.

Tammy went over much the same ground as the police had already covered without finding anything new. Eleanor could think of no-one who would want to kill the children, although she was aware her husband had many enemies. Ask him who his enemies are, she'd said.

"Mrs Goldcrest, you said your husband had taken the little girls for a walk. Do you remember what time he left home?"

"It was in the morning. I remember thinking it was bit early to be going for a walk. But he said he wanted the girls to get a bit of sun. Then I wondered where he was; he was so long away. I was going to call him, but then the police arrived."

"Do you remember what time the police came around here?"

"I don't know," she said. Maybe 2.00 pm, 3.00 pm."

"Were you in all day waiting for them to get back?"

"No, I did a shop when I couldn't see them."

"Was that late morning? Early afternoon?"

Eleanor closed her eyes for a moment. "It would have been late morning. Eric left the house at about 10.00 am and I got tired of waiting for him. He was supposed to help with the shop. He always gets out of it if he can."

Eleanor looked down at the mug of now cold tea as if she didn't know what it was doing in her grasp, and replaced it on the coffee table.

"Do you remember what time you left the house?" said Tammy.

"God knows." She paused and thought about it. "I can't think. No, it must have been around 11.00 am. I went to the Tesco on West Street, Axminster. I did the weekly shop, while Eric took the girls."

She stopped talking as if she'd realised for the first time, or perhaps yet again, all she had lost. She looked so desperate, her face creased with agony, that Tammy changed tack.

Hauling herself out of the deep armchair, Tammy wandered towards the French windows. Afternoon was drawing on, casting lengthening shadows across the lawns and the countryside beyond. She turned back into the room and asked, "Mrs Goldcrest, tell me about your relationship with your husband?"

"Do we have to do this? Do we have to, Ms Pierre? I mean, don't the police have this under control?"

"Of course, Mrs Goldcrest. Of course, they do. It's just that your husband felt that the police and the press had already anticipated the outcome of the case and decided he was involved. He asked me to take a look at things, possibly from a different perspective."

She shrugged. "I suppose that's not unreasonable."

"Is there any possibility at all that your husband could have hurt the girls?"

"There was always; there is always," she corrected herself, "the threat of violence in the man. I screamed at him. Accused him of being involved. I was distraught. Told the police it must have been him. No wonder he's run off. I still can't believe what's happened."

Eleanor looked at the backs of her hands, then placed them in her lap. "He loved the girls, though. No. No, I don't think he could have hurt them, despite what I said. Why would he? To hurt me? Never! We rowed, often, but tried not to in front of the babes. He had no reason to hurt them."

"Fathers and stepchildren, Mrs Goldcrest? You know. It happens."

"No. No. It doesn't make any sense. Does it? Could it?" Eleanor looked utterly distracted. "Oh God, I'm so confused. I just don't know. I'm sorry to be this useless." She started to weep silently, and, extracting a handkerchief from a pocket in her slacks, blew her nose.

Walking towards her, Tammy said, "We'll leave you now, Mrs Goldcrest. I'm so sorry to have upset you."

"It's alright. Don't worry."

Unfolding himself from the armchair into which he'd been slouched, Dov got to his feet. Towering over Eleanor, he spoke for practically the first time, "Would you mind if I used your facilities before we go, Mrs Goldcrest?" He caught Tammy's eye as he said it, and she got the drift.

"Yes, of course; there's a loo down the hall, where you came in."

"Thanks," he said and strode off through the living room double doors.

"I wonder if I might too, Mrs Goldcrest?"

"What? Oh yes, there's one upstairs to the right at the top of the landing."

The banisters and area each side of the fawn thick-pile carpet hugging the elegant Y-shaped flight of stairs were pale oak, giving the space a sense of great expanse.

She couldn't resist the temptation to push open a couple of the doors leading off the landing, and, noticing a double bed in one of the rooms, tiptoed in. Mirrored built-in cupboards lined a wall opposite, and an arched doorway leading off the bedroom lead into an en-suite facility. Taking a deep breath, Tammy stole into the luxury bathroom. White porcelain, mixed chrome and gold fittings, a further walk-in shower area shielded by a patterned glass screen; all spoke of casual wealth. A shelf running the full length of the jacuzzi-style bath was festooned with bottles and jars, many showing labels indicating tranquillisers, some with dates more than a year old. It seemed Mrs Goldcrest was under a great deal of stress. How much of it due to Mr Goldcrest? Tammy wondered.

There were further jars and bottles of tranquillisers on a shelf in the single loo, also situated off the landing. They were arranged haphazardly, and Tammy had to prevent herself from tidying the items according to size and content.

Hoping she wasn't pushing her luck, she peeped into what was clearly the bedroom of the little girls. Three little beds, with mobiles and toys everywhere. Children's books, paints, colouring books and on a sideboard, three tiny brown teddy bears with pink ribbons round their necks.

Downstairs again, Tammy and Dov took their leave just as a black Mercedes S400h saloon pulled up on the drive, all eighty thousand pounds of it, and a large, overweight middle-aged man in a rumpled pullover, jeans and trainers climbed out. With his dull grey hair pulled back into a ponytail, his bushy eyebrows knit in an angry stare, he confronted Tammy and Dov, then looked over at Eleanor Goldcrest, who was standing at her front door, and said, "Who the fuck are these two, Elly?"

"They're private detectives, dad. She's Ms Tammy Pierre and that's her partner Mr Dov Jordan."

"Oh yeah?" he said, advancing towards Tammy. "And who the fuck called you in, with your poncey names?"

She stood square to him, about the same height, and said softly, "Your son-in-law, Eric, asked me to look at the case, sir. He felt the police were jumping to too many conclusions."

Dov came and stood next to Tammy, but she moved away from him. "It's okay Dov," she said. "I can handle this." She could feel Dov's breath close to her cheek. He was angry, but controlled.

Eleanor's father said, "I don't know where that little piss artist is, but if I see him anywhere near here or Elly, I'll break his fuckin' neck. I don't care what he's been up to, him and the crap he mixes with, and I don't want to know. As for you two," he said, addressing Tammy and Dov, "you can also piss off. You're not wanted here."

Then he looked at Tammy and frowned, "Did you say, Ms Pierre, Elly? Christ! You a bloke or a bird? Why dontcha' grow some hair?"

Returning to their car, Tammy called back, "Phone me if you need anything, Mrs Goldcrest."

It was then that Tammy glimpsed the neighbour to the right of Eleanor's waving at her, she thought, frantically through the window. Tammy nodded at her and raised a hand, palm forward as if to indicate she knew the neighbour wanted to talk.

CHAPTER 10 DAY 3

TAMMY AND DOV WERE BACK in the hotel she'd stayed in previously, The Royal. She'd not told Ginny which hotel in case she called and found that her lover was not alone.

Dov was restless, marching to and fro like a caged lion. He'd stripped down to his black boxer shorts and T-shirt, and now opened the minibar and extracted a miniature bottle of whisky, which he poured into a tumbler before demolishing it in one.

"As I see it," he said, "you're getting nowhere with this. No clues, no motive, no sightings. Nothing."

He stood facing Tammy who was sitting upright on the coverlet of the bed, her back propped against pillows on the backboard. She'd stripped down to a white lacy bra and knickers. With the bandanna removed, she tenderly touched along the scar on the side of her head, feeling the sharp edges of the stitches against her fingertips.

"How is it?" Dov asked, one hand on his hip, the other grasping the empty tumbler.

"Bit tender," said Tammy. "I've taken three Nurofen, so that should help."

"And the ribs?"

"Same," she replied. "And Dov, will you please sit down. You're making me nervous."

"Sure, sure," he said, flopping down in one of the armchairs and stretching his legs out comfortably.

"So, do you have any idea at all who attacked you the other night?"

"None. If I'm being warned off something, then someone needs to tell me precisely what. I do know that in a few days' time I'm booked to accompany a member of a so-called extremist political/religious group to a safe house. I'm still awaiting details. It'll pay well, and business has been quiet for months now. So much so that we may need to vacate Bruton Street."

"How do you feel about safeguarding the life of a potential terrorist?"

"Dov," she sighed. "In the first place, I don't yet know who it is I'm being retained to protect. Second, it's not my job to make political judgements, unless the individual is a convicted criminal. I'm reassured that this is not the case here.

"Third, will you please pour me a vodka, and add some ice from the fridge, and stop fussing?"

"Okay," Dov said, hauling himself out of the armchair and reaching into the minibar for another miniature.

"I have to say, this contract disturbs me, Tammy. Can't you drop it?" he added, handing Tammy the iced vodka.

"No, Dov. I can't. And anyway, I've already been given a considerable sum on account. I'm not about to refund it."

Wandering back to the armchair, Dov dropped into its comfortable confines. "Okay."

He raised his hands in an enquiring gesture. "So, to change the subject, what're you going to do about making some sort of progress with this Goldcrest thing?"

Tammy sipped from the chilled drink, felt it lace her insides comfortingly. She needed a line but not while Dov was around. He'd be furious.

And also, her habit was the only thing that ever made Ginny really angry. Otherwise the younger woman was as placid and agreeable as it was possible to be. That reminded Tammy she'd not spoken to Ginny for most of the day.

"I need to call Ginny," she announced, picking up her mobile and punching in the single digit speed dial.

Ginny picked up on the first ring. "Tammy?" she said, breathlessly.

"Hi Ginny. Everything okay?"

"Yes, darling."

"Any enquiries?"

"A couple."

"Let me guess. Surveillance jobs for potential divorcees?"

"'Fraid so."

"Oh well. Better than nothing I suppose."

"Hmm. I guess. How's your head, Tams?"

"Bit sore. Look, I'm turning in now. I'm tired. Getting nowhere with the Goldcrest thing."

"Why don't you call your friend at the Met?"

Tammy swallowed the last of her drink, closed her eyes for a moment, savoured the taste at the back of her throat.

"I will, tomorrow. Chief Superintendent Bob Walker owes me a favour. I need an intro into the Lyme Regis nick, and a chance to look at any CCTV footage they might have. Bob should be able to shoehorn me in."

"How long do you think you'll be away, darling?"

"Don't know, Ginny. Probably just overnight. I'll let you know as soon as I do."

"I miss you, Tammy."

"I miss you too, darling. Now I must sleep. I guess I'll see you tomorrow."

"Okay. Love you."

"Love you too."

Tammy rang off and looked across at Dov. "I feel so guilty, Dov."

Dov leant forward, putting his hands on the armrests as though he was about to lever himself out of the armchair.

"Do you want me to go, Tammy?"

"No dammit, no. I want you to stay."

CHAPTER 11 DAY 3

"WHAT THE HELL are you doing now, Tammy?"

She was grabbing at a pair of grey slacks and a white blouse, hauling on black bootees. "That neighbour. The one next door to Eleanor."

"The one that waved at you?"

"That's right. I'm going back to talk to her."

"What now? I thought we were looking for an early night?"

"We were," said Tammy, picking up the room 'phone and calling reception to order her a taxi.

"And now we're not."

Dov ran both hands through his hair; he looked utterly exasperated. "Hell, Tammy. I wish you'd make up your mind what you want to do."

"Why should I? I'm a woman."

"Do you want me to come with you?"

Tammy pondered for a moment, squeezing the back of her neck, deep in thought.

"No, I don't think so," she responded. "I'll keep this one woman to woman."

The taxi dropped her right outside the neighbour's front door. Thankfully, Eleanor's front curtains were closed. It wouldn't be any help if she were drawn into a dialogue with Tammy regarding anything the neighbour might or might not know about the Goldcrests.

The house was slightly smaller than the Goldcrests' and set back further from the road. Tammy was shown into a living room with older, more traditional furnishings than Eric's and Eleanor's, and highly polished parquet flooring instead of carpeting, but with the same glorious views from the back windows.

Introducing herself as the neighbour, Beatrice Cumming, a plump, late middle-aged woman dressed in a flowered housecoat, explained she was a widow living alone, her husband having died some ten years previously. Seated in the armchair opposite Tammy, Beatrice said, "Call me Bea, my dear, everyone does."

She regarded Tammy with what looked like a hopeful smile. "Can I offer you anything? Tea? Coffee? Something stronger?"

Refusing the offer of refreshment with a shake of the head, she replied, "I'm Tammy Pierre, a private investigator. But," she added, when Bea glanced quizzically at her ID, "I've police accreditation under the Police Reform Act 2002 that allows me to use a police-style warrant card.

"It gives me, among other things, powers of arrest. Of course, it helps, when applying for one of these, if, like me, you're ex-Met. You'll appreciate, they're not exactly handed out wholesale."

"Ooer!" exclaimed Bea. "That sounds really impressive."

"So, talk to me, Bea."

"I have to say, I didn't think, somehow, you looked like police, although you and that handsome young man you were with seemed sort of official. It was worth taking a chance on beckoning you.

"The police had dashed off in a hurry. I wasn't sure what to do right then, but knew I wanted to do something. Talk to someone. Then they came back again a bit later anyway. At least one of them did. That was Sergeant Trevelyan."

Bea frowned as she recalled the conversation she'd had. "Unpleasant woman. Rude. You'd have thought I was involved somehow."

"They'll be back again, Bea. They'll want to talk to all the neighbours in the area, which they probably have already. And no doubt will again. Find out what they can. See who knows what."

"Tammy; may I call you Tammy?"

"Of course, you can."

"Those poor lambs," said Bea. Her face went pink and she looked so distressed Tammy thought she might burst into tears at any minute.

"Oh, I'm so sorry," she went on, raking some stray curls behind her ear, "but when I heard. Oh my! Oh my!"

Tammy waited until the older woman had recovered herself somewhat, then, "Mr Goldcrest is no longer home, I understand."

Bea gazed up at the ceiling as though recalling the man. "My God, he's a strange one and no mistake."

"Do you think he is, or was, ever violent towards his wife?"

Smoothing the lap of her housecoat, Bea replied, "I keep myself to myself, but I've heard them in summer when their windows have been open. He sounds pretty intimidating when he shouts, I can tell you. And once, in their back garden, I saw him yell at her and then clap his hands close to her face. It made a sound like something exploding. She shrank away from him as if she were terrified. But no, I can't say I've ever been aware of him actually hitting her."

"An unpredictably violent man," Tammy mused.

"He already has a record of cautions with the police for violent affrays you know, albeit minor issues, but still... Bea, do you think Eric Goldcrest could have harmed the little girls in any way?"

"Never!" she exclaimed, staring Tammy in the eye. "He doted on them."

Tammy sat up and steepled her fingers. "I've spoken with him and he seems to think the police have marked him out as a suspect."

"No way. Absolutely no way."

Sitting back in the armchair once more, Tammy clasped her hands together in her lap. "So, Bea; what is it you have for me? What can I do for you?"

"Kristof is back," she whispered.

"Sorry, who?"

"I'm forgetting, you're not from the area are you? Obviously, I'd know if you were. My! I could hardly miss you, could I? You're so tall. And beautiful."

And then, as if focusing on it for the first time, "But my dear, your head? What…what…?"

Realising in her hurry she'd forgotten the bandanna, Tammy's hand flew to her head.

"Oh, now I've embarrassed you. I didn't mean…"

The poor woman appeared nonplussed, but Tammy flapped away the comment, "Just an accident. Nothing more."

"Yes but…"

"Bea. Please. Who is Kristof? What makes him so important?"

"Leonard Kristof is a child killer," she breathed. "Nine-year-old kiddie from hereabouts. Raped her first, then strangled her."

Recalling the pictures Eleanor Goldcrest had shown her of the murdered children, a shiver rippled around Tammy's stomach.

"The forensics people said it was his…his…"

"His semen?" Tammy prompted, shaking her head as though to expunge the recollection of the Goldcrest children.

"Horrible. Horrible. I mean how could anyone? Damned animal." Bea had closed her eyes as though it might shut out the memory of what had happened.

"Always claimed he was innocent," she continued. "Then when he was sentenced to life with a minimum of twenty years, he was dragged to the cells screaming blue murder and injustice. At least, that's what the papers said. Screaming blue murder."

"When did he come out then?"

"According to that Sergeant Trevelyan, a month ago. There'd been a whisper among the neighbours before she told me anyway. And before that there'd been press warnings about his imminent release, but they didn't seem aware of exactly when he'd be out, or where he'd be going. That's all I know. I ask myself, is it safe around here now? The locals will want him gone. If you ask me... Well..."

"It's not that straightforward, Bea. He'll effectively be out on licence. He'll need to report regularly to a probation officer. The local police will, of course, know of his whereabouts. He'll be watched like a hawk."

"I suppose so," said Bea. "But they can't watch him twenty-four hours a day can they?"

Then, she paled as though she'd just remembered something. "You know, I thought I saw him last night, and also the night before, through the back window here, looking out onto the garden," she added, twisting in her chair and pointing towards the rear of the living room.

"Tall; a shadowy figure moving between the trees. Long wavy hair, tatty-looking clothes. The security light came on and as soon as he was caught in the glare he ran off. Then last night again, although he stayed out of range, so it wasn't so clear. But it was him alright. I mean, who else could it possibly have been? It frightened me."

"Bea, have you reported it to the police? You should, you know."

"I didn't want to trouble them."

"But that's what they're there for, Bea," she replied gently.

"I will, I will," she said, humbly.

"Does anyone have any idea where he's living right now?"

"He's not been seen by anyone else, far as I know, but I'm guessing he'd most likely have gone back to the home he was brought up in, just north of town off the Woodberry Road, there's a little cul-de-sac. I doubt the place has been lived in for years. His mum, a widow, was there for a while after the sentencing, but she died a couple of years later. They say she never came to terms with what he'd done. Not surprising really."

"His father?"

"Died when Kristof was in his late teens. Heart attack. His mother soldiered on alone. Must have been hard for her. Still, I heard he had some insurance for the mortgage, so that would have been taken care of. She always looked careworn to me."

"Did you know him? Kristof, that is?"

"Not really. We'd been married ten years when we moved here. My husband was a stamp dealer. Always said he didn't need to worry about carrying foreign currency when we travelled. Just kept a few valuable stamps in his wallet, and did deals when we needed local cash."

She paused for a moment, looking concerned. "Tammy, are you sure I can't get you anything? You seem tired, my dear."

"I'm fine; really. Tell me more about his appearance. I mean, when you knew him as a lad, what did he look like?"

"Well, I saw the boy from time to time. Odd looking creature. Not his fault I suppose, but very tall and stooped, like a giraffe. Sticky out ears and a long nose. No chin. Face like a ferret."

"It was him the other night," she repeated. "I know it. All the local girls used to steer clear, not that he ever tried chatting any of them up."

"Bea, I'm going to look for him. I'd like to speak with him as soon as possible."

"What, now?"

"Now."

"Do you think you should? I mean, he could be dangerous."

"I doubt it; he's interested in little nine-year-olds, not women of my age. I can take care of myself," she said, grinning. "And, I'll have my boyfriend book a taxi and come with me," she said, dialling Dov's number on her mobile.

Twenty minutes later Tammy took her leave of Beatrice, climbing into the taxi with an exasperated-looking Dov. "You've been a great help, Bea. Thank you so much."

"I'm really glad to have met you, Tammy. You've reassured me no end. I think I shall sleep tonight a little less troubled. But, just you take care, my dear," said Bea as she waved them both off.

A matter of minutes and the couple found the cul-de-sac and the house, standing on its own, looking pretty run down.

"Wait here, please," Tammy instructed the driver, as she and Dov alighted.

The place, a tiny detached house with crumbling pebbledash, looked derelict. The front garden was overgrown and the timbered window frames and front door were apparently rotting. Through the faded ground-floor curtains a dim light was just discernible.

"What are you going to ask him?" said Dov.

Tammy paused mid-step as she extracted her ID. "God knows, Dov. I've not the slightest idea. But I'd better decide pretty quickly, because look!" she exclaimed.

A tall scruffy figure, with wild hair and wilder eyes, came out of the front door of the house ranting, "Who the fuck are you? Go on, get off my land before I move you off myself!"

*****

So much safer now, Bea thought, recalling the chat with Tammy as she snuggled down beneath the duvet.

Meanwhile, as she slept, and out of the range of the security lights, a stooped figure roamed about in the garden of Beatrice Cumming's home.

CHAPTER 12 DAY 4

SHE'D CAUGHT AN EARLY TRAIN and reached the office in Bruton Street at 10.00 am, Ginny having arrived at 6.00 am. Tammy had a mountain of emails to catch up on and lists to compile of things to do over the next few days. The sun beaming into the office lifted her spirits somewhat, the attack of a few days ago having left her more shaken than she was wont to admit.

Then, too, there'd been the confrontation the previous evening with Leonard Kristof, as unpleasant a piece of work as she'd ever come across.

"The filth again is it?" he'd snarled.

"No, Mr Kristof. We're not police."

"Look like the filth to me." He advanced toward Tammy, peering at her through bloodshot eyes.

Tammy felt Dov move forward as though to protect her. "No Dov," she muttered. "Wait." She could hear Dov's strained breathing as he contained himself.

Pointing at Dov and then Tammy, Kristof spluttered, "Don't you bastards ever leave a man alone? I didn't do it, you know. Twenty years of my life gone down the toilet. Now you're back again."

Tammy studied the man's face. Could a guilty man put on such an impassioned show of innocence? she wondered. "They found pornographic literature in this house, Mr Kristof. Lots of it. The guilty verdict wasn't founded on air."

"So what? So bloody what?" Kristof stood back and folded his arms defiantly. He looked exactly as Bea had described seeing him the other night, in tatty clothing, torn trousers, grubby shirt open at the neck, worn-out trainers, with hair a tangled mess.

"None of your business if I jerk off to pictures of little girls. The big ones always laughed at me." He was waving his arms about, looking manic. "So, it's my business what I do in private. And, I told the police at the time I had all those pictures. I knew they'd make a business out of it. See, they didn't have to search for anything. I told them where it all was. I never touched an underage in my life. I just used to look that's all. Still do, if you must know. Little girls. Just look."

She realised she was going to make no progress at all this evening. "Thank you for your time, Mr Kristof."

"That wasn't my cum they found in her."

Pausing for a moment before retreating to the waiting taxi, Tammy reminded him, "There was DNA evidence, Mr Kristof."

"DNA can be wrong. Cops are bent. Anything for a conviction. All bullshit. It was wrong. Not mine. You hear me? Not mine!" he shouted.

"We won't trouble you further tonight." She could smell his body odour and rank breath.

"You don't believe me, do you? Bitch. Fucking bitch."

"On the contrary, Mr Kristof. I think you were subject to an appalling miscarriage of justice."

"What?" he exclaimed, as they left him standing on his pathway, mouth wide open.

Leaning towards her in the back of the cab, his brow furrowed, Dov asked, "Really, Tammy? A miscarriage?"

"It's just possible. I'll get more from him next time if he thinks I might be on his side."

"Women." Dov smiled. "All beyond me."

"Exactly," she said grinning, as she thumped him playfully on the shoulder.

An exhausting evening altogether, she thought, about to be lightened by a welcome exchange with her old Super.

"Hi, Bob. It's me, Tammy."

"Tammy," the deep baritone of the superintendent was raised several notes in surprised delight. "How good to hear your voice. What's your news? How are things in the world of private investigations?"

"Unpredictable."

"As ever, I'd imagine."

"I'm afraid so."

"You've not wrecked any cars recently, have you?" he said with a trace of mirth in his voice.

"No sir," she responded, recalling the run-in she'd had with him that had nearly resulted in an ignominious and premature end to her career with the police. Strange he should bring it up, and in that fashion. He wasn't usually a man who joked about.

"So, tell me, what's prompted your call?"

"I'm dealing with a client in the Lyme Regis area."

"Something to do with that horrific baby murder?"

"Actually, it was babies. Three of them. You've read about it?"

"Of course. But how are you involved? Surely the local nick are on to things?"

"Presumably, yes. I'm being retained by the stepfather, Eric Goldcrest, who feels he's being hung out to dry. I've not spoken to anyone at the Lyme Regis nick, but I'd like to. I could use an in?"

"Do you know who's in charge?"

"Apparently, it's one DI Margaret Copeland."

"Hmmm. Can't say I know her. But I'll call her anyway, see what I can do."

"I understand her Super is a man called Downey?"

"Ah," Walker said, "I have come across him."

"What sort of man?"

Walker paused for a moment, then said, "Let's just say he's got a reputation."

"A reputation?"

"That's right. He's a top man. Doesn't suffer fools. But he's said to be difficult. Some might say, impossible. He terrorises the lower ranks. Gives them a really hard time. Finds fault, picks arguments. Sometimes jumps to conclusions too quickly. I could go on."

"I think I've got the picture," sighed Tammy.

"The thing is, apart from one or two episodes of, shall we call it, overenthusiasm, on the whole, he gets results. And he'll want the credit for any arrests made in this case."

"Okay. Point taken."

"In particular, he won't want any outsiders meddling. I'll talk to Copeland, see if she'll assist. I'll put it to her that she might score some points with Downey, get some of the credit for any progress assisted by an outside influence."

"Thanks, Bob. That's really appreciated."

Tammy knew the type. Downey. She'd come across them all too often in her professional life. Overbearing, bullying, loud, obnoxious. Usually using their behaviour as a cover for their own inadequacies. But just occasionally, they were result-getters: achievers without patience for the lesser mortals of this world.

When she was a constable, albeit for a brief time, Tammy had had to bear the constant haranguing and harassment of her station detective chief inspector, Hubert Morris, a large, overweight, balding, red-faced individual who berated her at every turn. Nothing she did was acceptable. Nothing was ever right. He attacked her confidence on every possible occasion, and at every possible level, until she began to query her own competence. She even began to question the wisdom of her career choice.

That was until she achieved promotion to the rank of detective inspector, when she'd got to work one day to find the whole team with uncertain smiles across their faces, and a huge bunch of crimson peonies, her favourites, on her desk with a card which simply said, 'About bloody time. Huw.' How could he have known? she wondered. Then she'd understood everything.

Downey, she anticipated would not be so charitable.

She left it for a day. There was office administration to catch up on and a number of surveillances to plan, and wealth checks required for clients chasing outstanding debts, or contemplating divorce. These last she could leave Ginny to work on. It never failed to amaze Tammy that individuals running Bentleys, ten-bedroom mansions in Surrey's stockbroker belt, and holidaying in the world's most exclusive locations were frequently flat broke. The homes were rented, the cars on lease, the lives entirely on tick. In many cases businesses had failed, then been restarted only to fail again. How could they sleep at night? she wondered.

A physical attack she herself could face, the threat of assault was something she'd had to deal with all too often, but when it came to an overdue bill, that would keep her awake at night. Not that there'd been much in the way of overdue bills in her life, up to now. But business was slow; the rent on Bruton Street was coming up, the mortgage on their flat, crippling. The inherited funds had been all but utilised in setting herself up in the business and with Ginny in the apartment, as well as dad in retirement in his flat. The overindulgences, like the vodka, would have to go on hold. For the foreseeable future. As for the white powder. She reached for a cigar.

It was raining. Another monochrome grey London day when everything seems to go in slow motion, plodding, weary, wet.

Tammy's head was throbbing like the insistent beat of a base drum as she sat, elbows on her desk, resting her forehead in her palms. The cigar sat in the ashtray, smoke curling upwards. The stitches in her ribs were pulling like crab's claws and she was feeling anything but focused. Ginny had put off paying a couple of utility bills. Bless her, she'd said nothing to Tammy, but Tammy had seen the envelopes arrive in the post.

Not a good start to a working day, one where she'd need to persuade, or perhaps convince a possibly reluctant detective inspector to co-operate with her.

It was time to approach DI Copeland. Bob Walker had given Tammy both the station number, easily obtained, and Copeland's mobile, the better bet if discretion was to be preserved. Tammy sat looking at her own mobile for several moments contemplating how to deal with or counter a refusal from Copeland.

In the same instant, she gasped with pain as a feeling like the jagged teeth of a man-trap tore at her insides, doubling her over the desk while she grasped her stomach to try to ease the needle-sharp agony. It was happening too often now. For years she'd had the odd twinge, but over the last few months the discomfort had doubled and doubled once more. She should get it examined again, she knew, but there was too much on at the moment. She was well aware of what it was anyway. All a doctor could do would be to confirm the obvious.

A little more than a month ago she had found time to see her GP, Doctor Khan; short, greying, dynamic, committed to his patients and his profession, he was an inspiration. "It's endometriosis my dear. The clawing cramps you've been experiencing."

That's all I need right now, she'd thought, what with everything else going on in her life at the time. Still, she decided, she'd lived with it and put up with it for years and coped. Unlikely she would ever conceive, the doctor had said. What with that and her high levels of testosterone. The hormonal treatment he'd said would help ease the discomfort was something she'd consider in due course. Right now, she didn't need to see her oestrogen levels reduced any further. And, of course, there was no need to take precautions when she was with Dov. Still, a pall of sadness settled over her. Never to be a mother. Not to have the fulfilment of bearing her own child.

She sat quietly, taking deep breaths, calming herself down. She could deal with it. No problem.

As she sat tapping her pen contemplatively on the blotter, easier now, the barbed spasm receding at last, an email arrived. They arrived all the time. She tried to deal with them quickly if she was in the office, scanning them to extract the more urgent ones, or if they particularly attracted her attention. This one attracted her attention.

It was headed in large capitals, picked out in red. It said simply:

READ THIS NOW

> *You hurt Bear. Broke his cheek and nose. We don't find that amusing. Forget the Middle-East contract, or else make sure your Will is up to date. And a word to the wise, lay off the murder investigation.*

Tammy stared at the screen for some time. The language was what she would have called educated, middle class. In particular the phrase, 'We don't find that amusing.' Also, it was properly punctuated, with the hyphen correctly placed. It would have been less alarming had it been illiterate.

And that warning about the murder investigation, could only be a reference to Eric Goldcrest. Someone tapping some phones? No need to alert Mr Goldcrest at this stage, if at all. But who would have an interest in advising her to cry off here?

She pinched the bridge of her nose, puzzled. But then, even if she hadn't been in dire need of the fees the jobs would generate, Tammy would still have risen to the challenge like a Falcon Heavy, the world's most powerful rocket, taking off. "Bear, whoever he is, took me by surprise," she muttered. "Thanks for the warning. Next time I'll be ready."

Ginny, Tammy's one bright spark, came into the office with a hot mug of black coffee and a dish of garibaldi. Bright being the operative word, for Ginny was wearing a smart black dress, edged in red piping, a red chiffon scarf, and red toe-capped black shoes with zebra striped bows at the front. A short, matching black jacket was hanging in the cloakroom. The inevitable red spectacles teetered as usual at the end of her nose. Tammy looked her lover up and down. "My, my, Ginny."

"You like?" said Ginny, her head on one side. "You did see me getting dressed this morning. Didn't you?"

"I did." Tammy smiled. "But it hadn't registered till just now."

"You look very pale, Tammy," she said, staring closely.' "Is everything okay?"

"I'm fine, Ginny. Don't fuss, please."

"Okay! Okay! I was just asking. What's that, Tammy?" Ginny was standing over Tammy looking at the screen with, 'READ THIS NOW' facing her. Usually emails went straight through to Ginny if Tammy was out of the office. Not today. Ginny looked down, the copper curls falling forward fanning her cheeks, and quickly scanned the rest of the message. "'Make sure your Will is up to date?' Not sure I like the sound of that," she said.

"It seems our chum from the other night has friends, or accomplices more likely, who don't want me to take on the Middle-Eastern job. Don't look so worried, Ginny." Tammy looked up at the younger woman's worried frown. "The first rule of any contract murderer is not to telegraph your proposed target to warn them you might be in the area."

"Okay, understood. But look what that man did to you, Tammy. You can't just joke about them, can you?"

"I'm not joking, Gin. I know they're dangerous and I will take care. And while we're on about it, think what I did to him."

"Alright, I won't mention it again. At least, not for the time being." Ginny went back to the outer office where she was comfortable in her own little domain. Everything was neat and in place. Unlike Tammy, who, despite her otherwise obsessive tidiness, was the only one who could locate anything in her own paper-strewn office, while anyone could pinpoint whatever they needed in Ginny's well-ordered space.

* * * * *

They'd met five years previously by chance when Ginny had dropped her purse in Paddington Station, without realising it, while rushing for a train. Tammy spotted what had happened and scooped up the purse and dashed after Ginny, who, it seemed was travelling on the same train.

Ginny was going to see her parents, her father, a locally-based solicitor, and her mother, a primary school teacher, for a long weekend in South Wales; Tammy was on an assignment to the same place. It was a fortuitous meeting, for the two got on as though they'd known each other for years. From there, the friendship blossomed into an affair and finally into declarations of love, notwithstanding Tammy's predilection for men. At the time, Ginny was PA to the sixty percent owner of a Mayfair art gallery, an elderly Swiss gentleman, who with his brother, the forty percent co-owner, had built the business virtually from scratch.

Ginny was astonished to learn of Tammy's profession. "A detective?" she'd asked, incredulous. "With your looks, why aren't you a model, or something? You could be earning a fortune."

"Yes, and dying of boredom," came the response.

At about the time they moved in together to the flat in Queen's Park, Tammy announced that she was planning to leave the police force to go into business on her own, and did

Ginny know anyone who might want to be employed by her as a PA? By coincidence, it seemed, she did, joining Tammy after her three months' notice with the gallery expired.

Tammy was exotic. There was no denying it. At six feet tall with that tawny complexion, cropped hair and skin like velvet. Everything about her. Even her choice of perfume, Bandit by Piguet. The panatellas she favoured which gave her breath a delicious earthy essence. The way she moved, with catlike grace.

Perhaps, above all, came Tammy's absolute confidence in herself. She exuded a sort of male power which, coupled with a natural female sexuality, left Ginny in a constant froth of excitement and uncertainty. She was twelve years Tammy's junior. She didn't smoke. She seldom drank. There'd been a few unsatisfactory men before she'd met Tammy. Nothing that really excited. They were mostly in too much of a hurry, leaving her disappointed.

There'd been one that stood out, though for all the wrong reasons, in her last year at university. A young lecturer, gentle and effeminate. Floppy fair hair and long slender fingers. When he'd touched her hand, apparently by accident, it produced an unexpected response in her. On an invitation for a drink in his rooms at the university, before a meal out, she'd arrived to find him comically dressed in riding gear, waving a switch.

She had burst out laughing at the sight of him, and he calmly told her she'd need to be punished. Ignoring the warning signals in her head and succumbing to a frisson of excitement, she found herself in his arms. It was the first time she'd responded that enthusiastically to a man, but, after all, he was so much like a woman.

Then it had changed. In a moment, he'd thrown her forward on to his sofa, dragged up her mini skirt and used the switch to beat her across the buttocks and backs of her thighs. At first the blows were light and stung slightly. It was a game. She'd played doctors and nurses as a child. It was just a game. Something else told her she should get out of there. But what if it was just a game?

She should've screamed, she knew it. Then the blows became harder, more concentrated, savage even. She could hear him panting with the exertion, hear the thwack of the blows in the air, even before they landed on her. She was turned on her back, embarrassed, spread-eagled, her dress rucked up and he was on her. She could feel him nudging against her looking for a way in. She was stinging, burning where he'd beaten her, her buttocks and thighs bleeding against the furniture, and then he was in her, pushing and pushing. She felt filled with him; not what she wanted. Not like this.

But she was starting to let go, starting to come, despite herself. Her screams, when they started, were not for him to stop, this girly boy with his light weight barely felt against her, but for him to go on and on and in, till she found herself grasping at him, clutching him to her. She was rising to meet his every thrust, her ankles crossed and squeezing against his buttocks, pushing up and pushing up in a rhythmic dance with him, until she felt herself exploding around him, and him in her moments later. She was soaked with him, soaked and shivering.

Back in her own bedroom at the university, she admitted the word she'd denied herself at the time. She'd been raped. She never reported it to the police, her responses, filling her with guilt, prevented her. Every man's bloody dream, wasn't it? But the incident had left her wary of men, and there'd been no more boyfriends. More recently there'd been the one episode with Kurt, but she found herself in a sort of denial where he was concerned. It was just a single aberration.

There had been some brief liaisons with women of her own age, both before and after the incident with the lecturer, but nothing that set her on fire. He'd set her on fire. She'd become confused about her own sexuality. Was it male or female she wanted? One thing was plain to her, she would always feel safer with women. And there'd be no more risk-taking in future.

Then with all reasoning and sense thrown to the winds, Ginny was overtaken by the drug that was Tammy. A narcotic more addictive than heroine. A woman with the strength of a man and the gentleness of a woman. It was an extraordinary and serendipitous meeting of needs.

But it wasn't all pluses. There was the unpredictable temper that Ginny had been on the receiving end of on more than one occasion. And then too, Tammy arrived on Ginny's scene with a cocaine habit. One drug Ginny would not abide. One she wouldn't sanction. It was the one thing that made Ginny flare up.

"You're not bleddy Sherlock Holmes, you know," she'd stormed at Tammy on one occasion, in an oblique reference to the great detective's cocaine habit.

"I don't need you to tell me who I am and who I am not," came the rejoinder.

And so, Tammy had to be discreet when she needed a boost, reeling from exhaustion at times when she was faced with long hours at work on an assignment.

* * * * *

Tammy wondered right now whether to slip out to the ladies to do a line. But Ginny was being particularly vigilant these days. Better not to risk a flaming row at this moment.

Then her mobile sang out. She was wanted for a close personal security job. A gentleman, one Geoff Miggan, a licensed insolvency practitioner was scheduled to preside over a meeting of creditors the following morning, 11.00 am at the Doubletree Hilton in Southampton Row. A liquidator of an insolvent company was required to be appointed to wind up the company's affairs. There were a lot of very angry people involved, and telephoned threats had been made against both the company's director and Mr Miggan. Dov wasn't going to be available, she found, so she'd meet the practitioner there, an hour early to get the lie of the land, and otherwise handle the assignment alone. The cash would be welcome.

Getting on with matters immediately in hand, as soon as the superintendent had tendered it, Tammy had fed DI Copeland's number into the memory of her mobile, and now she pressed the speed dial and waited for the ringing tone. But it went to voicemail, and Tammy decided not to leave a message. She'd call again tomorrow.

7.00 pm, an early night. At first she thought nothing of the navy-blue Lexus Rx450h she spotted in her rear-view mirror as she and Ginny drove home. The car looked brand new, unlike Tammy's similar, but older model. Same colour as mine too, she thought. Very nice.

It was behind her every time she turned a corner. A coincidence? Didn't feel right. Shouldn't still be there. Tammy frowned, and abruptly swung her car to the right without indicating, on an amber light instead of driving forward on the normal route home. A couple of car horns sounded in protest. A pedestrian shook his clenched fist.

The Lexus was still behind her; it must have jumped a red light.

She was a trained security officer with police force experience of taking care of visiting VIPs. She matched this with a built-in instinct for spotting possible threats to her own safety, or that of her charges. But her five years with the police had never resulted in anything quite like the attack from the man called Bear. She made light of Ginny's concern, but frankly, it mirrored her own. The Lexus tailing her meant trouble.

"What is it?" Ginny said.

"Nothing, nothing. Just being paranoid."

But she didn't feel paranoid as she picked up the route home and watched while the Lexus followed her all the way, before finally accelerating away as Tammy came in to park at the kerb outside their block.

They're warning me off, she thought. There'll be more of the same, no doubt.

Then, as she and Ginny alighted from the car, she saw the Lexus again, this time passing their block in the opposite direction. But she had its number.

CHAPTER 13 DAY 5

SHE'D HAD A TROUBLED EVENING and turned in early, taking a single tiny square of Donormyl, a sleep remedy available over the counter from just about every chemist in Britain.

Eric Goldcrest had called during the day asking for updates, progress, whatever. But she had nothing to give him yet. He'd sounded alternately frantic, then bereft, and then frantic again, his mood beginning to get under her skin.

At 2.00 am, with the moon casting diagonal beams across the duvet through the vertical slatted blinds, Ginny became aware of Tammy moving about restlessly in the large bed.

The muffled sound of a car starting up filtered through the double glazing. Somewhere nearby a cat let out a strangled scream. Ginny, now fully awake, stared at the ceiling.

Tammy's arm, draped across her lover's stomach, shifted about restlessly. For a while Ginny lay still hoping Tammy would settle down. But when after an hour she thought she heard crying she reached for Tammy's shoulder and gently squeezed.

"Tams?" she whispered. "Are you okay?"

"What?" she murmured, cuddling up tight against Ginny's soft warmth and inhaling her delicious almond scent.

"You were crying, darling. In your sleep. What's wrong?"

"Crying? Was I?" Tammy was quiet for few moments, then, as though thinking aloud.

"I was having a bad dream. I forget what it was. No. I remember now," she said sitting up quickly, her elbows on her knees, head in her hands. "It was the girls, Ginny. I keep seeing them. The pictures. Those three little… How could anyone…?"

Ginny pushed herself into a sitting position next to Tammy, wrapping a warm arm around her shoulder. "I don't know, Tammy. But…"

Rubbing her eyes with her knuckled fists, she turned to Ginny. "I thought I was a hardened cop after five years in the Met."

"But this was no ordinary crime, my love. It was harmless children. God, Tams, how could you fail to be affected? You're a woman."

"So they tell me," said Tammy, wryly, remembering she'd recently protested as much to Dov.

"Men really don't understand or react like we do. They can't. Or they won't," she sighed. "It's just different for them, I suppose."

Distractedly running a hand over the shaven area of her scalp, feeling the ridge and lumps where the stitches held, Tammy tentatively asked, "Ginny?"

"Hmm?"

"Does it look very ugly?"

"What's that?"

"The scarring. Does it put you off me at all?"

"Tammy," she responded. "Don't be ridiculous. Nothing could put me off you. I love you, darling. You know that."

"Hold me, Ginny," said Tammy, taking the younger woman in her arms and feeling the softness of her breasts crushed against her own.

"Sometimes, Tammy, you seem so vulnerable. I'm just never sure about you."

Releasing Ginny, as though shrugging off the moment, Tammy said resolutely, "I'm making a tea." And, climbing out of bed, added, "Maybe I'll sleep after that. You want?"

"That'd be lovely," said Ginny, watching with something like dismay as Tammy's brief moment of fragility was swiftly camouflaged behind the usual concrete castle walls. Then brightening somewhat, she added, "And hey, you haven't seen since you got in; I've cleaned the fridge, shelves and all."

"Wonderful, darling," Tammy responded, having visions of a spotless fridge and the flooded floor she'd find when she went in to boil the kettle. Ginny's idea of cleaning was a bit like the scales of justice, what went up on one side, came down on the other. So Ginny's well intentioned spring cleaning generally left the flat looking like a war-zone.

Tammy had got to sleep eventually, and was greeted by an overcast morning, although the rain seemed to be holding off.

9.00 am and she was sipping her first coffee of the day. Ginny was out on assignment watching the movements of a financial man suspected of insider trading. His bosses simply wanted a tail on the man to give them an idea of where he went when not in their Canary Wharf office. It wasn't difficult. He was easily identifiable, being a man in his late sixties with thinning grey hair and unusually tall. Ginny would have put him at around six foot eight. He suspected nothing, and judging by his confident demeanour, clearly thought his bosses suspected nothing, and so Ginny, using taxis quickly summoned through the MyTaxi app, was easily able to check on and monitor his movements.

Some of Tammy's colleagues were still resident at her old nick in Westminster, and it was one of these whom she called now, former PC, now Sergeant Cherry 'Red' Stevens, before racing over to the Doubletree for that creditors' meeting. As with the planned call to DI Copeland, Tammy used Red's mobile. "Hi, Cherry."

"Tammy!" she responded without a pause. There'd been a short time when Tammy had wondered whether there might not be something between the two of them. It was inviting; Cherry was a blond voluptuous scatterbrain, who'd finally made sergeant against expectations due to simple bloody-minded determination and a desire to stopper some of her more sexist male peers' pathetic comments. Tammy had recognised something of herself in Cherry, and it was appealing. In the end, Tammy had demurred. Affairs with work colleagues were never a good idea, and in any case, she couldn't be certain which way Cherry leaned.

"How's tricks, Cherry?"

"Fine, all fine, all fine." She sounded excited to hear Tammy. "And you? What's happening in your life? How're things in the world of private investigations?"

"Let's just say, challenging."

"Hmm. All sounds very serious." Tammy could practically see Cherry's captivating smile as she spoke. Always bright, always optimistic. One of Cherry's most endearing qualities. "Let me guess, you want a favour?"

"I want a favour." Tammy smiled. "A car number to be traced. Not sure whether I was being followed or not, but it'd help if I had some information. Probably nothing. But, well, you know…"

"See what I can do. I'll try to link it to something we're on at the moment. If I can't justify it though, it could be problematic."

"I know. Look, don't take any unnecessary chances. If it can't be done, it's not that important. It's just me, looking over my shoulder."

Locking up the office, Tammy MyTaxied a cab and made it to the Hilton at 10.00 am, an hour before the meeting was due to start. She was directed by reception to a large conference room at the back of the hotel, which was laid out to accommodate some fifty or sixty people on chairs arranged theatre style with a centre aisle. At the head of the conference room was a top table with three chairs, a jug of water, tumblers, a bowl of sweets, a box of ballpoints and notepads.

Tammy had chosen to wear a black two-piece trouser suit with a white shirt and dark tie. Two-inch heels raised her to six foot two and she'd worn a short-tailed black bandanna to cover the scar. If there was to be some first-sight confusion about her gender among the attendees, so much the better.

Geoff Miggan, the presiding insolvency practitioner, wearing a sober dark suit, turned out to be a very short bald man, with no more than a cropped circle of hair around the perimeter of his skull, a bulbous forehead, a Roman nose between thick brown eyebrows and, she couldn't help noticing, unusually large hands and feet. Not every woman's idea of Brad Pitt, she mused. She changed her mind abruptly when he introduced himself. The handshake was firm and dry, the voice deep and commanding. The smile, from those full lips, warm and winning. Why was it? she wondered, that the most unlikely men could be so utterly attractive?

The company director, whom Geoff introduced to Tammy, was a Mr Akin Osuji, a tall well-built man in his early fifties, greying slightly at the temples, similarly soberly attired to Geoff. A doctor in private practice from Nigeria, based in the UK, he'd organised the shipping of a number of luxury cars from the UK to Nigeria, initially as a favour to friends, then later as a business when more and more people had sought his assistance. The medical practice had begun to take second place.

Mr Osuji had thought that the well-publicised problems of trade with Nigeria wouldn't impact him as he was from that country himself. He'd been sadly mistaken, with dozens of vehicles having gone missing recently, apparently in transit, and over a fairly short period of time after an apparently trouble-free start to the business. The company was showing a deficit of some £3 million, and creditors wanted their cars or their money back. They wouldn't be in the mood for excuses or debate.

Checking out the space, Tammy spotted what might constitute an escape route through double doors at the back of the conference room, if she needed to bundle the director and the insolvency practitioner away from trouble. She moved the front row of chairs back to ensure that any aggressive attendees wouldn't be too close to Geoff.

"Do things ever get rough where you've been involved?" Geoff enquired, as he surveyed the area, walking up and down the aisle. He seemed entirely unworried. "If so, can you handle dozens of angry people without resorting to violence yourself?"

Standing close to the top table, with arms folded, watching Geoff, she said, "Most people are amenable to reason, and calm down when spoken to softly. I've hardly ever been forced to get physical."

"And if there is violence? I presume you can handle yourself? As a woman, if I may say so, you'd hardly be in this business if ballet was your primary talent."

"Ah, ballet," she said. "It was, insofar as you mention it, my primary ambition in life. Unfortunately, the males couldn't lift me up. In fact, we were all much happier when I was lifting them."

Geoff Miggan smiled broadly. "Ms Pierre, I think you and I are going to get on famously."

People were beginning to arrive early. It was just 10.30 am and a number were starting to take their seats.

"Okay," said Tammy, "what's the format?"

"We start on the dot at 11.00 am. If we start either side of that people may complain. Mr Osuji and I will take our places, and you'll sit, I suppose, further back, but where you can be clearly seen?"

"Agreed," she said, taking one of the three chairs at the top table and moving it off to the left behind Geoff and the director to a place where she could both see the proceedings, and be seen.

"Then?" she enquired.

"Then we start." Geoff walked towards the spot he'd be seated and indicated Mr Osuji to take his place. "With you in a moment," he said quietly, and Tammy noticed the gentleman seemed nervous, constantly pulling at his collar and straightening his tie.

More creditors were drifting in, and from the buzz of conversation and angry looks in Mr Osuji's direction, Tammy could sense an early build-up of tension in the air.

Geoff continued, "After I've got everyone signed in, I'll introduce the meeting, say who I am and my role in assisting the director in preparing for this meeting of creditors, which is called for the purposes of appointing a liquidator, and also a liquidation committee, if required." Geoff and Tammy were standing almost next to each other, their heads inclined as though in intimate conversation, which of course they were.

Indicating where Tammy would be seated, they both walked towards the chair, and Geoff said, "I'll run through the company history, explain precisely what has happened, advise them of the liquidator's duty to both report on the conduct of the director and to trace any company assets. They'll all be given copies of the company history, and statement of affairs, detailing the company assets, which are, unfortunately, nil and its liabilities, running to some £3 million. Then I'll throw open the meeting to questions. That's the time things might start to get difficult. Once we get through that, assuming there's no bloodshed, sorry, I shouldn't joke, there'll just be the formalities of the appointment of liquidator and committee."

By now, the room was packed, showing a mix of people from both the UK and Nigeria, with dozens standing at the back where there'd been insufficient places to accommodate everyone.

Before taking her place behind the top table, Tammy had walked up and down the aisle, letting herself be seen. There were puzzled expressions wherever she looked, and in response to a number of enquiries about whether she was also a creditor, she'd merely responded that she was present to assist with the formalities. Conversation and the connections you made with it were one of the surest ways of nipping potential aggression in the bud. It's easier to attack a stranger than a friend.

Despite all that, Tammy was experiencing her usual pre-assignment nerves. Perhaps, not helped by the approaching time of the month. She was nearly always irregular, her mood swings becoming erratic and unpredictable, her temper unreliable. She recalled the car she'd wrecked in an act of almost uncontrolled rage. Nonetheless, these circumstances were different, and she knew that once proceedings began, her pulse would slow, she'd be ice cold and in control.

She'd already scoped the crowd and found, not surprisingly, a number of particularly large gentlemen had seated themselves in the front row, those places she'd thoughtfully moved some way back. They'd pointedly avoided her pre-meeting overtures. She noted they might be a problem.

And so she took her place and proceedings got under way. All seemed to follow the outlined procedure, until, as Geoff had predicted, creditors were allowed to put questions to the director. As far as they were concerned, the director was the one at fault. He had no adequate explanation for the loss of the vehicles. The meeting became heated, voices were raised. One of the attendees, a Nigerian national, who identified himself as a fellow doctor based in one of London's teaching hospitals, stood and said, poignantly, to Mr Osuji, "You know, you make our people ashamed to be seen in this country."

Mr Osuji looked bereft, unsure where to direct his gaze, but he had no answers. There was a moment of silence while people reflected the embarrassment of one man. It was just a moment, no more, before one of the large gentlemen at the front lumbered to his feet. Taller than Tammy, even in her two-inch heels, he was a man in his fifties, with thick black curly hair, black eyebrows and a prominent hooked nose, wearing a sports jacket and corduroys. "You," he said, pointing to the director. "Where's my car? Or what've you done with my bloody money? I want answers, mister, and I want them now."

As the man approached the top table, Tammy rose quietly from her seat.

Mr Osuji also stood to address the man's questions. His answers were clearly inadequate, and another of those at the front, an equally large gentleman, probably in his late thirties, in jeans and leather jacket, with shoulder-length hair, got to his feet and started adding his own comments.

A third and fourth on the front row, in their forties, both in suits and ties with slicked-back shiny hair, they might have been brothers, now joined in what was now developing into a forum for abuse rather than enquiry.

Time to act, thought Tammy, before it all gets any uglier. Advancing until she was level with the top table, she faced the now restless creditors. The noise in the room was becoming an uproar. Seeing her out of the corner of his eye, Geoff angled his head to one side in a gesture that said, not yet.

Then the first of those to have got up, the black-haired man, advanced until he was practically eye to eye with Mr Osuji. He'd been drinking from a polystyrene cup, which he suddenly swept across his front, drenching Mr Osuji and Geoff Miggan in coffee and dregs.

Tammy knew what to expect now. Experience said, expect a microsecond of calm before pandemonium.

Everything then happened very quickly.

Before anyone could move or speak, Geoff pointed at the black-haired man and said softly, "Sit down, Mr Dixon. You too, Mr Cranfield, and you, Mr Ezenagu, Mr Huxley."

"How d'you know all our names?" asked Mr Dixon, the black-haired one, as he stumbled about, looking at the others in perplexity.

"I know everyone's names here," said Geoff. "For heaven's sake, man, you've all signed the register of attendance."

Then Geoff looked beyond Dixon towards the back of the conference room and called out, "Mr Sekibo, I know you've a couple of queries, would you mind if we dealt with them after this meeting?"

Mr Sekibo, a dapper little man, who hadn't raised his hand with any questions, looked astonished at being singled out, but nodded politely.

The initiative was now with Geoff, and Tammy began to retreat towards her place, wondering what was coming next.

Looking awkward, the front row had resumed their places, and it was now Geoff's turn to approach them. "This is a disgraceful state of affairs," he said, in a voice so low they had to strain to hear him. "Never in all my years in the profession have I had to preside over such an unholy shambles. Do you have no dignity?"

Dixon started to apologise, with the rest of the front row watching without comment. As the apologies grew more profuse, Geoff held up his hand. "My role here is to examine and report to the appropriate authorities the conduct of the director and to locate missing, stolen or wrongfully sequestered assets.

"The formal business of this meeting, which I am now moving to, is the appointment of a liquidator. Does anyone wish to nominate another, other than myself as liquidator?" Geoff scanned the room for less than two seconds. "Carried," he said. "I am your duly appointed liquidator. Do creditors wish to form a committee?" A few looked at each other, but Geoff gave them no time for debate, before confirming that there'd be no committee, then how he would charge fees, and finally concluding the meeting.

"I would appreciate it," Geoff said, walking towards the exit to the conference room, where he proceeded to usher people out, "if creditors would kindly leave in an orderly manner. We're in a public place and I'd remind you to show some courtesy to others using the premises."

Tammy watched, somewhat bemused as the most aggressive of those in attendance left with muttered apologies to Geoff.

And then it was over. A pall of perspiration, anger and resignation hung in the air.

"Wow!" was all she said.

Then, "That was quite something. Did you really memorise all their names? I mean, there must have been more than sixty present."

"Of course not," said Geoff. "I just memorised some of the names of the big ones I thought might cause trouble, and one other name, Mr Sekibo, whom I couldn't see, who hadn't even asked a question. Except, of course, those at the front didn't know that, did they?"

"I have to admit, Mr Miggan, I am impressed. I'm also exhausted just watching you operate. You hardly needed me here at all."

"Oh, I think I did. Your presence gave me some measure of personal security, and it gave the meeting something to distract them. Incidentally, I'm also exhausted, Ms Pierre. I need to get Mr Osuji, who looks lost sitting over where we left him, to sign some things. Then, can I buy you a drink? My room is a bit quieter than the bar. I'm here overnight, then back to the family in Harrogate."

It was more of a suite than a room, with twin double beds, a kitchenette and bar, and armchairs arranged around an occasional table. There was modern art on the walls and bowls of fresh flowers everywhere. It was all lightwood and light upholstery. Bright sunshine flooded the room, dispelling the sombre mood of the past hour and a half.

"What can I get you," he asked, walking towards the bar.

Flopped back in one of the armchairs, legs stretched out, Tammy sighed, "Vodka, please. No ice."

"Think I may join you," he said, opening a bottle of Stolichnaya Blue Label and pouring two generous slugs. "Mind if I loosen my tie?" he asked, dragging the tie away from his neck.

"Not at all," she responded. Mind if I do too?"

An hour later, with naked bodies entwined, Tammy said, "That was nice."

"Only nice? All my hard work, and all you can say is, nice?"

"I'm aching everywhere," she said.

"Everywhere?"

Punching him in the chest, she said, "Everywhere that counts."

He lay back gazing up at the ceiling and smiled.

Draping herself comfortably across his chest, she said, "I have to say, Mr Miggan, you sure know how to please a girl. Tell me, do you have a nickname?"

"First, let me return the compliment, Ms Pierre. You sure know how to please a guy. As for the nickname, whatever makes you ask that?"

"No reason. Just wondered. You know, with all your, ah…skills shall we say? And…those hands and feet of yours? You know what they say."

He leaned up on one elbow and looked down at Tammy with that disarming full-lipped smile of his. "No. Tell me, what do they say?"

Tammy looked at him in amazement. "Are you being serious?"

"I'm always serious, Tammy. May I call you Tammy? You won't think me too familiar?"

"After. After what we've just…? Too familiar?"

"It's just that I should hate you to think I was taking advantage…"

"Heaven forfend. I mean, whatever could have given you that idea?"

"I couldn't possibly say."

She punched him on the chest again. "No sir, it's just that I couldn't help thinking, 'What big hands you have grandma'. You know, Little Red Riding Hood?"

"Is that all the little girl said?"

"No there was, 'What big feet you have grandma'."

He looked contemplative. "Hmm! I think I might be able to guess where this is leading."

"I wondered when you might," she laughed.

"Very well, I admit it," he said, holding his hands up in surrender. "Yes, I did have a nickname. And it rather fits in with your story. You see, it rhymed with my surname."

"Of course." She grinned. "It would."

In the shower, she scrubbed herself clean of any trace of Geoff, hoping Ginny wouldn't be in an amorous mood. She'd need to sleep this evening, and the day was barely half done. She really should feel guilty. She did feel guilty. Trouble was, it only heightened the pleasure. He was asleep when she emerged from the bathroom, so she dressed quietly, and giving Geoff a kiss on the top of his head, slipped out of the room. He'd contact her again, she decided, if he was in London and in need of a bit of personal security.

Early afternoon, Cherry got back to Tammy. The Lexus was a hire car. A company in Brentford. As Ginny's tail had apparently returned to the office, Tammy suggested she make her way to Brentford and effect some discreet enquiries about the driver of the Lexus. They weren't obliged to tell her anything, although client confidentiality was more the province of professional firms, but they might just assist, particularly if Ginny showed them her 'PA to Private Investigator' business card and exercised some of her wide-eyed charms on them.

It worked, but the hirer turned out to be a woman in her sixties. It didn't seem to fit the bill for a driver tailing Tammy. So, just coincidence? Probably. The only odd thing was, the old lady had paid the charges in cash. Still, they had a name and a mobile number to go on, if they were genuine. The name would certainly be, as a hirer was obliged to tender a driving licence as ID.

Copeland was apparently due back in the station by mid-afternoon, Tammy found on calling. So now was a good time to contact her mobile. DI Copeland picked up on the second ring, announcing her name and rank.

"Good afternoon DI Copeland; this is Tammy Pierre. I believe Superintendent Walker may have been in touch?"

"That's right, he was. Yesterday." She sounded guarded. "Something to do with an ex DI working for a client on the Lyme Regis murders. That you?"

"That's me."

"Look, we've got things well in hand. I really don't see how I can be of any use to you."

"No, but I may be of some use to you. If, like me, you've found little to go on regarding motive, I was thinking if we pool some of our efforts, we might make some progress. I'm happy to let you take the credit for anything I turn up."

Tammy heard Copeland sigh at the other end of the phone. Then, "What did you have in mind? I really don't see…"

"At this stage, I just thought…I assume you've still got Scene of Crime Officers involved?" Tammy went on without waiting for a reply.

"The area taped off? Disposable crime scene tent still in place? Someone keeping an eye on things?"

"For God's sake," muttered Copeland. "What do you take us for? A bunch of hillbillies?"

"Okay, okay," responded Tammy, placatingly. "I'll just take a discreet nose around if you don't mind, before I come in to see you."

"If you must," sighed Copeland. "But I can assure you we've already conducted an extensive and thorough fingertip search of the area."

"Understood," said Tammy, not wanting to undermine the DI. "Look, have you got any CCTV around about the time of the murders? We might be able to verify some movements of people. We've got to start somewhere."

"We have started," snapped Copeland. "You don't expect me to start giving you a report of everyone we've interviewed so far and what they've said, do you?"

Then, seeming to think better of it, said, "We're going through things at the moment."

She stopped for a moment as if thinking how to proceed, then said, "Come in tomorrow evening at 8.00 pm. My DCI's not going to be in. I'm telling you, if he finds out, forget your friend Walker. I'll be roasted alive. Christ, that's him coming now. Have to go."

The phone went dead.

CHAPTER 14 DAY 6

TAMMY HAD TAKEN the late-afternoon train to Sidmouth and checked in at the same hotel as before. Eric was paying her expenses, so it wasn't an unconscionable luxury, despite the agency's comparative lack of business.

Dressed casually in denim jeans and bomber jacket with black Nike trainers, which would be comfortable on the uneven shingle, she planned to spend no more than an hour, max, looking around. The search team will have gone over the place with a fine-tooth comb, but there'd be no harm in checking out the possibility, however remote, of something having been missed. Also, it would give her a chance to get a feel for the place. The spot where the murders had taken place. Police work sometimes produced unexpected and astonishing results purely based on the gut feeling of the officer or officers involved.

She'd decided to start her search around the perimeter of the tape which stretched about twenty metres by twenty, some four hundred metres square. She couldn't conceive of anything having been missed within that perimeter. The copper on duty, an eager young lad, had been notified by Copeland that Tammy might show, and merely nodded at her when she introduced herself, while she donned a pair of disposal Walgreen's vinyl police gloves. Tammy's preferred choice, the vinyl being tougher and more durable than latex.

There was a cool evening breeze and the bracing tang of the sea, a smell, three little ones would never get to know. From nearby could be heard the murmur of traffic, but nothing else. Onlookers had dispersed a couple of days ago. About a hundred yards away, two youngsters kicked a ball watched by anxious-looking parents, otherwise the beach was deserted. It wasn't yet dusk, and Tammy could still see reasonably clearly, but all the same, she extracted a small torch just to be sure she missed nothing. Fifteen minutes into her search she spotted something glinting in the late evening sun. It didn't require a torch for Tammy to make out what it was. But before bending down to retrieve it, she looked over to the tent to see if she could be observed, but the constable was out of sight.

Well, well, she thought. And what have we here? It was a heavy gold chain with a pendant on it. An expensive item to have been lost. Had it been reported missing? Would anyone claim it? And why hadn't it been picked up by the search team? It hadn't taken Tammy long to find it, working on her own. How could they possibly have missed it, even if it was outside the taped-off area?

Facing away from the duty policeman so he wouldn't see her, she turned the pendant around to get a closer look. It comprised a pair of hands, fingertips and thumbs touching to form an O-shape that framed a pair of initials. The initials 'EG'. As swiftly and unobtrusively as possible, she slipped the pendant and chain into an evidence bag just as she heard behind her the sound of footsteps crunching in the shingle and the copper's enquiry.

"Found something have you?"

As she turned to her right to face the approaching policeman, she casually slipped her left hand with the evidence bag containing the pendant into her left jacket pocket, leaving her hand there in a casual stance.

"No, nothing. Thought I'd seen something that might have been missed, but it was just the sun glinting off a smooth boulder. Say, young man, when did the fingertip search around here end?"

"This morning," he said.

"Have you seen anyone here since? Any onlookers poking around?"

"Nope," he replied. "Only the usual Council blokes cleaning up rubbish left on the beach. But I was told they're here every evening."

"Same ones?"

"Couldn't say; this is my first time here. You might ask at the station who else has been covering the site."

"And has this area been continually manned?"

"Pretty much. I took over a couple of hours ago; I was running a bit late, so there was a gap of maybe ten or fifteen minutes when no-one was here."

"Okay, thanks. I'm all done now," she announced, and sauntered off.

Before going to the police station to meet up with Copeland, Tammy took herself to the hotel located up the slope overlooking the beach for a drink and a ponder. The same hotel within whose grounds the girls had been lost. She found a quiet spot in the bar and relaxed over a large neat Smirnoff, before donning the vinyl gloves again and extracting the pendant, holding it by the chain for another look. If there were prints or DNA on the item, she didn't want to risk compromising any evidence.

'EG'. Eric Goldcrest? Or, come to think of it, Eleanor Goldcrest. She dismissed the idea of Eleanor. The pendant was a heavy male type, not the sort of thing an elegant woman like Eleanor would be seen wearing.

Eric then? Lots of possibilities here. If he were the guilty party, the pendant might have been accidentally dropped by him at the time of the murders. But then it didn't make sense for the search team to have missed it. And if he had dropped it at that time, surely, he would have immediately reported it as missing in order to divert attention from himself. But then again, if he were innocent, surely by now, he'd have reported it missing anyway.

The only other explanation was if he weren't aware it was missing. In which case, might somebody have planted it there? And presumably not until this afternoon, in order to bring the spotlight down on him. Other than Copeland, no-one locally knew Tammy was due in Lyme Regis this afternoon, so it couldn't have been planted with the express purpose of having her find it. On the other hand, there was always the chance, indeed the likelihood, that it had been deliberately dropped when there was less activity in the area. Specifically, therefore, at the first opportunity that became available, in the knowledge that it could hardly be overlooked indefinitely. Not necessarily Tammy, but someone was bound to find it.

Following on therefore, the next question was, if not Eric, then who? Somebody who wanted him to be collared for the crime? No other possibility presented itself as remotely plausible.

At this point, Tammy had run out of alternatives and decided to make her way to the Lyme Regis police station. As she was retained by Eric, she'd keep all knowledge of the pendant to herself, at least for the moment.

When Tammy arrived at the Lyme Regis police station, as arranged at 8.00 pm, Copeland was waiting for her. There were four other police present in the place, all concentrating on flickering screens. They looked tired and frustrated, like corralled horses looking to escape. The team needed to be larger, but numbers had been reduced as budgets were cut, and cut again.

On one wall was a large chart headed 'Operation Jurassic', with pictures of the three children's battered corpses, together with recent pictures of Eric and Eleanor Copeland. There were also headings covering Motives, Neighbour Comments, Paedophiles, Unusual Local Activities/Visitors to the Area, Random Sightings, and Any Other Thoughts. At this stage, there was pretty much nothing to tie anyone to the killings. The whole taped-off area of the beach had been photographed, but there was little else on the chart beyond what appeared to be random notes and suggestions.

The two women introduced themselves, Copeland with a degree of diffidence. She was wearing a somewhat tight-fitting grey two-piece suit which barely covered her fulsome frame. Tammy was similarly attired, although her suit was an immaculate fit on a honed physique.

"You're so tall," she said, looking up at Tammy.

"So they tell me," replied Tammy.

"I didn't mean..."

"Don't worry," said Tammy, noting the other's embarrassment. "I know I'm not what everyone expects."

Copeland sighed, clearly nervous, but apparently reassured by Tammy's response. "This way then," she said leading Tammy.

The place had a musty smell to it, coupled with that of takeaway chicken and stale burgers. Paint was chipped, desks scratched, wallpaper with damp patches and lifting in places. It all looked and felt tired.

"What happened to your head," Copeland enquired, cautiously.

Tammy's hands went self-consciously straight to the bandanna, which had slipped, revealing the stitches and the shaven area of her scalp. "An accident," she responded, straightening the scarf around her head to cover the scar.

"Pretty nasty. Car?"

"No," Tammy sighed. "Actually, it was an assault."

"Good heavens. Where?" Copeland stood with her hands on her hips, gazing up at the now covered area of Tammy's head as though it might reveal some answers.

"Here, as a matter of fact. In Lyme Regis. A few days ago."

Copeland's brow was creased in concern. "That's terrible. Do you know who or why?"

"Not sure. Think I'm being warned off a security job."

"Did they get away?"

"Not exactly."

"Not exactly?"

"I left the gentleman reclining in the gutter, in a somewhat worse condition than me."

"Wow!" Copeland breathed. "I bet you can take care of yourself," she said, looking Tammy up and down. "I mean, you're pretty big."

"Tall, perhaps. Not sure about the big."

Copeland smiled for the first time. "Security, you said. Isn't that dangerous? I know our diplomatic section have had a few incidents."

"I've done Diplomatic, and the general rule in any threatening situation is, avoid violence at all costs. If it can't be avoided, aim to win at all costs."

The DI looked uncertain how to go on, so Tammy prompted her, "Tell me, from what you've seen and done, those you've interviewed so far, any impressions? What about Eric Goldcrest? A murderer? A child killer? He seems to think you've already got him pegged for the crime. Were you hard on him?"

"Not really. If we're to eliminate people, you know, we have to press for facts. I was no tougher with him than I would be with any other possible suspect. His wife was hysterical. If anything, she gave him a much harder time than we did. I think she's calmed down a bit. But he's not returned home."

Tammy thought for a moment, then said, "You know, the world, the press, they always look to the new father where there are second marriages and children left behind from the previous one. It's as though the new man in a mother's life sees the children as a constant reminder that there was once someone else in her life. Someone whom she loved and was committed to as fully as he now believes, or wants to believe, she's committed to him. Also, there's this thing about the lady having been penetrated by another man who's left his calling card behind, as it were. The kids are a constant reminder of that previous presence. They're an affront to his masculinity. So, the story goes, he wants rid of them."

"When you put it like that. So, what do you think about Eric Goldcrest? Does he fit that category?" asked Copeland.

"I don't think he does. He's a nasty piece of work, admittedly. A natural crook, with a lot of enemies, I'm sure. But I think he genuinely loved the little girls. I interrupted him when he was about to tell me something, then didn't get back to it. I doubt he'll remember what it was. Now, what have you got for me?"

The DI had concentrated on images she thought would be of greatest use in the mass of recorded information from CCTVs from towns around the Lyme Regis area. "There's Eleanor," said Tammy, frowning at the screen. "What's she up to?"

"Looks like she's shopping?" said Copeland. They were seated in DI Copeland's office, a lot of papers randomly scattered about her desk. Much like her own work surface, Tammy mused.

"When's this dated?" Tammy asked.

"Two days before the murder."

"Do we know where this was filmed?"

Copeland looked down at the screen. "According to this, it was shot near the mainline station in Axminster. Look, you can see the station over the back on the left."

"I've got it. And she's with someone. Do you see? There," said Tammy, pointing to the screen.

"Is she with someone? Or does that man simply happen to be near her?"

"Look, look. She's talking to him," said Tammy, pointing at the screen again. "They seem pretty involved to me. In fact, if I didn't know she was already married, I'd say there was something going on between them."

"You could be right," admitted Copeland, reluctantly.

"Tell me, detective, do you have access to the latest facial recognition software?"

"You'll be lucky," said Copeland. "It's available to about a quarter of all UK nicks. And that's it."

Swinging round to face Copeland, Tammy said, "Come now, detective. Don't tell me you can't get some sort of in here."

"I don't know." She sounded doubtful.

"Listen lady." Tammy felt herself becoming impatient. "I've made it clear, any discoveries along the way and you'll get the credit. That should satisfy your man, Downey. I'm told he's hard to please."

"If I come up with something, or if you do, he'll want to know what, how and where the information came from." Copeland looked away from Tammy, refusing to make eye contact.

"That's as maybe. But you'll think of something." It felt as though it was slipping away from her. Copeland couldn't be persuaded to take the chance. She was basically a play safe, timid woman. One who'd only ever feel comfortable if she played it strictly by the book. Mr Goldcrest would be facing disappointment, or worse. Tammy would see the assignment as a personal failure, something she was loath to ever admit to.

As a last shot she raised her voice, "So I'm asking you. Do you want in or not? Are you proposing to remain a DI for the rest of your career, or are you prepared to make a half-step out on a limb and reap the rewards if there are any to be found?"

There was silence.

"For God's sake, woman, answer me. Are you married?"

"Yes," she said, quietly.

"Under your husband's thumb?"

"What?" Copeland had a vision of her husband, that insignificant individual who barely reached her shoulder, who, when he wasn't mute, tried unsuccessfully to humiliate and put her down at every turn.

She sat back in her chair and undid some of the front of her straining jacket, breathing in with relief. Wouldn't it be good to throw all his taunting back in his face with a victory in this of all cases? Mind you, he'd come good with Jessica's problem of bullying. It had stopped, and nothing more had been said by the Head. Perhaps she should give her husband a bit of credit.

"Well?" shouted Tammy.

Copeland stared at Tammy, fascinated by this bizarre woman. "I'll do it," she said, finally. "I'll find out what I can and get back to you."

"That's my girl," said Tammy. "I knew I could count on you."

The mood in Copeland's office had noticeably eased between the two women.

Then it changed. In the smallest moment.

"Christ," whispered Copeland. "There's someone coming in." She stood up from the desk. She'd gone very pale. "It's Downey. What's he doing here? He's supposed to be away." She sounded frantic.

His tie was crooked, and his dark suit creased and shiny. He was round-shouldered and thin to the point of skeletal. He had dark oily receding hair, a long nose and buck teeth protruding from mean lips. He was the closest thing to a rodent that Tammy had ever encountered in human form. Even the tremolo effect of his voice had the shrill timbre of a rat's squeak.

"Copeland," he sputtered. "What're you doing here at this time of night? And who the fuck's this?"

"My name is Tammy Pierre," she said, getting up from the desk. "And I'm a private investigator, retained by a client in the matter of the recent triple child murder here in Lyme Regis. I'd asked DI Copeland if she'd be good enough to spare me a few minutes of her time."

"Oh really? A few minutes of her time, eh? Well, Ms Pierre, or whatever your name is, the few minutes just ended. We don't need the help of an amateur. I'm on to someone already. A bit more time, and I'll have all the evidence I need."

He turned his attention from Tammy. "You!" he barked at Copeland, who was wide-eyed with astonishment. "In my office. NOW."

Then, pointing to Tammy, he rasped, "As for you, I want you out of here, now."

Turning on his heel, he barked, "Hear this, if I catch you in my nick again interfering with any of my staff, I'll have you for criminal trespass, unlawful entry and anything else I can think of."

As Tammy got up to leave, she whispered in Copeland's ear, "The Red Lion, soon as you can. On your own. I've got something for you."

CHAPTER 15 DAY 6

THERE WAS A HOLLOW SILENCE at the other end of the line. Then, faintly discernible, the sound of breathing.

"Who the fuck is this?" Goldcrest grabbed the phone as soon as it rang, putting it to his ear, not noticing who the caller was. He was exhausted, worn out. Burned out more like. Trying to keep tabs on what was happening at work while waiting for the Pierre woman to come up with something. The police were a waste of space. That self-satisfied bastard Downey didn't have a clue. Copeland? Nice lady, but out of her depth, he reckoned.

If he had his way, he'd shake up the police. Make 'em shape up. More government funding, bobbies on the beat again, re-open all those nicks they'd closed. Tougher sentencing. Bring back the birch. And hanging. No pissing around. Bloody do-gooders. 'Would you be prepared to witness a hanging, Mr Goldcrest?' asked some idiot at a dinner party a few years ago. Christ, he'd told her. He'd throw the bloody switch himself. He had sounded so belligerent, she'd started to cry, and he was forced, much to Eleanor's embarrassment, to apologise.

Eric's father, a generally mild-mannered accountant entirely under his wife's thumb, had been a flog 'em and hang 'em man. Perhaps as a foil to his otherwise apparent timidity. 'No messing around son,' he'd said to the boy when he was ten years old. 'Got to pay their debt to society. Too expensive to allow them the luxury of prison. If I had my way, I'd hang 'em all. Including burglars, muggers. You name it. And flogging never did anyone any harm. Look at Winston. Flogged till he bled at that boarding school of his. Won us the war though, didn't he?'

Like his father, Eric was at home with numbers and echoed his father's views on the value of corporal and capital punishment. It spoke volumes about his relationships both in society and in business.

Unlike his father, Eric was happy taking risks. The bigger the better. Also, for all his father's opinions on the punishment of offenders, he was otherwise an honest and honourable man. Colleagues would have been hard put to find the same qualities in Eric Goldcrest, whose ruthlessness in business gave him a reputation that preceded him. But which equally seemed to have contributed to his enormous financial success.

How often, Eric Goldcrest wondered, did they get major crimes in the sleepy town of Lyme Regis, anyway? All so very cosy there. Antique markets, Purbeck ice cream and Jurassic beaches. Goldcrest closed his eyes and shuddered at the thought of the boulders that now seemed only to lay in wait for the defenceless. All that Palaeolithic charm overtaken by a modern murder. It didn't seem possible.

At least the private eye had experience from her time at the Met. Good looking woman, in an odd sort of way. Not his type, though. Too assertive. A sort of man woman. He liked his women quiescent, like Penny his first wife had been. Like Eleanor, for all her bloody moods. Eric Goldcrest needed to be in charge. He also needed people who knew what they were about, like that Ms Pierre.

The silence continued. But something told him not to hang up right away, so he waited. At first there was only the sound of breathing. Then he heard it and heard it quite clearly: it was someone sobbing.

"Eleanor? Is that you?" Eric frowned into his whisky glass, his fourth double for the evening. Then, wearily replacing the tumbler on the glass topped occasional table with a clunk, he dragged himself out of his armchair and wandered to the window of his hotel bedroom overlooking Hyde Park. Dusk. There were joggers doing the rounds, cyclists, evening strollers and the usual moving tide of traffic on Park Lane. He'd be using room service for his evening meal, if he could find the appetite. He'd hardly eaten since the girls had been found.

"For God's sake Eleanor, I've got your number showing on my mobile screen. Either say something or hang up. I haven't got the patience for these games."

"When are you coming home?"

"What?"

"I miss you."

"You miss me?" Eric Goldcrest's voice had risen a couple of octaves. "You're the bloody reason I left in the first place."

In the three years they'd been married, Goldcrest thought he might have begun to understand some of his wife's temperamental inconsistencies. But she was so unpredictable he'd given up, realising the effort was in vain.

"You and that crew from the local nick, particularly that weasel, Downey, practically had me convicted from the word go."

"I know, I know and I'm so sorry, Eric. It was all my fault. When the police arrived..." Goldcrest could hear the sound of crying again. "Please come home. Please."

"Elly. I need time to think. I just can't get my head around what's happened. All three. The babies. Some fucking maniac. How could anyone...? If I could only get my hands on..." He gazed down at the greenery below, tears pricking the backs of his eyes.

"Don't, Eric. I can't bear it."

"Neither can I. Look, I've got this woman working on it."

"I know, Tammy Pierre. She's really helpful."

"Elly, we need more than helpful. We need bloody results."

"Try not to lose your temper with her, Eric. If the police can't come up with something, she's our only chance. You know how aggressive you can get with people. Don't suddenly dismiss her if she takes a time to get any sort of result."

"Eleanor, you've met Pierre. No-one, but no-one is going to tell her what to do. Christ, she's at least six feet tall, and nobody's fool."

"No, and neither are you. But she's not one of your employees. Do your best to treat her like the independent professional she is."

"Don't tell me what I should and shouldn't do, Eleanor." Goldcrest drained the last of his whisky. He could feel himself becoming irritable.

"I wasn't. I just... Eric, the place is so empty here."

"Eleanor, I'm having enough trouble coping myself, I can't deal with you as well."

"But I need you here."

"You should have thought of that before you started telling the police what you thought I'd been up to."

There was a long pause on the line, then, "Eric?"

"It's enough now, Eleanor. I'm tired. I need to rest."

"You, you, you. It's always you, isn't it, Eric?"

"And what the hell is that supposed to mean?"

"I mean, when it comes down to it, the only person you care about is yourself."

"Enough, Eleanor. It always ends up in a row with you, doesn't it? You're never satisfied until you really get my goat."

"Tell me something, Eric. Just for the record." She hesitated again. Not sure whether to go on. But she couldn't go back, not now. Couldn't stop herself, like a leaf caught in the rapids spinning out of control, till she opened up. "Did you kill the girls?"

The words hung in the air between them, the atmosphere charged with uncertainty. The mood so recently close, now cloying.

Eric Goldcrest ground his teeth, his lips curling back in a snarl of rage. "Did I kill the girls? Did I kill the girls? Are you completely off your trolley, Eleanor? Just for the record. Just for your files. No! Eleanor. I did not kill the girls. Now FUCK OFF!"

CHAPTER 16 DAY 6

"WHERE THE BLOODY HELL have you been? And what sort of time do you call this? Your dinner's stone cold and congealed. I'm buggered if I'm reheating it for you. You were supposed to be home hours ago. What do you think I am, your bloody skivvy? Cos if you do mister, you'd better bloody think again."

Doris Downey's estuary English had reached the piercing level of a scream, and heaven knows what the neighbours on the other side of their three-bed semi must have thought of the racket she made almost daily, berating her husband for every real or imagined minor transgression.

Doris Downey's father had been a train driver on Southern Rail until his death, years previously, in a freak accident on the railways. Her mother had married again, a funeral director with his own business in the country, and started to harbour middle-class aspirations which had rubbed off on her daughter.

Detective Chief Inspector Clive Downey was not a happy man. His wife, a chain-smoking, shrewish little woman who favoured dated, ankle-length skirts and faded grey cardigans and looked much as one might imagine one of Macbeth's three witches, was an angry fifty-year-old, who'd had ambitions for her husband she could no longer see him fulfilling. 'You're never going to make superintendent,' was her mantra. 'You're just a bloody failure.'

Downey would invariably shrug and mutter under his breath, 'Stupid woman,' before retiring, as now, to the study in dressing gown and slippers, to watch the latest episode in one of his boxed sets of Scandinavian detective thrillers. He favoured the logic of the police approach, and liked to model himself on the handsome detective, Henrik

Sabroe, played by the actor, Thure Lindhart, and with whom Downey had absolutely nothing in common. He'd gone so far as to try emulating the character's neat pencil moustache and pointy beard, but the growth he sported was too thin, and he just looked ridiculous. It was removed with a sense of regret and no minor feeling of personal humiliation.

At school, Downey had stood out, but for all the wrong reasons. Academically bright, but not brilliant; a loner, he was generally regarded as an impenetrable little creep. Something about the boy unnerved his fellows and he was never actually picked on. He got to realise this odd ascendancy he had over bigger, brighter, older boys, and played on it whenever he could. A sneered remark here, a put down there. His teachers were aware of the mutual dislike bordering on contempt that Downey and his peers had for each other. But as there were never any complaints by parents or boys, nothing was ever deemed necessary to be done.

One day, Downey would have been about fourteen at the time, a group of boys decided to drop him in the mire once and for all, and arranged a contrived theft of valuable items from the stationery cupboard which they planned to lay at Downey's door. Several of the school's laptops and a number of smart leather folios and briefcases for the sole use of staff were taken.

But he'd overheard snippets of their conversation and, putting two and two together, turned the tables on them. He surreptitiously photographed the boys stashing the stocks in his locker at the other end of the school, where they'd planned to 'discover' what Downey had been up to and report him, before his presumed plan to remove the items from the school's premises. But Downey beat them to the punch, and reported them first, to their astonishment, and, by providing photographic evidence, had them all suspended. After that they left him alone.

With an aptitude for cryptic crossword puzzles and an interest in stamps, which suited his tidy, ordered mind, his parents weren't surprised when their son opted for a career in the police, his stated aim being to excel one day as a detective. He'd done reasonably well in the force, though not as well as he'd hoped. Indeed, as a keen young copper his hard work and diligence had been noticed, as had his singular lack of imagination.

Still, he consoled himself, if genius was reckoned to be ninety percent perspiration and ten percent inspiration, his career shouldn't suffer too much. But, with his career seemingly stalled at the DCI level, he was now paying the price for his perceived shortcomings in himself, both as a detective and as a man. For all of his successes, Downey was known for browbeating suspects. At least one likely guilty party had been let go by the court when Downey was shown to have failed to properly explain the man's rights on arrest. Downey still harboured hopes of eventual further recognition of his talents with the appropriate promotion, however far remote that possibility seemed to be becoming.

He and Doris had never had children. They'd met when Downey was a sergeant attending a funeral organised by Doris's stepfather. The latter had hoped his stepdaughter would one day enter the business, but while she was prepared to help on occasions such as this, she was otherwise having none of it.

The deceased had died in suspicious circumstances and Downey was charged with the task of scoping out attendees at the event for future examination and possible questioning. He'd scoped out Doris, who at the time was a feisty twenty-two-year-old with a sharp tongue and a brazen sense of humour. She'd taken to the shy young sergeant and saw him, along with her drive, as a route away from her stepfather's ambitions.

Trouble was, Downey hadn't performed as well as they'd both hoped. They'd delayed starting a family, and as Doris became more frustrated with her husband's plodding career, the question of a family had remained on the back burner, until it was pretty much too late.

His own levels of disappointment and frustration grew with each passing season, and with every year he became more belligerent towards his team. His successes, based as much on that questionable attitude he showed towards suspects as on his skills as a policeman, were outweighed in the eyes of his staff who now referred to the perennially depressive and disgruntled man as 'Downer Downey'.

Now, Downey found he was having to deal with something entirely new in his experience, in the form of Tammy Pierre. He just couldn't fathom the woman. That is, man or woman? What was she? Butch, but feminine and beautiful at the same time. Despite himself, he found her attractive, sexy even, though he would never have admitted it to a living soul. Were he a single man, he knew full well he'd be the last person on earth she'd ever find attractive.

But still, he wanted to impress her. He was a DCI. Mightn't he still make superintendent? After all, he was Detective Henrik Sabroe, without the pencil-thin moustache or pointy beard. He realised he was jealous of Tammy. Her talent, her independence, her confidence. She towered over him and just about everyone else, whether she was in heels or not. He didn't want to feel belittled by her, although clearly, he did.

His sergeant, Trevelyan, openly loathed her, using every opportunity to pour scorn on her when Tammy was not at the station. Downey longed to endorse Trevelyan, but realised it was poor policy to slag off a fellow professional, albeit one no longer in the force.

And so, yes, Tammy's charisma was a thorn in Downey's side. It infuriated him, and he'd already determined he'd give her as hard a ride as he could. He ran his own nick in his own way, and he wasn't about to let her get in his way. And as for that bloody French accent. No damned frog was going to show him up in front of his own crowd.

But then, Downey needed a success if he was going to redeem himself in the eyes of his peers and subordinates. All he needed was one big case, one impressive arrest, and he'd be in line for consideration for that long-awaited promotion. He knew he had the ability. His own Super had said as much. But Downey couldn't conjure cases out of thin air. And time was running out for a man in his fifties who was up against youngsters with university degrees being fast-tracked to the dizzying heights he still cherished.

Still, the murder of those three kids might offer him a chance. If only he could get that lazy bunch of wasters in his nick to get off their arses and produce the goods. His DI, Copeland, was too bloody soft on them all. Always looked worn out and haunted. Troubles for some time with her daughter's school. Although of late, she seemed to have recovered some of her energy.

Then an idea struck Downey. An idea that had him smiling to himself. He'd settled down in the study with a glass of Dubonnet, having resolved to ignore Doris for the rest of the evening, and the rest of the week, if possible. Netflix was playing one of the Scandinavian boxed sets he'd already watched three times before. Detective Henrik Sabroe was having difficulty dealing with his sidekick, the autistic detective, Saga Noren, in the murder mystery series, The Bridge. The woman was impossible. Attractive, inscrutable, obstinate. If people like that didn't work on the side of the law, surmised Downey, chances were, they'd be found on the other side. If Saga Noren weren't a detective, who's to say she wouldn't be a killer?

How many times had Downey, on hearing do-gooders complaining that the prison system was supposed to be about rehabilitation of the socially challenged, thought to himself, Rubbish. Punishment. Retribution. It was in the Bible, wasn't it? The code of Hammurabi, king of righteousness: 'an eye for an eye, a tooth for a tooth.'

And it was then that the idea had occurred. It was really so simple. So obvious. So beautiful, he wondered why the idea hadn't crossed his mind before.

Billy Anderson. Local boy. Well, young man. And autistic. He'd been done once before already. Threatening behaviour. Some kiddie's mum had reported him and he'd been let off with a caution.

Caution? thought Downey. Caution? He'd have him. If the murders couldn't be pinned on anyone else, there'd be Billy Anderson waiting for him like a wrapped-up parcel, ready to go.

It was then that Doris Downey looked in at her husband and, pointing at the screen, screamed, "There's still the bloody drying up to do, while you're there on your fat arse imagining you're screwing that Swedish tart."

CHAPTER 17 DAY 7

TAMMY HAD TRAVELLED BACK to London the next morning and planned to spend a day in the office catching up on correspondence and paperwork.

She'd changed her mind yesterday evening and had handed over the gold pendant to Copeland when they'd met up at the Red Lion an hour after Tammy had left the police station, with the advice to say nothing to Downey for the moment. "Get it DNA tested as soon as you can before we decide how to proceed."

Copeland had protested that she had to submit the information to Downey. But, as Tammy had pointed out, if there was nothing incriminating, it would hardly matter, and if there were Downey would be apprised soon enough. From Tammy's point of view, she might just have bought a bit of time for her client, assuming he had an explanation for the pendant's presence near the scene of the murder.

The back-log of work facing her, the mess of the scar and the sometime congealed blood at the side of her head were depressing prospects.

Her head was pounding. Almost certainly the DNA of one the Goldcrests was going to be discovered on the pendant, probably Eric's. But that alone wouldn't put him in the frame. She pinched the bridge of her nose and sighed. Slow progress, she thought.

More depressing, or perhaps disturbing, had been her visit, on impulse and unaccompanied, to Kristof's home late the previous evening. Dov would not have been impressed. But then Dov wasn't going to know. Her approach the last time she'd met with him had produced the desired result as Kristof now cautiously invited her in. He was curious to know why she felt he was innocent.

His place stank of cabbage, sweat, tobacco and the clearly defined aroma of toilet. Tammy shuddered involuntarily, eschewing, with difficulty, thoughts of what she could achieve with a day or two spent cleaning the place. The windows were boarded, as she'd already seen, preventing the place from gaining any type of airing, and the ancient sofa and easy chairs added a musty character to the room.

"Keeps the kids from getting too close," he volunteered, seeing her staring at the timbered barriers. "Been a few nosing about the place. They'll be throwing stones next. Little fuckers."

"Mr Kristof, tell me, how do you live? I mean, how do you get food in? Shop, and so on?"

Leaning back in his armchair, Kristof, his bony fingers with elongated black-rimed nails grasping a roll-up that he constantly dragged on, explained how most of his needs were catered for by his supervising officer. His meagre requirements were covered by the local Council but amounted to a pittance. His supervising officer helped him collect the cash by going to an ATM with Kristof's PIN. With rumours and gossip swirling around, he'd have to move on before things got too difficult for him in the area. The house would have to be sold, if he could find an agent prepared to work for him.

"You know," he said, "thirty percent of released prisoners have nowhere to go, end up homeless and on the street or else they reoffend. At least they get food and shelter back inside. My SO's alright though. Young bloke. Idealist, poor sod. He'll learn. Anyway, for now, he's helping."

"Okay, so you had no choice. You also said the police had already been round here?"

Kristof pulled back a lock of the curling hair that had fallen over his forehead, tucking it behind his ear. "That's right. Coupla days ago. Greasy sod called Downey with some cow called Trevelyan."

Tammy raised an eyebrow at Kristof's description of Downey. "Go on," she prompted.

"Of course, the Prison Service will have told him about my release. Asked if he could have a few words with me. Where was I on the morning of the murder of those kids? I told him to fuck off. Don't think he liked that too much. Pointed a finger at me, said 'I've got you in my sights, scumbag.' I said, 'Aren't you supposed to treat the public with respect. I mean, you are a public servant, aren't you?'"

Despite herself, Tammy almost smiled.

"But you think I'm innocent?" His dull grey T-shirt was torn at the neck, as were the knees in his shapeless trousers, held up with what looked like a length of string for a belt. He was unshaven, and probably unwashed, his hair, having detached itself from behind his ear, was hanging lank and greasy. He sounded almost pathetic. He looked just like the ferret Bea had described him as. "So, what's this all about then?"

"Talk to me, Mr Kristof. Tell me about yourself." Tammy settled herself back in the armchair and crossed her legs, her hands in her lap rather than on the armrests of the filthy furniture.

"What's to tell," he said, shrugging. "I got fitted up by the cops. The night that kid was killed I was home with mum. She told them I was home, but she was getting forgetful, kept changing her story, got dates and times confused. It was pathetic seeing her in the witness box." His eyes seemed to glaze over as he recalled the events of the trial.

He went on, "Prosecutor made mincemeat out of her. Made mincemeat out of me, too. I was frightened. Looked a mess. Wasn't properly briefed by the counsel the court provided. The way everyone in that place looked at me, it was as if they'd made their minds up before the trial even started. Took the jury just one hour to reach a verdict. One bloody hour to decide the next twenty years of my life.

"'Have you reached a verdict upon which you are all agreed?' The judge looked in my direction as he asked the question. Practically sneered at me.

"'We have my lord.'

"'And how do you find the defendant, guilty or not guilty?'

"'Guilty my lord.'

"Witnesses said I'd been seen in the area at an hour which matched up with the time of the killing. Descriptions fitted. 'Tall and gangling,' one of them said, 'with grungy dark hair and no chin.' What a joke. Christ knows who it was they saw, but it wasn't bloody me.

"Then there was the DNA. Something about it being a close match. What the fuck does that mean? A close match? Twenty years ago that was enough to convict. I've read up about it since then. They now know it's not guaranteed infallible. But what am supposed to do? Lodge an appeal? Look at me." He raised his open hands in a gesture of hopelessness. "Not exactly film star material, am I? Who'd want to find me innocent?"

"Very well, Mr Kristof, but what about all the child porn the police found here?"

"Okay, I already admitted that didn't I? Last time you saw me? I get off on pictures of little girls. But not murder. I'm a fantasist. I've never touched a child in my life. Come to think of it, I've never touched a grown woman either. One glimpse of me and they run a mile. I've heard of the Dark Net. But that's not for me. Not that I've got any way of looking at it even if I wanted to." He gestured around the room. "See? No laptop, no TV, no nothing."

Kristof was becoming restive; he'd stubbed out the cigarette and was now apparently casting around for his tobacco tin and cigarette papers on the floor next to his easy chair.

"You've talked about your mother. What about your father? You haven't mentioned him at all."

"He died when I was in my teens. I hated him. Always saying he didn't want to be saddled with another man's child. Beat the shit out of me half the time. Mum was alright, God love her. Not strong enough to deal with him, though. Once he was gone, she pretty much brought me up on her own."

"Another man's child? I don't follow."

"I was taken in. Never knew who my real parents were. Kristof's a Hungarian name. I found that after I made enquiries about my birth name when I was in my twenties. Changed it from my adopted name of Nathan. Mum wasn't all that happy about it, but I wanted a proper identity. My real mother came to the UK when she was pregnant, on her own, single mother, aged just fourteen. My father must've liked little girls."

Kristof seemed to be wrestling with an idea. He twisted around in his seat uncomfortably, finally he looked Tammy in the eye, as if he'd reached some sort of conclusion.

Then, he admitted, "Something of me in there, I suppose. She died a year after I was born. Dropped dead in the street, which is why I was given up for adoption. There was an autopsy. Coroner's report said scars all over her body suggested she'd been subjected to a lot of abuse. Mum couldn't have kids. So… What with him being what he was, dad that is, I often wondered if she regretted persuading him to let her adopt."

He'd rolled another cigarette and drew on it, blowing smoke from his mouth and nostrils. "Look, lady, this is getting tedious. You said you thought I was innocent. Can we get on with this? What makes you say that?"

Tammy stared at the man for several seconds, apparently contemplating her answer.

Then, "Gut feeling. No more. It just seems to me as though there might have been a conviction on little more than circumstantial evidence, added to yours and your mother's poor showing in the witness box. Plus, as you've pointed out, DNA evidence isn't always one hundred percent reliable."

"So, what happens now?"

"I'm guessing that the police at some stage are going to put you in the frame for the killings of these three kiddies. Right now, though, I believe Downey may have his eye on someone else."

"Who's that then?"

"Not for me to say, at the moment. But it might just help if you submit without protest to their questioning, if it's called for. And I wonder whether a fresh DNA sample volunteered by you, might help you show willing in the current case, although to date there's been nothing found to link it to. But, maybe, just maybe, it might be worth a look at the original conviction. I should be able to get hold of a transcript, see what, if anything it, turns up."

"Why would you do this for me?" He stubbed out the remains of the roll-up in a cracked glass ashtray.

"Not you, Mr Kristof. For me. And my heightened sense of what is just and what is unjust."

She stood up, looking down at the clearly perplexed man and said, "Thanks for your time, Mr Kristof. Please don't get up, I'll see myself out."

"Ms Pierre?"

"Yes, Mr Kristof."

"Thank you. You're the first one that hasn't jumped to conclusions." He waited as though unsure whether to go on, then hesitantly, "You can call me Leo, if you want."

* * * * *

She was still thinking about the previous evening's interview, and the sense of mixed unease with the man, together with the grime and hopelessness that seemed to billow out from him, still clutched at her. A blistering hot shower when she'd got home, and another this morning had helped.

And now, she made an appointment for that lunchtime with her favourite hairdresser, Girligig, near Ladbroke Grove tube station. If anything could be counted on to raise her mood, it was a decent hair do. Mitch Janner, the owner, slim and with his customary cap covering a shiny dome, was a genius. His clientele, including both Caribbean and European, either with curls or wanting them, were treated to the artistry of a man who'd written a book on the subject of haircare.

She got back to the office feeling refreshed and light-headed. The bandanna would be needed for the time being, but she looked and felt wonderful. He'd even treated her to a glass of wine before she'd left. Another of the many pluses of his wonderful salon.

Ginny brought her up to date sitting opposite her, but not before admiring the hairdo. "You look lovely, Tams, isnet?" she'd said, with that relic of her Welsh tang.

A fringe bank had been in touch with an unusual request. They'd lent some £5.5 million to an entrepreneur who needed the cash for new plant and machinery for his manufacturing company in the Midlands. The loan required the businessman to contribute half a million pounds of his own cash to the deal. The bank smelled a rat, but couldn't nail it.

It was a safe contract from Tammy's point of view, and would yield a hefty fee if she could get to the bottom of things. Maybe they could manage to stay on at Bruton Street. Maybe not. Ginny ran the finances, with no arguments allowed.

Tammy was still awaiting details of the VIP security assignment to come through; she wondered whether, or if, any more warnings might arrive. The encounter with the man called Bear was still fresh in her mind. It had been a close call. Not one she'd fancy repeating.

There'd been no movement on the Lyme Regis murders. She'd heard nothing from DI Copeland, and wondered if there'd even be any further contact from her. Eric Goldcrest had called several times threatening to report her to her licensing authority, and upon being told that the Security Industry Authority, the SIA, operated with long delays due to both pressure of work and government cutbacks, promised instead to approach his local MP. She was able to calm him down when she explained how she'd enlisted the help of DI Copeland, and he'd just have to wait things out for the time being.

* * * * *

They were having an early evening in, pottering about in their night things: basically, shorts and T-shirts. Tammy wore sensible backless slippers while Ginny's were a fluffy dog-faced creation with droopy eyes, floppy ears and a little smile.

Ginny had thrown together a quick makeshift of rice with shredded chicken leftovers, chopped onion, cabbage, carrot and chilli peppers. Pretty much everything she could lay her hands on in the fridge. She seasoned it all with cumin, salt and pepper, garlic and herbs de Provence. They'd each had half an avocado with olive oil and balsamic vinegar to start with and finished with a simple fruit salad. Ginny had made the main dish a bit too peppery, and she looked sheepishly at an amused Tammy as she panted and flapped at her mouth with both hands until it all settled down.

They were snuggled up on the sofa watching an old black and white on DVD, a Danish film called *Babette's Feast*, the story of two sisters who take in Babette, a refugee who determines to repay the sisters' kindness, following a lottery win, by cooking a meal for them and the whole village with astonishing results.

They'd seen the film before, and would no doubt watch it again. It showed so many of the better aspects of human nature.

Tammy's mobile rang unexpectedly. Lifting her arm from Ginny's shoulder, she reached into the pocket of her shorts and pulled out the phone. Dov's name came up on the screen. Christ, she thought, her palms perspiring. Not now, please. Putting the mobile to her ear, she made as if to answer it and then quickly pressed the red button to end the call.

"That was quick," said Ginny.

"Hmm? Oh, yes," said Tammy. "One of those damned PPI sales calls. You know, the ones that begin, 'Is that Tamsin Pierre? Hiya there, Tamsin. How're you doing?'"

"You got all that? In just a moment?"

"No, not all. But once they start, you know how they go on."

"I always say, 'No thank you. I'm not interested today.'"

"Ginny Jones, you really are too sweet."

"I know, I know," she giggled.

"Honestly, what would I do without you?" said Tammy, kissing Ginny on the cheek. "Say, do you fancy an early…?"

She was interrupted by the mobile ringing again. "What the devil…?"

This time the caller ID said 'Copeland'. "Good evening, detective," said Tammy. "I was wondering when I might hear from you again. Incidentally, where are you calling from?"

"I'm home now."

"Okay. So, do you have anything for me? How did you get on with Downey?"

"Nothing yet," said Copeland. "At least nothing we can use. As for Downey, I've never seen anyone in such a rage. He more or less threatened to see me out of the force if I have anything more to do with you."

"And will you?"

"Will I?"

"Have anything more to do with me?"

"Yes, Tammy. May I call you Tammy?"

"Of course. So, what is happening, Margaret?"

"Meg, call me Meg. All my friends do. And yes, things are happening. But I don't like what I'm seeing."

"Tell me. I'm listening."

"Downey wants results. Wants them now, and doesn't care how he gets them. He says the public and the press want an arrest."

"Oh really? And who exactly did he have in mind? There are no suspects and to all appearances, no clues, no motive. Nothing."

"Downey has been following up a notion I reckon he's had right from the start. He knows about Kristof, of course. We both know that. But he's keeping him as a second string, as it were. No, he's been looking for something else, very specific on the CCTV images to back his idea. Apparently, he was up for hours after you left, staring at the screen. He's working on a theory which will give him an excuse to harass someone I think is almost certainly innocent. Not only that, but someone who's basically incapable, in my opinion, of hurting a fly."

Ginny had whispered that she'd make them both a coffee and had tiptoed out into the kitchen.

"I'm listening," said Tammy, sitting up. "Go on."

"We've a local lad, lives with his mum. Billy Anderson. About nineteen or twenty. He's very autistic, but totally harmless. You'd remember him if you saw him just the once. He's a big boy, I'd say very oversized, with short chopped off hair combed in a centre parting. I spoke to his mum once, and she just said he likes it that way. It's a bit odd looking, but no major issue.

"Some of the kids around seem wary when they're anywhere near him, but he's mostly, but not always, in a world of his own. Like so many of that sort he's a wizz with computers. Works on his laptop most of the day, apparently. Sometimes does odd jobs for the Council. Bit of pin money. His mum encourages it, gets him out, and there's always the possibility of a bit of human interaction. He hardly talks, but he understands and can follow instructions.

"A youngster who was new to this area tried to approach him when out with her own mother a while back, and Billy looked confused. Didn't respond. Tried to walk away, but the kiddie ran after him till Billy mumbled something incomprehensible. The kiddie's mum decided Billy was a threat and called the police, if you can believe. Downey arrested Billy, accused him of using threatening behaviour and eventually he was let off with a caution. Downey's been looking to scapegoat him for something ever since."

"God, that's terrible," said Tammy, getting up and walking restlessly around the room. "What happens next? What's Downey going to do? Arrest the boy?"

"It looks like it. Then watch this space. I'm guessing he'll call a press conference any time now and announce that he's pulled someone in for the crime."

"But he's got no motive."

"That won't stop him. If I know Downey, he'll find one. Or else he'll say the boy's mental and didn't know what he was doing."

"Charitable of him," said Tammy, nodding to Ginny as she put the mugs of coffee on the occasional table.

"Downey might even try to get the boy to sign a confession if he can bamboozle him, and just as importantly his mother, into foregoing legal assistance."

"Can he place this Billy anywhere near the scene on the day?"

"He's seen on CCTV in the vague vicinity late in the afternoon. He was in overalls. Could have been doing a bit of Council work. Sweeping a street, clearing rubbish. And that's it. Not only that, on screen it looks as though he's been out shopping with his mum too, a bit later on."

"You know, Meg, he'll never get a conviction with what he's got. Even if the boy confesses, I doubt the CPS would ever give it the time of day. Is Downey really going to suggest the lad was wearing gloves when he attacked the little girls? Or will he insist that Billy knew what he was doing and wiped the stones clean?"

"I know it's crazy, Tammy. In the end, he'll just make himself look foolish."

"You've sent the pendant off for DNA testing?"

"Yes," Meg whispered, as though she might be overheard. "I'm out on a limb for you, Tammy. I could be out of the force, you know."

"Meg, you're a star. Let's see what they come up with. If there's nothing of substance and we have to declare it to Downey, you give it back to me and I'll say I picked it up."

"And if anything is found?"

"It depends what. If there is a link to anyone, you can say you sent it off in a hurry and neglected to tell Downey. He'll give you some flack, but will bask in the glory of a possible conviction."

Meg Copeland sounded doubtful. "Alright, Tammy; whatever you say."

"You'd better keep me in the loop."

"Don't worry, I will."

"What's happening, Tammy?" Ginny asked after the call ended.

Tammy flopped back onto the sofa, drawing up her long legs, settling her knees under her chin and wiggling her toes.

"You heard me talking to Meg Copeland?"

"Yes, what was that all about?"

Tammy explained the matter of the pendant she'd found.

"But shouldn't Meg be letting her boss know about that?" Ginny asked. "I mean, she could be in real trouble…"

"Don't, Ginny. I know I'm asking a lot. But Downey keeps jumping to conclusions. I'm just seeking to protect my client from misguided pressure or assumptions being made suggesting his involvement, until we've got more."

"I still think Meg should have let someone know about the find, don't you?"

"To be honest, heaven knows. This man Downey, Meg's boss, is tilting at windmills. For an experienced and qualified policeman, he's acting like a loose cannon. Right now, he's very likely considering hauling in a local autistic lad called Billy Anderson, and Meg thinks he's going to give him a hard time."

She leaned over and picked up a mug and started to sip the coffee as Ginny snuggled back under the protection of Tammy's free arm.

"Tell you what, though," Tammy mused, "I'm wondering about the man seen on video with Eleanor."

"What did he look like?"

"Hard to say. The picture wasn't all that clear. But I'd guess he was fiftyish. Fair hair, with oddly dark eyebrows. Maybe his hair was white? Don't know."

Tammy let her feet drop to the floor as she thought about it.

"You know, he was wearing a suit and tie. Not the sort of thing you'd necessarily wear if you were out shopping. They were filmed on a camera near Axminster, not far from the station. If you ask me, he might've just left work and come down from London. But what would he want to see Eleanor about?"

Ginny stuck her fingers in her hair and ruffled it, frowning with concentration. "You don't suppose they could be having an affair?"

"I wonder. And if they are? I can't see what it would have to do with the murders."

The two pondered for a moment. An instant of quiet reflexion. Then Tammy's phone bleeped again.

She pressed the answer button and heard Meg Copeland's voice bark at her, "Sky News. Now!"

CHAPTER 18 DAY 7

BILLY ANDERSON PICKED UP a blue pencil and started sketching in the sky. He'd been drawing for hours on a white sheet of A3 laid out on the living room floor, head down, totally absorbed in an apparently random set of curls and swirls that made no immediate sense.

That is, until he began to bring the whole picture together, filling in the detail that now brought something tangible out of the morass of disjointed multi-coloured lines. His mother knew better than to interrupt him, as he'd get confused and tearful if his train of thought was broken. But she could already make out the familiar lines of local countryside, a church, a brook. It was beautiful and made her want to cry.

No-one would see it, and no-one would buy it. Billy discarded everything he produced as soon as it was finished. It broke Mavis's heart, but there was no reasoning with her withdrawn son, who'd simply pull down the shutters if she suggested keeping anything he'd drawn.

She'd known something was wrong as soon as the midwife handed the huge baby to her. She'd wanted a baby for the twelve years she'd been married to Horace, a ruddy-cheeked man from Cornwall, big, be-whiskered and prematurely grey. He'd decided to come to Lyme Regis for no particular reason he'd ever proffered, to work in commercial angling, concentrating on line caught bass which he sold to local fishmongers and hotels. He left their home as soon as he saw his new-born son. Mavis was forty-five.

"Something not right with him. Boy don't look proper to me, none. Fishing's good in Cornwall this time of year," he'd observed, before packing a bag and departing without ceremony. Mavis Anderson never heard another word from her husband, and was left with the daunting task of bringing up an autistic boy on her own.

Mavis Anderson's grandmother had been in service to a wealthy farming family in Dorset in the early years of the twentieth century, when it was still common to have hordes of servants. Her daughter, Mavis's mother, was a charwoman and daily help all her life, working until she was in her late eighties, finally succumbing to a heart attack when trying to lift and turn a heavy mattress, despite the pleas of her employers to ease up.

"I'm as good as any man. And anyway, what'll I do with meself if I retire now?" she'd protested. And so, she'd died on the job. She probably wouldn't have wanted it any other way. When Mavis was born, her mother had taken the day off work, and then, "Got back to what needed doing in the house."

Mavis was never sure who her father was, but suspected it was the man of the house her mother was employed in. A short and stocky individual of somewhat retiring disposition, whom Mavis undoubtedly resembled in both appearance and demeanour. If the man's wife was aware of Mavis's probable pedigree, she wasn't sufficiently affected to end the marriage.

One thing was certain, whatever her mother's modest circumstances, Mavis never went hungry or short of clothes. Furthermore, the rent of their terraced house was never mentioned by Mavis's mother, so the daughter drew her own conclusions, and later confirmed in her own mind when, on her mother's death, she found she'd inherited what was in fact her mother's house after all.

For herself, Mavis eked out a living doing occasional charring, as her mother had taught her, or else lived off benefits while struggling to educate her son.

School had proved to be impossible. So it was all down to Mavis. And she worked herself to a frazzle. The boy hardly spoke, so his mother was amazed when she'd found her attempts to teach him the rudiments of reading were superfluous. Before she'd even attempted a school, Billy had taught himself to read. He was just three years old when Mavis caught him reading a newspaper she'd left lying around. He'd not heard her enter the room, so she stood quietly and watched as he formed the words and whispered them under his breath, his shoulder-length curly blond hair, that he wouldn't let Mavis touch, bobbing in time with the murmured syllables. It was the first time she'd heard him form a complete sentence. He still only conversed in monosyllables to her, though.

Fairly early on, Mavis had tried a nearby institution that catered to children like her son. Five classes of six children, each with a dedicated teacher. Billy, a big lad, bigger than the other five-year-olds in his class, interacted with no-one, despite the heroic efforts of his teachers. Although one teacher, a slender Malaysian girl called June Tay, fresh out of college, seemed to be making some progress with Billy.

She had her teacher's training diploma, and had supplemented that with an Ofsted rated course dealing with children with special educational needs, or SEN. The syllabus was challenging and encouraged participants to think outside the box. There were few rules beyond listening and observing and then, above all else, patience, patience, patience.

She'd read *The Spark,* by Kristine Barnett, the mother of autistic genius, Jake Barnett. Kristine had concentrated on encouraging Jake, and other children with whom she'd worked, to explore any avenues in which they showed a specific bent. In one case, a little girl had exhibited a particular interest in cooking. Kristine had given the child free rein and in doing so had begun to effect a connection, providing whatever the girl had needed from ingredients to facilities, always showing an interest in her ideas, drawing her out.

The notion she could make a difference excited June. As a child she'd wanted to be a nurse. She played at being a nurse, she'd been given a nurse's uniform for her sixth birthday. She was a natural carer. But as she got older, the sight of her diabetic grandmother slowly dying, the amputations of both her legs, the suffering she experienced, made June realise that the medical profession was not for her. She would be unable to cope with such suffering.

But as a carer she could teach, and she could concentrate her efforts on children with learning or behavioural difficulties. Just watching the youngsters coming into her class each morning gave her a fluttering feeling in the pit of her stomach. They were a challenge, her challenge. She wrote home to her parents telling them what she was up to, and talked about Billy all the time to her flat mate, a mature student nurse with an optimistic take on life, called Barbara.

June would look for any tiny signs of response from her charges, and when she saw them, she'd redouble her efforts to build trust, make progress. And progress was precisely what she had begun to make with Billy, albeit cautious. Mavis had let June know that Billy could read, although it was plain to see, and furthermore, that he was able to cope with mathematics his mother couldn't even begin to comprehend. And he produced beautiful pictures.

So it was his art that June first concentrated on. Presenting Billy with a choice of paper, canvases, pencils, crayons, chalks, pens, paints and brushes, she watched, marvelled and praised what he produced. Endlessly persevering, she observed him producing pictures of mesmeric beauty: a piece of scenery, a still life, farm animals, abstracts, but never a portrait, nothing with people. Then it would all be spoiled in an instant when he screwed them up, discarding them without an apparent second thought. June couldn't get into Billy's head. She couldn't prevent him from destroying everything once it was completed. It was something that presented a challenge to her.

Barbara warned her she was getting too involved with Billy, that she might one day face disappointment, but June wouldn't be deterred. The time would come, June felt certain, when something would be kept, preserved, shown to others. She worked on that, not merely observing, but commenting on Billy's work, describing what she saw, giving her interpretation of his mysterious abstracts, always wondering what went on in that secret mind of his. But always, she avoided physical contact with him. He'd scream if he was touched by anyone, and so she was scrupulous about maintaining her distance at all times.

And then there'd be numbers, and numbers, and numbers. He'd cover the virgin white sheets with webs of numerals, so June bought him mathematics books which he soaked up like a sponge. Apart from his pictures, he didn't damage anything else though, and when, at June's suggestion Mavis bought him a laptop computer, he was entirely in his element, working away, undisturbed for hours at a time.

Billy could sometimes be heard whispering, particularly when working on the laptop, much as he had when Mavis had caught him reading to himself. June tried to listen in, to overhear, but could only try to guess what Billy was saying. It sounded much like a recitation of the mathematical formulae that June observed on the laptop screen. But none of it made any sense to her.

The boy was pink-cheeked and chubby, with an insistence on combing his curly hair in a centre parting for no reason June could ever deduce. She was forming a real affection for the boy. At times she felt she could just pick him up and hug him to bits. Billy still avoided eye contact with her, but she noticed on occasions when she praised him he would sigh, as though in response. The first signs of a breakthrough? she wondered with a stab of optimism.

Then it was all spoiled. Just like that. Ruined irrevocably.

June, forgetting for the merest instant he didn't like to be touched, thoughtlessly patted Billy's arm in a moment of affection. The lad snapped his arm away as though he'd been stung and turned resolutely away from her. In that second June knew she'd lost him, and it upset her more than she could say.

Billy simply closed down, started screaming, even when he was addressed softly by anyone, and, eventually, Mavis had to take him away from school. She liaised with the local Council, keeping them informed of what she was doing in regard to Billy's welfare. No formal teaching was required in the boy's case. Council tests had shown Billy's IQ to be off the scale.

And so Billy had spent his formative years at home with his mother, his art, his mathematics and his voracious reading. After the incident with June Tay, Billy had taken scissors and cut off the long curls, leaving the short cut he favoured. As he got older, he took to walking about the town, where he was largely left alone. He was big, he was harmless, he was known and liked, although he never actually connected with anybody.

All that was until the incident that left Billy with a caution for harassment.

CHAPTER 19 DAY 8

SO, THERE IT WAS. On television the night before, and now in all the national newspapers.

Tammy was at her desk looking at Sky News. The announcement, now repeated in the morning summary, had been made by a smug-looking Detective Chief Inspector Downey at a hurriedly called press conference that a suspect was being questioned. One who had been cautioned in the past for harassing a child. Further news would follow, but no charges had yet been made. Downey had refused to answer any of the barrage of questions that had been flung at him, merely hurriedly stalking off, his stony countenance disguising the satisfaction he was feeling over developments.

Tammy was impatient to learn more, but knew she'd have to wait for Meg's update. She busied herself instead with enquiries into the fringe bank's £5.5 million loan assignment, which kept her occupied for much of the morning.

Meg Copeland called later that day. She whispered, "I'm at the nick right now. Can't talk long, Tammy. Downey's had him in all last night and all day today. Kid's weeping and totally confused. They won't let his mother near him. He's over eighteen, so they say he can make his own decisions. He's not been properly arrested, nor read his rights. Downey's insisting the boy agreed to come in and assist with enquiries. They've offered to allow him one phone call. He's been told it'll all go away quicker if he doesn't bother with a lawyer. Billy has no idea what they're talking about. His mother's been here all day too, crying, poor lass. Downey is totally overstepping the mark. He's said he's going to get a superintendent to authorise keeping Billy in for questioning for thirty-six hours, or more if he makes an application to the local magistrates. Have to go now." The line went dead.

Then Tammy's phone rang again. This time it was Eric Goldcrest. He sounded jubilant. "So they got the bastard. That Downey's on the ball. Good man. Told you I wasn't involved. Now will you believe me?"

"Mr Goldcrest," said Tammy, reaching for and lighting a Wintermans, "I didn't doubt you in the first place. If I had, I wouldn't have taken you on as a client." She blew a jet of smoke at the ceiling. "But I wouldn't hold my breath if I were you. The boy they've arrested is autistic. His original caution for harassment was a nonsense. He had no motive—"

"He didn't need a motive. That scum murdered the babies. They'll put him away for good. He's a bloody nutter. Can't you see?"

"No, Mr Goldcrest, can't you see? There is no case to answer here. It won't ever make it to court. Trust me. DCI Downey might even be censured and Billy eligible for aggravated damages, if half of what I've heard is true."

"You're mad. Call yourself a professional? Do you really think our boys in blue, bless them, would risk any of what you're accusing them if they didn't have a case?"

"I'm not criticising our boys in blue, Mr Goldcrest. Just one of them. I don't believe Downey can be trusted for one minute, and—"

"Forget it, Pierre. I'm hauling you off the case."

"Your choice," she sighed.

"That's right, lady, my choice."

"I'll let you have my bill."

Goldcrest laughed. "Your bill? You'll be lucky," he said and rang off.

Then Tammy's phone went again, just as Ginny came in with a pile of post. She paused as Tammy answered, "It's Meg," she mouthed to Ginny. "Hi Meg, I've just seen Sky news again. That poor boy."

But Meg didn't respond to the comment, she sounded breathless. "Tammy, I've managed to get an ID on the man with Eleanor."

"Well done, Meg. That's excellent."

"It's someone called George Derby. And guess what? He's one of Eric's partners."

"Now that is a piece of news."

"What are you going to do next, Tammy?"

Tammy drew on the panatella, then flapped smoke away from her eyes. "I think I'm going to pay a visit to Eric's business in Shoreditch, London International Investments Corporation, see what they have to say about all this."

"You'll let me know what you come up with, if anything?"

"Of course I will."

Tammy debated whether to make an appointment with the four partners or simply turn up unannounced. She decided on the latter, being impatient for some sort of progress. If the partners had commitments, they'd be unlikely to change their arrangements just for her. If they were available, curiosity would probably persuade them to give her an audience.

LIIC occupied about twenty thousand square feet of office space in a listed eighteenth-century building on Shoreditch High Street. The carpet felt as thick as a sprung mattress and the place exuded wealth and opulence, being decorated mainly in pastel shades with the mandatory glass partitions and abstract art on walls and pedestals.

She wore a navy-blue trouser suit with matching blouse and four-inch heels, not wanting to tower over or intimidate anybody more than necessary. The bandanna was navy to match the suit. Tammy made sure it was firmly in place before announcing herself.

There were two girls at reception, the one nearest as Tammy approached had dark hair cut in a bob, not much longer than Tammy's crop, and wore a turquoise-lapelled blouse. The other girl had blond side-parted straight hair to her shoulders and the same style blouse, which presumably comprised the company's brand image, tying in as it did with the colour of the reception desk and other random furnishings picked out in turquoise in the area and contrasting with other muted colours.

"Can I help you?" the first girl enquired, smiling.

Tammy explained, without detailing more than she needed to, who she was and why she was there without revealing the name of her erstwhile client.

The receptionist looked doubtful until Tammy added that she had been retained in the matter of the Lyme Regis murders. Then the receptionist's eyes opened wide, and said she'd see what she could do if Tammy would just take a seat.

Sinking into one of the several vast turquoise leather armchairs, Tammy didn't have long to wait before the receptionist beckoned her over and let her know that two of the partners were in, Mr George Derby and Mr Nigel Cudlipp. Mr Samuel Goldblatt, the managing partner, was in Antigua, and Mr Eric Goldcrest was presently away on business. They weren't sure of his whereabouts, nor when he was scheduled back in the office.

Derby came into the conference room that Tammy had been ushered into. He was white-haired with black eyebrows, somewhat reminiscent of the Labour politician, Alistair Darling, and looked to be closer to sixty than fifty. His immaculate dark suit and tie were clearly expensive, and he wore an ostentatious yellow gold US university graduation ring set with a blue cabochon stone, which Tammy presumed was sapphire. He spoke with a broad New York accent.

Tammy stood up to shake hands with him, and Derby looked up at her as though surprised at her height, reaching a level about six inches shorter than her. His face was heavily lined and he had the pale, harassed look of a man with something on his mind.

"What can I do for you, Ms Pierre, was it?"

They sat facing each other over a mirror-shiny teak surface, Derby with his hands on the table top, Tammy with her hands in her lap.

"I'll come straight to the point, Mr Derby; I had been retained by one of your partners, Eric Goldcrest, in the matter of the Lyme Regis murders."

Derby sat back and folded his arms defensively. "What's that supposed to do with me? And you said 'had' been retained by Eric? Aren't you anymore?"

"No, Mr Derby. Eric has withdrawn his instruction to me."

"And why's that, may I ask?"

"Because the police are holding someone else for questioning in the matter, and Mr Goldcrest feels he is no longer a suspect."

"I see." Derby sat staring at Tammy, with a puzzled expression. "So what's your take on this? Why are you here if you're no longer retained?"

"Call it my social conscience," said Tammy. "I don't believe the lad they're holding had anything to do with the murders, and I'm going to do a bit of rooting about for the time being."

Tammy placed her long fingers on the table in an assertive movement, spreading them out, the pearl-lacquered nails contrasting with her natural honey complexion. Derby looked down at her hands, then up into Tammy's eyes.

"So what's any of this to do with me? And why are you wasting my time, lady?" The same mode of address that Eric Goldcrest had used. Rude and possibly belittling to one more reticent than Tammy.

"I just thought you might be able to help as you were seen in Lyme Regis with Eleanor Goldcrest, your partner's wife, around the time of the murder.

Derby looked as though someone had punched him in the face. "You're talking crap, lady." That term again.

"I've never been in Lyme Regis in my life. I don't care who says they've seen me there or anywhere else. Get this. I don't socialise with my partners, or their wives. So I think it's time you got your pretty ass outa here before I start calling security."

"Of course, Mr Derby," Tammy said, getting to her feet. "Incidentally, you're quite right, we don't yet have witnesses to your presence with Eleanor; what we have is both of you on CCTV with dates and times."

She smiled politely at Derby and proffered a business card. "Call me if you'd like to talk at any time. I'll be happy to make myself available. I'm sure you had nothing whatever to do with the murders. Though the police might want to chat with you at some time. They may just see things differently."

As Tammy walked out of reception the girl there asked whether she'd like to see Nigel Cudlipp, who was available, but Tammy said no, it would wait for now.

She got back to the office after 7.00 pm. Ginny had sent a text saying she was going on home to cook and she'd keep the food warm. Tammy missed Ginny when she wasn't around. Ridiculous, as they worked together. She called her now and Ginny picked up immediately. "Hiya Tams. Food's on and cookin'. You going to be long, lover?"

"Half hour, darling." Tammy smiled to herself, a warm glow spreading over her till she was enveloped by it.

Then her phone went. Goldcrest? she thought. Derby? The mood was broken.

"Tammy?" It was Dov. It sounded urgent. "We need to talk."

CHAPTER 20 DAYS 8 AND 9

TAMMY WAS LATE AGAIN. Ginny glanced at her watch, the Rolex Tammy had given her for her birthday. 10.00 pm. The meal would be overcooked, the chicken dry, the parboiled roast potatoes spoiled.

Ginny was in her night shorts and T-shirt, both bright red. She stood with an elbow cupped in her palm, the other hand propping her chin. Tammy was late getting home more frequently, instead of travelling back together with Ginny at a reasonable hour. And, Tammy was always tired these days too. She looked worn out, the lines on her face becoming more prominent, her eyes bloodshot. The attack hadn't helped, and whether Tammy was prepared to admit it or not, the man with the knife had left her badly shaken up. The stitches in her head, which had not yet dissolved, were still prominent, and Ginny knew they gave Tammy a lot of discomfort, although she would never complain. Ditto those in her ribs.

But if Tammy had always appeared invincible, untouchable, now she was becoming unreachable. The sudden thought that Tammy might be seeing someone else crossed Ginny's mind. The time spent in Lyme Regis? she wondered. Pretty well all accounted for. The odd telephone call where Tammy hung up protesting they were sales pitches? Couldn't be someone else. So Ginny killed the idea. Tammy would never betray the trust Ginny had in her.

There was still the one major issue ongoing: Ginny suspected Tammy of continuing to use cocaine despite the warnings that she'd leave her. There'd been traces of the white powder on the edge of the handbasin in the loo, not completely wiped away. Tammy's smoking was acceptable, vodka at £100 per bottle had been acceptable up to now, but would be no longer.

Ginny kept a tight hold of the budget, and Tammy's more expensive habits were going on hold. There simply wasn't the business there to justify those sorts of indulgences.

*****

Tammy was dressing frantically. "I've got to get home, Dov. Ginny's going to start suspecting something."

She was ready in moments, the navy trouser suit and blouse all neat, black shoes on, bandanna in place as Tammy checked her MyTaxi app for a cab to take her back to where the car was parked. Three minutes, it said. She'd be home by 10.30 pm.

Ginny had called once already, at the most inopportune of moments. It had been all Tammy could do to sound calm, as though she were just packing up at the office. Worry about the lack of business and at the same time the double life she was leading was beginning to tell on her. She looked weary, she felt it and knew it. She'd seen Ginny staring at her on more than one occasion when she thought she wouldn't notice, as though she was trying to work something out. Trying to appear cheerful and upbeat when it was the last thing she felt was like trying to run an uphill marathon when you were suffering from influenza. She hoped there wouldn't be a row when she got home.

Dov's parting shot was, "Tammy, I already said, we need to talk. We were supposed to talk tonight, not to…"

"I know, I know, Dov. Just give me a bit more time. There're things I need to discuss with you too."

*****

She got to the office early next morning. Ginny was still asleep when she'd left the flat and she was at her desk by 6.00 am dialing her father's number. His voice came on the line, "Matthew Pierre?"

"It's me, Papa."

There was a pause, during which Tammy could envisage the old man sitting up in bed and putting on his spectacles. "Tamsin!"

He sounded strong this morning, and somewhat bemused. "So it's Papa today, not Daddy. We back talkin' French now. Tings mus' be bad. What's happenin'? How's de head?"

"Oh, the head's okay. Healing up. Stitches still there."

"So what's it all about, love? Your Papa am listenin'."

"Oh Papa, it's just everything right now. There's not enough work coming in to meet expenses. I'm making Ginny cross with me. Dov doesn't know where he stands and I can't go on messing him about for ever. There're things he doesn't know that I need to discuss with him.

"On top of all that, I've been looking into the Lyme Regis murders."

"I've seen it in the papers and on the telly."

"What am I going to do, Papa?"

"I'll tell you what you gonna do, love. Y'all gonna carry on at work and let matters take care of their selves. You dealin' with the murders of the little kiddies. Focus on that. Who's your client?"

"That's just it, Papa; I don't have one. The man I was representing, the stepfather of the little girls, withdrew his instruction as soon as they made an arrest."

"So, who's paying you for your time?"

"No-one, at the moment."

"Is that sensible? Why you carrying on den?"

"The man they've arrested, little more than a boy really, he's autistic. I think they want to pin the thing on him. I'd like to help."

"You a good girl, Tamsin. You go an' help de boy, and leave you own troubles on hold."

"Love you, Papa," she whispered.

"Love you too, dahlin."

As she hung up, her phone went again. Someone had been trying to get through as she spoke to her father, but before she could check the phone log, she found herself answering the call. Other than Ginny, or her father, she couldn't think who would want to call her at this hour.

"Ms Pierre?" the familiar American drawl.

"Mr Derby?"

"I think I may have been a little short with you when we met."

"I think you might," said Tammy.

"Could you see me today, do you think?"

"Where are you now?"

"At the office."

"I'll be there in twenty-five," she said and hung up.

At the same moment, Ginny marched into the office; she was in a black skirt and blouse with plain red shoes and a red stole. "You left without me," she wailed, grinning at Tammy.

"You were still asleep, lover."

"Calls at this time of the morning? Is that the man in your life?" enquired Ginny.

"What?" said Tammy, shocked.

"Only joking, you dolt."

"Oh, yes. Yes, of course." Tammy smiled, but it took an effort.

"So? Who was it?"

"Hmm?"

"On the phone. Hello there! Where are you, Tammy?"

"Sorry, sorry. It was George Derby; he wants another chat."

"Mr Derby. That's interesting. I wonder what he's about. He was rude to you, wasn't he? Probably having second thoughts now he knows he's been seen in the area with Mrs G."

"That's what I think. I'm off there now. I'll let you know how I get on."

"Any other plans for the day? I thought you were going back to Lyme Regis shortly. That boy they've got?"

"I'm going down after I've spoken to Derby. They may try to prevent me from seeing him. I'm going to bluster my way in, force it if I have to. He's entitled to the assistance of a qualified representative, which I am. I may be late back, or else stop over."

"Okay," said Ginny, coming over to Tammy and, putting her hands on Tammy's shoulders, kissed her on the nose. "You just make sure you behave yourself. No hanky-panky."

Another moment of shocked silence, then recovering herself with a weak attempt at a carefree smile. "No hanky-panky, darling," said Tammy, kissing Ginny on the cheek before grabbing her handbag from the desk and dashing off.

Derby was waiting to greet her as soon as she arrived at the offices of LIIC. It was just 6.50 am. He ushered her into the same boardroom as their previous encounter, mouthing at one of the girls, already at reception, to bring in coffee.

They sat opposite each other, as before. Derby's large hairy-backed knuckled hands, which Tammy had noticed before, belligerently bunched on the boardroom table like a boxer about to fight.

"So, what's all this about me and CCTV in Lyme Regis?"

Tammy stared him out for a while, contemplating how to deal with the man, her own hands on the table, the fingers placidly interlocked. She decided on the direct approach.

"Are you having an affair with Mrs Goldcrest?" she asked quietly.

Derby stared back at Tammy, his black eyebrows beetling, the malignant grey eyes boring into her. He and Eric Goldcrest, thought Tammy: equally unpleasant individuals, both financial predators and highly appropriate partners. She could see the rise and fall of his chest as he considered his reply, but she wrong-footed him again by answering for him.

"I think the answer must be yes, Mr Derby. Or else you'd have denied it by now."

"Well, what if I am?" he growled. "What's it to you anyway?"

They were interrupted by the receptionist with the bob coming in with a tray of cups, biscuits and a cafetière of coffee. Derby waved her away impatiently, and she left without a word.

"You asked to see me," said Tammy, ignoring Derby's question. "How can I help?"

"How d'you think Eric fits in with this whole thing? D'you think he could'a' done it?"

"Not for one moment."

"What about me then? You say I'm on CCTV in the area."

"That's right."

"So, tell me, does that put me in the frame?" He sounded apprehensive, his voice low as though afraid he might be heard.

"You tell me, Mr Derby. I asked you a straight question; are you having an affair with Mrs Goldcrest?"

"And if I am?"

"All sorts of possibilities. For one thing, I can't think of any motive you'd have for murdering three innocent children, even if it was in supposed revenge for any grudge you might have had against Mr Goldcrest."

"So, that eliminates me."

"In my eyes, maybe. But the police may take a different view if they can't make charges stick against Billy Anderson, and they won't. They've been looking for anything they can lay their hands on. DCI Downey is a man who shoots from the hip. They say he gets results. He also gets things wrong. He's an impatient man. Shortly, they're going to have to let Billy go. That's when Downey will start looking for new ideas. Make no mistake. You'll be in the frame, at least for a while."

"Shit!" he muttered. "That'll do my reputation a lot of good. Be great for the business," he said with no trace of irony.

"Might the police look for a revenge motive? Did Eric Goldcrest ever do you any wrong?"

"Too right he did. And got away with it. A lot of money was involved. I mean, a lot." Derby put his hands together in an attitude of prayer.

"I could have wrung the fucker's neck. There were rumours. If you, or the police start nosing around in the industry, there'll be enough people out there willing to try to screw me by detailing what was involved. Or what they believe was involved. It'll be pretty obvious I wanted his guts. We couldn't get rid of Goldcrest; the mutha had something on all of us. Well, maybe not Sam."

"Sam? Is that Samuel Goldblatt, the managing partner."

"Right. Man's clean as a whistle. Don't think he realised what he was climbing into bed with when he collared me together with Eric and Nigel. He thought our talent would more than make up for our shenanigans. Thought his honesty and knowledge of the people in this industry and how to deal with them would iron out any problems. Felt the whole was better than the individual parts."

"What one might refer to as a symbiotic partnership."

"How's that?" Derby looked puzzled, his head on one side.

"Nothing," she responded. "I have to say, you and your industry don't inspire confidence, Mr Derby."

"Yeah, I know. A lotta not very nice people. I don't pretend to be any better than the rest of the buggers. But I'm no killer, Ms Pierre, for Chrissake."

"No, Mr Derby. I don't believe you are." She paused.

"So then, tell me about your relationship with Eleanor Goldcrest."

"Oh that. Well, it started sorta casually. We'd see each other socially, at gatherings, partners' dinners, and so on. Only when we had to," he added.

The coffee hadn't been touched. "Can I?" Derby pointed to the cafetière and Tammy nodded. "She made all the running. Flirted when he wasn't looking. Dropped hints, found reasons to touch my hand, like if she was passing a glass of something my way. I didn't get it. Thought she was happily married, if anyone could be to that piece of—"

"And?"

"Seems she wasn't. So, we started meeting up at the hotel in Axminster. It was just far enough away from Lyme Regis for her not to be known, she hoped, and close enough for her to be around for the little ones."

"You were noted on the hotel register as having been there on the evening before and the morning of the murders, Mr Derby."

"Jesus!" He sighed. "How'd you know that?"

"I'm a private investigator, Mr Derby. I make it my business to know."

"So it could look bad for me?"

"Too soon to say. But it might give Downey an opportunity to haul you in for some fairly unpleasant questioning."

"Christ. Look Ms Pierre, if things start to get, how shall I put it...difficult? Could I maybe employ your services? You know, to help me out a bit?"

"I see we've had a slight change of heart here, Mr Derby."

"Look, I apologised for being rude the other day." He held up his hands in submission. "I was out of order."

Getting up, Tammy smiled politely at Derby. "You have my number, Mr Derby. Call me if you need me."

"I will," he replied, and, getting up to shake hands with Tammy, added, "It may be sooner than you think."

CHAPTER 21 DAY 8

SCREAMS ECHOED ABOUT HIS HEAD like birds' wings flapping in his face, at his ears, his throat. In a blizzard of noise, men's voices, hoarse, commanding, brutal, assailed his consciousness.

A woman shouted, "Hold him, hold him!" And through it all the screams continued.

Hands grasped his arms, bruising them, dragging him up from where he'd been sitting at his laptop in the bedroom.

"Here we go, sonny. Here we go, sonny…" The voice, or was it voices, advanced then faded, back and forth, disappearing into the distance.

His mother was screaming.

He should help her. He was trying. Trying so hard, but, "Mum, mum, mum, mum, mum," was all he could manage.

He was reaching out for her, felt the warm softness of her hand in his before it was savagely wrenched from him. "None of that now laddie. We'll have no more of that, son."

He recognised one of the voices. Higher-pitched than those of the other men. The caution he'd received in the past. It blazed in his memory. The man had shouted at him, that time. Called him a paedo. The magistrate had used words like unfortunate incident. No intentional harassment. And, misunderstanding. But he'd cautioned him anyway. So Billy had a criminal record.

The hubbub went on. He was shoved this way and that, pummelled like an oversized punch bag. He swayed about from side to side and, finally losing his balance, fell awkwardly, knocking his hip against a chair which cracked under his weight.

"Leave him be. Leave him be," Mavis's hysterical voice pleaded. "He's done nothing wrong. Why won't you leave him alone?"

Disjointed words filtered through. Another familiar voice. Female this time. A pale, mean-faced woman. Thin with faded mousy-coloured hair. "William Anderson…warrant for your arrest. Anything you say…"

* * * * *

Following his arrest at home last evening, he'd been kept in a cell all night. Mavis, his mother had managed to calm herself down for a time, then become frantic again when DCI Downey refused to let her accompany her son to the station.

"Can he have Eeyore?" Mavis brandished the ancient soft toy, some of its stuffing leaking from the feet and tail.

"What?" Downey muttered irritably.

"It helps him to sleep. He won't be any trouble. Billy's a good boy, really." Mavis tried to hand the toy to Downey, who furiously brushed her aside.

"For Christ's sake," he snarled. "Your son's going to the nick, not fucking kindergarten.

"He likes muesli and fruit before he goes to bed," Mavis had pleaded in a final effort with Downey, who'd simply been heard to mutter something about bread and water being more like it, if he had his way.

Mavis had stayed awake all night sitting in an ancient armchair, Billy's favourite in the house, as though it would bring her nearer to him. Wringing her hands in silent desperation, she'd willed her boy to be alright. To be strong. To be able to cope, knowing only too well he wouldn't. How could he cope when he hadn't the slightest idea what was going on?

Mavis was supposed to protect her son, but when he needed her most, she was powerless to help him. Weren't they supposed to give you a lawyer? Maybe Billy would get one in the morning. Yes, that was it, in the morning. She sighed. Everything would be alright. Of course it would. It had to be. Didn't it?

Then the bald realisation of her son's predicament burst that brief bubble of optimism. It was all too obvious: Mr Downey had it in for her Billy.

Someone must know what to do? Maybe she could get some help from Mrs Goldcrest? But no. It'd be selfish, the woman was suffering too much already.

Perhaps that Detective Inspector Copeland? She'd looked concerned and worried when they all came around last night. Tried to say something to Mr Downey about helping Billy understand what was happening. But he'd just told her to be quiet.

In the morning, Mavis was exhausted, stiff and desolate. The house was empty without her boy. She'd made herself a cup of tea in the early hours. It stood cold and untouched on a side table. They didn't talk much when they were together, just the two of them. It was enough for each to know the other was there. They had their own largely unspoken language. Signs, nods, smiles. Signals mutually understood, which would never be picked up by anyone else, let alone a policeman who'd already decided her son had committed an unspeakable crime. She'd go to the police station this morning and see if they'd let her see her son. If she asked really politely.

* * * * *

It had been a chill night for Billy, and the bed hard with only a single threadbare blanket for cover. A stale ham sandwich, with green mould at the corners, had been provided with a cup of water. He wanted his mum to be with him. He missed her. Why couldn't she be with him?

"Cuffs," the man had barked when they came to fetch Billy from his cell, as the early light filtered through, pointing at the young man's wrists as though the other officer, the same thin woman in a blue uniform who'd sneered at him last night, needed to be shown where the shackles should go.

"Cuff him now."

Billy looked at the manacles that held his fists together. Tears streamed down his face, their salt taste running into his mouth. The metal bracelets dug into his flesh, and hurt. Billy's heart was pounding in his chest so hard it felt as though he might burst.

Her hands had touched his while she manoeuvred them into position to apply the fetters. They were clammy and cold and made Billy's skin crawl. Billy didn't want to be touched by her. He didn't want to be touched by anyone, except maybe by mum, and sometimes that Mrs Goldcrest.

She was nice, Mrs Goldcrest. Billy called her Mrs El, when he could get the words out, and had begun to let her take his arm occasionally when they walked together. She had a gentle voice, and Billy tried to respond to her, but couldn't always get out what it was he wanted to say, no matter how hard he struggled.

He tried to move away from the officer, that woman, but she said, "Not so fast, big boy. We know what you've been up to, sonny. We'll have you. There'll be no bloody cautions this time."

"Now," she added, "before we get down to the formal stuff." She then proceeded to put question after question to Billy, who merely sat mute on the bed. Eventually, she withdrew exasperated.

"You try, sir," she said to Downey. "Thought I might soften him up a bit for you, sir. No chance. I give up."

He knew this place. He'd been here before, seen the same man last time. He had a yellowy, lined face, thin lips, buck teeth and greasy hair. He looked angry. There was a deep ridge between his eyes and a vein pulsed at his temple. His fists were bunched as though he might hit someone. Billy didn't know why he was here. Didn't know what he was supposed to have done. He only knew the man frightened him.

The Detective Chief Inspector. He smelled a bit like their loft at home, fusty, decaying, as though he needed a wash. He was small, had to look up at Billy, that is until they were both seated on grey plastic stacking chairs in a shabby little room with peeling green painted walls and a table between them, bare but for tape-recording equipment.

The other policewoman, the one who'd just tried unsuccessfully to question Billy, stood by the door to the interview room saying nothing. Her boss would know how to handle the creep. He was experienced in that sort of thing.

Sometimes, concentrating on mathematics for long periods could give Billy a soft headache. He didn't mind; if he'd managed to work something out, managed to understand something previously insoluble, he got a delicious fluttering in the pit of his stomach. He started to recite pi to himself. He knew it to dozens of decimal places, hundreds possibly.

The handcuffs bit deep. Billy's hands were becoming numb and turning blue with the lack of circulation. He tried to adjust his wrists, but the iron clamps were too fast. In the background, Downey's voice, like a mewing cat, cut into Billy's head which began to throb. Billy needed to concentrate on something else.

"Now, sonny. We know what you've done, don't we? Eh? Hurt those little girls? Tell me all about it and we can let you go home to your mum. We know you didn't mean to..." Having barely sat down, Downey got up from the chair, scraping it back, and started pacing the room restlessly.

What little girls? What was he talking about? He'd never hurt anyone in his life.

Billy closed his eyes and concentrated: *the square on the hypotenuse is equal to the sum of the squares on the other two sides. Pythagoras was a mastermind…*

"All you need to do is admit it. Then we can all go and have a nice cup of tea, can't we?" Downey stood over Billy, his arms folded. Billy could smell his breath: warm and sour. It made him want to gag.

Andrew Wiles was a genius. He'd solved Fermat's last theorem in 1994, some 358 years after Pierre de Fermat, the mathematician, had claimed that the proof was too large to fit in the margin of a copy of his Arithmetica…. Billy had read the proof over and over, and felt he was beginning to get close to an understanding of Wiles's brilliant exposition.

There was a tap at the door to the interview room and as DI Copeland entered the room, Downey looked over his shoulder, frowning with irritation.

"I was watching, sir, on the monitor."

"So?" snapped Downey.

"Shouldn't you be reading Billy his rights, sir?"

Downey harrumphed. "He wouldn't understand if I did. Anyway, you were there and saw he got them read last night when he was arrested."

"This interview is being recorded, sir," she offered. "And even so."

"Even so! Even so! Anything else on your mind, DI Copeland?"

"Sir," Copeland said softly, "Billy is entitled to have someone accompany him. And those cuffs, sir?"

"He's over eighteen, isn't he?" said Downey, ignoring the reference to the manacles.

"He's a vulnerable person, sir. He's…"

"When I want someone to tell me my job, I'll bloody ask them. You can sit in if you want, or else you can piss off. Make up your mind." Downey was looking for an approach. A way through to this dummy.

How would Henrik Sabroe' have handled the situation? Downey thought.

The man's pencil-thin moustache would have curved in parallel to his confident smile as he persuaded the prisoner, through subtle questioning, to trip himself up. Sabroe would reign triumphant. He'd make mincemeat of this blubbering, overweight idiot. But he could be equally subtle, drawing the lad out, playing him like a toreador leading a bull by the nose at the end of his swirling cape, before seeing the boy charged with murder. The press would sing his praises. His Super would be delighted. He'd left the moron to cool off through the night. Today would be an example to his team of how to crush a cretin into submission.

"I'll sit in, sir," said DI Copeland.

"What?" spluttered Downey, his reverie interrupted.

"I said, I'll sit in sir," repeated Copeland, taking the chair Downey had been sitting in and arranging herself with her hands in her lap. At least her presence would give Downey pause before he abused the lad any further.

Downey's voice lost its wheedling tone, his hero's subtlety rapidly consigned to distant memory as the DCI became ever louder and more insistent, until he was practically shouting. "Look, we can make things hard for you, laddie. It's your choice. I haven't got all day. But believe me son, if it takes all day. If it takes all bloody week!"

Fidelio was Ludwig van Beethoven's only opera, composed in 1805 and finalised in 1814. Mozart composed twenty-two musical dramas, forty-one symphonies and twenty-seven piano concertos before dying of exhaustion in 1791 at the age of just thirty-five. Thelonious Monk was bi-polar, and a visionary jazz pianist and composer…

Billy's vision was becoming blurred; tears flooded his cheeks once more. Downey's voice rattled on in the back of Billy's head like a dog yapping far off in the distance.

"...entitled to legal representation, but things...must understand...trying to understand...want to be polite... must co-operate...more swiftly if you don't mind answering a few questions. You have no choice in the matter."

The onslaught was again becoming more febrile, more pervasive, until it was as shrill as the shriek of a cockatiel.

Billy was rocking back and forth, back and forth. He was on a swing in their garden. Mummy was pushing him. It was a sunny day, and he felt happy. He was swinging higher and higher. Mummy was laughing. He was smiling. He was rocking faster than ever. More, mummy. More, mummy. More, mummy...

Downey's voice rasped on in Billy's head, the sound of it fading into the far distance as Billy withdrew from his situation. The lad finally felt at peace. At last. It was all going away. He understood, and had it all worked out like the mathematician, Andrew Wiles. Billy looked up and actually smiled as he rocked up and down, his mother pushing him back and forth.

Downey was relentless, his tones as effective as a pair of hands pushing Billy on his swing. Billy tipped over on his chair, falling forward, cracking his skull against the edge of the metal table and crashing to the floor, where he remained, silent and still, blood pooling about the yawning gash in his forehead.

CHAPTER 22 DAY 9

THE WEATHER HAD HELD. Having started crisp and bright, it had now warmed up and the journey by train had been pleasant.

Tammy wondered how pleasant her visit to the Lyme Regis police station was likely to be. She'd not planned anything particular in regard to an approach, but would simply wing it, depending on whether Downey was there or not.

The reception area was very down and out, with peeling paintwork and worn woodwork. A couple of people sat side by side on those stackable plastic chairs, waiting to be seen, she supposed. An elderly man in a shabby overcoat and a woman, who might have been his wife, also in an overcoat, despite the warm weather. The woman, looking decidedly agitated, constantly turned to the man and muttered in his ear as if she'd just thought of something else he needed to know.

Standing the other side of a glass screen was a skinny young woman with faded mousy hair and a long-faced, sullen expression. She would have been about thirty, but already looked as though she'd endured the trials and tribulations of the world for twice that time.

"Are you the skipper here?" enquired Tammy.

"Who wants to know?" said the policewoman, looking up and down at Tammy's tall appearance. Then she glanced up at the bandanna. "You that Peter woman? The investigator or something?"

Tammy's hand went self-consciously to her head, but the bandanna was straight. "I'm Tammy Pierre, private investigator."

"Yeah, I know all about you. Been dealing with my DI, Meg Copeland haven't you?"

"We've had a couple of conversations. And you are?"

Shoving some paperwork to one side, as if to clear her mind, she replied, "I'm the skipper of this nick, Detective Sergeant Trevelyan."

"I believe you're holding Billy Anderson here on suspicion of the murder of the three little girls?"

"That's right. So, what's it got to do with you?" Trevelyan sounded belligerent, though Tammy could think of no reason why.

"I'd like to have a word with Billy." Tammy smiled down at Trevelyan, trying to look as agreeable as possible.

"You his lawyer then?"

"No, but I have reason to believe he is not being legally advised."

"Where'd you hear that from? No, let me guess. Miss Goody Two Shoes, Copeland." Trevelyan had got up from her chair to face Tammy. "Anyway, it's not down to me."

Tammy clenched her fists in annoyance. "Let me remind you, sergeant, Miss Goody Two Shoes is your superior officer."

Trevelyan shrugged but said nothing.

"Is Meg in today?"

"No. She's got problems at home. Something to do with her daughter and school. You'll need to talk to DCI Downey."

"Is he the senior investigating officer in this case?"

"That's right. And I'm the custody sergeant."

"You've interviewed Billy?"

"I have," she said, her chin raised in defiance. "Sort of. He wouldn't answer anything I asked him, and if you ask me, he is guilty as hell."

"Thank you, Sergeant. I'm not asking you. But I would like to see DCI Downey, if you don't mind."

"I'll go get him. I can tell you, he won't be pleased to see you," Trevelyan smirked. "He's gunning for you, you know."

Tammy had little time to plan any strategy with the man as a few moments later, Downey emerged from a side door in the reception area. Looking much the same and just as slovenly as before, he came up to Tammy on the blind side of the elderly couple and hissed, "I thought I told you to stay the fuck outa my nick."

She felt her face go hot. Tammy's hands started to shake with fury but she realised if she didn't bring her bubbling rage under control, she would be no help to Billy. "I believe your suspect is entitled to legal advice, Detective Chief Inspector."

"He's been given the chance."

"You know very well the lad is autistic. How well have you explained to him and his mother his rights?"

"We've done all the explaining we're obliged to do, and he's had all he's going to get." Noticing the elderly couple showing some interest in their exchange, Downey, turning on his heel and opening the door from whence he'd emerged, said, "Not out here."

He hurried on in short mincing steps, with Tammy striding behind, until they'd reached his office, where he promptly sat behind his large and immaculately tidy desk. He seemed more confident looking at Tammy where she stood, and she didn't wait to be invited before taking the chair opposite his desk.

"I didn't invite you to sit down," he croaked.

"You didn't need to, Mr Downey."

"Look, Miss?" Downey attempted a smile.

"Ms, if you don't mind," she said, sitting back and crossing her legs comfortably. He wouldn't be difficult to manage, she thought. He was basically a weak and foolish individual who would crumble at the first real opposition from anyone. He wanted and needed the self-satisfaction of a quick arrest, but hadn't factored in the consequences of having insufficient evidence to make a case against the boy.

"Alright then, Ms. Look, what are you looking for here? We've got the bugger. What more do you want? I mean, what's your interest anyway? You're a private investigator, what do you know about police work? Why don't you just leave all this to the experts?"

"But I am an expert, Mr Downey."

"How's that then?" Downey leaned forward solicitously in the manner of one talking to a backward child.

"Because I'm an ex DI, Mr Downey. I was with the Met for five years, so I know my way around. Now I'd like to talk to your prisoner, if you don't mind."

"You? An ex-copper? Blimey! Whatever next?"

"Your prisoner, please, Downey. He is entitled to legal advice."

Downey sat back in his chair, a look of triumph on his face. "You're no lawyer."

"I don't need to be. You know perfectly well The Police and Criminal Evidence Act grants suspects the right to legal advice. I am an accredited representative. Check it out if you like. And, I've interviewed innumerable suspects."

The older man stared at Tammy, drumming his fingers on the desktop. "You call yourself a private investigator, right?"

"Perceptive of you, Mr Downey."

Chewing his lower lip in irritation, Downey asked, "Just where do you get your info from? You're not in the force anymore, so how'd you do it?"

"I've still got my contacts in forces around the country. I know coroners, pathologists, press, IT experts. I can get into pretty much any bank account in the country. I don't just work for private clients. Governments here and abroad can use my services if they need them."

"Very clever, I'm sure." Downey continued to stare at Tammy. Then he ventured, "What's that accent of yours?"

"I beg your pardon?"

"You've got an accent."

"I've got dual French-English nationality. Part of my education was in France. The Sorbonne. English is my second language."

"Very exotic, I'm sure."

"Can we move on, Chief Inspector?"

"I'll give you ten minutes with him, the murderer."

Uncrossing her legs, Tammy leaned forward to press her point.

"Don't be bloody ridiculous, man. You've not even charged him yet, let alone got a conviction." She sat back again, folded her arms. "The boy's autistic. I want an hour with him, minimum.

"Then I'm coming back again if I think it's going to be necessary."

"Never," barked Downey.

"What are you afraid of, Downey? The verbal confession you might have bullied out of the boy, to use a well-known phrase, won't be worth the paper it's written on. If he's guilty you'll get the credit. If he's innocent and you're shown to have been wrong without having given him a fair chance, you'll just damage your own reputation."

"Alright then." Downey breathed in deeply as though the future of the country rested on his decision. Finally, he replied, grudgingly, "You've got an hour. And that's it. One hour. No more."

"Generous of you, Chief Inspector. By the way, I called Mrs Anderson and asked her to sit in on the interview. She should've been here by now."

Picking up his phone, Downey buzzed the reception area. "Anyone out there?" he asked.

Tammy heard Trevelyan's voice, "We've got Mrs Anderson here, sir."

Downey said nothing.

Two young female officers brought Billy into the interview room, an angry looking Downey standing by with folded arms. The lad was dressed in baggy grey trousers and a rumpled jacket with his shirt collar awry. He was sweating profusely; he'd clearly been crying and there were signs of bruising on his cheek. He was handcuffed.

The two young officers exited, both looking somewhat embarrassed. A moment later, Sergeant Trevelyan ushered in Billy's mother. She was probably in her mid-forties, but she looked older and weary. A little woman, slightly overweight with greying, blond hair drawn back in an old-fashioned bun. She wore brown-framed spectacles and a dark brown coat over a floral dress.

Tammy, having spoken to Mrs Anderson over the phone, now shook hands with her. Billy's mother looked up at Tammy as though she were her saviour, and said, simply, "My!" Then she looked in horror at her handcuffed son. She seemed bewildered and close to tears.

Turning to Downey Tammy snapped, "I want the cuffs off him."

"But he's a danger," whined Downey.

"To what, Downey? Your self-esteem?"

Without a word, Downey looked at Trevelyan and pointed to the handcuffs. She had the keys with her and proceeded to remove them. Billy looked at his mother, appeared to want to say something.

Indicating two chairs on one side of the interview table, Mrs Anderson took the prompt, seated herself and guided Billy into the seat next to her. Then Tammy sat down.

"Satisfied now?" enquired Downey.

Ignoring him, Tammy addressed Billy's mother, "Mrs Anderson, you must be parched. Would you like a cup of tea?"

"Ooh!" she said. "Do you think I could?"

"And what about Billy here? Do you think he'd like a cup too?"

"Oh, he'd love one. He has it strong with three sugars. I like mine milky with one teaspoon. 'That's awfully kind of you, Miss Pierre."

Making no comment about the minor error in address, though noticing Downey's smug amusement, Tammy turned to Trevelyan, "Thank you, Sergeant," she said. "Two teas, please. And I'll have a black coffee, if you don't mind. No sugar."

Downey, nodding at Trevelyan, stalked off in a fury, muttering under his breath, "They'll be opening a bloody tea shop for murderers next."

CHAPTER 23 DAY 9

"I NEED TO SPEAK with you now. Right away, Mrs Copeland. It is most urgent." The voice was cultured, educated; it sounded agitated. Almost frantic.

"I'm sorry, but who is this? Is it—"

"It's Olivia Fordham, Jessica's headmistress. And I need to see you to discuss your daughter, regarding that chat we had a week or so ago."

"My daughter?"

"Well, who else do you have at this school?" There was a pause. Then, "No, I'm sorry, that was quite out of order. Your daughter has been involved in a fight."

"A fight?" said Meg, horrified.

"Actually, several fights. I only learned of this late last night, which is why I'm calling you now."

"Jessica? It can't be. Not our Jess."

It was 8.30 am and she was ready for work. They'd all raced through breakfast, as usual. Jess and her Coco Pops with milk, Reg with his Ready Brek and weak tea, and Meg with two slices of white toast smothered in salted butter and Marmite, gulped back with a strong black coffee.

The three of them were standing in their hall. Reg would be taking Jess to school in a moment. He was still complaining about having the flu. But then he was always complaining about something, and Meg, with a murder on her watch, and possibly on her mind, didn't have time to mother her husband or put up with his constant whining.

"I've got a really busy day today, Ms Fordham."

"It's Mrs Fordham," snapped the headmistress, "and I've been in since 6.00 am this morning, and expect to be here until 10.00 pm tonight. We all have busy schedules, Mrs Copeland."

Meg considered correcting the head's form of address, preferring to be a Ms, but demurred. The woman was already angry enough. This was a very different person to the one who'd previously counselled patience to be exercised by Jessica in the hope that given time the child would tough out the bullying.

"My husband and I will be in shortly. I'll cancel everything I've got on this morning."

"I wish you would," said the head, who then hung up.

Meg looked at her husband. "You heard all that?"

"More or less." He shrugged.

Then she turned to her daughter, who was decked out in the school's smart green-jacketed green and white tartan uniform. With those pink-cheeked freckles and wide blue eyes, she looked angelic and innocent. She was innocent. God knows what the head thought Jess had been up to, but her daughter had not, and would not ever get involved in a fight. Of that Meg was absolutely certain. And what mother doesn't truly know their youngster's mind? Particularly that of a timid child like her Jess. So, Meg asked herself, what was it that had really happened?

"Jess," she said, "what happened at school yesterday?"

Jess gazed at the floor, hands again behind her back. "Nothing, mum."

"Show mum your hands, Jess. Come on," she prompted when the child didn't move.

"Jess!" Her tone was more commanding, and then immediately softened. "Jess, no-one is going to be cross with you. I just want to look at your hands."

The child reluctantly brought her hands from behind her back, and showed them to her mother, palms uppermost.

Meg had a hand on Jessica's shoulder. "And the backs, Jess. Come on, for heaven's sake, sweetie, Mrs Fordham is waiting for us."

Jess turned her hands over so her parents could see the backs, which were torn and had clearly been bleeding.

"God, Jess. What's happened? How come I never saw your hands? I wondered why you seemed to be keeping them under the table most of the time we were eating breakfast." She took her daughter's hands in her own and looked them over. "Reg? Do you know about this? Well, you must do; I can see there's cream on these cuts."

Reg said nothing.

"Let me guess; someone's pushed you over? Yes? But then, why is it the backs of your hands and not your palms that are cut?" She waited for an answer, but when none came, she said, "Look, Mrs Fordham wants to talk to us about something, she says you had a fight, well, fights at school yesterday. Did you?"

There was still no response from the little girl, whom Meg proceeded to bundle into the car, not taking up time with any further questioning. She was followed by her husband, before driving quickly to the school.

The Meadow School stood in magnificent parkland in the heart of Yeovil. An imposing one hundred and sixty-year-old, two-storey building in Cotswold grey stone, its ethos is one that encourages mutual support through trust, respect, and friendship.

The school had produced a nine-page document which specifically addresses the problem of bullying. Pupils are encouraged to report incidents of harassment to staff as soon as they occur so they may be dealt with immediately. Disciplinary measures, if needed, are clearly set out, and parents are expected to assist teachers in identifying and coping with issues as soon as they arise.

The happiness and safety of children is paramount in everything the school does.

The headmistress's study looked out onto immaculate green lawns. It was a picture of English country calm and order. The room itself was covered in an oatmeal carpet, with the headmistress's desk of a light beech to one side of the wide window. There was a green glass-shaded table lamp on a brass base together with various framed photographs, presumably of family members, on the desk. The walls of the study had a variety of scenic prints and one or two were of horses or horse races that looked like works by Stubbs.

The family were all seated in leather armchairs opposite Mrs Fordham, who looked distinctly ill at ease. Wearing a brown tweed skirt and white blouse with tasselled bow at the neck, she'd ushered them into her room. Jessica was between her parents, Meg in her usual two-piece working jacket and skirt with, today, a pink blouse, Reg in a shabby grey suit. His tie was crooked, his shoes scuffed, and he looked untidy and worn. Meg surveyed her husband with mixed pity and contempt. Was that really the best he could do? she wondered.

There was an atmosphere in the room, which was hardly surprising. The headmistress spoke first. "I think you know why I've called you in today, Mr Copeland? Mrs Copeland? Jessica?"

"Something about bullying, you said," responded Meg.

"I'm afraid to have to tell you that Jessica has been reported by a number of the pupils here for bullying."

"Are you being serious?" asked Meg.

"It's not the sort of thing I'd make jokes about," responded Mrs Fordham.

"But have you forgotten what's been happening to Jessica these last weeks? She's been coming home with abrasions, cuts and bruises where the others have been attacking her," said Meg. "We've had all this out last time we spoke."

"Mrs Copeland, that's the first I've heard that things had reached such a state. We discussed the bullying a week or so ago, yes. But that was the bullying that Jessica was complaining of. This is an entirely different situation. Jessica is now the one being accused of harassment."

Meg turned to her daughter. "Jess? What's this all about?"

The child looked down, remained stubbornly silent.

"Jess! Talk to me. NOW! What is going on here?"

"They were kicking me. And punching me. And laughing at me."

"Who was?"

"I don't want to tell who."

"Well, how many of them were there?"

Jessica looked up at the ceiling as though she were making a mental calculation, then said, "Six."

"Six? You're telling us you were set on by six children?"

She nodded in meek acquiescence.

"Were they from your year?" Meg was sounding increasingly perplexed.

"No," said Jessica, "they were all from year eight."

"But 'they're twelve and thirteen-year-olds."

Meg turned her attention back to Mrs Fordham. "Can you please tell me exactly what happened here?"

"It seems that Jessica had six separate fights with these pupils. She made one girl's eye bleed and another was given a bloody nose. Two more had teeth loosened when Jessica punched them in the face. We simply cannot sanction that sort of behaviour here."

That accounted for the cuts and abrasions on the back of Jessica's hands, thought Meg, who responded, "And you're calling our Jessica a bully? She's set upon by six others, bigger and older than her, then defends herself, and now she's the one in the dock? And you can't sanction, what? An outnumbered child fighting back? That's a strange sense of priorities if you ask me."

"Well, we simply can't have that sort of thing going on here."

"No, you're right we can't." Meg started getting to her feet. "My husband and I have scrimped and scraped to send our daughter to what we consider to be the best school in the area. We still rate it."

Maintaining the initiative, against Mrs Fordham's attempts to interject, Meg went on, "I'll let you know how we decide to proceed in the next week or two. In the meantime, we'd be obliged if you'd remind some of the other parents here of their obligations to keep their young hoodlums in check."

"Well. I mean. Really," said Mrs Fordham, clearly nonplussed by Meg's outburst.

They left Jessica at school with strict instructions not to get involved in any fights, no matter how far she was provoked.

Meg drove Reg back to the house to collect his own car.

"I'll need a cuppa after that lot before I'm off to the nick."

Reg had said not a word throughout the whole episode. Now, in their own kitchen, Meg asked him, "You've said nothing all morning. So, tell me now, what did you make of all that? Our little girl? Crikey! She took on six of them." Meg sat down on one of the kitchen chairs with a clump. "And won? She beat them all? But I specifically told her, no violence. Reg? Can't you say something? Lost your voice?"

He sat opposite her at the breakfast table. "I knew it."

"You what?" She looked puzzled, irritated.

"I knew what she could do if she got set on again. So I told her to fight back for once."

"You told her what?" Meg's eyes were blazing.

"Tell me again, Reg. Do I really believe what I am hearing?" She looked as though she might attack her husband at any moment, so angry did she appear.

"I told her, she's as much right to be at that school as anyone else there," his voice sounded timorous. "I told her you can't walk away for ever, because there's some see it as a weakness and they'll never stop coming after you. I told her I'd always run away from a fight, and I wasn't proud of it. I told her she was as strong as any of them. She's good at gym and swimming and she's watched that girl in the Olympics win the gold at boxing a dozen times. I just said, go to it girl. You've nothing to lose."

"My God, Reg. My God. And I thought I knew you. And I thought I knew our Jessica."

"Did I do wrong, then? Did I do wrong, Meg. You look so annoyed."

"Did you do wrong? What? No, love," she said, smiling at last. "For once, you did absolutely right."

CHAPTER 24 DAY 9

THE THREE OF THEM SAT in the interview room sipping their drinks quietly. Billy occasionally dribbled tea, holding the cup awkwardly with two hands, but his mother swiftly mopped his chin with her handkerchief each time.

"He doesn't say much, my Billy. But he'd never hurt a fly. That man Downey, he's got it in for my boy. I know he has," she said, fiercely. "We're awfully grateful to you, Miss Pierre. But honestly, I don't know what you can do to help."

Caring for an autistic son, Tammy thought, a lifetime's work and commitment with little recognition from the outside world, and precious few thanks. And what could she possibly offer or promise this woman who seemed to be hoping for so much from her.

"To be honest, Mrs Anderson, there probably isn't a great deal I can do. I just thought someone should attempt to give the lad some sort of hearing. I realise he may say nothing to me, to either of us, come to think of it. But perhaps I can persuade Downey to eliminate the boy from his enquiries and let him go sooner. He can't hold him for more than thirty-six hours without an order from a magistrate, anyway." Reaching into her bag, Tammy extracted an iPad. "I'll just make a few notes on this, Mrs Anderson, if you don't mind."

"Oh no dear, you go right ahead."

Billy had finished his tea and now sat with his hands on the table in front of him. Small, chubby child's hands, which he stared at without moving. But how to make any sort of contact with the lad, Tammy wondered, when he was so quietly remote?

"Mrs Anderson, is there anything at all that gets through to Billy? Anything I can say? Anything you could tell him about why he's here?"

Mrs Anderson smiled sadly. "Oh, I think he understands things. I'm sure he knows what's going on here. He just has difficulty talking back. You know, making himself understood. He struggles all the time, but he finds it really hard."

Tammy drank the last of her coffee and pushed the cup to one side.

"But, from what you're saying, Mrs Anderson, Billy sometimes communicates with you. Can you say what it is that triggers that response? I mean, do you actually know?"

"Not really, dear. I just sit holding his hands and it seems to relax him and let him concentrate a bit."

"And that's it? You hold his hands, and it seems to help him to open up a bit?"

"That's right dear. That's all I do."

"Do you think Billy would mind if I held his hands?"

"You could try, dear. I don't suppose it would do any harm. It might even help. But don't be offended if he pulls away. He can be really funny that way, you know. He generally hates being touched. But…"

Tammy reached forward slowly, covering Billy's hands with her own, barely touching them. They were warm and felt soft and spongy to her. For a moment Billy flinched, drew back a bit, then he gradually relaxed and let Tammy's grip become more obvious, but he otherwise gave no indication he was aware of her presence.

Tammy stared up at the ceiling of the interview room, her hands still on Billy's. If walls could talk, she thought. This place would have a few stories to tell. Stories of bullying and confession. Stories of suspects refusing to talk, or simply refusing to co-operate. Stories of interrogators using techniques that were unexpected to get a suspect to talk.

Getting up from her chair, Tammy let go of Billy's hands and walked around the table until she was standing over him. Something registered in the boy, because he looked up at her in alarm. His alarm grew as Tammy leaned down, took his face in both hands and kissed him on both cheeks. Mrs Anderson looked astonished. Billy's response was still more unexpected, because he burst into tears.

"Oh, Miss Pierre," exclaimed Billy's mother, "Billy's never, he's never..."

Billy dropped his head as though it was too heavy to bear and interlaced his fingers at the back of his neck. "She said to do it," he sobbed. "Mrs El. Mrs El said to do it."

Tammy felt herself go cold. Turning to Mrs Anderson, she asked, "Do you know what he means? And do you know who Mrs El happens to be?"

"He means Mrs Goldcrest. Eleanor Goldcrest. Billy calls her Mrs El. Oh dear, that's why Billy's here isn't it? Those poor babies." Mrs Anderson looked at her son wiping his tears away with the back of his hand, then back at Tammy, as if she were searching for words. The right words.

"She's a nice lady, Mrs Goldcrest. Chats to everyone in town. She often talks to Billy, and he listens to her when she comes up to him. He doesn't walk away like he's scared, like with other people. Like that caution he got. She was only a little girl, but she scared Billy. She ran after him you know. She meant well, didn't she? No harm intended. But there you are.

"See, Mrs Goldcrest, now she doesn't look down her nose at him, as though he's a type of freak. Told me the boy should try to get some sort of work. He's done a bit of Council work, sweeping streets, for one thing. But he's better than that. He's really clever on the computers, you know, but only if he's working alone. He wouldn't be able to cope with working for no-one else like, cos he doesn't communicate much." Mavis was becoming more animated, as though encouraged to open up with Tammy there to hear her.

"What he needs, is something, anything, to try to bring him out of hisself a bit. I told her he can sort of manage if there's a routine involved, but I'd never given it much thought till she suggested it. You know, Billy actually having a job and that. Said she'd ask around. Billy might do alright stacking shelves, I told her. So, she said, 'How about Tesco? These big organisations have a policy for taking on disabled, and Billy might fit in there. Worth a try.' We were due to make an appointment."

Mrs Anderson sighed. "Then all this happened."

Having resumed her seat, Tammy rested her palms on Billy's clasped hands once more. He'd calmed down and stopped crying, and didn't try to pull his hands away from her. "Hello, Billy," she said softly. Leaning forward and looking up at him, Tammy tried to bring her eyes into focus with his, to seek a response. "Hello in there? Is anybody home?"

But Billy wouldn't look up. So Tammy waited patiently while the seconds and then the minutes ticked away. Yet, there'd been a response, albeit a shocked one, to her show of affection. Those two kisses. Apart from his mother, Tammy doubted anyone had ever shown Billy much in the way of affection in his life. Then a thought occurred, "Tell me about Mrs El, Billy. Was she nice to you?" Tammy gave Billy's hands a little squeeze.

"Like I said, he doesn't usually like to be touched by no-one," repeated Mrs Anderson. "But, I dunno, sometimes he responds. You can never tell when he will, though."

Billy's attention seemed fixated on Tammy's pearl-lacquered nails. He gave the barest of nods and whispered, "Nice. Mrs El."

Billy's mother raised her eyebrows at Tammy. "Don't stop dear, not now."

"Did she talk to you, Billy? Mrs El?"

"Ask him about the walks, Miss Pierre. Mrs Goldcrest used to go for walks with him along the Ware Cliffs nearby. He's happy there. No crowds of people. They also used to go walking along the Cobb. That's that stone-built wall around the bay. Been there for hundreds of years. It makes a harbour. He sometimes lets her take his arm. She said she's even got him to say a few words. Not much, though. Just little things like, 'nice', or 'warm'."

Mrs Anderson became enthusiastic. "She once brought those little girls with her. The three that…"

She stopped talking for a moment as though it was too painful to continue. Then, brightening a bit, "You should've seen Billy. He responded at once. More than I've ever seen him before."

Looking up, Billy surprised Tammy by catching her eye. "Nice," he said. There was a long pause as Billy fought to say the words. The room was quiet, almost oppressive in the continuing silence. Billy closed his eyes, scrunching them up with the effort of trying to express what he had in his mind. Then, "Little girls. Mrs El told me."

"What did she tell you Billy. Is it a secret?"

"She told me to," he said, and repeated, "She told me to." Staring at nothing in particular, he looked to be far away.

"She told me to do it," he whispered under his breath.

Billy kept his eyes on Tammy and opened his mouth to make another comment when Downey stormed in. "You satisfied now, Ms Pierre? He's all but admitted it. And he's trying to blame it on Mrs Goldcrest. He's pathetic. Should be locked up for all time."

Turning on Downey, Tammy snapped, "Mrs Goldcrest told him to try and get a job, for God's sake. A proper job, not just occasionally sweeping streets for the Council. Which you don't seem to know anything about. You've obviously not been listening in to the whole interview. Or if you have, you've chosen to pick up the one comment that you think supports your case.

"And while we're about it," she added, "what possible motive would Eleanor Goldcrest have for getting someone to kill the daughters she adored? You didn't see her after she'd heard the news. I did. Face it, Downey, you're clutching at straws. We were just beginning to make some progress as well, and you've managed, or contrived, to spoil it."

Downey stood with his hands insolently in his pockets, his creased and shiny suit hanging from his spare frame. "This interview is over. As far as I'm concerned, he's guilty as hell. And he knows it."

At that moment Meg Copeland walked into the police station. She looked harassed and tired, although the day was barely half over. She looked over at Tammy and mouthed, "Okay?" and Tammy acknowledged with a nod.

Then, getting to her feet Tammy regarded Downey. "You're holding the wrong man, Detective, and I'm going to prove it. I'll need to see Billy again."

"No chance. You've had enough time here, now I want you outta my nick."

CHAPTER 25 DAYS 9 AND 10

SHE WAS BONE WEARY but elected to take the train back to London instead of spending the night in Lyme Regis. It was getting dark, and the approach to Waterloo more dismal than usual, with its lines of derelict warehouses, graffitied walls along the rail track and rubbish between the lines. She'd catch up with Meg Copeland in the morning and see what she had to report.

It was late; she'd called ahead and told Ginny to expect her, but not to worry about food as she'd eat on the train to Waterloo. On the journey back to town, she'd experienced those same raking claws in her stomach she'd suffered a few days ago. They'd passed after a few minutes, but she knew she could no longer put things off; she would have to find the time to see the doctor again and think about hormonal therapy.

She'd picked up a cab almost immediately at Waterloo and was home in about twenty-five minutes.

From outside the flat, Tammy heard a soft and repetitive, boom, boom, boom, boom. What on earth, she thought? Once inside the noise got louder, and walking into the living room Tammy found a barefoot Ginny in her tiny red shorts and shortie red nightie dancing round and round with her hands over her head, crossed at the wrist, fingers splayed. "Hiya, lover," she giggled as she saw Tammy come in, spinning around some more. "Isn't it brilliant?"

"Yes, but what is it, or who is it?" Tammy grinned, slipping out of her coat and shoes to join Ginny as she spun round, the singer's voice at once that of an old man, and in the next moment a soprano, assuming it was the one person. "The rhythm's irresistible," she admitted, ignoring her tiredness.

"It's 'Heavenly Light' by Laura Pergolizzi. I bought it today. She leans the same way as us," Ginny whispered as though someone might be listening in. You must hear, 'Lost on You' as well," she said. "I'll play it next, all about the break up with her lover of five years. It made me cry. Isn't she fantastic?"

"I think you're fantastic, Virginia Jones," laughed Tammy, grabbing Ginny round the waist as they danced together. "I don't know where you get the energy."

* * * * *

She slept badly. There were things on her mind, decisions to make, things to discuss. They couldn't be put off indefinitely. Dov was becoming more impatient, but she had no answers for him. Thrashing about during the night, she was afraid she'd wake Ginny, but she needn't have worried, Ginny slept on undisturbed.

Dawn thrust its way through the vertical slats of the Venetian blinds making zebra stripes across the room. Ginny was on her back still fast asleep, her baby face peeping over the duvet which was pulled up to her chin, the copper curls forming a halo on the pillow. She was making little snuffling, puppy-dog noises at the back of her throat.

Tammy ached from head to toe. Drained, she thought. Ready to drop. Not a good way to start the day. She turned on to her side away from Ginny and gazed at the far wall, focusing on nothing in particular.

Poor Billy, she thought. They'd have to let him go. Defenceless kid. Her heart went out to him, watching him desperately trying to express himself. She couldn't wait to see Downey trying to justify bringing the lad in.

Climbing gingerly out of bed so as not to disturb Ginny, she wandered into the spare room in her navy shorts and T-shirt, and worked out on the rowing machine then the exercise bike, ignoring the stitches pulling at her ribs, till she'd built up a proper sweat. After a blistering hot shower, she felt better. Still, she thought, I could use a break.

* * * * *

Ginny sat up and stretched. Tammy had left early for the office again. Ginny would make her own way in. But first she'd go for an early jog in Queen's Park nearby. The pillow slips would need changing: Tammy hadn't noticed the tiny spots of blood left from her scarred head when she left for work.

Ginny donned her black tracksuit and red trainers, and felt ready for anything. The rain during the night had given over to a fresh clear morning. Ginny had also been putting in the hours at work, so a run would help rid the cobwebs before the start of the day. There were few other joggers out at this time of the morning: one very elderly, white-haired gentleman in a baggy blue tracksuit and a couple of slow moving, overweight middle-aged women, both in pink. There was also a lovely lift in the feel of the morning provided by the splash of autumn colour, with phlox, beardtongue, tickseed, and asters all prominent.

The bank contract regarding the loan of £5.5 million had been delegated to Ginny to try to sort. Tammy had made the early running, but was now too involved in the Lyme Regis murders to give this contract the time it needed. Ginny was pretty sure she'd finally cracked it. Couldn't wait to tell Tammy. There'd be a substantial fee, and Tammy, not to say the bank, should be delighted. Tammy was trusting her with more and more responsibilities, and she was revelling in the challenge.

It was as well. Tammy was looking ever wearier these days, as though she had the world of worries to contend with. Okay, so business wasn't great, but it wasn't catastrophically bad. Plenty of other similar-type agencies survived on less business, though they weren't having to support luxury offices in Bruton Street.

The scarring looked dreadful, red and angry when contrasted with the snake of black sutures ranged through the shaven area of her skull. She might have lost her, Ginny thought. It was that close, and the idea brought her to the edge of tears.

Ginny had introduced Tammy to her parents two or three years ago, when the couple's relationship was well established. The elderly couple had been overawed by this tall charismatic figure. They might not now recognise the fraught individual she presented in her current state.

At various times in their affair, Ginny's mother had quietly berated her daughter for, 'Carrying on like this.' Telling her that she thought Tammy was a lovely person, but really, it wasn't natural. And anyway, didn't Ginny want children one day? Of course, Ginny wanted children, but she had no answers either for her mother or for herself right now.

Ginny had showered and changed, a plain black two-piece today, and it was time for work.

* * * * *

In the office that morning, Tammy called Meg Copeland. "Any progress at your end, Meg?"

"Nothing. We've had teams on the shingle again where the kids were found, looking for anything. But so far, nothing's turned up. The autopsy report confirms what we already know, that the murder weapon was convex judging by the concavity of the wounds. So, almost certainly just that single bloodied stone found by the bodies, and nothing else to look for."

"Anything yet on the pendant?"

"It's too soon, Tammy. I've tried to gee things up, but I'm afraid if I make too much fuss, you know, attract attention, forensics might just report to Downey rather than me first."

"What about time of death, or rather, deaths?"

"Bodies were discovered at around midday, maybe a bit later. Mr Patel wasn't sure of the time. Rigor hadn't set in, so it's likely the time of death was somewhere in the region of 10.30 to 11.00 am. Eric Goldcrest says he left home with the girls about 10.00 am and this ties in with when Mrs Goldcrest says he went off with them. We're rechecking all the CCTV in the surrounding areas at those times."

"Meg, do me a favour?"

"Of course."

"When we watched the CCTV images at your nick, I remember seeing another guy pop up. Didn't really register at the time. But thinking about it again, each time I saw him he was somewhere in the picture near Mrs Goldcrest and George Derby. He should be easy to spot. Very tall, with elephant's ears, a long bony nose, and medium brown hair over his ears and collar, probably trying to hide the ears. Looked really worried, or maybe just intense. Light colour suit and tie. If you can spot him, maybe your facial recognition people can ID him."

"See what I can do. No promises. I've leaned on them once already."

Copeland called back a couple of hours later. "Believe it or not, I've got a name."

"Well done, Meg. So, tell me."

"It's Nigel Cudlipp."

"Of LIIC?"

"The very same. Nasty piece of work by all accounts. Likes to push his weight around. The man's a first-class bully."

"I've met the type. And not just the adults, you know. Kids are even worse."

"Don't I know it." Meg sighed.

"Talking of which, I heard at your nick there'd been some problems with your Jessica being bullied at school."

"Too right. I always told her to walk away from an argument. It takes two to tango."

"And did she?"

"Did she?"

"Walk away from a fight?"

"No. It seems my other half told her to stand up for herself for once. I couldn't believe it, he's normally such a whimp."

"What happened then?"

"She took on six of them over the course of a day. Made one girl's eye bleed. The Head was furious. Blamed it all on Jessica. I couldn't believe it of our little girl."

"Sometimes people give you no choice, Meg. My friend and self-defence coach Dov Jordan told me, if you're ever attacked, run like hell. If you're cornered, fight like hell. Your Jessica did just the right thing."

"I'll bet no-one ever bullied you, Tammy."

"You'd be wrong there, Meg."

"Really? I'd never have believed it. How old were you when it happened?"

"I was six. She was bigger and older than me. She'd been baiting me for ages, pinching, scratching, kicking."

"How did you deal with it?"

"When I knew I'd had enough, knew I wasn't going to let it go any further, I lashed out at her. Knocked her into the waste paper bin. She left me alone after that. She used some pretty choice racist insults. Upset my mother badly. But not me. No ma'am. I'd won. Don't you worry about Jessica. She did what she had to, when she knew she had no other choices."

"Thanks, Tammy. That's a real help."

"So, talk to me about our friend Cudlipp."

"Well, I did a bit of digging around. Found out his first wife left him, accused him of trying it on with her thirteen-year-old from her own previous marriage. Mr Cudlipp has a reputation for liking little girls."

"Where did you get all that from, and so quickly?"

"Took a chance. Called LIIC, said I was Fraud Squad looking into various unnamed financial irregularities, without being specific. Making a few generalised preliminary enquiries. Seems the partners there are hated by everyone they come into contact with, not least each other, and as they were all out when I called, the girls on reception felt free to talk, and talk they did."

"Meg, you are a genius. It would never have occurred to me to have taken that tack."

"Thanks, Tammy, but I'm sure you'd have taken that route eventually." Copeland sounded delighted with the compliment she'd received. "But there's more."

"There is?" exclaimed Tammy, reaching for the coffee Ginny had just placed on her desk.

"Cudlipp confided in the girl I was speaking to on reception that a couple of months ago Eric Goldcrest had stormed round to his house accusing him of every financial impropriety under the sun. Very funny coming from him. Talk about the kettle and the pot. He also wanted to know if Cudlipp was involved with Eleanor."

"What? Come on. I mean, really?"

"Cudlipp told Eric to piss off just as his own daughter, a five-year-old, came in to ask Daddy for a story. By this time Eric was beginning to lose the plot, and actually hit out at Cudlipp, missing him but knocking the little girl over, almost certainly by accident, with the backswing of the attempted blow. She fell over and started crying and Eric told her to fucking shut up.

"That did it for Cudlipp, who it seems is okay about abusing other people's kids, but not too happy about anyone else abusing his. He admitted to his receptionist he'd said something like, 'You'd better watch out for you and yours,' before throwing Eric out."

"What a nest of vipers," Tammy mused. "Would that be provocation enough for Cudlipp to kill Eric's daughters, do you think?"

"Search me, Tammy. Financial people in general, with their advanced mathematics, their algorithms and whatever else, and this lot in particular, are from another planet, if you ask me."

"No honour amongst thieves, is there, Meg?" The coffee had got cold, and Tammy buzzed Ginny for another.

"Any progress?" Ginny mouthed.

"Tell you later," Tammy mouthed back.

"So, Meg, what in hell keeps this lot together? Apart that is, from the shedloads of loot they're making?"

"Apparently, it's the absent partner, the one in Antigua at the moment. He's the moderating influence. Without him, the whole thing would have fallen apart by now. Loot or no loot."

"Meg, that's excellent. I'm on my way to see Cudlipp now, if he's in," said Tammy, grabbing her jacket from the back of her chair and dashing past Ginny. "Back soon, Gin," she gasped.

* * * * *

Nigel Cudlipp was exactly as Tammy had pictured him in the glimpsed CCTV pictures, odder if anything. He had a front tooth missing, which gave him the most peculiar aspect. With his wealth, one would've thought it would have been dealt with immediately rather than being left. Might it have been the result of a recent fight with someone?

Seated in the same chair George Derby had sat in when Tammy had first met him, Cudlipp, speaking in a cut-glass English accent, spun a story of double dealing, betrayal and suspected affairs. Having had Derby professionally shadowed on a couple of occasions with no conclusive result, and wondering about a possible involvement between Derby and his own wife, he'd decided to follow Derby himself and had found, to his astonishment, that there was every likelihood Derby was having an affair with, of all people, Eric Goldcrest's wife, Eleanor. Eric had been right about Eleanor's involvement with someone else, but had picked the wrong person.

"You're on CCTV, Mr Cudlipp, at the back of the hotel where Eric played hide and seek with the little girls. And on the day of the murders, too."

Cudlipp shrugged. "So what? Doesn't mean I had anything to do with their killing, does it?"

"Not on its own, no. But you had opportunity, and you had a motive." Tammy smoothed her skirt with the back of her hand and watched for Cudlipp's reaction.

"What do you mean, the financial fiddles Eric had shafted me with? Are you calling that a motive for murder?"

"Believe me, Mr Cudlipp, I've come across more mundane motives than that for murder."

"Spur-of-the-moment vandalism may presage murder. But premeditated? How could I know what Eric's movements might be on any given day?"

"Who said anything about premeditated? You hated Eric, knew he'd been double dealing you; you followed Derby down here suspecting him of having an affair with your wife, found him instead involved with Eleanor, and then I'm guessing you spotted Eric and the girls by chance. You can't have met him, or he'd have mentioned it to me. The murder of the little girls would have been unplanned, spur of the moment. I don't know how you lured them away, or whether you just grabbed them and ran hoping they wouldn't scream. I hear you were also raging with Eric for knocking over your little girl during a recent argument you had with him."

"Where'd you hear that one?" Cudlipp asked, looking perplexed. Then, "Don't tell me." He inclined his head towards the reception area door.

Tammy shrugged, but offered no comment. Then she asked, "Mr Cudlipp, what was the actual time you were in Lyme Regis on the day of the murders?"

Cudlipp seemed thrown for a moment. "I was there at midday," he said.

"Not before?"

"No, not before. I'm certain of that because I remember checking my watch as the church bells rang midday."

"You're lying, Mr Cudlipp. Why would you lie unless you had something to hide?"

"It was twelve noon when I was at Lyme Regis. I'm not lying."

"Oh, but you are, Mr Cudlipp; you see, the time you were recorded at the back of that hotel was 10.15 am, some fifteen to thirty minutes before the girls were killed. As I've already said, you had both motive and opportunity. I'm surprised you didn't bump into Eric at some stage."

Cudlipp just shrugged. But Tammy noticed his forehead was sweating somewhat, and he displayed the same intense, or possibly worried, expression visible on the CCTV images.

"Then at twelve noon you were actually recorded, and not far from that same hotel looking somewhat dishevelled. What did you do to those little girls, Mr Cudlipp?"

"Well, I must have got my times wrong. When I realised there was nothing going on between Derby and my wife, I left." Cudlipp was sweating profusely by now.

He went on, "Maybe that was twelve. If I looked a mess, it's probably because I'd been running around the place like a blue-arsed fly trying to catch out Derby and my wife.

"Look, Ms Pierre, I said I'd be happy to assist, but this has gone far enough. You're not the police, and I'm neither obliged nor prepared to waste any more of my time in this nonsensical parade of conjecture."

"There are times, Mr Cudlipp," said Tammy, getting to her feet, "when silence says more than a thousand words."

CHAPTER 26 DAY 11

SHE'D TAKEN THE TUBE to Bond Street and was walking down towards Bruton Street instead of having driven in as she usually did. Ginny had gone on ahead of her to open up.

Traffic was light at that time of the morning, so she could hardly fail to notice the same dark blue Lexus trailing along a little behind her. At first she thought she'd ignore it. But then decided, dammit, why should I? Turning on her heel, she stepped off the kerb and swiftly approached the car which swerved ever so slightly as she got close and then quickly accelerated away. She tried to get a glimpse of the driver, but it all happened too quickly.

In the office Ginny told Tammy to take a look at her emails as there was one odd one with no sender ID. It read:

READ THIS NOW

Cancel the Middle-East contract. You must know you're out of your depth here. We want him. We'll get him. He won't bother with another security firm. We've warned off the largest, and the smaller ones won't take the chance. We're keeping an eye on you. Also, drop the murder hunt. Be sensible. Remember, you're just an expendable Falasha.

"What do you think?" asked Ginny. "Will you still be going ahead with the job? I mean, you might have been killed. And what's an expendable Falasha?"

Tammy paced the office reception area restlessly; she ignored Ginny's enquiry. "Why would these people, whoever they are, be warning me off like this? If the target is to be attacked, why give us the time to prepare? As for threatening all the small security firms, that's nonsense."

"You think so?" asked Ginny nervously, running her fingers through her curls.

"Of course. There're over one hundred close protection firms in the UK. If they'd all been warned off, word would have got around by now, and I've heard nothing."

"So why do you think you're being sent these emails?"

"This is a large contract, which could lead to more of the same, if we keep our heads. We need to show that as a boutique security firm we can handle a job like this with ease, competence, and discretion. And particularly, not be frightened off by threats."

"And do you think we can?" sighed Ginny.

"Yes, of course we can. Someone is trying to bully us out of a lot of highly lucrative work, which I'd place bets they want for themselves. They're not about to kill or kidnap anyone. That's just a blind to put us off. I've got a hunch that their man, Bear, a gentleman of apparently limited intelligence, overstepped the mark with his knife."

Tammy, still pacing back and forth, stared at Ginny. "And they want me to leave the Goldcrest investigation alone. That's got me stumped. Someone has it in for him, and this isn't just to do with financial shenanigens. But who'd want to pin a murder on him? Unless they know something we don't. In which case, why not go straight to the police?"

"Tammy," said Ginny, quietly. "You haven't answered my question. Please, what's a Falasha?"

Tammy finally stopped promenading the area and addressed her lover, "Alright, Ginny. I've not wanted to frighten you, so I've deliberately been avoiding the obvious. At least, the obvious to me."

"Tell me, Tammy. It's to do with that word, isn't it?"

"I'm afraid so, darling. I'd better explain. You'll need to know anyway. In case one day things ever become really nasty. The Falasha, Ginny, are Ethiopian Jews."

"Is that bad then, Tams? What's wrong with Ethiopian Jews?"

Turning to face Ginny, Tammy put her hands on her shoulders, as though to reassure her. "For heaven's sake, my dearest darling naïve Ginny, the Falasha are black Jews. These emails are simply the work of racist anti-Semites who don't want my skills, the skills of a black Jew, employed in the protection of fellow Jews, or the equivalent, Israelis. Or anyone else, by the look of it."

"My God! Tammy!"

The telephone interrupted them and Ginny, quickly composing herself, answered. She still sounded somewhat breathless with the shock of Tammy's revelation but spoke firmly and briefly with the caller before turning to Tammy. "It's the bank; they want to know what progress we've made on the investigation into the £5.5 million loan. You heard me tell them I'll get back to them shortly with our report."

Stepping over to the filter coffee maker, Tammy poured herself a generous mug of the coal black liquid, then looked over at Ginny enquiringly, but Ginny signalled she was okay.

Back on the sofa sipping the scalding beverage, Tammy enquired, "Do you want to bring me up to date then?"

"Well," Ginny breathed. "I've sorted the whole thing out. But really, shouldn't we be talking some more about that email and the threats implied? I mean, what would you do if…?"

"No Ginny. No." Tammy overruled. "Just get on and tell me about the bank contract. I can't wait to hear. Go on, talk to me," she said, smiling.

"Okay then, if you really insist. But… Alright, Tammy," she exclaimed, holding her hands up in submission, seeing Tammy about to get annoyed.

"Right then, so. The bank's customer, a Mr Walter Thoms, manufactures and supplies car parts, specifically for luxury sports cars and racing motors around the world. Thoms Turbo is a big business, with big turnover and profits. But the sector is highly competitive and machine tools need constant updating."

Tammy smiled again but said nothing, merely concentrating on her coffee.

Ginny went on, "Thoms urgently needed £5 million to replace outdated machine tools, and the bank refused to countenance a loan unless Thoms himself contributed half a million, which he didn't have and couldn't find, because his home in Whetstone, his principal asset, worth around £10 million is mortgaged up to the hilt."

"Ginny," said Tammy, "you have been busy, haven't you? So, what about the scam?"

"Wait till you hear this," said Ginny. "It seems that Mr Thoms went back to the bank, said he had to have not £5 million, but £5.5 million if he was to fulfil current orders. The bank still insisted he put in half a million.

"So now, and this is the neat bit, he went to the supplier and said he wanted them to sell him the five million pounds worth of machine tools he needed, but to load the invoice, actually billing him for £5.5 million. He then said that they, the supplier, should pay him back that half million pounds surplus once the bank had advanced the requested £5.5 million, that is, the half million he needed to satisfy the bank, which he decided to call commission on their sale to him."

"And did they?"

"That's exactly what they did. It meant they'd received the £5 million they required for the sale of that quantity of goods, plus the added half million which they handed over to Thoms, who'd properly invoiced them that sum for his commission. He then promptly put the half million back into his company as the bank had required."

"But Ginny, didn't Thoms have to show the bank he'd put in his half million before they'd advance the £5.5 million to the supplier?"

"You'd think so, wouldn't you? But no. Thoms had anticipated that and persuaded the bank to transfer the money to his own solicitor to be held in escrow with his own half million contribution from the supplier, the two payments being made concurrently. That is, to the supplier from the bank via the lawyer and to Thoms's company from the supplier via the same lawyer, when all parties were agreed on the deal."

"Ginny, I'm impressed. That is quite a result, you know."

"Are you pleased then, Tammy?" Ginny said, pushing at the bridge of her glasses with her forefinger and looking anxiously at Tammy.

"Am I pleased? Darling, whatever do you think?"

"How do you guess the bank will react?"

"Well now," said Tammy, getting to her feet to fetch another coffee. "That's the question, isn't it?"

"Tell you what I think?"

"I'll be interested to hear. Just what do you think the bank will do?"

"Nothing."

"Nothing?" exclaimed Tammy, surprised.

"Okay." Ginny picked up a ballpoint pen and started purposefully doodling on a post-it pad on the desk in front of her.

"So, the bank already has a fixed charge over the company's freehold premises for their current loans. What they'll have done now is to take a chattel mortgage over the company's new plant, to cover this further £5.5 million loan."

"Do they tell Thoms what you've found out?"

"Of course, they must."

"Otherwise?"

"Otherwise, who knows what he thinks he may be able to get away with in the future?"

Tammy smiled. "You've done really well, Ginny. But now, if the bank tells Thoms what it knows and does nothing about it, they lose face. What do they do to save face?"

"They let him know they could have him for fraud. Then, whatever the shortfall in equity on his home they take a further charge against it anyway. And finally, if they haven't already, they get him to sign a personal guarantee."

"Might they consider calling in the loan at this stage, before things run the risk of deterioration?"

"No way. If they jeopardise a profitable business, whatever its current cash flow issues, they risk losing out if assets in an insolvency are subject to a forced sale."

Tammy sat back on the sofa, her arms crossed and studied Ginny's face. Her head ached under the bandanna and her ribs were sore. She must have appeared annoyed because the younger woman looked uncomfortable under her scrutiny.

"Is that okay?" said Ginny. Tammy seemed angry a lot of the time these days, and Ginny wasn't sure how to approach her.

"Ginny. I have to say this, but I couldn't have done better myself. Not even sure I could have done it as well."

Ginny's face lit up. "Really?" she said. "You're being honest with me?"

"Yes darling, really, honestly. How did you get so much inside info?"

"I hope you won't be cross with me, Tammy."

"What did you do? Break into the supplier's premises?"

"No, nothing like that," said Ginny, aghast.

"Darling, I was only joking."

Ginny started speaking more quickly, "No, what I did was, I turned up at the supplier, Fidelity Manufacture, just outside Hertford in Hertfordshire, on a day when you were in Lyme Regis."

"And left the office unattended?" enquired Tammy.

"Did I do the wrong thing?"

"No Ginny. I'm teasing you again."

"Okay. Right. Well, I wore my dark grey two-piece, a black blouse, low heel, black shoes and tied all my hair back in a bun. I put on the black-framed specs, you know the ones, and wore a pale shade of lipstick. I was so nervous when I got there I could hardly breathe. I'd called ahead and said I wanted to meet with the CEO on an urgent matter which was of some delicacy.

"When I got there, I gave him my card."

"You mean the card for this agency?"

"That's right."

"Okay, go on."

"I thought it best to be up front. So I said we'd been approached by the Fraud Squad."

"The Fraud Squad, Ginny? Good grief."

"The Fraud Squad. To make some discreet private enquiries into a series of transactions involving Mr Thoms and, among others, Fidelity. I explained to a pretty alarmed CEO that neither he nor his company were in the frame. But we needed answers. After that, he couldn't stop talking. I got all I needed from him. In the end he was so reassured by me he asked if we could assist with his company's own security issues."

"Ginny, that is brilliant. You know it's high time we started talking about me making you a partner in this business."

"Oh wow, Tammy. What can I say? I mean—"

Ginny was interrupted when the telephone rang again and she picked up. Tammy saw her frown slightly, then, "Very well. I'll tell her." She looked up at Tammy. "Eric Goldcrest. Breathing hot and cold. Wants to know what's happening. Where are you? Et cetera, et cetera."

Tammy was pacing the area again, an elbow in her cupped palm, chin on her knuckles. "What do you think, Ginny? What do you make of the man?"

"I wonder if he is involved? If he had any inkling of his wife's affair with Mr Derby, might he have killed the girls in a moment of spite? Eleanor was with Derby that morning, wasn't she? And they're not Eric's girls after all. Enough stepfathers have been convicted of stepchild murder without the provocation of an affair."

"So why would he have employed us?"

"If he thinks the police could yet be likely to harass him, he might hope that we can either put the suspicion permanently elsewhere, or simply continue to divert attention from him. Although, it seems they've got poor Billy Anderson firmly in their sights right now."

"You could be right, Ginny Gin. Time I had another chat with Mr G."

"Tammy, I don't want to harp on about it, but we're not earning any money for the Lyme Regis time spent, you know."

"I do know. Promise I'll call a halt as soon as I see Billy off the hook and free. Someone's got to look out for him."

"And the other thing? That warned-off contract?"

Tammy touched the side of her nose conspiratorially. "Leave that to me," she said, smiling.

CHAPTER 27 DAYS 11 TO 14

"THANKS FOR AGREEING TO SEE ME again, Mrs Goldcrest. May I call you Eleanor?"

"Yes, yes of course. Is it Tammy?"

"Absolutely."

They were seated in Eleanor's living room. Late afternoon. The constant commute was wearying, but she would persevere for the time being. Tammy had turned down the offer of hospitality, saying she only wanted a few moments of the woman's time. Eleanor looked tired, her hair was dull and the floral dress she wore seemed overlarge for her. She was clearly losing weight.

Tammy wore a brown jacket with matching slacks and bandanna. The pain from the scar had begun to ease up, but it would be some time before her hair had recovered sufficiently to go without the added covering.

"Eleanor, I hope you won't be offended if I'm brutally blunt."

"No please, you go right ahead."

"Very well. Tell me, are you and George Derby having an affair?"

Eleanor didn't respond immediately, merely remained sitting quietly with her hands folded in her lap staring ahead.

"I think I'll take that as a yes, Eleanor?"

Dropping her face in her hands, Eleanor started crying. "It was never planned," she said.

"Eric could be heartless at times. Coarse, unfeeling, pitiless. He frightened me. And though he never laid a finger on me, there was always that underlying threat of violence in the man.

"George was kind. He was gentle. It just happened gradually. His own marriage was falling apart. He made the usual excuse to his wife that he was away on business. If she ever suspected, I wasn't aware of it. We both needed to be needed. He gave me a non-demanding love and attention that lent me a feeling of worth once more."

"How did you get away to meet George? Wasn't Eric suspicious?"

"I'd only been seeing George for a few weeks. Seems silly I know, but we'd meet up at the Regis Carlton Hotel near Axminster station, always on a Friday evening. It was chancy, because it's only about ten or fifteen-minutes' drive from here. But, to be honest, it added to the excitement, knowing how close by Eric was.

"I'd tell Eric I was going to see mother; she lives on her own in Exeter St David's, about an hour on the train from Axminster. He offered to drive me to the station each time. Bit of an irony when you think of it. I'd tell him not to bother waiting, which he was happy to do. George would be parked nearby in a hire car so there'd be no chance of Eric recognising him. Then he'd pick me up and we'd check in to the Regis. We'd stay overnight and George would drop me off at Axminster station for Eric to pick me up on the Saturday afternoon. Saturday morning Eric would play with the kids, take them shopping.

"Oh, I don't know. I should never have…" Eleanor started weeping again.

Getting up from the armchair, Tammy went and sat next to Eleanor, putting her arm around the woman's shoulder.

"Eleanor," she said gently. "It wasn't your fault."

"Yes, but…"

"Yes, but nothing. Now, can I get you anything?"

"You're very kind, but no. I shall be alright."

"You've been seen by the police liaison officer. PC Deyton?"

"Yes. Pattie. Older woman. Lovely lady. Been a help. Don't know how I'd have coped without her."

"By the way, Billy Anderson, you were friendly with him. Did you ever give him any advice of any sort?"

"Billy's autistic."

"I know."

"He's very timid. You know, withdrawn. I used to take his arm, walk with him along the Ware Cliffs high over Lyme Regis. I told him he should try to get a job. Anything. He looked frightened, but I said, 'Just do it. I'll come with you if you like.'"

"That's very much what Billy told me."

"I saw that man Downey on the news. He looked pretty smug to me."

"Tell me, Eleanor, is there any way Billy could have done this to the girls?"

"Never. Not in a million years."

Standing up to leave, Tammy smoothed the front of her slacks. "Eleanor, thank you so much for your time. I'll try not to bother you again. My cab's been waiting outside. He'll be wondering what's happened to me."

Once settled in the cab, Tammy called Meg Copeland before they drove off.

"Hi, Meg, it's me."

"Hi, Tammy."

"Anything to report?"

"Nothing at all. After your visit, Downey decided to make sure he had Billy all sewn up properly, so there'd be no accusations of undue pressure. He produced a duty lawyer who told Billy to say nothing. Not too difficult. His mum's still pretty upset, but your visit helped and obviously got Downey thinking. Thing is, he's seething because he's got no evidence against Billy and he knows he's going to have to let him go. That is, unless he can get a magistrate to extend the time he can hold on to Billy."

"Thanks, Meg. Look, I've got a commission to work on so I'm going to be away for a couple of days. Hopefully nothing will blow up till I get back."

"Keep in touch, Tammy."

"I'll try, but I can't promise."

Next she called Ginny. "On my way home. I'm bushed."

"I'll bet you are, darling. You need a break."

"Badly. But not just yet. I got a text today telling me to pick up instructions from our accommodation postbox. They're not taking chances with emails or telephone calls. It's all on paper. I'll check it out with you when I get home."

It was nearly midnight when Tammy walked into the flat. She had the letter with her. It was in a nondescript brown envelope which she showed Ginny, who was in bed but still awake. "There it is."

"Have you read it yet?"

"Yes. You might want to take a look. It's brief."

It simply read:

Lisle Airport. 8.00 pm. Collect parcel and deliver safely. Goods are new. Weight and dimensions. 1 meter 65 approx 60k. Fragile.

Ginny shrugged. "Do you know what all that means?"

"If it weren't for the dust up with this so called Bear, I'd have wondered if it was genuine. I've not had one of these types of contact for a while. But I reckon it's the real thing. Only one way to find out."

"What's that then?"

"Go ahead with the instruction."

"Could it be a trap?"

"Mmm. Possibly. But I don't think anyone's going to attack me in broad daylight in the middle of an international airport, albeit a small one."

"So who's the contact from?"

"Not generally known, Ginny, but MI5 and MI6 occasionally subcontract one-off jobs to firms like us. All we've needed up to now has been emailed instructions, albeit in the same crude code. It's discreet and informal, attracting little if any attention. But even with the most sophisticated encryption, there's the rare but successful hacking; hence the occasional instruction in an envelope is left at an accommodation address. So, I'm taking this seriously. Now let me explain.

"The parcel is the person I'm meeting. Deliver safely means we take the individual to a safe house. Goods are new, says the individual is young. 1 meter 65 is the height. 60k is the weight. 'Fragile' is sexist, I'm afraid, for female."

"Really? What's the code for male then?"

Tammy smiled. "It's 'robust.' All pretty basic, but I don't have time or patience for sophisticated codes. And anyway, no-one will have seen this. I checked at the accommodation address and the envelope was safely locked away.

"Oh, and there is one more encouraging item, Ginny."

"There is? Surprise me. What could possibly be encouraging?"

"Our unpleasant correspondent has no idea whom we're supposed to be protecting, other than they've correctly deduced it's someone important."

"How can you be so sure?"

"Think about it, Ginny. That last email warning us off referred to male. Remember, 'We want him. We'll have him.' But you see, we're protecting a 'her', not a 'him'. She, whoever she is, is safe. They, whoever they are, merely want to take the work away from us. That's all."

She paused. Then, with a troubled look, she added, "Somehow, they know the date though."

Ginny said, "But Tammy, isn't this the sort of work only done by governments? How are you involved? I don't like the sound of it, you know. That warning email? Someone knows what's going on with you. And I thought government work was contracted to agencies. We're not government, are we?"

"It's true, Ginny. It's government work, but when they're stretched as they are right now with terrorist atrocities, they sometimes effectively subcontract work out to trusted people, such as those who are ex-Met, like me. Also, I do have Home Office clearance.

"I know, I know," she protested, holding her hands up in surrender. "I've not mentioned it before. But that's because in all the time we've known each other, this is the first engagement of its type I've been asked to do.

"As far as everyone is concerned, it's all done by government anyway. No-one knows about me, my involvement or who I am. Contact is different each time. Sometimes we meet at an agreed spot in London. The text simply says something like 'Meet. One hour.'"

"It worries me, Tammy. What if anything happens to you? How do you know this person isn't a terrorist herself? Or a fugitive from justice? These people who are threatening you. I mean, you could be the target. You could be killed."

"In that event, dear Ginny, the security services can't afford to be compromised. They'll deny all knowledge of who I am and why I might have been wherever I am found."

"Where you're found. My God, Tammy. You mean, wherever your body is found."

Tammy shrugged a response, but added nothing.

Ginny fidgeted with the sheets, shook her head despairingly. "I wish you wouldn't do this, Tammy. You know, I've just got a bad feeling about it."

Rubbing the back of her aching neck, Tammy thought, what the hell must she think of me? I look old and tired. Bloodshot eyes, face lined, head scarred. Not up to taking on risky assignments like this one anymore. She shook off the thought.

"I'll be fine, Ginny. I'll be away two nights, max, and it'll open the doors to a lot more, big-ticket work."

"But won't you be alone?"

"No. I'll take one of the big lads I know from my years at the Met. I'll fly to Lisle by six-seater early tomorrow. Get a feel for things. Our parcel, will arrive in time, probably by car, for us to take off at approximately 8.00 pm."

"What will you be flying in?"

"I'm hiring a Beech G58 Baron. It's a twin engine beaut that'll do over 200 knots, climbing at 1700 feet per second."

"I see you've done your research."

"Absolutely. I want us back here asap. I'll aim for Blackbushe Airport in Surrey. We'll complete a gendec stating whom we're carrying etc."

"So, what's a gendec?" Having climbed out of bed, it was Ginny's turn to start pacing about distractedly, the shortie red nightie looking incongruously inviting.

"Ginny, sit down, or get back into bed, for heaven's sake. You're putting me on edge. A gendec is a general declaration of who's on board: passengers and crew; health issues, if any, and places of departure and arrival.

"So customs will have the info at Lisle, and Border Control will know at this end. But no-one else, other than our principals, will have had access to any detail until we meet our parcel in Lisle.

"Let me put your mind at rest; we're not using any unlicensed airports or procedures. Everything is by the book.

"If it still sounds imprecise, it's meant to be. We won't even have a name at that stage. We'll simply look out for someone who fits the description then take it from there. She'll be looking for us, so it shouldn't be too difficult. We'll be in jeans, flight jackets and baseball caps.

"Also, I'm hiring a high-performance motor with run flat tyres fitted and false plates. It's costing, but we're not paying. From the airport we'll go M3 to M25, off at Junction

10, then A3 and side roads to Oxshott village where there's a safe house in a cul-de-sac off the main A244."

"Safe house? Which one is this? All new to me. Since when did we—"

"Just stop fretting," Tammy interrupted.

* * * * *

She fitted the description. In high heels and carrying a neat shoulder bag, she was about forty, looked Middle Eastern with short dark hair, wearing a black jacket and skirt, split at the knee.

She was accompanied by a heavyset, crop-headed individual in jeans, Timberland walking boots and leather bomber jacket. She spotted Tammy, who was with Dov, at once and, smiling nervously, approached them with her minder in tow.

"Oh," the woman exclaimed, looking them up and down, "I thought you were two men." Then to Tammy, "Are you? I mean, can you?"

Leaning forward, Tammy touched her shoulder reassuringly. "You'll be fine," she said. "No-one knows you're here. We've got throw away mobiles for emergencies. I assume you've been in touch with no-one either?"

"Only to say which airport we're flying to, and our approximate time of arrival."

Frowning in irritation, Tammy asked, "Who's idea was that?"

"Those were our instructions. Our people said they need to know where we are at all times."

Tammy said nothing, shaking her head in frustration. To their pilot, Dave, a stocky young man with pockmarked cheeks, she snapped, "Better get the flight plan filed and us underway."

"Yup," he said and went off to the office.

Forty-five minutes later they were airborne. She was called Gila, he was Caleb. As Tammy had guessed, they were Israeli. And the woman wasn't a terrorist, or a fugitive from justice. She was a top mediator. Important cargo. And in the UK for two nights, max. Beyond that, and the fact that she was to meet someone in London the next morning, she said little. She did ask, "Are we safe? You seemed worried about my informing my people..."

"We're not worried," Tammy spoke over her. "You'll be fine. Someone tried to warn us off this job, that's all. We'll keep a sharp eye open and deal with anything that comes up."

Gila and Caleb glanced enquiringly at each other. He just shrugged. "I heard they're good," he muttered, looking at Tammy and Dov.

The landing was smooth, customs a formality. The Porsche Panamera was waiting where she'd left it in the car park. With acceleration of 0 to 62 in 4.2 seconds and a top speed of 188 mph, they should be able to outrun anything seeking to impede their progress.

They were going to need to.

It was dark, and the M3 was almost deserted, as was the M25 where they joined it at Junction 12. They'd leave the 25 at Junction 10 as planned and pick up the A3, thence to Oxshott, the safe house and a slug of vodka. Comforting thought.

A sheen on the road surface from recent rain reflected the car's twin headlights. Tammy, driving with lamps on full beam, took the car up to the 70 limit. No point in attracting attention unnecessarily. The Porsche drove as smooth as velvet, sweet as honey. Dov was next to her, saying little, as always. The two passengers sat comfortably in the back, hand luggage on laps. Not a vehicle in sight. A sigh of relief. Well on their way now. What was that number by the Pergolizzi woman? *Heavenly Light*. Tammy hummed it to herself.

She kept to the middle lane, eyes constantly scanning the rear-view and wing mirrors for anything out of the ordinary. Junction 10 loomed as they approached the exit slip from the M25. A short hop to Oxshott and the safe house.

The elephantine presence of a grey SUV on her offside caught Tammy's attention. Then a second similar vehicle looked to be about to overtake her on the inside lane. She was momentarily hemmed in. Caleb shifted about in his seat uncomfortably.

Tammy was left in no doubt about what was happening when the interior of the Porsche was lit up by a blaze of lights from a third following vehicle reflected in her rear-view mirror.

Her pulse raced and a vein throbbed in her neck. The flanking vehicles gently closed in on her, bumping the sides of the Porsche, shunting it this way and that. Gila screamed. Caleb swore under his breath. Tammy's palms remained dry and she gripped the steering wheel firmly as the two grey SUVs moved ahead of her so she could neither drive through them nor round them.

Something like bits of iron junk was thrown from the windows of both leading cars. The Porsche crunching over the gritty debris, lurched unsteadily, quickly regaining its poise. Caltrops, she thought. Four-pronged, palm-sized steel teeth for bursting tyres. Problem: she'd have thirty miles at best before the run flat tyres gave up on her. Far less if she pushed the car hard, which was just what she was aiming to do.

The vehicle following moved closer till it touched the tail of the Porsche, which seemed to literally stagger under the impact. Tammy could no longer be certain they'd get away. She'd thought the emailed warnings had been directed at herself. But the situation was more confused than she'd reckoned. Things were becoming unpredictable.

Junction 10 led to the A3, which they'd aimed for, but would now be too slow for them to outrun the SUVs. There was no time to consider options. Gila was screaming hysterically and banging on her side window as though trying to escape the vehicle. Caleb had pulled what looked like a plastic gun from the inside of his bomber jacket.

"Put that bloody thing away," barked Tammy, in the next moment reaching forward for the switch to the rear fog lamps.

"What the fuck's she thinks she's doing now?" scowled Caleb.

The flash of the rear reds looked like she was braking and the following motor immediately hauled back, giving her a window to stamp on the brakes, adding to the eruption of light at the tail-end of the Porsche and allowing her to fall back herself, out of the clutches of the two big greys.

Now, dragging the wheel left and forced unwillingly onto the exit slip, with the two SUVs running on her offside wing, she immediately swung the wheel to the right again, swerving in front of the two big motors and back onto the main body of the motorway, then she floored the throttle. The car responded like a SpaceX rocket, roaring ahead of the three following motors, leaving them stuttering in her wake as she approached 180 mph. Now her palms ran wet. The tyres could go at any second, and with that, all control of the car.

Gila was still screaming, Caleb cursing, as Tammy said softly, "We're about six miles from Junction 9. There in two minutes. At say, half our speed they'll be there in four, that's three miles behind us. I'm guessing, or hoping, they'll reckon we'll use our greater speed to take us further round the motorway. But we'll come off at 9 anyway, then find the A244 to Oxshott.

"And this is us, now," she said almost at once, and braked hard. "Dov? Anything?"

"Nothing behind," said Dov, with obvious relief, looking over his shoulder. "You should maybe slow down a bit Tammy? The tyres are gone, you know."

"I know, Dov. Let's try to get home first."

"If you can," he said quietly.

She was on the rims, sparks flying as the Porsche careered along the last mile of the A244 to Oxshott village. If she stopped now they'd not be able to move again, the car simply being carried forward at this stage on its own momentum and a silent prayer. Tammy suddenly realised that the wrought-iron gates to the cul-de-sac would need to be opened and that's where their journey would end. If they were still being chased, their pursuers would be with them in no more than a couple of minutes.

As she swung the car left towards where the gates should have been, her confidence now failing, she saw that the housekeeper had thoughtfully left them open together with the up and over doors to the double garage in the safe house, an eight-bedroom red brick mansion at the end of the cul-de-sac. In the distance could be heard the growl of fast-moving motors.

Through the iron gates, the pair starting to close automatically behind them, the sounds of the other cars came ever nearer.

They'd be just too late. Glaringly clear. Now, in the double garage, the up and overs closing agonisingly slowly, the sound of the other three SUVs screamed at them, then whispered past, just as the doors clicked shut. Tammy breathed. "Home."

"Pretty tight," said Caleb. "The wheels must have melted by now." Turning to Gila, he said, "Are you alright?"

"Yes, I'm alright. I'm sorry I… You know…"

"You don't need to apologise for anything," said Dov.

The four people sat unmoving for several moments, the car seemingly filled with the echoing sounds of the chase. Then Caleb said, "She should never have driven. You should have taken the car, Dov."

"I would have," said Dov. "Only I can't drive like Tammy. In fact, I don't know anyone else who can."

They were welcomed indoors by Mrs Evans, the elderly housekeeper, her grey hair in curlers, who had a hot meal and clean sheets waiting for them.

Gila's appointments for the next two days were in London. It was agreed that Tammy would drop her, as a further precautionary measure, at Claygate, the mainline station after Oxshott, in the morning and collect her late afternoon. She'd use the Ford Focus already parked in the garage as she'd requested.

Gila and Caleb would book scheduled flights from Gatwick to Israel, on the day they proposed returning, with Tammy dropping them at Claygate again.

She was too weary to respond to Dov's advances and slept like the dead that night and the next, restricting herself to a texted, 'All okay' to Ginny on each of the two evenings, finally returning home still worn out, but exhilarated on the third evening.

* * * * *

Late evening, she practically burst into the flat, still in jeans, flight jacket and baseball cap. "Not what we were expecting at all," she announced excitedly to a puzzled-looking Ginny.

"No idea whether they were after me or the couple we were ferrying. Could have been a bit tricky, but what a buzz. Fantastic motor. Porsche Turbo S. Gunned it to 180 like it was an afternoon canter.

"Ginny, I am on a high. I'm literally floating. What a fizz.

"Ginny? You're not saying anything to me. Darling, what's wrong? Is anything the matter?"

"Tammy. Billy's dead."

CHAPTER 28 DAY 14

"JUST TELL ME, what the FUCK is going on here? I leave you sons of bitches alone for five minutes while I take a break in the sun, and what happens? I get your crap following me all the way here, through four thousand miles and five hours' time difference."

Samuel Goldblatt spoke with the same New York burr as his partner, George Derby.

"Can't you muthas be left to your own devices without seein' the whole of the LIIC edifice falling apart at the seams? Who's in today? Who've we got?"

George Derby and Nigel Cudlipp were sitting in the latter's office, Cudlipp behind his desk and Derby in one of a pair of maroon leather easy chairs in front of him. They both shifted about uneasily.

The office had been decorated by Nigel Cudlipp's wife in her own favourite colours, involving a magnificent high-gloss finish, sycamore-inlaid, forty-eight thousand-pound David Linley Riviera Rouge desk, featuring a Santos rosewood top. On the floor, a burgundy carpet overlaid with a Persian rug that must itself have cost a fortune, and etchings and lithographs on the walls. The rosewood credenza supported a lead crystal decanter with matching wine and whisky glasses on an antique Georgian silver tray. There was also an eighteen hundred-pound Miele bean to cup, self-cleaning coffee machine, producing every possible permutation of drinks. The illuminated glass-fronted cupboards at either end of the credenza contained ornaments in silver and porcelain.

The room was testament to Mrs Cudlipp's contempt for her husband. "The bastard thinks I don't know about his sordid little secrets," she complained to a friend. "Well, one way or another I'm making him pay. He doesn't know it yet, but he's buying me a Mercedes Benz SL class. It'll set him back at least seventy-four grand."

"It's me, Sam," said Cudlipp, leaning forward as though to get closer to Goldblatt, his public-school English contrasting acutely with the accents of the other two. "And I've got George with me here."

"So, where the hell is Goldcrest? I said in my email, you should all be there. Like now!"

"Eric's gone awol, Sam," said Derby. "He figured the cops were after him, so he employed a big black private eye to look out for him. He's shown his face from time to time, but he's just laying low for now, I guess."

"I heard about her. Pierre somebody? Supposed to be ex-Met. She any good? Know what she's about?"

Cudlipp, resting on his elbows, moved till he was practically hovering over the phone, which was on speaker, said, "She's asking a lot of questions. We all seem to have been in her sights from time to time."

"Yeah, I know. Your wives have both been on the blower screaming at me. Jesus! As if I didn't have enough to do sorting out the shit you to schlemiels keep getting us into."

Derby and Cudlipp looked at each other sheepishly, but didn't respond.

"You two lost your voices? George, do me a favour, your wife's decided you're having an affair with someone. Seems to think it's Eric's wife. Are you?"

Again, Derby said nothing.

"Okay, George, the silence tells me all I need to know. So what happened, you don't got enough pussy in London to keep you happy? Are you out of your fuckin' cups? How many times do I got to tell you, you don't spit on your own doorstep. Eric finds out? Then what? We ain't got trouble enough already? He'll break up the partnership. Assuming he doesn't go to jail first. That'll be a blast, won't it? Publicity'll wipe us out, totally. Gonna take the lawyers till the next century to sort out who gets what."

"It won't come to that, Sam," said Cudlipp.

"First off," said Goldblatt, ignoring Cudlipp, "you, George, have got me real worried. Eric screwed you big time. I know. I also know you can be an unpredictable sonofabitch. How can I be sure you didn't use Eleanor as a cover to kill the kids? It's just the sort of thing you'd go and do."

"Hey, now hold on, Sam." Derby was sounding increasingly agitated, running his fingers through his white-flowing locks.

But Sam ploughed on, "I had Eleanor on the phone to me when it happened. Poor kid's outta her mind. I mean, three kids who never did nuthin to no-one? Gotta be one sick bastard. You know, George? if anyone fits the bill—"

"Now just look here Sam—"

"Don't, 'just look here' me, George. Come to think of it, and while we're on, I wanna know all about you and Eleanor."

"What's to tell?"

"George, if I catch you dropping your wife in the shit..."

"It was just a fling, Sam. Eric's been giving her a hard time, so I gave her a bit of comfort."

"I'll bet you did. As if she didn't have enough on her plate. Since when did you give anyone any comfort, George? Jesus Christ!"

"But..." tried Derby.

"As you for, Nigel," Goldblatt went on, ignoring Derby's protests, "think I don't know about your predilection for little girls. Your wife tells me she found a stack of porn with what looks like 10-year-olds on it."

"She what?"

"You heard, you fuckin' pathetic... You had to have paperwork and leave it lying around, didn't you? If you're that hard up, couldn't you have gone online then deleted it, or something? No, I s'pose not. Everything on computer's traceable these days. What were you doin' in Lyme Regis anyway? Fancy Eric's kids did you? Things go wrong for you? Kids started screaming?"

"Sam, for God's sake," Cudlipp protested.

"So, tell me, wise guy; what did you got to do in Lyme Regis? There for the air, were you?"

"If you must know – "

"Yeah, buster, I must know. Tell me what're you doin' pissin' around in Regis, same time as George?"

"I was following George."

"What?" Goldblatt exploded. "Yer follerin' George? What in Christ's name for? You in love with him or something?"

"I thought my wife and he..."

There was a long pause, then, "You have got to be kiddin' me. I ask myself, what in hell was I thinking of when I teamed up with you three? I mean, what've I gotten myself into here? Talent, I told myself. They've all got talent. It'll override everything else. We'll do okay. I forgot. Integrity's supposed to count for something too. Now I see, with you three it's the one thing that counts for nuthin'.

"I'm back in a few days. So now hear this. If you dummies don't sort yourselves out, I'm closing down the partnership, whatever it costs. Do I make myself clear?"

CHAPTER 29 DAY 14

IT FELT LIKE BEING KICKED in the gut. Tammy's overnight bag dropped from her grasp, falling to the floor with a dull thud.

"Dead? Billy? How's he dead?" Her voice was hoarse. "Ginny? What's happened? Tell me. How's Billy dead? I thought he was supposed to be in custody."

Ginny came and put her palms on Tammy's cheeks, looked into her face.

"Oh, Tammy. Downey got the borough superintendent to give the necessary to keep Billy in custody for thirty-six hours, but couldn't get a magistrate to sanction a further thirty-six too, so he had to let him go. That was the day after you left for this security job."

Ginny spoke slowly and deliberately. "Downey had already gone beyond the limit, but Meg said he'd made it clear, no-one was likely to know or contest it. And anyway, he insisted it was in the interests of public safety."

"How'd it happen, Ginny? Where was Billy found?"

"Billy was found at the foot of the Ware Cliffs, you know, where he loved to go walking. Meg Copeland's been trying to get in touch. It's horrible. Downey's been on television insisting that Billy committed suicide because of the murders so that proves it. Downey says Billy knew he'd eventually be found guilty and that he couldn't live with it."

Flopping into an easy chair, Tammy cupped her face in her hands. She visualised the three murdered Goldcrest kiddies and her throat tightened, but she held back her tears. "What a bloody mess. What's Meg had to say?"

Sitting in the armchair opposite Tammy, Ginny gazed at her lover. She looked like a cage fighter who'd just lost a major bout, the euphoria of a few minutes ago replaced by a look of confused dejection. "Meg says that all the usual is happening. SOCA are all over the scene, and will be for days. The area's completely taped off. Billy's body is at the pathologists, with the PM scheduled for today or tomorrow. Probably tomorrow, now.

"Apparently, Downey's blowing hot and cold about everything, but he's announced that the case will be closed as soon as Billy's suicide is confirmed."

"Suicide be damned. Billy's been murdered. I'd stake my own life on it. After that first televised appearance of our friend Downey, there'd be enough people out there with a motive."

"And Tammy, there's something else you don't know."

Tammy was overtaken by a dreaded feeling she was going to hear something she really didn't want to. "What is it, Ginny?"

"It seems that Meg Copeland..."

"Is this going to be bad news?"

"It depends on how you look at it. See, Meg got a terrible dressing down for not telling Downey about the pendant."

"Oh bugger! I'm sorry about that. I shouldn't have asked her to keep it to herself at all. I feel terribly guilty. Probably damaged her career…"

"No, Tammy, no. You see, it all ended fine because Downey now says he was proved right all along about the Goldcrest murders."

"What! How's that then? Sorry, you've lost me completely."

"Well, it seems that a few days ago Meg found a pendant on the beach near the site where the children were killed." Ginny raised an eyebrow. "If you see what I mean?"

"Yes, Ginny. Don't keep me in suspense."

"So, with all the toing and froing, press, public and so on, she claims she forgot to tell Downey about the pendant, which she sent off for DNA testing. They've not yet gone public, but they're pretty sure they've found Billy's DNA on the item."

"Ginny, that's just not possible. What would Billy be doing with a pendant that might belong to Eric Goldcrest? Where would he have got it? Why wasn't it found before I found it? How would Billy have got it there? None of this stacks up."

"Tams, you told me the constable on duty at the site where you found the item said the only people he saw on the beach, once the onlookers had given up, were the Council sweepers and cleaners. On the day you went down there, there was a gap of a few minutes between the police shifts, you said. Billy Anderson did some work from time to time tidying the beach. He could have dropped it then, during the time between the police shifts. Even if he'd been seen that day, everyone in the area knows Billy, he wouldn't have attracted attention."

"Alright, so we say Billy dropped it. It's got his identifying DNA. It still doesn't answer any of the questions I've put. He didn't drop it at the time of the murders or it would have been found then. If you ask me, someone is playing games here. But God knows who. The only possible motive is to somehow involve poor Billy. Which is exactly what seems to have been achieved. Enough for one day, Ginny."

"Let me get you something. Tea? Coffee? You look all in."

"Vodka, Ginny. And make it a large one, no ice?"

She was back in a couple of moments with a tumbler of the clear spirit which she handed to Tammy, who drank a third of it in one.

"Hang on," said Ginny, "I'll just grab a coffee."

A few moments later she was seated again opposite Tammy cradling a burning hot mug in her palms. "So, where next, do you think?"

"Another word with Mr Goldcrest, I guess. I'll try to see him, or at least talk to him on the phone."

"How's the head?" said Ginny, changing the subject.

"Improving slowly," said Tammy, self-consciously adjusting the bandanna.

"Let me see."

"It's still horrible. See?" she said and dragged the bandanna to one side.

"No, it's not so bad now. Your hair's starting to grow back and the scarring isn't so angry. It doesn't matter to me, Tammy. The bandanna doesn't stay in place overnight anyway."

"You are a darling, Ginny. Now I must get some sleep. Early start tomorrow," she said, inclining her head towards the door.

CHAPTER 30 DAY 15

TAMMY WAS IN THE OFFICE before Ginny. Feeling physically wrecked, she wondered how she'd get through the day, let alone the rest of the week. Glancing at her watch she saw it was 7.00 am. Ginny should be in in about half an hour. She'd just have time.

In the ladies she unzipped the inner pocket of her shoulder bag, and extracting from it a concealed plastic bag, poured some of the white powder it held onto the cistern lid. Cutting it into two lines with a credit card, she then quickly inhaled before guiltily stealing back to her desk.

Its effects were swift and in a matter of moments she felt rejuvenated, positive, strong, even light-headed, ready to take on anything and anyone. It was too early to start making calls so she spent a couple of hours catching up on emails.

She'd greeted Ginny with a broad smile when she'd shown up at around 7.30 am. But Ginny had seemed unimpressed, merely remarking, "You seem to have woken up suddenly. I thought you were all in."

* * * * *

Eric Goldcrest was in London and reluctantly agreed to meet Tammy, but not in his office. They were in the American bar of The Beaumont Hotel, located in Mayfair, close to Tammy's office. Elegant, quiet, all browns and creams. A haven of peace in the centre of London's busy whirl.

"You know, Mr Goldcrest, Starbucks would have been just as convenient." Tammy was in one of her workaday two-piece light grey suits. She sat back in the comfortable armchair and crossed her legs, a fruit drink on the table between them. She'd taken to wearing a turban instead of the usual bandanna.

Eric Goldcrest looked less distraught than he had at their previous meeting in her office. This time he wore a smart, if sober, charcoal grey suit with white shirt and pencil-thin tie. Tammy recalled how edgy he'd been at the prospect of his expensive jacket being marked. He was nursing a whisky despite the hour, not yet noon.

"You wanted to see me?" Goldcrest looked Tammy up and down, gazed insolently at the crossed legs, the glimpse of thigh.

"May we talk about you for a moment, Mr Goldcrest?"

"Me? Why would you want to talk about me? For one thing, I've disinstructed you. I'm not paying you a bean, so what's the point of all this?"

"I'm trying to get my brain around all the individuals in this case. I simply can't make head nor tail of any of it. Why would anyone want to murder three innocent little girls?"

"You tell me. That's supposed to be your job, isn't it?" He sounded aggressive, defensive, even.

"Humour me." Tammy gazed at him intently, wondering, just what does make this man tick? "Tell me," she said, "can I start by asking you what sort of family life did you yourself have as youngster?"

"Really?" Goldcrest took a gulp of his whisky, the ice rattling in the glass. "I fail to see what that has to do with anything."

"Go on. Let me be the judge."

Goldcrest sighed. "I should think it was pretty standard. Three older sisters. All arrogant bitches. Probably took a lead from their mother who wrote the book. If dad ever upset her, the smallest thing, she'd hit him, for God's sake. I grew up thinking domestic abuse was something women visited upon men, not the other way around."

Goldcrest had raised his voice, but now lowered it when he realised he was attracting attention. People at tables nearby were glancing in his direction with concerned looks.

"Dad worked in the accounts department of the local authority health department in Bromley, where I grew up. Nice man, but weak. I decided no-one, and certainly no woman, was ever going to push me around. I suppose I became as big a bastard as the women in my family. I developed a thick skin. Nothing touched me. Nothing hurt me. Helped me to take on some of the scum in my industry. I was always good at maths. So finance was a natural world for me to inhabit. Screw my co-directors if they don't like me. I've helped them get rich. They don't complain about that, do they?

"On the female front, I wanted to marry a compliant woman. One who knows what it is to be feminine, not feminist, and I found what I was looking for in my first wife, Penny, and then again in Eleanor. Eleanor's background was the exact opposite of mine. Strong, even brutal father."

"I know," interrupted Tammy. "I met him briefly. Can't say I was impressed. Still, if that's what Eleanor was looking for in a man..."

"Hmm," responded Goldcrest noncommittally, before continuing. "Weak ineffectual mother. She was looking for a strong man, one she could rely on as she'd relied on her father. She found me. We suited each other. But she's frightened now, and that's a shame. Not what I ever wanted. Not of my doing."

Goldcrest caught the eye of a passing waiter, and, pointing to his glass, indicated a double, please, with soda. The waiter nodded his understanding and hurried off towards the bar to comply.

A short time later the whisky arrived, and Goldcrest immediately poured a measure of soda, then took a long pull on the drink before depositing the large cut-glass tumbler on the side table with an emphatic clunk.

Now was the time, thought Tammy, to test a response. "Mr Goldcrest," she said. "What do you know about a gold pendant comprising two hands framing the initials 'EG'?"

Goldcrest immediately coloured bright red. Tammy noticed the man had acquired a sheen of sweat on his brow. This was more than she'd expected, so soon. But equally, she couldn't decide how to interpret the reaction. So, she said nothing, merely waited.

"I lost it," he said eventually.

"Clearly," said Tammy.

"Where was it found? When was it found?" He was casting his eyes this way and that, in an apparent fog of confusion.

"It was picked up close to the site where the crime took place," she said, avoiding the use of the word 'murders'. "It's with the police. They're testing it right now for DNA."

"They'll find my DNA on it, won't they?" He seemed to have quickly composed himself once more.

"If it belonged to you, then of course."

"I'd better tell you then. I doubt you'll understand."

"Try me. I can be quite understanding, given the chance."

"After my first wife died of breast cancer, I realised for the first time in my life how vulnerable we all are. How vulnerable I was. I worked in a world of alpha males, and here I was crying all the time.

"Not at work," he added hastily. "But at home where I could grieve quietly and in peace."

"And that worked?"

"At a stretch. The hours I put in at the office, you know, they helped take my mind off things. But I was going through the motions. I was lost, lonely, at a loose end. Just existing, really."

He turned away from Tammy, as though something had embarrassed him. He stopped talking for several moments as though unsure whether to continue. Then he said softly, "I had an affair."

"Is that so wrong? Presumably it didn't last? Where did you meet this person?"

Goldcrest pulled at the collar of his shirt. He seemed uncomfortable. "It was a man."

"A man?" Tammy had tried not to sound too shocked.

"I knew you'd find it strange."

"Well, go on then."

"Met him by chance, then I got chatting to him. He was dropping his boy off at school, whole crowd outside the gates, he had a sort of lost look about him. I thought I recognised something there. I was right.

"Seems his wife had also died of cancer. The pancreatic variety. It had taken her eighteen months, during which time he'd taken care of his son and nursed his wife when the district nurse, or nurses weren't there."

Goldcrest took another long draught of his drink, and, replacing the tumbler, sat looking at the back of his hands for several moments.

"He was short and stocky, the man. Nothing special to look at. A jeweller. Bisexual, he told me. His wife, whom he adored, had been the stronger of the two. It was an odd marriage, but one that worked; like so many of the most successful partnerships, it was an entirely unpredictable relationship."

"You fell in love with him?" Tammy asked speculatively, as though testing the water.

"The man was more feminine than any woman I've known, and in desperate trouble. Practically suicidal. As I said earlier, I work in a world of macho men. Here was something for which I was completely unprepared. You see, I'd never met a man so gentle and in need of comfort and affection. We met up for drinks. I encouraged him to think of his boy, of the lad's future. Told him he'd eventually find someone else. Time was a great healer. All that."

Goldcrest faced Tammy and smiled. "I felt really needed for the first time in my life, and not for money. Don't get me wrong, I loved Penny. She loved me, but she was also an independent soul. She wanted me. I'm not sure she needed me. Two different things, aren't they? Does that make sense? Does that surprise you? Just for once I felt like giving something to another adult human being, rather than taking what was on offer."

"You don't have to answer this if you'd rather not, but was the affair physical?" Tammy wondered.

"A hug and a kiss. A teenage fumble once or twice. I'm not queer, you know." Goldcrest sounded a bit more like the belligerent individual Tammy had come to recognise. But for all that, he had the guilty look of someone caught pilfering from the local supermarket.

"So, this man gave you a memento. The gold pendant with the initials."

"That's right. We exchanged pendants. Mine, made by him for me, was heavy. I paid another jeweller to make one for him, but in a lighter weight. Nothing too male, as it were."

"I understand. Did Eleanor ever get to know about this relationship?"

"To tell the truth, I'm not sure. It had ended about the time I met her. That's probably what finished it, you know, when she came on the scene." He finished the last of his whisky and beckoned for yet another. His capacity seemed inexhaustible.

"I told her the pendant had been my grandfather Edward Goldcrest's, given to me a couple of years before he died. He was a good old boy. A bloody sight better as a father than my own had ever been. Did Eleanor know?" he pondered out loud.

"He phoned once, you know. The man. His name was Henry. Eleanor got there first, she was in the bedroom. I picked up a few moments later downstairs in the hall. I'd only just got home. Heard no more than bits, but couldn't make out much. He sounded unhappy. I was tempted, but couldn't risk my marriage. I put my extension down quietly. I don't think much of substance was said. She never mentioned anything to me of any importance. Just said that someone had called for me. She'd not heard me come in, and when she'd told him I wasn't home, he'd said he'd call back another time. He never did. And I didn't follow it up."

"Then you lost the pendant." A statement, not a question.

"Right. It saddened me greatly."

"But you never reported it lost? A valuable piece, with sentimental associations? Why not?"

"I was sure I'd find it. I didn't want to make a big deal, just in case anything had been said during that call. I mean, I couldn't very well ask Eleanor could I? Or maybe I could've, on reflexion. God knows. Also, I was pretty sure I'd lost it a few days before…before the…" He looked close to tears again.

Another whisky arrived, and he sat gazing at it for a few moments before picking it up and drawing on it. It seemed to calm him. "I sometimes play golf. When I get the chance. Helps me unwind when things are getting on top of me. What with all that had happened, I wasn't thinking about bits of lost jewellery. But it crossed my mind it might be on the course, or in the club house, maybe the showers. I don't know. Not top of the list of priorities however much I missed having it."

Goldcrest looked pensive, unsettled. For the first time Tammy had to admit she might have been wrong about the man. And yet, with the loss of the little girls and the belief that Billy might have been the one, what more motive might an angry, bereaved father have, even if the little ones were only stepdaughters? "You know Downey's insisting that Billy committed suicide. What do you think?"

"How would I know?"

"You had a motive. You had every reason, not just to want him dead, but to do the job yourself."

"Don't be ridiculous." He looked irritated, knocked back the last of his whisky in one gulp.

"Anderson killed himself two days ago. I was in London for meetings. Check with my PA. I wasn't anywhere near Lyme Regis that day. Come to think of it, if I had been, you'd have seen me on CCTV somewhere."

He got up suddenly, checked his watch. "Look, I've got to make a move now."

Tammy stood up as well. "I appreciate your time, Mr Goldcrest."

"Yes well…" He shrugged noncommittally.

"A truly terrible thing losing not just one, but three. We can come to love our stepchildren every bit as much as if they were our own, I'm sure." Tammy stared at him levelly.

"Sorry?" Goldcrest looked at her quizzically. "Stepchildren? Who said anything about stepchildren?"

"Your stepchildren, Eric."

"I don't remember saying anything about stepchildren. Where did that idea come from? Is that what you've been thinking all along? The old stepfather kills another man's children idea?"

"Weren't they? I mean, you've been married only a year, the girls were six years old. Weren't they Eleanor's children?"

"The hell they were. Is that it? And Eleanor and I had been together for three years prior to getting married. Have the police and everyone been assuming from the start that I'm the stepfather?"

"When I mentioned fathers and stepchildren to Eleanor as though the girls were not yours, she didn't correct me."

"I wonder why?" Goldcrest scratched his jaw thoughfully. Then looking up at Tammy.

"These were my daughters, Tammy. My little girls. Penny's and mine. I adored them. I'd have died for them. What reason on earth could I have for killing them?"

Tammy stared at him. "I'd...I'd just thought..."

"I can see what you thought. It's my fault. I just assumed... I should have made it clear. I started to say, when we first met, but then got diverted." He looked down at the floor, shaking his head in despair. "I should have made it clear," he repeated. "I've been distraught, bewildered. I don't know...I didn't realise."

"I'm so sorry, Eric," she said, using his Christian name again. "It's as much my fault as yours. I suppose even the most experienced among us miss the obvious, make wrong assumptions."

Tammy sat down again. "You know that puts a whole new complexion on things," she said.

"Look, before we finish, can you just tell me something about your marriage, Mr Goldcrest, if you don't mind? Then I won't trouble you further. May I ask, has it been all you hoped?"

"It started out well enough," said Goldcrest, resuming his place, though glancing at his watch again. "But I was always involved with the girls. I couldn't expect Eleanor to be as committed as me.

"And, I admit, I excluded her too much. They were my children, not hers. I think she began to resent it, possibly from quite early on in the marriage. She wanted kids of her own, practically begged me. But, I kept thinking that if I gave her children I'd in some way be being unfaithful to the memory of the girls' mother, Penny.

"Also, something I learned about Eleanor after we wed might have given me pause if I'd known at the time. She was mildly bipolar. She had bouts of depression. Albeit they were rare. But it was another reason I kept on delaying having kids with her. Ridiculous I know, but it was an increasing source of tension between us.

"I reckon that apart from the obvious hard work, having children of your very own can focus the mind on problems other than yourself. I mean, it stared me in the face. Eleanor was just great with my three. Amy, Poppy and Petra. I see that now. They adored her. Called her mama. If anything could help lift those occasional depressions, being with the kids did.

"So we began rowing a lot. Shouldn't have happened. My fault. Badly judged. Selfish of me. She'd have made a good mother. Instead, the arguments made the little ones cry. They know what's going on, kids, from an early age. Breaks my heart when I think of it."

Reaching forward, Tammy touched Goldcrest lightly on the shoulder. "Look, I've really gone on long enough. Thank you again for your time. I really appreciate it."

Goldcrest shrugged, gazing off distractedly, but didn't reply immediately, then, "No problem," he said, brightening slightly.

"Look, Eric, I've got some calls to make so I'll wait on here for a bit, but I needn't detain you."

"No that's fine," he said, reaching out and shaking hands with her.

"Oh, and I hope you won't mind my pointing out, but you've nicked yourself shaving. Again," she said, faintly amused.

"Hmm? Oh, thanks. Yes," he said, raising his hand somewhat sheepishly to his chin. "Always in too much of a hurry."

Tammy sat down again to finish her fruit drink and ponder Goldcrest. Strange man. A set of contradictions. She'd even found herself warming to him. She wondered if he had any idea about the affair Eleanor was involved in with Derby.

On impulse, she picked up the whisky tumbler Goldcrest had been drinking from and put it in an evidence bag she always carried with her. Then she called Meg. "Hi, Meg. It's me. Anything happening?"

"Hi, Tammy. Pathologist's report is in."

"Suicide?"

"Murder!"

"Murder! Are they absolutely sure?" She sat back in the chair, shocked.

"They're certain. No doubt about it. But listen. It's likely he was pushed from the cliff. It was raining that day, and there was mud on his shoes from the cliff top. But, and this is the terrible thing. He was still alive when he hit the ground."

"Oh my God. How long did it take him to die then?"

"Not long, Tammy. You see, someone finished him off."

"How's that? Meg, this just keeps getting worse."

"He was bludgeoned to death with a large stone from the beach, just like the little girls. His head smashed in. The rock was left lying by him. Like some sort of trophy. And, just as before, there were no prints. Oh, and one other thing. The blows were all on the right side of his head. The assailant must have been left-handed."

"Does that tie in with the children?"

"You tell me, Tammy. You saw the pictures. The kiddies were so badly battered it'd be nigh on impossible to tell for sure. But we had thought left-handed as well, hadn't we?"

CHAPTER 31 DAYS 14 AND 15

"MEG, WILL YOU GET ANY STICK from Downey if I come around and look at a few hours of CCTV at your nick?"

"Downey's in a bind, he can't decide whether to ignore the pathologist's report and insist it's suicide, which is rubbish. It's more than his professional life is worth. So he'll have to drop that notion shortly. On the other hand, he's totally at sea. Back to square one on the little girls, and now without a clue as to who could have killed Billy."

"Meg, I'll bet he could use some help. I'm an experienced copper, after all. Tell him I'm coming in tomorrow. Perhaps he'll even be polite."

Next, she called Ginny, "Hi, darling. Look, there's been one helluva development. You won't believe." She paused as though debating the magnitude of what she was about announce. Then, softly, "Billy's been murdered."

"No," Ginny breathed.

"I know. I couldn't believe it myself at first. I'm going to grab an overnight bag, train down there, turn in early and see Meg first thing in the morning. Look at CCTV. See if anything pops up."

"Okay. I'm in the office for another couple of hours. Call me in the morning?"

"Of course. Sleep tight."

"You too."

She looked at her watch. It was 5.00 pm. Dov would be home at the flat. She called. He didn't sound over enthusiastic. "I never hear from you, Tammy."

"Come on, Dov, we saw each other only yesterday."

"That was business," he said gloomily. "When do we get to see each other properly? Just you and me?"

"How about tonight? I've got to be in Lyme Regis tomorrow. I told Ginny I'd be travelling up tonight. I could come round to you then catch an early train tomorrow."

"What about your girlfriend?"

"Don't, Dov. That's not fair. You know I love her."

"But you won't be telling her."

"How can I? It's deceitful what I'm doing. And yes, I do feel bad about it, if you must know."

"How long?"

"Give me an hour, two at most."

She'd taken a quick shower and left with an overnight bag. Instead of the bandanna, she wore a navy sweatband. She'd chosen a mini flared pale blue V-neck dress; she wore it with heels and without stockings. All thighs, calves and cleavage tonight, she thought. I wonder how he'll react.

It was a dry chill evening, and she was aware of the shifting breeze as it swirled like trespassing hands up and around her bare thighs. Grabbing a cab, she was at his place in twenty minutes.

Despite herself, she felt a shiver of excitement. Dov was a highly competent lover. Better than the drug which picked her up, Dov's attention would relax her completely. Help her unwind. She'd denied him the other night. There'd be no denials tonight.

He greeted her at the door wearing slim-fitting black slacks and a white open-necked shirt with bloused sleeves he'd had tailor-made. He was clean shaven and smelled of something expensive. He angled his head towards the flat in a gesture that said, "Come in." He hardly looked at her.

He'd cooked, she could smell it, and her mouth watered. Her favourite, lamb casserole marinated with red wine, chopped mint, cumin and coriander, garlic and onion. It would be accompanied by mashed Cyprus potatoes and fresh runner beans.

There was something incredibly sexy about a man who could cook. But then, everything about Dov was sexy. He was a highly capable individual, one upon whom she felt she could rely in any given situation. She was in love with Ginny, of course, but had witnessed her affection for Dov grow in a way she'd not deny. More than just an occasional lover, he was a friend.

The flat looked homely for once. Dov had gone to some trouble. Mountains of books had been tidied away, and antique pieces locked up. There were two lit candles on the dining table, which was laid with a pink cloth and contrasting wine-coloured napkins. A couple of joss sticks smouldered on a sideboard lending the flat a slightly exotic feel.

She went into the tiny kitchen and reached for the fridge door, but Dov, leaning over her, pushed it shut. "No peeping," he admonished.

"Really? I just wanted to see what you'd done for dessert." She felt disconcerted, abashed, embarrassed even. Her cheeks flushed, and she wondered if he was aware of her discomfiture.

"Sit," he instructed, pointing at the dining table.

He'd made a trifle. The base was finger biscuits soaked in medium dry sherry, topped with a layer of whipped cream. On top of that were sliced plums and cut-up segments of orange into which he'd mixed red currants. A layer of custard had been added, and the whole topped off with a further blanket of whipped cream, sprinkled with chocolate powder and chopped blanched almonds. The whole meal must surely have taken ages, and yet she'd given him barely a couple of hours' notice she was coming.

*****

She sat back, very full. It had been all it promised to be and more. She'd need to do some work in the gym or on the exercise machines at home. But it was heaven, and she told him so. And for the first time since she'd arrived, he smiled.

Then he said simply, "Bed." It was neither request nor instruction. He got up and came to her side of the table and reached out as though he were about to help a child across the road. And she took his hand, compliantly, and let him lead her into the bedroom.

"Let me," he said, as Tammy started to unbutton the dress.

He moved unhurriedly, undoing one button at a time until the front of the dress hung open revealing a tiny pair of transparent white knickers and nothing else. She'd always been self-conscious about her small breasts, and covered them now with her hands.

"Don't be silly," he said softly, pulling them away.

"But they're so small," she said shyly.

"Tammy, I'm making love to a woman, not just to a pair of breasts. You're one of the most beautiful women I've ever known."

"But…"

"Enough of the buts, Tammy."

Flinging her arms around his neck, she said, "I love you, Dov Jordan."

"I love you too, Tammy Pierre."

* * * * *

He slept on as she showered in the early morning, and she crept out of the flat without disturbing him. She ached deliciously from Dov's attention, and looking over him before leaving, one suntanned arm outside the duvet, he looked so much at peace she longed to kiss him, knowing if he woke, they'd make love again.

* * * * *

Late morning. The 'Operation Jurassic' board was covered with images and comments; ideas and theories; photographs of the Goldcrests, as before, together with George Derby, Nigel Cudlipp, even the recently released child killer, Leonard Kristof. Various others with names Tammy presumed had come into the picture at some time or another.

They'd spent hours at Meg's desk trawling through CCTV images of Lyme Regis and surrounding areas on the day of Billy's murder, and then the several days immediately before and after, without finding anything of value. Nothing that is, until this moment.

"Look, Meg." Tammy, dressed casually today in denim jeans and a burgundy V-neck sweater, pointed animatedly at the screen.

Meg, looking more matronly than usual, was in a brown skirt and jacket, the fuzz of incipient moustache more prominent, a fresh soapy smell about her. She wore pebble round wire spectacles that Tammy hadn't seen her in before. Her desk supported an array of immaculately laid out papers. Some of the stress brought on by her daughter's travails at school seemed to have diminished, and she appeared able to concentrate less distractedly on her work.

"What have you spotted, Tammy? Oh, I see now," she said, peering closely at the image. "I know who that is. He's up on our board there," she said, pointing to the operations display. "We had reports he was being released more than a month ago, so I Googled him. Downey went to see him with Sue, a week or ten days back, and they got short shrift there. Downey came back apoplectic. Said if he couldn't nail Billy, he was going for Kristof."

"I met him," Tammy said quietly.

"You met him? When? You never said."

"I wanted to get an impression of the man without letting any other views impact, so I said nothing to you. That is, until now."

"And?"

"And, I have to say, he is one strange character."

"How so?"

Turning away from the screen, Tammy faced Meg, crossed her arms and looked contemplatively up at the ceiling. "Okay," she said, addressing the DI directly. "He's very tall. Grimy. Adopted, apparently. Hungarian mother had him at fourteen, little more than a child herself. Likely to have been subjected to prolonged abuse, possibly by Kristof's birth father. He actually volunteered his fancy for little girls could be inherited. If such a thing can be? Insisted he wasn't violent; adamant he'd never attacked anyone in his life. And he was clearly devoted to his adoptive mother whom he felt had had a raw deal in court."

"What do you think?"

Shaking her head, Tammy said, "I just don't know what to think. The man's a series of paradoxes. He's so unsavoury to look at, and yet, I almost felt myself sympathising with him. Certainly, the case against him doesn't look to have been too strong to me, from what he says. The transcript might reveal more when I get hold of it." She shrugged. "He said to call him Leo."

"A real oddball, I see," Meg agreed.

"You know, if Downey does decide to chase Kristof as his second string, he's nothing to go on, nothing to go with, short of trying to bully a confession out of him."

"Same as he's tried with Billy." Tammy squinted back at the frozen image on the screen.

One of the young uniformed officers quietly deposited two mugs of black coffee on Meg's desk. "Thanks, Jenny," said Meg, lifting the drink to her lips and blowing on it.

Tammy nodded her thanks to Jenny, then said, "Something in this picture doesn't stack up. He's in the street, so I can't be sure. It's not all that clear. Move on a bit. We had some views inside Tesco.

"Look, there!" She pointed as Meg took the recording on further. "That's him. Kristof. Who's he talking to? Can you make out anyone?"

"I can't see, Tammy. They're obscured behind that plant display. We need the image to be enhanced. It's almost as though they're hiding. He looks animated enough. Talking sixty to the dozen. We need a lipreading expert. I'll see what can be done."

"Hmm! One who can read lips in profile. No, there's something else here. I've got it," she said, slapping the top of the desk. "He's had a haircut. He actually looks clean. He's in a decent, smart dark tracksuit, with clean trainers. Looks like someone's waved a magic wand over him."

"Downey said he stank. Torn and filthy clothing. So what's transformed him—"

"Hey, Meg!" Tammy interrupted. "What the hell's he doing in the shops anyway? When are these images dated?"

Meg leaned forward again. "Look here," she said, pointing. "They're dated two days ago."

"And I saw him just over a week ago. I suppose he could have cleaned himself up since then. But he looks different. He looks, I don't know, poised. He even holds himself more erect. I don't get it. Kristof told me he couldn't be seen in town. Afraid of facing abuse. Said his shopping was done for him by his supervising officer. Something very strange is going on if you ask me. Could we have a Jekyll and Hyde character here? Have we been looking in the wrong place all along? I'm going to pay another visit to Mr 'call me Leo' Kristof just as soon as I can."

The station was busy, but seemed subdued, as though everyone there had been affected in some way by Billy's death. Someone had decided to spray the place with air freshener. It had made little inroads into the cloying smell of perspiration. No-one had thought to open a window.

A tired-looking wasp landed on a file on Meg's desk. One of the men looking over said, "Swat the bloody thing."

But Meg, ignoring him, carefully picked up her file with the sleepy wasp on it, and walked down steadily to one of the windows which she opened with one hand, while retaining the file in the other. Then she shook the file gently until the wasp flew off. As though reading Tammy's thoughts she said, "I know. But if we leave the windows open, every gust blows papers all over the place."

Downey had gazed over the shoulders of the two women from time to time. He was looking for inspiration, but finding none, had confined himself to inconsequential, but frequently spiteful mutterings. He'd reluctantly agreed to Tammy's presence, accepting that his lack of anything to go on and her experience in the force might produce something. But his dislike of her was obvious, and his comments were peppered with oblique references to her dual nationality and mixed race.

"We don't have many people of your persuasion in this neck of the woods," he'd sneered on more than one occasion. He was more stooped than ever, and his suit, the same suit, like his hair, was lank and shiny. He was a morose and spectral presence whom Tammy pointedly ignored.

Tammy spread her arms behind her head, her back and neck aching from the hours of concentration. She indulged herself in thoughts of Dov for a moment, and of last night. He knew how to be gentle with her, how to drag things out, when to be rough to the point of brutality. She could sense little points of pain and pleasure still apparent all over her body. Her thoughts drifted for a moment back to Geoff Miggan. Some men just had what it takes. Peggy Lee's record, *Some Cats Know*, came to mind and she must have gasped, because Meg looked at her concerned. "You okay, Tammy?"

"I'm fine," she replied, embarrassed, as though Meg might have read her mind.

"Another coffee?" asked Meg, getting up from the desk.

"What the doctor ordered. And then, I tell you what, why don't we go back to the time of the first murders. Take another look. See if we can find anything that might link the events. While I think of it, I know I've already asked you about chats with the Goldcrest neighbours, but I'm assuming there wasn't anything of any use, either before or this time?"

"Nothing," said Meg. "The Goldcrests seem to have largely kept to themselves. Eric was seen by one of the neighbours taking the girls out the morning they went missing. But there was nothing that appeared odd or worth commenting on. You've made contact with Bea Cumming. Lovely lady. I spoke to her too. She didn't like Eric. Thought him bad tempered, menacing and unpredictable."

Meg disappeared and was back in a few moments with the coffees. "I could use a smoke," said Tammy.

"Not in here, you know."

"Yes, I do know."

"If you want to go outside, I can always wait."

"No, let's get on. I'm told I smoke too much anyway. Bad for the complexion."

"Yours is wonderful, Tammy. You've got nothing to worry about. What do you use, if you don't mind my asking?" said Meg wistfully.

"I hardly bother. Lucky really. A bit of Oil of Olay at night. That's all."

They turned back to the screen and resumed searching for anything that might help. Downey marched by from time to time, his dislike of Tammy, almost palpable. "That moron killed himself. I'm telling you, pathology's got it wrong, and when you two time-wasters give up chasing ghosts, I'm going to start looking at other possibilities."

He stalked off, and Meg caught Tammy's eye and merely shrugged.

It was Meg who spotted something first. "Look, Tammy, who's that?"

They were re-running the images from the day of the first murders.

"Where?"

The woman was petite and wore a dark tracksuit with her face almost obscured by a hoodie. The time showed as 10.15 am.

"Is that Eleanor?" said Tammy.

"Wait while I go back to 10.00 am. There's a camera outside the Carlton."

"You're right," said Tammy. "Look, that's her coming out of the hotel, looking as if she's on a mission somewhere. But where? And to do what?"

"Looks as though she's getting into George Derby's hire car."

On an impulse Tammy said, "Flip forward a few minutes. Let's see if she goes into town. See what else has been picked up."

They started searching camera image after image without success. Then Meg spotted her again. "Look, there," she said.

"Where?"

"She's on Broad Street, according to the camera. She's not far from Tesco Express. Nothing remarkable there. S'pose she's been doing a bit of shopping, that's all. See the carrier bag? Except, there's a Tesco in Axminster, so why bother driving into Lyme Regis? And why risk being seen by your husband when you're supposed to be having an affair?"

"But it's not a Tesco carrier. Tesco bags are white with a blue-lined motif and red lettering. That bag Eleanor's carrying doesn't have that distinctive motif or lettering."

"And it's too small for a food shop," said Meg. "I was thinking, there's a dolls' hospital along Broad Street. Sells new toys as well. She might have crept in on the quiet to buy the babes a little gift. A guilt offering? Supposedly bought from wherever she goes to meet her mother."

"One of us will have to ask her. I guess we should think again about the day of Billy's murder. We should see if Eric was anywhere in the vicinity. He says he can prove he was in London that day. But if anyone had a motive to kill Billy, he did."

Tammy stretched her arms and spine again and yawned. "Popping out for a smoke, Meg. Simply screaming for one."

It was bright out for once, and fresh. There was little going on in the car park at the back of the station. She breathed in deeply, clear of the claustrophobia of the police station. The slim cigar was smooth and comforting as she inhaled it, noting the absurd irony of the action. What she wanted was a line. She needed a boost, was desperate for a kick. The car chase had drained her more than she wanted to accept. She was tired. Nothing new there.

Dov was pressing her. Ginny was quietly unhappy about the lack of attention. Work came first. Work came before everything.

Meg joined her a moment later. "Pathologist's been in touch. I got a call just as you left the office. They've found something under Billy's nails."

"Did they say what? Is it going to help us at all?"

"Tiny fragment of skin under one nail, and some sort of fibre under another. They couldn't identify it."

Back at Meg's desk Tammy reached into her shoulder bag and extracted the plastic evidence pouch.

"Meg, I saw Eric the other day for a chat. It may not be admissible. It possibly isn't ethical, but," she said, taking out the whisky tumbler, "he drank from this. Might be an idea to DNA it and compare it to the DNA on the fragment of skin found under Billy's nail. A long shot. Pretty unlikely. But worth a look."

"Tammy, look. At the side of the screen. That's Eric Goldcrest. Isn't it? On Church Street. Hang on, though. No, can't be sure. What do you think?"

"I think that's our man, Meg."

"Shall we bring him in for a chat?"

"I can't wait. Meanwhile I'm going back to see our friend Leo first."

"I'll come with you, Tammy. If that's okay? We'll take a pool car."

CHAPTER 32 DAY 15

HE WAS THERE, Leonard Kristof, walking almost jauntily along the tree-lined Woodberry Road towards the wreck of a place he was presently inhabiting.

He appeared much as he had in the recent CCTV image, that is, infinitely cleaner than he'd been when Tammy had first interviewed him face-to-face. Meg pulled up the car just past him, and Tammy leaned out of the passenger side window. "Leo?" she asked, a little uncertainly.

"That's me," he said with a bright smile.

Meg leaned across Tammy and flashed her badge at Kristof. "Could we have a moment?"

"Always happy to oblige the good ladies of the constabulary."

Again, the thought came to her, Jekyll and Hyde. Tammy frowned. How could this be the same man? And the accent? She didn't recall that from her meeting with him. And yet is was him, indisputably so. How could he be so changed, and in so dramatic a fashion?

"Where would be convenient, Mr Kristof? Your home? Or the station?" Meg asked.

"Station's okay by me," he said, smiling, and, reaching for the back door of the saloon, he climbed in.

"Back to the station alright with you, Tammy?" Meg asked.

"I'm fine."

Where was all that timidity? The anger? The regrets? Tammy shook her head imperceptibly. She was missing something here.

They were seated in one of the interview rooms, coffee having been provided for Kristof and the other two by the young PC, Jenny again. Little had been said during the brief drive back to the station. Time for a closer inspection. Kristof was groomed, that much was all too apparent. To be precise, he was immaculate. His nails were trimmed. His hair had been cut and styled. His blue tracksuit was spotless. He smelled of soap and aftershave.

This was the very same man they'd seen on CCTV talking animatedly in profile to someone only barely visible to the CCTV camera. The same man whom Tammy had found stinking filthy, cowering and fearful. When had he found the time, or come to think of it, the money to have himself re-kitted out? He was supposed to be terrified about meeting up with some sort of confrontation if he showed himself in the town centre. This didn't look like a man afraid of anything. He still resembled a ferret, but one for whom things were indisputably looking up.

Tammy said nothing. She just watched and waited as Meg began her interchange.

"Mr Kristof, this is an informal interview, and you are here voluntarily. Am I correct?"

"That's about the size of it." He leaned back in his chair and surveyed the two women with apparent interest. He looked almost smug.

Meg sighed but kept going, "This interview is being recorded. Do you understand?"

"Yup. Carry on."

"Mr Kristof, do you think we might ask for a 'Yes' for the recording?'

"Yes. Yes. Yes." He grinned.

Meg went on, looking somewhat exasperated, "Will you please state your name for the tape?"

"I am Leo Kristof, presently of this manor. Now can we please get on with this? I'm a very busy man."

Busy doing what? Tammy asked herself.

"Before we start, Mr Kristof, I have to caution you. You have the right to remain silent. You do not have to say anything, but it may harm your defence if you fail to mention something that you later rely on in court. Anything you do say maybe given in evidence. Do you understand?"

"Hey! Wow!" said Kristof. "That's quite a mouthful. Defence, did you say? What defence? You ain't charged me with any crime. Anything more?"

All this, from a man recently released from jail, pursuant to a murder conviction twenty years previously, who must have heard similar at the time of his earlier arrest. Tammy watched the man's eyes. They were open and ingenuous, as though he had absolutely nothing to hide, nothing to fear. There had to be a chink in the armour, or else Leonard Kristof was an actor worthy of an Oscar nomination.

Meg continued as though nothing daunted, "You have the right to legal representation, should you wish it. But if you do decide to be assisted by a lawyer—"

Kristof held up his hands. "No lawyers needed ladies. Like I said, I ain't under suspicion for doin' nuthin'. Just here to help you good folks if I can."

The accent seemed to have become more pronounced with Kristof's apparent increasing confidence. It sounded contrived. A show of bravado?

"Very well." Meg insisted that Kristof state he appreciated the interview was being recorded. She'd already referred to the tape when asking his name. Kristof again nodded his understanding.

"For the record then, you are Leo Kristof?"

"That's me," he said smiling, and noisily slurped his coffee.

"May I start by asking you where you were on Saturday, September 2nd between the hours of 9.00 am and 2.00 pm?"

Kristof hung his head, his shoulders slumped in a gesture of defeat. His mood seemed to have changed in an instant. From bright to dark. Day to night. The speed of the change was quite extraordinary. He'd become sombre, seemed lost in thought. But after such a simple enquiry? Silence ensued for several seconds, then, "Hmm?"

"Mr Kristof?" prompted Meg.

No response. Kristof appeared utterly morose. He looked vacant. Meg turned to Tammy questioningly, but Tammy simply shrugged as if to say, 'Don't ask me!' What was going on?

"Leo?" Tammy tried.

At last, as though imparting a closely held secret, he said, "I was with my brother most of the day, from about 11.30 am onwards."

Meg and Tammy glanced at each other in astonishment.

"Before that," he added, "I'd taken myself for a little morning walk along the clifftops. Shake off the cobwebs. Clear away the blues. I got back and he said he'd been for a walk too. On the beach for some fresh air."

On the beach, thought Tammy. In the morning. And brother? This was something new. Then again, a walk? On the morning of the murders? Did the man know what he was suggesting?

"We ate lunch together," he went on. "Then had a bit of shuteye in the afternoon. Turned in early. A right shithole of a place he's got there. Shoulda stayed in my nice hotel."

"What's that you say? Your brother?" Meg enquired.

"That's right."

"Which brother is that, Mr Kristof? We've no record of you having a brother. Can you explain?" asked Meg.

"No, please. Let me guess," interrupted Tammy. "We're talking about one Mr Leonard 'Leo' Kristof, aren't we?"

"Yeah." He smiled. "Right on."

"But you're also Leo?" Meg asked. "Aren't you?"

"Leopold. Not Leonard. We're identical twins. Leonard didn't ever know he had a twin. I found out by chance years ago. When I heard he'd been found guilty of rape and murder twenty years back, I wasn't sure what to do. I never visited him in prison. Seemed no point."

"And now?" Meg asked.

"I heard he was coming out. Saw it in the press." Kristof seemed to be brightening at recollections of his brother. "Thought I'd pay him a little visit. See if there was any way his bro could help him get back on his feet. The papers said where he could be found. I was in the area for a few days before I finally decided to introduce myself. It was that same Saturday, September 2nd you said? Day of the murder of those sisters. He was in a right state, I can tell you. Dirty, disorganised, in that dump of a place."

"And was he surprised to see you? To learn he had a brother?" said Meg.

"Yes, ma'am. Told him I'd been in the States these last twenty years and done okay for myself. Now back in the old UK and a spot of early retirement."

Tammy blew on the surface of her piping hot coffee. So that accounted for the accent, she thought. "You say you were in the area for a few days before going over to your brother's place?"

"Sure was."

The man's attitude was infuriating, but Tammy kept her cool.

"Where were you staying before you went to your brother's home?" Meg said.

"Why, I was at your marvellous local, The Regis Carlton."

A thought occurred to Tammy. "While you were staying there, Mr Kristof, did you happen at any time to meet Mrs Eleanor Goldcrest?"

"Who?" Kristof responded blankly. But Tammy noticed his gaze had dropped as he responded.

"Mrs Eleanor Goldcrest, Mr Kristof. You know who I'm talking about. The mother of the murdered girls. You say you were in the area a few days before the killings. Was it just a few days, or was it perhaps a week or two? Mrs Goldcrest stayed at that hotel from time to time. I'd like to know if you ever saw her or talked to her.

"As for your appearance, people change over time. Press reports with photos of you, or more pertinently your brother, wouldn't have shown you as you are today. More likely as your brother was twenty years ago. You could have walked around unaccosted, at least until the press got hold of some current pictures, which anyway would have shown a pretty poor specimen of a man. I believe there've been one or two recent long-range shots of your brother, but there's nothing remotely resembling you as you are today.

"Obviously, your brother's done his level best to keep out of the public eye. So, I ask you again. Did you see or speak with Eleanor Goldcrest at any time?"

Then, as though hit by a revelation, Tammy asked, "Did you bully her? Hmm? Eleanor? Mr Kristof? Is that what pleases you? Do you like to see people squirm?"

In the next moment another thought crossed her mind, "I wonder, have you also come back to harass your brother? Is that what this is all about?"

But Tammy quickly dismissed the former notion, however appealing. If there'd been any contact between Eleanor and this man, it would have been one of the first things she'd have mentioned to the police after the killings.

Being approached by a recently freed child killer, if she'd recognised him as such, and if she'd deigned to talk to him, then when? Before the killings? Hardly. After them? An equally implausible scenario. Still, she waited for Kristof's response.

"Damn fool nonsense," Kristof retorted. "As if I'd come back just to start laying into people. Why that poor lady—"

"Oh, please, Mr Kristof; spare me the tears. Alright then," said Tammy, "moving on. Was that all, Mr Kristof? Did Leonard have anything to offer?"

"Well now, since you ask, I have to tell you he was crying truly awful. Kept saying that he'd done something terrible that morning. I had the devil's job getting it out of him. Said he couldn't help himself. He'd done it before and he had to do it again. It was like a drug. Those three kiddies."

Meg and Tammy gazed at each other.

Tammy shrugged. "Are you being serious, Mr Kristof?"

"God's truth," he replied.

Tammy smiled at Kristof encouragingly. God's truth? she thought. Wherever did God fit in with this man's scheme of things? "Go on then, Mr Kristof. Tell us what he told you."

"Cracked their skulls open with stones on the beach, that's how he put it." Kristof sat back with the self-satisfied expression of a major lottery winner.

The room lapsed into stunned silence. The two women stared at Kristof as though waiting for more, but neither one said anything for the moment. Kristof simply beamed, continuing to look mighty pleased with himself, having recovered his earlier buoyancy.

Tammy was first to break the quiet. "Cracked their skulls, did he? Your brother?"

"The very same. It's what he said."

"Did he say how many stones he'd used?" Tammy prompted.

"One in each hand, is what he told me."

"I think not, Mr Kristof," Tammy said emphatically.

She'd pushed her chair back and started restlessly pacing the little room. "Those wounds were caused by a single stone, and were all on the right-hand side of the children's skulls, suggesting a left-handed person.

You're left-handed, aren't you, Mr Kristof?" she observed, watching him hold his mug of coffee.

"Your brother's right-handed. Not unusual in identical twins. Are you actually trying to help your brother, or are you up to some sort of mischief? I mean, just who're you trying to fool, sir? Did you in fact kill those children yourself, Mr Kristof? And are you now, for some perverted reason trying to implicate your brother?"

"Of course not. I'm trying to help him."

"How, by attributing a murder to him he probably had nothing to do with? Furthermore, I saw Leonard a few days after the killings. He said nothing about having seen you. Nor did he say he'd just found out he had a twin brother."

"I told him to say nothing about seeing me. I read about that first trial. Fitted up, Lenny told me. Had no money to defend himself. It's different now. I'm going to pay for his defence, if he needs one. I'm comfortably off. Like I said, done pretty well over the years."

"And when were you going to let us in on this little secret?" Meg asked.

"Only if you picked him up and charged him."

"But you're telling us all this now, and we haven't charged him," said Meg.

"For God's sake man, we've nothing to charge him with. No evidence whatsoever. All you're doing by coming here is hanging your brother out to dry before he's been accused of anything. We've got others in the frame for this murder. Not Leonard. Mr Kristof, why don't you leave us to get on with our job without going out of your way to muddy the waters by incriminating a possibly innocent man?"

Standing up, Kristof shrugged. "Your call," he said. "Now if there's nothing further?"

"There is one thing," said Tammy. "The neighbour on one side of the Goldcrests, Beatrice Cumming, thought she saw someone around midnight in her back garden answering the description of your brother. At least insofar as the tracksuit and trainers were tattered and filthy. She phoned it in to the police who logged the call. The someone was spotted the day after I'd had a chat with her, that would be three days after the murders. Ring any bells, does it?"

"It might do," sneered Kristof.

"Come on, Mr Kristof. Was that you, in your brother's clothes? He was too frightened to venture out of the house, so it had to be you, didn't it?"

"Maybe," he said sullenly.

"What were you hoping to achieve by impersonating your brother?"

Kristof shrugged noncommittally. "Just nosing around, tryin' to get the lie of the land. Not sure what I was hoping to find."

"At midnight? For someone ostensibly here to help your brother, you sure don't do him any favours."

"Can I go now?" Kristof snapped as he started for the door.

"I'm all done here," said Tammy.

"Mr Kristof," said Meg. "I'd like you to keep in contact. Can you give us a mobile number in case we need your assistance? I'll assume you're residing with your brother?"

"Sure," he replied. "Happy to help."

After he'd gone Tammy sat down again, she said, "I wonder? Meg, are you thinking what I'm thinking?"

"What's on your mind, Tammy?"

"Why is this man Leopold in Lyme Regis at all? What's brought him here? Charitable feelings about his long-lost brother? I don't think so. Did he kill the Goldcrest girls and then come up with this story about helping out his brother as spur of the moment thing? With not enough time to think of anything else right after we invited him back here, talking about two stones instead of one to do the murder would have been a neat way of diverting attention from himself. The man's a dangerous troublemaker."

Tammy leaned back in her chair. "You know what? I'm beginning to wonder about that first murder all those years ago. Might just as easily have been Leopold. Same face, same description. Same man, for all anybody knew. If Leonard had no idea he had an identical twin, who else could have known about him at the time? Leonard complained to me the DNA evidence found on the child he was convicted of killing might have been close but not conclusive. He'd been reading up on the subject recently.

"I didn't comment either way when I saw him, but I do know, identical twins aren't necessarily as clearly defined as they once were by their DNA. Recent advances involving what is known as 'Melting the DNA' based on research into the varied lifestyles, environment and or disease experienced by either or both of the two twins, modifying the results of the tests carried out, has meant they can be identified separately within a matter of hours. They're referred to as 'epigenetic' changes in the DNA."

"Wow, Tammy. I'm impressed."

"Don't be. I still know enough people in the business to tap old friends for info."

"I'd better make enquiries of our forensic people," said Meg. "See what they know and if they can come up with anything. Is the research likely to be expensive?"

"I've no idea, Meg. You'll need to ask. We are talking several murders here, present and historic. A past miscarriage of justice? Who knows. A present attempt at a repeat performance from a highly convincing psychopath? I wonder.

"See what you can come up with. We need something other than hunches about what might have happened if we're going to progress this case. Maybe we're about to get a clue to the question of who murdered the little girls. Was it Leo? Or was it Leo? Take your pick."

"What a conniving bastard," Meg whispered.

"And how very macabre would it be?" mused Tammy. "If the brother, Leopold committed the first murder, then cleverly watched his brother, Leonard swing for it, and has now used Leonard's release from prison as a golden opportunity to do the same thing again, while indulging his passion for child killing?"

"You know, we've still got other avenues to explore, Tammy. But we'll keep close to Mr Leopold. I've never met his like before."

"Whatever," Tammy concluded, shuddering as icy hands ran down her spine, "I think we've been in the presence here of something truly malefic."

CHAPTER 33 DAY 16

IN AN APARTMENT off the Edgware Road, Dov moved about restlessly. He'd been contacted by a client who wanted him to undertake a substantial contract in Dubai.

The home was palatial, and the client wanted it festooned with the finest pictures, antiques and objets d'art. Dov would work with an interior designer to ensure that colours, styles and textures matched. If the contract was a success, others would follow. Dov would be away from the UK for many months.

In all the years he'd known Tammy, she'd kept him religiously at arm's length. The other evening was the first time she'd declared her love for him. He'd been shocked, overjoyed.

But then she'd seemed withdrawn, become defensive, insisted it was Ginny she loved and was committed to. He was in his forties, had always wanted a family but never found the right one. Tammy was the one. Her own biological clock must be ticking.

Several times the other day she'd started to say something, then stopped. What was it she'd wanted to tell him but couldn't?

* * * * *

Meanwhile in the Queen's Park flat Ginny was agitated. She'd showered and shampooed, and her hair was tied in a turban towel. She seldom drank, but, restless and ill at ease, she'd helped herself to some of Tammy's ludicrously expensive vodka from the freezer, and she now sat in a red towelling robe unseeingly as Sky News unfolded.

Tammy was holding something back and nothing Ginny said could persuade it out of her. She was depressed and by turns, irritable, snappy or simply silent with her own thoughts for long periods. The other evening, sitting in watching a film together on Netflix, Tammy had barked at her over some trivial comment she'd made. Then she hadn't seemed to be aware of Ginny quietly leaving the room to go into their bedroom where she'd put a tissue to her eyes before going back to the film. Ginny's upbringing had been a happy one. Her parents were ideally suited, and although they'd hoped for a second child, Ginny as an only child had received all the love that two might have otherwise expected.

Apart from the university incident, about which she tried not to dwell, and the more recent episode with Kurt, both of which had left her confused, the few boyfriends in the pre-university years had left her feeling incomplete. There had to be something more. Tammy was the something more. Dynamic, exciting, unpredictable. Lovemaking with Tammy was an exercise in total abandon. Or it had been until recently when Tammy's mind had seemed to be elsewhere.

And, Tammy had her issues too. She'd confided to Ginny that she'd had an abortion when she was fifteen. Her parents had known nothing about it, and the job had nearly gone disastrously wrong. She wasn't sure whether she could still have children. The revelation carried with it the implied desire for a family. Although, with Tammy's levels of testosterone, it was surprising she'd conceived at all, still less likely she would again.

But what if she were to, against all the odds, where would that leave Ginny? And then, she thought, she would also want to be a mother one day. The twin notions left her inexpressibly sad.

Hanging all the towelling to dry in the bathroom, Ginny wandered into the bedroom, pulled on a long white cotton nightie, shook out her curls and climbed under the duvet. She didn't go to sleep immediately, it was still early, although it had been a busy day in the office with more enquiries for work coming in.

So she sat up in bed, her arms around her knees, surveying her life. Tammy had suggested making her a partner in the business. She could see the easy smile on Tammy's face as she'd made that announcement with a sort of casual enthusiasm. It had never occurred to Ginny she would be anything more than a PA. Her parents had been delighted at the news. Ginny had been overwhelmed.

Again, there was the ever-lurking question of the drugs. Cocaine was becoming an increasing problem. Tammy would be exhausted one moment, and then full of life after briefly exiting the room or office. One didn't need to be an expert to know what was going on.

Ginny had a natural deference about her, accommodating, albeit misleadingly, to the point of servility. Despite that one-off with Kurt where she'd been intoxicatingly in total control, she was generally happy to have Tammy take the lead in just about everything. Ginny had never been consistently unhappy at any stage in her life. Hers had always been a sunny outlook, and that was going to continue, whatever it took to make Tammy content.

Whatever, that is, except where the drug was concerned. On that issue there was no room for negotiation.

Tammy was due back, but Ginny wasn't sure just when; she hadn't called. Increasingly, this was happening. Ginny didn't want to appear to be checking up on her, but Tammy was forgetting to tell her when and where she'd be at any given time.

On that thought, she drifted into a restless sleep.

*****

Having forgotten to draw the curtains, the sun had streamed in early, rousing her before she was ready to be woken. Her head felt as though something was hammering at it from the inside trying to get out.

She'd eaten something last night in the hotel restaurant that had disagreed with her, leaving her violently sick in the morning. Or was it the several vodkas in the hotel bar? Or perhaps it was the lines of coke she'd indulged in, knowing there was no Ginny to admonish her. Her mouth was sour and her stomach still heaving.

"Blast it," she said out loud. "Blast it, blast it, blast it. Ginny! How could I have forgotten?" She punched the speed dial at the same time as she downed an Alka-Seltzer in the en-suite.

"Hi Ginny." Her voice echoed off the tiled walls in the bathroom.

"I was worried, Tammy. Your phone's always off, or you tell me not to call because you will. Then you don't. What am I to think? I feel very alone. Very vulnerable. Can you not see that?"

"I am so sorry, darling. I'll make it up to you, I swear, just as soon as this business is over. How does a week in Tobago sound?"

"Too good to be true?"

"I miss you, Gins."

"I miss you too. Do you know when you're going to be back this time?"

"Tonight. Promise.

"Meg's bringing Eric in for questioning under caution. He won't be under arrest, but we think we spotted him on camera in Lyme Regis the day Billy died. He's our prime suspect, but before he gets charged, we need to hear what he has to say. I've got the weirdest feeling that if Eric did murder the children after all, for God knows what reason, Billy's previous caution and now the recent questioning would have given Eric what he'd have seen as a heaven-sent opportunity to kill him, allowing that fool Downey to conclude that Billy had committed suicide after killing the girls. Trouble is, neither Eric nor Downey could have reckoned on pathology concluding that Billy's death wasn't suicide but murder."

* * * * *

Eric Goldcrest sat on one side of the interview table, his hands in his lap; he was casually dressed in a denim jacket, jeans and open-neck white shirt. He looked drawn and haggard. DI Copeland and Tammy, both in grey suits, sat opposite him. The tape machine was running, making a barely perceptible hum.

Copeland opened the interview.

"Thank you for agreeing to come in, Mr Goldcrest. As I've explained, this interview is entirely voluntary. You are not under arrest, but you have been cautioned."

"Yes, well get on with it then." Goldcrest looked around the room as though he might be seeking an escape route. He glanced up at the camera recording the event, and then back at the two women. "You know it's me should be questioning you two."

"Really?" said Copeland.

"I employed Ms Pierre here to do something about getting the police off my back, since everyone assumed from day one I'd murdered the children. But I've explained to Ms Pierre that the girls were my daughters, not Eleanor's. There's no way I'd have harmed a hair of their heads."

"Mr Goldcrest," said Copeland patiently. "Until you are specifically eliminated from our enquiries, we have to keep an open mind. The investigation into the murders of the girls is still ongoing."

"And getting nowhere, from what I can see." Goldcrest had leaned forward, his hands and elbows flat on the table, looking earnestly into the eyes of the women opposite him. "Am I still in the frame? Or can I be eliminated from your investigations?" He sounded sarcastic.

"No-one has yet been eliminated. The first three murders have been complicated by the possibility that Billy Anderson's murder is connected to them in some way."

"Anderson committed suicide. Your DCI Downey's made that clear."

"Pathology thinks otherwise. They've concluded that Billy was murdered."

"And what? You think I had something to do with it? Do you really think I'd be that obvious?" Goldcrest had pushed his chair back and was wandering restlessly around the small room.

"Would you mind please sitting down, Mr Goldcrest. We need your comments to be recorded clearly, and they can't be if you're nowhere near the tape," said Copeland. "And let's be clear, you had every motive to kill Billy."

"But no opportunity. If you've talked to my PA she'll have confirmed I had appointments all day, the day Billy was murdered." Goldcrest had stopped walking about and now stood facing the women, his hands defiantly on his hips.

"Your PA told us your second appointment failed to turn up, so you'd have had the time..."

"Now just a minute. That second appointment in town? CEO of an FX company. Offices near the Shard."

"FX?" enquired Copeland.

"Foreign exchange," said Tammy softly. It was the first time she'd spoken.

Goldcrest, who'd resumed his seat, looked surprised, as though he'd not really been aware of her presence up till now. Turning back to Copeland he went on, "I waited in reception for an hour on the promise she'd show. I only left when her PA couldn't get a response from her phone. A wasted hour. You can check it out if you don't believe me."

"We will, Mr Goldcrest," said Copeland. "You see we have you on camera in Lyme Regis on the day of Billy's murder."

"Impossible."

"You'd have just had time to get the train from London..."

"Train? Train, did you say? So, where's this camera evidence? Inside or outside the Axminster railway station?"

"Neither," said Copeland. "It's—"

"It's where?" said Goldcrest, sounding increasingly aggressive. "If I'd wanted to avoid the stations and drive down, I'd have had to break the speed limits twice over to get here, commit murder and then get back for my next appointment, and all in the time you say I did. Please, don't make me laugh."

"As DI Copeland said, Mr Goldcrest, your assertion you were in London all day will be looked into." Tammy had pushed her chair away from the table and sat back apparently relaxed and unconcerned. Looking Goldcrest in the eye, she said softly, "Meanwhile, you are on camera on the day of Billy's murder."

"Impossible!" thundered Goldcrest. "If it had been my intention to come to Regis undetected, it would have been easy. You see, I live here. I know where to look for all the bloody cameras."

"Well thank you for that, Mr Goldcrest." Tammy risked the hint of a smile in Meg's direction.

It was Copeland's turn to look triumphant. Turning to the wall-mounted screen behind her, she operated the remote and said, "I presume you'll recognise yourself in this clip, Mr Goldcrest? Unmistakeable really. Same grey hair, height, build." She paused for emphasis, then said, "Same denim jacket as the one you're wearing now?"

The film started to run, with Goldcrest squinting up at it. The image appeared, somewhat grainy, but clearly showed

Eric Goldcrest walking along. "Where's that supposed to be? Looks like Church Street to me."

"That's exactly where it is."

"Hah!" exploded Goldcrest. "And you think that's me, do you?"

"Well, who else do you think it might be?" asked Tammy.

"Well, it sure as hell isn't me," growled Goldcrest.

"You seem very certain, Mr Goldcrest," said Copeland.

"Can you zoom in on it?" he asked.

Copeland froze the picture, then brought it up close till the portrait of Goldcrest occupied the whole screen. It appeared more granular than before, but as Eric Goldcrest examined the enlarged image of himself like a jeweller sizing up a precious stone, he was looking hugely amused. "That's really supposed to be me, is it?" he smirked.

"Well if it's not you, Mr Goldcrest, who do we suppose it might be?" Tammy looked at him quizzically.

"How the hell should I know? I do bloody know that that is not me," he spat, pointing at the image.

"We're listening, Mr Goldcrest."

"Haven't you two geniuses of observation noticed that the man you've got on video has an earring in his left pierced ear? I don't wear any earrings, and furthermore my ears aren't pierced. Look," he said, pulling his left lobe forward in demonstration. "Neither is the right ear pierced. See?" he said, demonstrating in the same way.

Then holding both lobes between fingers and thumbs he got to his feet, looked down at the two women contemptuously and said, "Enough of this nonsense. Time I was off. Perhaps you'd be so kind as to eliminate me from your enquiries now? Or, at the very least stop wasting my time." His voice was rising to a self-righteous rage as he walked to the door.

Turning on his heel for a moment, he said, "How about doing what you're paid to do and looking for some killers?"

Meg Copeland looked at Tammy, clearly embarrassed, her cheeks flushing pink. She felt as uncomfortable as she appeared. Her jacket felt tight and she squirmed in her seat.

To Meg's astonishment, Tammy smiled up at Goldcrest knowingly and said, "We're not done yet, Mr Goldcrest. And you're certainly not eliminated from enquiries. Would you mind resuming your seat?" She pointed down at it authoritatively.

Goldcrest stared at her for a moment, then, scraping the chair back, sat down again, his arms folded defensively across his chest.

"Mr Goldcrest," Tammy enquired, "I have to ask this; are you aware your wife is involved in an affair with your partner, Mr George Derby?"

Several moments passed. Goldcrest gazed at the floor, his elbows on his knees. He looked like someone wrestling with myriad problems. When he spoke, it was to say, softly, "I knew something was happening. She was unhappy. That much was clear. Had been for weeks. Months. I don't know. I'd never have guessed what. She is a private person. Doesn't confide much. And George? God! Why him?"

"Perhaps she was looking for comfort? Affection? You're very involved with your work. Were you neglecting her, so she looked elsewhere for attention?" Tammy glanced at Meg to see if she agreed, and got a brief nod of acquiescence.

"Are you sure of all this? Have you spoken to Elly or George?" said Goldcrest.

"Both," said Tammy. "And we have your wife on CCTV going into the Regis Carlton, usually on a Friday..."

"Usually?" said Goldcrest. "Usually? How long had this been going on?"

Tammy shifted her position to make herself more comfortable. "We gather for quite some time. Your wife had you drop her at Axminster station on a Friday evening, then collect her on the Sunday using the excuse..."

"I know what the excuse was," said Goldcrest, irritably. "She was seeing her mother. So, where'd they go? Eleanor and George?"

"I told you, the Regis Carlton."

"That's a bit close to home, isn't it? Anyone could have spotted them if they came into town."

"We have your wife on CCTV in Lyme Regis on the day of the murders outside the dolls' hospital on Broad Street. She's carrying a bag of something that might have been bought in the shop."

"What colour bag was it?"

"Sorry?"

"It's a simple question. What colour was the bag she was carrying?"

Tammy again looked at Meg, who shrugged her shoulders. "It was pink."

"And you're sure it was Eleanor? I mean waltzing into town, done up to the nines, when she was supposed to be…"

"Done up to the nines?"

"All these weekends away. You'd have thought she was going to a five-star hotel." Goldcrest stopped as though the irony of the remark had just occurred to him.

"When we have her on camera, Mrs Goldcrest is dressed in a tracksuit with hoodie covering her face. She clearly didn't want to be spotted."

Goldcrest stretched, as though he'd just got out of bed. "Well anyway, that answers a lot of questions."

"How's that?" asked Meg. "What questions, Mr Goldcrest?"

"Every weekend she went away, she'd come back with toys for the girls. Guilt offerings, I suppose." Shoving his chair back, Goldcrest got to his feet once more. "I'm off," he said. "This is all going nowhere." He was starting to sound angry again.

"I'm leaving this bloody circus behind." Barely looking over his shoulder, he stormed out. The door slammed and he was gone.

The room reverberated with the echoes of his voice. Tammy and Meg sat in silence for several moments, Meg's breathing being the only sound apparent. "You sounded pretty sure of yourself, Tammy."

"Oh, I am, Meg. We're not done with Mr Goldcrest just yet, my dear. He's still high on my list of suspects for the children's murders."

"Why would he, Tammy? They were his own daughters, after all."

"Meg, I don't have a motive. Mr Goldcrest is a complete enigma. I'm just looking at what we've got to work with. I'll worry about motive if and when I can prove he's guilty."

"It really doesn't add up to me," said Meg, shaking her head. "And even if we find the evidence, will it be enough to convict?"

"Only time will tell. Maybe I'm relying too much on gut feeling. They always say, go with your gut, get the proof later. Many a criminal has been collared after an experienced copper followed their intuition. But even if Goldcrest hasn't murdered his daughters, he'd still have every reason to have gone after Billy. Let's wait and see if DNA gives us anything further."

There was a discreet knock at the door as Meg and Tammy got up to leave, and a matronly middle-aged uniformed constable looked in. "Come in Pattie," said Meg.

Then turning to Tammy, she said, "This is our family liaison, Pattie Deyton. Pattie, this is Tammy Pierre, a private investigator who's been lending us a bit of her time and experience."

"Hi, Tammy," said Pattie, smiling and extending a hand. "We've all been talking about you here at the station."

"All good things, I hope," said Tammy, taking Pattie's soft dry palm in her own.

"Oh yes," she said, smiling. "All very good. You're an ex DI aren't you, Tammy?"

"That's right. Based in London, the Met. All seems like a long time ago."

"Well," said Pattie. "We've got some more from pathology with accompanying DNA results."

"As an ex-copper, Tammy, I think you're going to find the results pretty interesting.

CHAPTER 34 DAY 17

PATHOLOGY HAD FOUND a tiny trace of human skin under one of Billy's fingernails. It was so small it had been missed on the first examination of the body, but with little else to go on they'd taken another thorough look and come up with this find.

They'd also discovered a shred of fibre under another of Billy's nails, as yet unidentified. Pale blue in colour, it might have been a piece of face flannel or a fragment of towel, or towelling from a robe. Again, it could have been from an article of clothing. A shirt or blouse? Trousers, or pyjamas?

Maddeningly, Tammy's whisky glass hadn't yet been looked at, so there was no way its DNA could be compared to any other. In any event, the police would be seeking DNA samples from anyone and everyone who'd ever had any contact with Billy. There was the sliver of skin, that had been located under one of the nails on Billy's left hand, and the fragment of cloth found under a nail of his right hand. Beyond that, nothing.

She'd indulged in a line in the ladies at Axminster station, and felt high and heady. She was in jeans and denim bomber jacket. Her hair was recovering and the stitches melting. She felt ready for anything. She'd enjoyed a smoke on the platform while waiting for the train to Waterloo, then several vodkas as she relaxed in the comfort of first class.

She probably wasn't doing her body any favours, but the stresses of the case, and the need to give Dov an answer, were telling on her. Her solutions to her problems gave her temporary respite from the gnawing need to make a decision about what direction to take next. Her mood began to darken again.

She'd texted on ahead to tell Ginny to expect her by 8.00 pm and to book a table at the Black Swan, their local gastro pub. Its owner, Eddie Bray, produced the very best in British cuisine, and her mouth watered at the prospect.

She'd been with Ginny for five years now, and had watched the younger woman gradually mature and grow in confidence. The forensic work on the five hundred grand-scam had been impressive. Tammy had been absolutely serious when she'd offered Ginny a partnership in the business. How strange, the way things turn out, she thought.

As a little girl, at her bilingual kindergarten in Paris, Tammy had been taller than the rest from the word go. At six years of age she could have easily passed for ten. A gentle child, she was always the one to go to the rescue if another kiddie was missing a parent, had a fall or hurt themselves in any way.

Four years above her, though only slightly taller, was Linda Backman, the school's tormentor-in-chief. Tammy was terrified of her and kept out of her way. Despite that, Backman terrorised Tammy whenever the opportunity presented itself; on one occasion, she pinched Tammy's neck and turned the flesh in her nails until it looked as though a cyst had erupted there. On collecting her from school that afternoon maman was furious when Tammy explained what had happened, but was absolutely forbidden, by Tammy, to make any mention of it at the school.

A week later, a few minutes before maman was due to collect her at the end of the day, Tammy was assaulted by Backman in the school foyer where the coats were hung. The older girl started pushing her around and calling her names. For the first time in her life Tammy found herself the subject of prejudice when Backman repeatedly called her a brown girl.

Puzzled by the abuse, but infuriated by the assault, Tammy, unthinkingly, punched the older girl in the stomach. Backman looked stunned.

"Cochon brun!" she screamed. "Brown pig, brown pig, brown pig!"

Tammy felt cold. Her hands and feet were cold. Her face was cold. She could see the other girl, watch the insults being formed in her mouth, but no longer actually hear what Backman was saying.

The next time Tammy punched Backman it was in the face, drawing blood from the other girl's nose. She stared at Tammy, unbelievingly. "Cochon. Cochon. Cochon," she spat. "Vous etês mort. You're dead."

The abuse and the persecution had to be stopped. And that meant now.

Tammy punched her again. Then again, and again, and again; the blows hit her randomly in the face and chest. Backman started retreating, her arms wind-milling as she shuffled backwards, and then suddenly half falling she sat down in a waste paper basket from where she looked up at Tammy, helplessly.

Maman had walked in just as the fight was coming to an end. One of the other newer teachers who'd arrived on the scene just before her and who didn't know Tammy, simply said to Mme Pierre, "Quelle petite fille aggressive. What an aggressive little girl."

"Je pense pas, I think not," responded Tammy's mother. "Elle et généralement três gentille. She's usually quite kind."

On the way home Tammy asked, "Maman, que'est-ce qu'un cochon brun? What is a brown pig?" It was the only occasion she ever saw her mother cry.

The incident was the first time Tammy had realised her own strength. Backman didn't bother her again, or any of the other young ones when Tammy was around.

The incident would govern her life. With the weaker ones she came across, particularly with girls, she was always wont to seek to protect.

When she'd first met her, Ginny had been timid, yet feisty. Confident, yet vulnerable. That word: vulnerable. She'd heard Ginny use it only yesterday. She felt terribly responsible.

Then she thought about Dov, and her heart sank. Here was a man in whom she could seek support, love, even protection. Gentle and patient, and, above all, not intimidated by her like so many other men.

Physically both bigger and stronger, he was happy to acknowledge her strengths in so many of those small but significant ways. The fact that she could handle a car better than he didn't impact his masculinity. Her ability to multitask, while he could only focus on one thing at a time. She was even more skilled than he with a handgun. None of this bothered him, and she knew he wanted to make their relationship permanent.

She thought back on the various men in her life. Apart from Geoff Miggan, the only other man who'd measured up to Dov had been a boyfriend in his last year when she was at the Sorbonne. Simon was short, like Miggan, and with prematurely thinning fair hair, a fragile physique and a sense of humour that left her breathless with laughter at times. All the women found him irresistible. Whispers about his sexual prowess were a challenge she refused to ignore, and all proved true. Not even Dov could make her come like Simon. They'd stayed together for a year before he finished his studies and secured a high-paid posting in Dubai. She was on her way to Cambridge university anyway, and inevitably they lost contact.

Her train was pulling in to Waterloo. She felt troubled, but wouldn't let it spoil her evening or Ginny's.

As she climbed out of the train with her overnight bag, she thought she'd spotted Ginny on the other side of the ticket barrier.

Then she realised it was Ginny, running towards her with her arms outstretched. She was in a red coat with black piping, and red butterfly shoes. Her hair was loose and bounced around like a million bed springs. Tammy's grey mood lifted, dispersed like swirling vapour.

They flung their arms around each other as though they'd been apart for weeks, Ginny saying, "I missed you, Tammy. I missed you so much."

"I missed you too, darling," Tammy replied, laughing. "But I'm home now, silly. Let's go eat, I'm starved."

CHAPTER 35 DAY 18

SEATED AT HER DESK in the Bruton Street premises, Tammy fidgeted with a Bic ballpoint, doodling on the blotter. She'd dialled Meg's mobile earlier but found the number tied up. It was ringing now.

"Meg Copeland. Can I help?"

"Hi, Meg, it's me, Tammy."

"Hi there, Tammy."

"Any news? Is there anything happening at all?"

"We're still awaiting further reports on the DNA items."

"Where are we going with all this, Meg? It's been seventeen days since the murders of the kiddies. Whatever trail there might have been will be stone cold by now. Except there never was a trail. We're no further with the murder of the little tots. No motive presents itself. We're agreed the killing wasn't random. But who in God's name would plan such a thing?"

Tammy paused to light up a smoke just as Ginny came in with coffees.

She mouthed, "Not supposed to in the office," pointing at the cigar.

And Tammy mouthed back, "I know," before blowing a jet of smoke to the ceiling.

Then she went on to Meg, "I think we're going to have to revisit the notion that Mr Goldcrest is involved. Other than him there's only Mrs Goldcrest. And that's a dead end. Her own stepdaughters? Hardly. And on the day of the murders she was in town, apparently buying a toy or toys for the girls, and what's more, she's involved with George Derby. Her time is well taken up."

"You're right, Tammy. I think we need to get Mr Goldcrest back for further questioning. Certainly on the matter of Billy's murder. If he thought for one moment that Billy had anything to do with the deaths of his daughters, what with his past cautions for violence, I wouldn't put anything past him."

"Will you call me as soon as those results are in?"

"Of course I will."

Tammy turned to Ginny. "What do you think, Ginny?"

Ginny sat nursing a steaming coffee, clicking a rhythm on the side of the mug with the crimson-lacquered fingernails of one hand. She looked over at Tammy and said, "Well, according to Conan Doyle, 'Once you eliminate the impossible, whatever remains, however improbable, must be the truth.'"

"Trouble is, Ginny, all we have is the impossible. We don't have anything that could be classed as improbable. We have absolutely nothing. Frankly, my head is beginning to spin. We've got to get a break sometime. But right now, there is a blank horizon in view."

As Ginny left Tammy's office to go back to her reception desk, Tammy's mobile buzzed a text message. She waited until Ginny had shut the office door behind her then looked at the phone to see who had messaged her. It was from Dov, asking to see Tammy over lunch.

Telling Ginny she had some shopping to do, she took a cab to Villandry in Great Portland Street. It was a dull day with not many people about. There were a few tables occupied in the restaurant, but it was still early for the lunchtime crowd. Principally the place was quiet and discreet.

She got there first and ordered a plain tomato juice with ice and lemon. He arrived ten minutes later. For one moment she hadn't recognised him, merely seen a tall broad-shouldered man striding confidently into the restaurant. The mirror of an incident the first time he'd taken her for a meal and not realised who she was. A couple of heads turned. Women who glanced at him speculatively. Her pulse had quickened, then she'd realised and smiled to herself. He was shaven and groomed, wearing a charcoal grey suit with white shirt and tie. His black Burberry Chelsea boots had a mirror shine to them.

"You look very handsome, Dov. Is this just for me?"

"Well, yes. Sort of," he said shyly, as he sat down opposite her. "You see, I had a meeting this morning with someone who wants me to work in Dubai."

"Dubai?" said Tammy. "I'm impressed. So, not just for me then?"

"No, Tammy. Not just for you. But you never see me in anything but jeans, so I thought for once, as I was looking a bit more formal."

"That's very sweet of you, Dov. So tell me about Dubai. Drink?"

"I'll have the same as you," he said, beckoning the waiter and pointing to Tammy's glass. Then he looked back at Tammy. "You look fantastic, Tammy. The head's pretty much healed, I see. No more bandannas. And the ribs?"

"Dov?" she enquired. "You wanted to talk to me?"

He seemed troubled, as though he had forgotten what it was that he wanted to say. Eventually, "Tammy, they want me in Dubai. It's a big contract. I won't get many chances like this one. If it works out, they'll recommend me to other clients. It could be the making of me."

She reached forward to place her hand over his. "Dov, I'm so pleased for you."

The waiter arrived with the tomato juice, and Dov nodded thanks to him.

"It means I'm going to be away for months at a time. Possibly permanently. Is that really what you want?"

"No, of course it isn't." She stopped to take a drink from the glass of tomato juice. And Dov followed her example. "But you can't just leave your career on hold."

"I know that. But..."

Dov started absently moving the condiments around the table as though they were chess pieces. "Tammy, I came to England because of you. But what did I do that for? You're involved with Ginny, not me. I hardly see or hear from you, unless its business. It's like I'm your pet puppy, and I feel abandoned."

"I'm so sorry you feel that way. I know it's all my fault. I don't know what I was hoping for. I love you, Dov. Next to Ginny you're the best thing that ever happened to me. But I'm in love with Ginny. I can't just abandon her."

"Marry me, Tammy. I don't care if you carry on the affair with Ginny. I'm forty-four; I'd hoped to have a family one day. You once told me you'd wanted a family too. We're neither of us too old, but the clock is ticking. How much longer can we both afford to wait? Just marry me.

"You can even keep running the business if you want. Travel out to Dubai to see me from time to time. If there is a child or children, we can work something out. That's all I want." He was looking down at the tablecloth, as though he was afraid to catch her eye. As though doing so might break the spell he hoped he'd created.

The restaurant was beginning to fill up, tables were being occupied and staff were taking orders for food. The sound of murmured conversations and muted laughter were becoming apparent. Outside, the day had brightened. A black cab horn sounded and smiling tourists could be seen, cameras slung around their necks, hurrying across Great Portland Street. With the sunshine came a sense of the endless possibilities that London offered.

She felt her throat tighten with sadness. "Give me a couple of days, Dov. Hmm? Perhaps I can come up with something."

"Okay. A couple of days. But after that I have to go. I'm already packed."

"Do you want to eat?"

"To tell the truth, Tammy, I'm not really hungry."

"Me neither," she said. "Shall we just go?"

* * * * *

In the office, Ginny looked at the time. Tammy had been gone over two hours, when she normally only grabbed a sandwich. Business lunches were kept to strictly one hour, unless there was the question of a significant or on-going contract.

Tammy had been restless for weeks. Restless and remote. It was as though she was somewhere else half the time. Ginny was becoming afraid for their relationship, beginning to think the unthinkable, that perhaps there might be someone else in Tammy's life. Her parents had liked Tammy, taken to her immediately.

But her father had quietly told her one day, "Ginny, love; she's an exciting woman. A beautiful woman. Just don't bank on her staying around for ever. I'm not saying she won't, but I would hate to see you hurt, love. Mam agrees with me. Just take care, that's all we're saying."

* * * * *

The telephone rang as Tammy re-entered the office. It was Meg Copeland. Ginny had the handpiece to her ear. "I'll tell her," Tammy heard her say.

"Progress, Tammy." Ginny punched the air. "A possible break, at last? Meg says the results are in and they've got a DNA match. She wants you down there asap. They're bringing in Eric Goldcrest for questioning again."

CHAPTER 36 DAY 19

DOV SURVEYED THE MOUNDS and mountains of books that had re-emerged after Tammy's last visit. There were antiques and artefacts carelessly left lying around. A day's work at least in packing for removal, shipping or storage.

He felt alternately optimistic and in the next moment, dejected. The day was warm and he'd opened the windows in the flat. London had a unique buzz. He'd always found the place to be friendly, with an old-world charm. People said, 'please' and 'thank you', held doors open for you. Queuing was for the most part de rigueur. Hyde Park, just up the road, was a wonderful open space, in common with London's other parks. A place to walk, sit, swim, boat or simply laze about on sunny summer days.

It would soon be past tense. She hadn't come back to him yet about that proposal. Admittedly, it was only yesterday he'd asked. But surely, if that's what she wanted he'd have heard by now.

How could she be so undecided? Ginny, he thought, answering his own question. Always Ginny. But Ginny couldn't give her babies.

His phone buzzed and he looked at the caller ID.

He said, "Esther! Where are you? I thought you were in Tel Aviv."

"I was," she said. "But now I'm in Dubai."

"Dubai," he said, sitting down in the armchair. "What are you doing there?"

"Waiting for you, Dov."

"Look." He sounded awkward. "I've asked Tammy to marry me."

Their's had been an intermittent affair during the last three years. She was a year older than Dov, with two grown sons. She worked in the Tel Aviv Museum of Art, which was where she'd met Dov one day when he was trawling for information on the origins of a particular artefact that had come into his possession. She was fair-haired with an hourglass figure and a bubbling sense of humour. She made the all too frequently dour attitude that Dov carried with him everywhere a little less of an overshadowing presence. She was also down to earth, pragmatic and, in her own words, the best thing that had ever happened to Dov.

There was a long pause, then she said, "And has she agreed?"

"Not yet."

"Dov," she whispered, "she hasn't and she won't. She loves you, Dov. But she's in love with the other one."

"Maybe. Give me just a bit longer. I know it's not fair to ask. But…"

"Alright then. I love you too. Dov, without any second thoughts, hesitations, or reservations. But I won't wait for ever. Don't leave it too late, my darling. A girl needs to feel wanted, not regarded as an also ran."

"I'm sorry…" he started to say, but she'd hung up on him.

CHAPTER 37 DAY 19

IT WAS ANOTHER warm autumn day. Tammy had caught the earliest train down to Lyme Regis, the views from her carriage window of fields, farms and countryside all reflecting the glorious reds and golds of the time of year.

She was now seated in the stuffy interview room of the Lyme Regis police station next to Meg Copeland, opposite a smug-looking Eric Goldcrest accompanied by his lawyer. The tall, slender, intense-looking young man was constantly fiddling with his fat black Mont Blanc pen and various items of paperwork, which couldn't have had much bearing on the case as his client had not yet been subjected to any detailed questioning.

The two men were soberly dressed in dark suits and ties; the women, both in their customary workaday grey jackets and skirts with, in Meg's case, a white high-necked blouse, and in Tammy's, a blue blouse, open at the neck. A jug of water and tumblers adorned the centre of the table, which otherwise bore only notebooks and writing implements.

Meg started, "Mr Goldcrest, first let me thank you for agreeing to come in voluntarily and be questioned today. Sitting in with me is Ms Tamsin Pierre, a private investigator whom you retained briefly and with whom you are, of course, familiar. As I'm sure you will be aware, we are recording this interview. And you are being questioned under caution."

"Yes, yes," he responded testily. "I know the damn format." Then he glanced towards his lawyer, and back to Meg and Tammy, then said simply, "Steven Velacroft, my lawyer." Tammy faced a clean cut, if somewhat hyper-active young man, immaculately turned out and displaying the sort of self-assurance normally suggestive of a privileged background and education.

Meg nodded to the solicitor, who acknowledged her by no more than a flicker of his eyelids, then she continued, "Just the same, Mr Goldcrest, I have to caution you that you do not have to say anything. But it may harm your defence if you do not mention when questioned, something which you later rely on in court."

"Oh, for God's sake get on with it, woman." Tammy felt the trace of warmth she'd momentarily experienced during her previous interview with Goldcrest at The Beaumont Hotel evaporate.

Goldcrest's solicitor looked at his client with a pained expression, but refrained from comment.

Meg continued, "I'm going to be questioning you today, specifically about the murder of William, that's Billy, Anderson. Mr Goldcrest, I'll get straight to the point—"

"I wish you would," he interrupted, frowning in annoyance.

"Our forensic people have identified a fragment of human skin under one of Billy's nails, and we have reason to believe that that skin is yours."

"Oh, really? You've taken no DNA samples from me, so what makes you think the skin under Billy's nails is mine?"

"I understand you met with Ms Pierre for a drink and a chat at The Beaumont Hotel in Mayfair recently."

"What if I did? That's no crime." He looked still more irritated.

Tammy surreptitiously rubbed her ribs which were still bruised from the assault more than two weeks ago. The side of her head itched but she resisted the temptation to scratch it. She no longer wore the bandanna and had carefully combed her recovering hair over the scar which she didn't want to risk exposing. She noticed Velacroft looking at her head on more than one occasion and found herself slightly self-consciously turning away from his inspection.

There was a pause in the proceedings. Goldcrest's solicitor took out a large white handkerchief from his jacket pocket and blew his nose.

Goldcrest glanced conspicuously at his gold watch as though he had another appointment to dash off to, and Meg, who rearranged herself on the uncomfortable plastic chair, taking time straightening her jacket, before homing in.

"Mr Goldcrest, when you left Ms Pierre on that day, she had the presence of mind to keep the glass from which you drank your whisky and to give it to us for forensic testing."

"I doubt that's permissible..."

"Oh, but it is, Mr Goldcrest. I can assure you it is. We may in due course ask you to agree to a formal test, but the one we've conducted has persuasive effect."

Goldcrest looked to his left to where his lawyer was seated, and the younger man just nodded, then added as an afterthought, "DNA evidence no matter how obtained is admissible in court. And further, if there were any debate about the manner in which the sample had been obtained, the police could simply apply for a Court Order requiring a suspect to give a DNA sample if they refused it voluntarily."

Then Tammy broke in, "I saw you the day after the murder, didn't I, Mr Goldcrest? And you said you'd nicked your face shaving."

"I'm always nicking my face shaving. So what?"

Tammy leaned forward staring into Goldcrest's eyes, searching for some weakness, but finding none, continued, "The sliver of skin was found under one of the nails on Billy's left hand. The scratch on your face was on the right, and it therefore follows that it was Billy who scratched you, presumably while you struggled with him."

"Struggled now, is it? What's your next suggestion going be? That Billy and I had an intimate discussion of the pros and cons of Brexit? Is that really it then? All you've got? Conjecture, surmise, and waffle. Doesn't exactly add up to an indefensible case of murder does it?"

"No, Mr Goldcrest, that's not all we've got." It was Meg's turn to come in. "You see, pathology found a shred of blue material under another of Billy's nails. At first forensics couldn't place it. They decided it was an expensive wool product, possibly a pullover, or, more likely because of the weight, a jacket. Tammy?" Meg looked to Tammy to take up the narrative.

She took her time, pouring herself a tumbler of water from the jug on the table before offering the others. She then drank it down slowly to the evident chagrin of Goldcrest who folded and unfolded his arms in increasing impatience, before turning to his lawyer.

"Do we have to go on sitting here through this bloody pantomime?" He appeared agitated, fidgeting with his cuffs and constantly adjusting the way he was seated.

"Ms Pierre, if you've something more, don't you think we might hear what you have to say without any further delay?" Despite his youthful appearance, Velacroft spoke with deliberation and calm confidence.

"Of course," said Tammy, smiling.

"Mr Goldcrest, on the second occasion that you visited my office in Bruton Street, you were concerned when my PA nearly spilled coffee on your expensive sports jacket. You said you'd paid approximately two thousand pounds for a Brunello Cucinelli jacket. I recall it was pale blue. Forensics are pretty sure the shred of wool found under Billy's fingernail was from that particularly expensive and almost unique product. Forensics have really been most diligent in their researches," she added.

"Prove it," snapped Goldcrest. "Prove it's from my jacket and then prove it means I'm involved in the Anderson boy's murder."

"I'm not sure we need to, Mr Goldcrest." Tammy had cocked her head sympathetically to one side. "Why don't you just bring the jacket in for us to examine?"

"I'll think about it," muttered Goldcrest.

"And so, we seem to have motive, means and opportunity," she went on.

"Rubbish." Goldcrest seemed genuinely furious. His face was red and he was perspiring freely. "What means? The newspapers said Anderson was found at the foot of the cliffs. Where does that give me the means? As for opportunity, I've already told you I was in meetings all day the day Anderson was killed."

Tammy laced her fingers and rested her bunched hands on the table in front of her. "Very well, let's look at means first, shall we? We're pretty sure Billy was pushed from the top of the Ware Cliffs. But that fall wasn't enough to kill him. Pathology tells us he was still alive when he hit the shingle at the bottom."

Goldcrest's attitude had changed, and he now affected a mood of complete boredom. "Really?" he said. "So how did I kill him then?"

"He was killed in an act of unspeakable savagery by a blow or blows to the right side of the head, delivered as he lay dying by, we presume, a left-handed person."

"So, let me get this right, you're saying I pushed him from the cliff top, and then someone else finished him off. A murder involving two people."

"Perhaps. But purely surmise at this point."

"Which two people did you have in mind, then?"

"I should have thought that obvious, Mr Goldcrest. Why, you and your wife. You can't have forgotten, Eleanor is left-handed. You both had the motive of revenge with the killing of your children, at first attributed by DCI Downey to Billy Anderson. Of course, you had the opportunity. You told us yourself you knew how to evade the CCTV cameras. And the means consisted of the cliffs and the rocks below. Add to that the skin and fabric samples…"

"Now look here, Ms Pierre, I've had just about enough of all this nonsense. Let me enlighten you on a few points. Alright, I did approach the Anderson boy before he was arrested. I wanted to sound him out, see if I could get him to talk. I'd heard a whisper he might get hauled in for questioning so I followed him, must have been the day before he was picked up by you lot.

"Eleanor told me he walks the Cobb and also the Ware Cliffs, and that's where I found him. I engaged him by simply showing him the static on that expensive Italian jacket, scratching the surface with a nail. It sparked and made him laugh. So I let him try. He got some of the fibres and obviously a trace of my skin under his nails."

"Very neat, Mr Goldcrest. But frankly, I don't believe a word of it, and I doubt a court of law would either. You didn't engage Billy before he was arrested, you killed him after he was freed because there was absolutely no evidence with which to charge him. Billy was first arrested twelve days ago, the skin found under his nail was fresh. Not more than a few days old, according to pathology. You sought retribution from an innocent man."

Goldcrest closed his eyes for a moment as though lost in thought, then, "Left-handed," he muttered under his breath. "She knew where he walked; she spent enough time walking with him. She knew how I felt."

He looked at the two women facing him. "Know what?" he practically shouted, pointing a finger at them both in turn. "I think she had every reason to want him dead. Add to that, with lover boy George to keep her company, what better way to get me out of the picture than by stitching me up for a murder knowing the police were dim enough to swallow it whole?"

"On the other hand," broke in Meg, "you might have pushed Billy from the cliff top, then gone on down to inspect your handiwork. On finding him still alive, you decided to finish him off. I put it to you that you deliberately smashed Billy's skull, using your left hand knowing you'd implicate the wife from whom you were effectively estranged. I rather prefer my theory to yours."

"And that's all it is," said Goldcrest, scraping his chair back and getting to his feet. "A bloody theory.

"Furthermore, I didn't even know my wife was having an affair, until you told me three days ago. And you forget, I'm left-handed too."

"Hmm," mused Tammy. "You'd have done better to use your right hand."

"Don't get funny with me, lady. I've killed nobody. You're just scratching around looking for ideas. Meanwhile, what the hell are you doing about finding the murderer of my children? It's been three weeks and what have you got? I'll tell you what you've got. Nothing. Absolutely nothing."

He turned to Velacroft, said, "Is that why they've dragged me in here with this half-baked rubbish that I'm somehow involved in the killing of Anderson? Eh? To cover up their other shortcomings?"

He turned back to look down at the two women. "If you're not charging me right now, I'm leaving. Steven?"

The lawyer nodded, also stood up, and said, "If you're not arresting him, my client has nothing further at this stage."

Meg announced for the tape that the two men were leaving and that the interview was at an end. She quoted the time.

In Meg's office over coffee, she said, "Of course he's right, Goldcrest. They both had a motive to kill Billy: Eric and Eleanor. And they both had the chance.

"We've seen Eleanor on CCTV the day the children were killed. I wonder if we could find her in town the day Billy was murdered? She might not have been as fly as Eric on the positioning of the cameras."

"True. But my money's still on Eric Goldcrest. He's as devious as they come. And he's got a history of violence. Thing is, how do we ever nail him?"

A moment later and to the sound of shuffled footsteps, DCI Downey looked into Meg's office. He was as colourless as usual. "Got you two on the ropes, hasn't he? You're no further than you were two weeks ago. Bloody farce," he complained, and stalked off.

"We need to talk with Eleanor," said Tammy. "I'm back in London this afternoon. Tomorrow?"

"If she's free. Leave it to me. I'll organise it. We'll chat at her home. Keep it informal. Midday okay with you?"

"I'll see you then. If anyone can unlock this mystery, I've a feeling that Eleanor can."

CHAPTER 38 DAY 20

"MORNING, DARLING." Ginny was standing at the hob in red mules, a tiny red nightie and negligee, which barely acknowledged its intended purpose of modesty. The mass of copper curls was held back from her face in a giant pony tail; she looked youthful, fresh and full of the joys of autumn.

The smell of sizzling bacon with fried eggs, mushrooms, tomatoes and fried bread all ready to eat made her mouth water. "Are you ready for breakfast?" she asked, beginning to slide food onto a ready-warmed plate.

"Not sure I can," Tammy said, smiling. She'd wandered in with sleep in her eyes, wearing the shorts and T-shirt she slept in.

"Upset tum again?"

"Something I ate at Lyme Regis? I don't know. Stress probably. This bloody case. I'll make a coffee. You?"

"Tea for me, please," said Ginny, taking an overflowing plate to the breakfast bar and perching on a stool. "Plans for today?" she said as she began wolfing down the food. "Any real progress?"

Handing Ginny her tea and leaning an elbow on the breakfast bar where she sat, Tammy said, "It's been a tangle, with nothing from the start. No motives, no pointers, no clues."

She sipped from her coffee as Ginny went on packing her cheeks. "We're going to talk to Eleanor Goldcrest today. It's a long shot. Any info she can give us. She was too upset to be much help the first time I saw her. Maybe she'll be a little calmer this time. You know, even if she suspected Billy of killing the girls, which she doesn't, I still cannot see her murdering him in revenge."

"And the children? Anything happening there?"

"Nothing. Absolutely no progress. We've been drawing a blank." She drank some more of her coffee, her eyes half shut as she contemplated where next.

"Yes." She sighed. "We'll see what Eleanor has to add. I think we'll find she's the key to all this. She must know something. But what?" she said, catching Ginny's eye. "Sometime we must get a break here."

The sound of Tammy's phone brought them both up with a start. Glancing at her watch as she picked the phone up off the breakfast bar, she remarked, "5.00 am? Who the devil calls at this time of the morning?" Putting the phone to her ear, she answered, "Tammy Pierre."

The voice at the other end was a primeval scream, "You fucking bitch. You mutha fucker!"

Tammy held the phone away from her ear. "What the…"

"She's dead, you fuck. She's dead and it's all your fault."

"Who's dead? Who are you? Will you just try to stop for long enough to tell me who it is that died?"

Someone else was trying to get through on Tammy's line, but she wouldn't interrupt the caller to find out who.

For a moment the phone went quiet, then the man said, "My daughter's dead, and it's all your fault."

At the other end of the phone Tammy could hear what sounded like someone sobbing uncontrollably. "Sir," she said, "who is your daughter? Please tell me who you are?"

"My daughter's Eleanor Goldcrest. And she's dead because of you. If you hadn't come down and interfered. Anyway, I'll have you, you bitch. If it's the last thing I do."

He rang off just as Tammy's phone warbled again. She was chilled with shock, uncomprehending, dazed. "Tammy Pierre," she announced.

"Tammy, it's me, Meg. We've just heard…"

"I know. I've just had Eleanor's father on the line threatening me. How? Where? When?"

"Same place as before. At the foot of the Ware Cliffs. But hear this, she was strangled before she was thrown, and then her head was battered with a large stone. And guess what? All on the right side. So, either we've got a left-handed person, again, or else a sicko with a warped sense of humour."

"Meg, I need time to think. Give me a while. I'll be down later, but I need to go over some things in my mind first."

"We've got a team meeting first thing. I'll brief you on what's happening when you get here. Downey looks like a man paddling a canoe in a storm at sea."

"I can imagine."

"We need your input, Tammy. I mean, who's next?"

"Soon as I can, Meg."

Her coffee had gone cold. She wrapped her arms around herself. Ginny sat down next to her, put an arm across her shoulders. "I heard," she said.

"Who'd want to kill her, Ginny? Little bird-like creature. Utterly defenceless. Harmless. I tell you, Ginny, I'm lost on this."

Ginny pondered, "Do you think the husband can have had anything to do with it?"

Tammy shook her head. "With what for a motive? The affair with Derby? I don't think so. He'd half guessed what was going on, just didn't know who was involved." She started rubbing her temples, moving the tips of her fingers in circles.

"Here, let me do that," Ginny said as she took over massaging Tammy's forehead and temples. "Better?"

"A bit. Yes, better."

Tammy's phone buzzed again, and she pressed the green button. "Tammy Pierre."

"It's me," said the voice.

"Sorry?"

"I owe you an apology." The voice was familiar. Then she realised who it was.

"I was out of order just now. It's Michael Blackburn."

"Eleanor's father?"

"That's right. The police here don't have a clue. Their DCI Downey is as much use as a lead-lined lifejacket. Copeland is doing her best from what I can gather. I've spoken to her and him. She's bright, but admits there's nothing to go on."

Blackburn had stopped talking.

"Mr Blackburn?"

"I can't believe Elly's dead. Who'd want to do it? That little shit she's married to? He's all piss and fart. A big mouth and a cheap crook. He threatened her once or twice. But she told me he'd never touched her. No, there's something else going on here, isn't there? Am I going to be next? Christ! Am I?"

"I've got your number, Mr Blackburn. I'll call you if there's anything you need to know."

They rang off and Tammy turned to Ginny. "Help me here."

"Of course. Let me get you a hot coffee first."

Leaning back on the bar stool, Tammy said, "If we take this step by step: we start with three kiddies being killed. We've no motive and no clues.

"Let's see who's involved. Eric Goldcrest. That would make no sense. Despite my suspicions. I have to say, why would he bring me in if my investigations ended up by damning him along with what he claims the police and press had decided? Neither of whom, incidentally, have put him under any pressure since the start anyway. Not even Eleanor, after her initial reaction, really felt it was anything to do with him. And she confirmed he adored the girls.

"Who's next? George Derby. He disliked Goldcrest, and, along with a lot of others, had lost money one way or another because of him. He was down in Lyme Regis at the time of the murders, but he was also down there on many other occasions. Plus, his time was being taken up with Eleanor. Why would he kill his mistress's children? Or, for that matter, her stepchildren? No, Derby is definitely out of the picture.

"What about Eric's partner then? Nigel Cudlipp lied about the time he was in Lyme Regis, sure. But that was because he'd read somewhere the approximate time of the murders. Realising I knew about the quarrel with Eric who'd accused him of being involved with Eleanor, he didn't want me to conclude that that was a motive to murder Eric's children. Perfectly understandable in the circumstances. Furthermore, his assertion that he wanted to know if George Derby was having an affair with his wife is quite plausible.

"Then there's Billy Anderson. A child molester? I think not. He was cautioned for what amounted to an absurd accusation, followed up by that fool DCI Downey making something out of nothing.

"Then we have to ask ourselves, who'd want to kill Billy? Eric, with his rage over the deaths of the girls and his habit of jumping to conclusions, abetted by Downey's initial assertions? That, plus the DNA evidence, which I'd have thought would nail it. But there are doubts, even there. Maybe Eric was telling the truth about seeing Billy before the killings and having him scratch the surface of the jacket.

"Personally, I doubt it, but we've got to give it room space until we get something better. Something unarguable. In court, reasonable room for doubt would let Eric, or any other guilty party, walk free. And that will not do.

"Then we have the Kristof twins. What a puzzle there. Leonard? Grimy, timid, just out of prison protesting his innocence. Would any six-year-old have been inclined to go with someone who looked like some sort of ghoul? I doubt it.

"Then we have Leopold. There's a real puzzle. Nothing to link him to the murders. Seen on CCTV talking to someone unidentified. Did he kill the child his brother served twenty years for murdering? Stranger things have happened. When I get a chance, I'm going to call in some favours and get the DNA on the original semen specimen re-examined.

"So, we're left with Eleanor. I was thinking of your Conan Doyle quote, 'Once you eliminate the impossible, whatever remains, however improbable, must be the truth.' Would Eleanor kill her own stepchildren? If so, why? What possible motive would she have? Look at the state she was in when she first learned of their murder. An act? I doubt it. A man may revolt against the idea of raising another's progeny. The maternal instinct is to protect a child. Any child. Anyway, she's dead. That means that right now, we're left with nothing possible and, frankly, nothing even improbable.

"You know, there is one other possibility we're forgetting."

"Go on," said Ginny. "Are you thinking about something like a spur-of-the-moment killing?"

"Exactly. We could be looking at a purely random killing. Some lunatic on the prowl for just such an opportunity as the girls on their own. Or on the other hand, we might be looking for a killer or killers who are children themselves."

"That's an angle I hadn't considered," Ginny pondered.

"Look at the two killers of the toddler, Jamie Bulger. They were just ten years old, and were the youngest convicted killers in British history.

"Or what about Mary Bell? She tortured and murdered Brian Howe aged three and Martin Brown who was four. She was just eleven at the time.

"If this is what we're up against, and we might well be, then in the absence of any witnesses or other forensic evidence, these Goldcrest children's murders might well go unsolved.

"Anyway, I'll be interested to know the outcome of the station meeting when I get down to Lyme Regis later today. Downey has insisted we get Goldcrest in for questioning again. I think he may consider charging him with Billy Anderson's murder. About time, if you ask me."

"Tammy." Ginny had climbed off the bar stool and stood before Tammy with her arms folded. She looked like a little red pixie from a children's book.

Tammy, spinning round on her bar stool to face Ginny, smiled half to herself, saying, "You look so serious, darling. What is it?"

There was a single plop from the kitchen tap. The clock on the wall ticked away quietly.

"Just for one minute. I know you're very tied up with this case. But I wanted to ask you. I know it's not really relevant, but...you would tell me if there was anything you felt I should know, wouldn't you?" Ginny nervously fidgeted with her red negligee.

"Why yes. Of course. What am I supposed to be telling you that I haven't?"

"I don't know. I just have this feeling that something isn't right. With you? With us? I don't know. You often stay in Lyme Regis and don't tell me till the last moment. When you do, your phone is always switched off."

She turned to look down and away from Tammy, like a child that's in trouble.

Climbing off her bar stool, Tammy bent down and enveloped Ginny in her arms. "You dolt. I told you I need peace in the evening to unwind. You can and you do call as often as you want during the day. Don't you?"

"I suppose," she said, sighing. "I was just frightened you might be seeing someone else."

"What? Ginny for heaven's sake. Whatever next?" Even as she said it, Tammy felt waves of cold guilt wash over her like a winter sea, only colder.

"I mean, you've been sick several times in the morning. You're not…?"

"No Ginny. I am definitely not pregnant."

She felt the pit she was digging herself into getting deeper and deeper, with no sight of the bottom and, worse still, no way of getting out.

CHAPTER 39 DAY 20

SHE'D SPREAD PAPERWORK and files on the carriage table in front of her, then restlessly shoved them back in her attaché. Rain spattered the windows as the train hummed on, and there were lightning flashes ahead.

The case was becoming a nightmare. She spent nights half-awake looking for something. Anything. As a DI she'd experienced sufficient intractable cases, but always with some sort of clues to juggle with. Here, she was staring into a black void. Eric was the only possible link to something. Meg was bringing him in this afternoon for another session under caution, it seems at Goldcrest's behest.

On top of everything, Michael Blackburn seemed convinced he was next. It would have to be considered later. There was no reason to suppose he was under any more threat than anyone else.

* * * * *

Of course, she was pregnant. Having put off finding out for as long as she could, she'd felt devastated at the time she tested positive, only the previous evening; and that against all the odds. Too many issues crowded in on her. She'd felt stifled by the knowledge.

She was actually two months late, but had deluded herself into thinking that it was her usual irregular cycle. She hadn't stopped her drinking, and was still doing lines whenever she felt too worn out to carry on.

She couldn't be expecting if she was still experiencing the stomach cramps, could she? She'd telephoned Doctor Khan. Apparently, she could.

She rested her cheeks in her palms. God knows what she'd tell Ginny. Another month and she might be showing; already there was the early hint of some swelling of the abdomen, albeit too slight to be noticed.

But there was something more. Something she couldn't deny. A sense of victory. A confirmation of her womanhood. And a personal feeling she would never be able to put into words: simply, 'I am going to have a baby.' A brief moment of understanding.

But then there was Dov. It felt as though her world was unravelling. She thought about Daddy. Papa. Not fair to call him, not in his condition. Just thinking about him was a comfort. She wondered, what would he advise? Then realised he'd have no more idea than she. How could he?

Her head was starting to ache along the scar, and though she'd absolutely resolved not to, she took herself off to the loo where she laid out two lines of coke. If Ginny could see her now…

But she came out and resumed her seat feeling refreshed and in control again. She'd stop the drug as soon as things settled. Whenever that was.

Then her phone went. For a moment, she dreaded Ginny might be calling. Then she saw it was Dov. "Tammy, it's me."

"Yes, Dov; I can see."

"Where are you?"

"I'm on my way down to Lyme Regis."

"Nothing resolved as yet?"

"Nothing," she said shortly.

"Are you staying overnight?"

"I hadn't planned to. Why?"

"I'd like to see you, Tammy. I hope it won't be for the last time, but just the same."

"I'll be in the Carlton. Meet me in the lounge at 7.00 pm."

It would be another night away from Ginny without explanation. She closed her eyes. She'd have to decide. About one thing she would not change her mind, she wanted this baby. Dov's baby.

*****

Outside the police station it was pouring with rain and chill. Inside, the place was warm and abuzz with activity. Officers looked up as she came in, and she got lots of smiles and hellos. She was becoming as familiar a face in the station as their own staff.

Even DCI Downey, as stooped, oily and grey-faced as ever, nodded in her direction. "I'll watch," he announced under his breath.

A waste of time, he thought. Goldcrest had killed Billy Anderson, that much was clear to him, but his smug-faced lawyer was already contesting the evidence. Turning the arguments upside down. Looking for ways out for his client. The Pierre woman had tried to rope in Goldcrest. The DNA evidence should have been enough to initiate charges, even if the manner of its retrieval was debatable.

He admitted, albeit grudgingly, that the woman had been persistent. Like a leopard stalking its prey. Only, the prey was about to escape, and there'd be nothing to show for all her efforts. Quite why Goldcrest had called for this interview he couldn't imagine. To threaten Pierre with proceedings for harassment? To humiliate the police? There was enough there.

He thought uncomfortably about the consequences that would ensue over his botched handling of Billy Anderson's arrest and questioning. He'd fouled up there. Badly. So, what did Goldcrest want? Probably to finally put the whole thing to bed.

Downey was waiting impatiently to find out.

Eric Goldcrest was already seated in the interview room, together with his lawyer, when Tammy and Meg walked in and took their places opposite the two men. All four were in dark two-piece suits.

Meg went through the now familiar preamble, but Goldcrest looked troubled and impatient to get things under way. He was frowning and fidgeting with the tumbler in front of him. His face was grey and drawn; he looked dishevelled, his collar undone and his tie hanging loose. He'd not shaved properly; Tammy couldn't help noticing. There were tufts of stubble on his chin and cheeks, but, Tammy thought wryly, no cuts or scratches this time. He didn't seem able to concentrate on anything for more than a moment. He looked as though he was about to say something, but his lawyer spoke first, looking earnestly at his client.

"Are you sure this is what you want to do, Eric? It's not too late to change your mind." He spoke in a soft, confident tone. "No-one here can touch you. There's no solid evidence to tie you to anything. Consider what you're about to do. Your business? Your future? Your whole way of life? Is that really what you want to put on the line? Furthermore, you really should have let me listen to this first, you know." He leaned towards his client, putting a hand on Goldcrest's forearm, as if he might persuade him to rethink whatever it was he was proposing.

Goldcrest, hunching his shoulders, pulled his arm away from Velacroft and thrust his hands in his jacket pockets as though they were cold. Then he took one hand out and with great deliberation placed a mobile phone on the table. No-one said anything.

The women looked at each other, puzzled; the lawyer shrugged in a show of resignation. "Madness," he murmured under his breath, "absolute madness."

"I'm tired," said Goldcrest, massaging his forehead with the tips of his forefingers. "This has all got out of hand. It's running away with me. It was never supposed to be like this. I may be a financial thug, but I'm not a career criminal. At least, I never thought I was. I just can't live with all that's happened." He glanced up at Meg as he spoke.

"I'm going out of my mind. You've hounded me to the ends of the earth," he said, turning to Tammy. "You!" he said, pointing a finger accusingly at her. "You were supposed to get me off the hook when I hired you. Instead it feels as though wherever I turn all I see is you. You'll never give up, will you?"

"No, Mr Goldcrest, I won't," Tammy responded quietly, knowing she was fast running out of time.

"I. Have. Got. To. Have. Closure. And if this is the only way I'm going to get there, so be it. I don't give a damn about the consequences anymore."

He leaned forward with his elbows on his knees, chin in his cupped palms, and sat like that for at least two minutes. It seemed like an hour. No-one in the room made a sound. No-one moved a muscle.

All the arrogance had disappeared, the confidence evaporated. He was like a shell of the man Tammy had first encountered in her office. His hair had become greyer in the last few weeks, until it was almost white. Tammy noticed it had started to thin at the crown.

Maybe there would finally be some answers. Tammy could no longer afford to neglect her own business, but Goldcrest didn't need to know that. This interview might well be her final involvement, a last throw of the dice in one of the weirdest sets of crimes she'd ever come across.

Except, she thought, she hadn't actually been hounding Goldcrest, however he saw it. A few interviews, with some problematic evidence in regard to Billy Anderson, and still less to implicate the man in the murders of his own children. She'd suggested to Meg that gut feeling told her otherwise, that it was evidence that counted. But all things considered, there was far more to implicate him in the Anderson killing than that of the children, where there was no discernible motive. Still, if her persistence was about to pay dividends…

Her old Super, Bob Walker, had once advised her, 'Tammy, if you've nothing to go on, don't stop. Keep going. You never know what you might turn up. You never know if the suspect will start to wilt under pressure and throw in the towel.' Goldcrest's lawyer was right. The man should shut up.

Stifling a yawn, Tammy wearily rubbed her eyes with the heels of her hands and waited with the others in the room for Goldcrest to continue.

Finally, he looked up. He sounded hesitant, almost apologetic. As though he shouldn't be taking up their time. "I don't know what I was hoping to find when I recorded this," he said softly. "I'd come home to pick up some fresh clothes and did this on impulse. She was home, Eleanor. I felt she was sneering at me. Silently laughing at me. Couldn't put my finger on it. I kept the mobile in my top jacket pocket. It's a bit muffled, but clear enough. It should explain everything. Or nearly everything. Perhaps you'd listen to the whole of it before commenting."

Goldcrest's lawyer reached out a hand and laid it on his client's forearm once more. "Leave it, Eric. You don't have to do this." His brow was furrowed; he was practically pleading.

Goldcrest, ignoring his lawyer's exhortations, leaned forward pressing an icon on the phone as he did so. Then he propped the mobile against the tumbler he'd been fiddling with, the better for all to hear what was being played back.

Voices were heard in conversation, a slight hollowness suggesting it was coming from the couple's kitchen. Goldcrest's voice was easily recognisable. It was the other voice, low and sinister, that wasn't immediately obvious.

"It's Eleanor," whispered Tammy. But Goldcrest held up his hand for silence.

Goldcrest: "Why don't you admit it, Elly, you're having an affair. I've guessed something was going on. I just didn't know who or where. I'm not completely gullible you know."

Eleanor: in a flat monotone, "No, but you're completely boring, Eric. You have been for years. We do nothing, go nowhere. It's just business, business, business with you, all the time."

Goldcrest: "It's George, isn't it. That private eye told me."

Eleanor: "The big black one? Nice girl. Your type, is she?"

Goldcrest: "How long, Elly?"

Eleanor: "How long what?"

Goldcrest: "You and George. How long has it been going on?"

Eleanor: "I don't know, two or three years. Who cares?"

Goldcrest: "Two or three years?" He sounds incredulous. "So, you admit it? You actually admit it?"

Eleanor: "What's not to admit?" She sighs. "Anyway, who cares?"

Goldcrest: "Who cares? Who cares? What do you mean, who cares? I care, Elly. I care. Or thought I did. Why? We planned to get married. We got married. What happened?"

Eleanor: "I'll tell you what happened; you kept me waiting. Kept me on a string for years. I thought things might change if we tied the knot. More fool me. Nothing changed. I decided to keep my options open."

Goldcrest: muttering, "Scheming bitch." Then aloud, "What happened with the girls, Elly?"

Eleanor: "How should I know? Police aren't making much headway are they? Did you kill them, Eric? Did you?"

Goldcrest: "Don't be bloody ridiculous, Elly. Why would I do such a thing?"

There was a pause in the recording, followed by the sound of people rearranging themselves on chairs.

Goldcrest: "I took the girls to the park at the back of that hotel overlooking the sea. The usual Saturday morning, as you well know. Kids ran around. Played hide and seek. Where were you, Elly? Not with your mother, that much we now know, but a few minutes up the road screwing your boyfriend. How romantic."

Eleanor: "Better than being stuck at home while you piss off for your kiddies' games. Three little coats. Three little hats. Three tiny teddy bears." She stops talking abruptly, as though she's said too much.

Goldcrest: "That's right. Their tiny teddies. One each. Only, one of the girls dropped hers, didn't she? I picked it up and brought it home. You're on CCTV on the morning of the murder with a bag outside the shop that sells those toys. When I came home that day, just before everything blew up, I noticed the single teddy in the kids' room. But I was holding the missing teddy. I didn't understand at the time. But I do now, don't I?"

Eleanor: "I don't know, do you?" She sounds disinterested. As though she's eavesdropping a conversation she's not involved in.

The tension in the police interview room was palpable. The air seemed heavy with it. In the distance came the muffled sound of a police car siren. Then the throb of a passenger jet passing overhead. Neither of the women said a word. Tammy was worried the slightest movement might put Goldcrest off, have him change his mind and kill the recording. She hardly dared breathe, while willing Meg to remain similarly still.

Then it looked as though the mood was broken anyway as Meg rearranged the way she was sitting. Goldcrest looked up, irritated, just as the recording seemed to have been reaching a critical point.

But Meg was only re-crossing her legs, and Tammy's glance, with one restraining finger raised, was sufficient for Meg to immediately cease moving. She looked embarrassed, but Tammy shook her head reassuringly, as if to say, no harm done.

Still, Goldcrest started tapping his fingers on the table as though he was undecided about whether to go on. Tammy reckoned the playback was about to be stopped, just as it had looked as though everything was coming out into the open. The momentum lost.

Adding to the air of uncertainty, Goldcrest's lawyer seemed as though he might take the initiative and turn off the mobile at any moment. He kept trying to catch his client's eye, to no avail. Tiny beads of sweat appeared on his brow, and he sighed loudly as though willing Goldcrest to see reason and take things no further. But despite the threatened interruption, the moment passed. Tammy quietly breathed. The recording played on.

Goldcrest: "How could you have known one of the teddies was missing if you hadn't been with the girls that morning? I had the missing one, and you thought you'd better replace it by getting it home before I got home. Pointless. One teddy on its own in the house? As if one of the girls had forgotten to take it with? Which wouldn't have happened, as I always handed them their tiny teddies myself to hold on to whenever we went out. But you always were pretty dim, weren't you Eleanor. You could have left well alone and no-one would have been the wiser."

Eleanor: "I don't know what you're talking about."

Goldcrest: "Why did you do it, Eleanor?"

Eleanor: "Why did I do what?"

Goldcrest: "For fuck's sake, Eleanor, why did you kill my daughters?" There was the crack of a fist smashing into a palm.

At first Eleanor doesn't reply. It seems she is considering her response.

Eleanor: then, defiantly, "That's it, isn't it? Your daughters. Your bloody daughters. Not mine."

Goldcrest: "The police and the press had me nailed for killing your daughters. The usual stepfather thing. It's always the stepfather, isn't it? Only I'm not the stepfather, am I? They were my daughters, Elly. My kiddies. You're the step-parent, not me."

Eleanor: "Thanks for reminding me. As if I need reminding. I always wanted children. My own, not some other bitch's. I put up with your brats for as long as I could. You and them. Always them. Years of it. Four bloody years of your never-ending shit. You were happy. You made that clear enough. You didn't need more children you said, when I begged you to give me a chance."

Goldcrest: "But you had everything. I'd never have known about the affair. In the name of God, why kill the babes? Why throw everything away? Did you think you wouldn't go to jail? That you wouldn't be found out?"

Tammy inhaled deeply, softly. She closed her eyes, willing Goldcrest not to interrupt everything now. Almost there, she thought. So near. What would Eleanor say next? Confess? Deny? Until now, there'd been broad hints but nothing actually admitted.

Dear, timid Eleanor Goldcrest living with a brute who'd denied her a family of her own. Maybe not so timid Eleanor after all, but she was certainly no murderer. Not possible. Was it? Tammy had her answer in the next few moments. The response, entirely unexpected, left her aghast.

Eleanor: "I was prepared to take that chance. I wanted out. I wanted the kids gone and you gone. I wanted to see you suffer the way you made me suffer. You knew my time was limited. The clock was ticking, but you just ignored it. You laughed at me. You always had to be one up on everyone, didn't you? But against your own wife? George has promised me the lifestyle I want, and if we're not too late, a family. And he's rich. At least as rich as you."

Goldcrest: "Hah!" he storms. "George is married. Or had you forgotten? And I promise you, he'll never leave his wife. She'd clean him out, and he knows it. Money's all that matters to George. You're just there to be played with. A brief diversion."

Eleanor: ignoring Goldcrest's remarks and sounding triumphant, "And he's going to leave her for me. Hear that? For me!"

Goldcrest: "Well if he does, which he won't, he's welcome to you. Tell him I'll send flowers to the wedding. Or better still, a wreath. Poor man, doesn't have a clue what he'd be letting himself in for. Maybe I'll visit you in prison. It was you, wasn't it, Elly? For God's sake, why won't you just bloody admit it?"

There's the sound of someone moving around the room, a restless sound. The heavy tread of a man. Then, what seems to be someone weeping.

Goldcrest: "How could you, Elly? How could you do it? They were harmless little tots."

Eleanor: as though thinking aloud, "I wasn't sure I could go through with it. The brats. I was looking for help from some quarter. Then I heard about the Kristof release. Manna from heaven, I thought. I'd Googled him so I knew what to look for. A real creep. I collared him in the supermarket."

"It was those two, then," Meg whispered. "On the CCTV, partially obscured." Tammy put a finger to her lips and Goldcrest held up a hand again for quiet. He looked more than ever like death. Heavy bags under his eyes, sunken cheeks, dry white lips. His eyes were bloodshot as though he'd not slept for a week.

The recording was still playing, and Eleanor's cryptic tones hadn't changed.

Eleanor: "He looked cleaner than I expected," she goes on. "Had an American accent. I thought he was in a UK prison. He didn't want money. I asked him to kill the girls, said I'd pay him. He didn't want money, just to implicate his brother. I said, what brother? Then he explained. He is one peculiar man. I think he gets off on seeing others pay for the crimes he commits. Especially his brother. He hinted he'd done the killing his brother served time for. Mad if you ask me."

Goldcrest: "Mad? You're calling him mad? Fuck's sake, woman, what does that make you? You're offering to pay a child killer to kill my kids?"

There's the sound of chairs shifting again, and someone - Goldcrest? - pacing back and forth. The volume of his voice is varied as though he's moving around the room.

Eleanor's next remarks had Tammy and Meg staring at each other in wide-eyed disbelief.

Eleanor: "I waited, but the opportunity never arose, and I got tired of hanging about for him to get on with it, so I thought, Go to hell. I'll do it myself. So I did. I did it myself. Never realised how easy it would be. Wham bam. Sorted. Long overdue."

Goldcrest: sounding incredulous, "Wham bam? Wham bam? I don't believe what I'm hearing. Not possible. Helpless toddlers. For God's sake. Totally crazy. And you want children of your own? I thought you loved them. When Penny died…"

Eleanor: "I never knew Penny. And I certainly wasn't interested in yours. They were the baggage that came with a rich man. A rich mug."

Goldcrest: "For Christ's sake, Eleanor, I loved you."

Eleanor: "Yeah, yeah. I'm crying." Then in an unexpected switch to a baby voice, Eleanor goes on, "I miss you. Please come home. Please."

Goldcrest: realising what Eleanor is reminding him of, "That time you called me in London and wouldn't talk right away. To think you nearly had me taken in. God, what a fool I've been." There's a moment's silence, then, "They were my daughters, Eleanor. Mine. Not yours to kill." His voice sounds strange, as though he's trying to contain himself, rein in his rage while attempting to learn more, find out everything concerning the death of the little girls.

Eleanor: "I put up with them."

Goldcrest: "You planned everything."

Eleanor: "I wasn't away every weekend, true. But when I was, I walked the same spot you take, keeping a careful look out for you. Scoping the area for alternative routes to the beach. Looking to see who I might bump into when I did the deed. Would have spoiled things a bit if we'd run into each other. I was always at the Carlton. A good alibi. When I went into town, I always left the hotel by a back entrance, and I wore a tracksuit with a hoodie, so I wouldn't be recognised."

Goldcrest: "But you were recognised. Outside the dolls' hospital on Broad Street, where you bought the replacement tiny teddy that you didn't need to replace, on the morning of the murders."

Eleanor: "So what are you going to do about it? Run to mummy?"

There was the sound of laughter on the recording. Eleanor's laughter.

Eleanor: "It was so easy. They were playing hide and seek. I watched them go into one of those sheds at the back of the hotel, then I followed them in. You were nowhere around. Come on girls, I whispered. Mummy's got a new game to play. They weighed nothing, the three kids. I scooped them up, one piggy back, two in my arms, and took them down to the shingle by a path I guessed we wouldn't be seen. Wouldn't have mattered if we were. Mummy and babies."

Eleanor pauses for several seconds before resuming her narrative, sounding thoughtful now, but doleful.

Eleanor: "Then I smashed their fucking skulls in. I even used my left hand to do it so the wounds would be on the right side of their heads."

Goldcrest: "What the hell do you mean, you used your left hand?"

Eleanor: "You, you cretin. You're left-handed, aren't you?"

Goldcrest: "You mean you were trying to implicate me right from the start?"

Eleanor: "My God. The man has a brain."

Goldcrest: "But can't you see, you stupid bitch, you're left-handed too? You'd have done better to use your right hand. That's what that private eye told me I might have done to the Anderson boy. Making a lot of assumptions about my guilt on that front, wasn't she? A real comedienne, that woman. Except I've killed no-one. As far as you're concerned, at least you'd have diverted some attention away from yourself. But I wouldn't expect you to have worked that one out."

Eleanor: ignoring her husband's comment, "Ah, yes."

Goldcrest: "What's, 'Ah, yes'?"

Eleanor: laughing, "Your precious private eye."

Goldcrest: "Well, what's so funny about her?"

Eleanor: "Not her. You! You idiot."

Goldcrest: "I'm all ears. Something else I don't know?"

Eleanor: sounding resigned, "Alright, I'll tell you. You may as well know. Your partners gave the lady a hard time."

Goldcrest: after a long pause, "The Pierre woman who was working for me?"

Eleanor: "Your partners, the brotherhood, have had your phones bugged for years. Looking for any way to get back at you for all the shit you've shoved their way. When you chased out of the house that day, afraid the police had you marked out for the killings, they knew, your partners. Hey, we all knew you'd hired a private dic to hold your hand. I suggested they organise a little welcome for her. Big boy, called Bear. Frighten her off, and let you convict yourself in the eyes of the police. Like I said, you ran off. Bad move. The innocent stay put. We just didn't reckon on her being so bloody persisitent."

Goldcrest: sounding incredulous, "Christ almighty."

Eleanor: "He won't help you. Partners got a taste for it from the start. Sent her some menacing emails telling her to butt-out. Had her followed a couple of times too, around her work and home. A smart blue hired Lexus. She couldn't fail to notice it. Annoyed she wouldn't let go, they decided to give the lady a proper second dose. Keep worrying her with any threats they could think up. Wear her out. Told her she was an expendable Falasha."

Goldcrest: sounding clearly puzzled, "What's that supposed to mean? Falasha?"

Eleanor: "A black Jew."

Goldcrest: his voice hoarse with rage, "Bitch!"

Eleanor: "It was lovely. Such fun. They organised a chase when she brought in some Israeli mediator. My idea again. Hee hee. Just wanted to demoralise her generally. Leave her exhausted. Get her to drop everything for a time, particularly your case. But after all that, you were the one who dropped her. What a laugh. And she still wouldn't let up. I'll say one thing for her, she's got balls. Say, is she actually a woman? Or a bloke in disguise?"

Goldcrest: "And you want to be a mother? You could teach Lucifer a thing or two. Killing my kids without a second thought."

Tammy, turning to Meg, felt as though her skin was laced with ice. Shaking her head imperceptibly, she felt Meg's hand gentle on her arm, and she nodded in acknowledgement. It was at that moment, Tammy realised all was lost, as she bent forward in a paroxysm of agony, jagged splinters of glass tearing at her insides in a spasm of endometriosis.

"Merde alors," she intoned quietly. No way could she disguise her pain, and she waited now for the recording to be interrupted. Goldcrest, not immediately realising what was occurring let the playing continue, barely registering what Tammy was going through.

But the lawyer had seen what was happening, and barked, "Enough!"

Tammy gripping her stomach with both hands, muttered, "No! I'll be fine. Really." But she realised it was all over. Not enough there to charge, let alone convict anyone. "Let it play," she urged, her voice barely audible. "Don't call a halt on my account. We need to hear this out."

Ignoring Tammy, Goldcrest's lawyer, now insistent, exclaimed, "I said, enough! This woman is clearly in pain." And in smug tones, "Problem there? Time of the month is it Ms Pierre?"

Then, turning to his client, "Look Eric, we can resume another time, if you still feel you must. Which, if I have anything to do with it, you won't. Right now, I'm calling a halt to this circus. Nothing we've heard here this afternoon involves or implicates my client in any crime. We're going." Getting to his feet, Velacroft looked at Goldcrest.

"Come Eric," he said assertively, "time to leave." Reaching forward, Velacroft touched the icon on the mobile phone, stopping the playback.

Looking slightly dazed, Eric got to his feet. He cast about him as though unsure which way to go, until his lawyer took hold of his arm and started to lead him to the door, Eric's phone in his hand.

For a moment, Tammy held her head in her palms. Admitted to herself, I've blown it. How stupid is that? Had him. Now he's adrift and we won't get him back.

Idly handling the amulet at her neck, its Hebrew inscription under her fingertips, she tried to imagine what her father would advise. It wasn't too difficult. When all is lost, he would counsel, say something, anything. You've nothing to lose.

Ignoring the pain and getting slowly to her feet, one hand on the table for support, Tammy addressed the man, "Mr Goldcrest," she said, "you came here today looking for closure. If you leave now, you may never achieve what you were seeking. Is that really what you want? Is that how it all ends for you? Because if it is, no-one is going to prevent you from leaving."

She let the words sink in, then, pointing at the door, she added softly, "Your choice."

Several moments passed, and then Velacroft said, "We're going. Come on Eric."

But Goldcrest didn't move. He just stood in deep contemplation. Then he said to his lawyer, "She's right."

"No, Eric. She's not. It doesn't have to be this way. Let's just get out of here."

"No, Steven. I'm going to finish this thing, once and for all. That's what I came here to do." Taking the phone from his lawyer's hand, he resumed his seat and turned on the recording once again.

Velacroft, visibly reddening, looked as though he might spontaneously combust with frustration and rage as Goldcrest sat back with his arms folded, his eyes closed.

Eleanor: "See, it wasn't them I was killing, it was you, you pathetic apology for a man: you and them. What you might call, cathartic."

Goldcrest: his voice getting louder to the point of hysteria, "Cathartic was it? That's a big word for you, Eleanor. You're not just bipolar, you're a fucking psychopath."

Eleanor: "Psychopath, am I? That's a big word for you, Eric." Eleanor can be heard laughing to herself.

Then, sounding sly, "Tell me, have you recently lost something, Eric?"

Goldcrest: guardedly, "Like what?"

Eleanor: "Like a gold pendant with the initials 'EG' on it?"

Goldcrest: "What! What do you know about a gold pendant?"

Eleanor: "I believe one was found on the beach."

Goldcrest: pondering aloud, "There was a leak from the police station here. Billy's DNA was found on a gold pendant. I thought…I thought…"

Eleanor: "Ah yes, the famous pendant. Lovely gold thing. Nice and heavy. Eighteen carat. How come I've never seen you wearing it? But of course, you and your queer friend. Wouldn't do if I'd known about him, would it? Thing is, I wasn't born yesterday. I know that whimpering tone when I hear it. Henry, wasn't it? On the telephone that time? Your dearly beloved."

Goldcrest: pensively, "I mislaid it a while back." The truth dawns. "You must have taken it. It was found near the spot. But how the hell did you…?"

Eleanor: "I gave Billy Anderson a bit of pocket money. Told him where and when to drop it. Your pendant, your initials. Possibly your DNA. Someone was going to be implicated. You? Maybe. Police might have hauled you in. On the other hand, Billy's thumbprint on it. Fingers too."

Eleanor can be heard in fits of giggles. "He was so trusting. Dearest Billy. That temper of yours, Eric. Always knew it would get you into real trouble one day. Pity you had to go and kill the boy. All for nothing."

Goldcrest: "You did what? Pocket money? You piece of shit. My God! What have I done…? What have you made me do? You fucking freak."

There was a break in the recording at that moment. Then a noise like Eric screaming and frantic activity in the room, furniture being overturned, before the obvious sounds of a person slowly choking, choking, choking to death. Then there's nothing but silence.

Goldcrest reached forward and turned off the mobile. No-one in the room made any move to speak. Echoes of the voices on the recording clouded the air.

Then Goldcrest spoke, his voice gravelly, "You see, I told you, I couldn't have killed them. Remember? They were my children. Not hers." His hands were shaking, tears coursing down his cheeks.

"That bitch," he muttered. "And I was so sure it was Billy. It had to be him. I mean, he had that conviction in the papers for molesting a little girl. And then there was the DNA evidence. There was no-one else there? Who else could there have been?"

Goldcrest got up and started restlessly pacing the room, running his fingers wildly through his hair. He was like a caged animal looking for a way out.

Goldcrest's lawyer looked bewildered. "Eric," he said, and made as if to get up to try and salvage something for his client. "For God's sake stop, man. This can still be dealt with."

Ignoring his lawyer, Goldcrest raved, "What have I done? It was her, that maniac, not me. She planted the evidence. It was her made me do it." He slumped back in his seat, his head in his hands. "That poor kid. Billy. My God, Billy."

"Eleanor's body was found at the foot of the Ware Cliffs. Eric?" Tammy probed as gently as she could.

"What?" Goldcrest looked dazed.

"Eleanor's body?" she repeated.

"I drove her there at night. 2.00 am. No-one was around. Threw her from the top. Heard her crunch on the shingle. It wasn't enough. I went down there, picked up the largest boulder I could find and smashed her fucking skull to a pulp. Cathartic, she said. Killing my babies. Well, it wasn't cathartic for me, killing her. It's not enough. It'll never be enough." He was sobbing now, uncontrollably.

A moment later, DCI Downey strode in purposefully. At last they had a result. The open ends, the question of the DNA leak, would have to be dealt with at a later date.

But for now, he said, "Arrest him, DI Copeland. Read him his rights, then charge him with the murders of Eleanor Goldcrest and William Anderson."

CHAPTER 40 DAY 20

"I'M DROPPING, DOV. Totally shattered. We've got our arrest, but it feels as though nothing has actually been achieved."

Tammy was seated on the edge of the bed in the Sidmouth hotel. She'd slipped off her shoes, but was still in her working suit.

Dov, in his usual denim and trainers, was slouched in an armchair, a whisky from the minibar in his hand. "Tammy, we have got to talk. I need to know where I stand. You're not being fair on me."

"Please, Dov. Can it wait until the morning? If I don't sleep, I think I'm going to black out."

He threw back the drink in a single gulp, savouring the taste at the back of his throat. "Okay. But I'm booked on a flight to Dubai from Heathrow tomorrow afternoon. I'll have to leave here early. We'll talk in the morning." He was shaking his head as though already anticipating a disappointing outcome.

She should have called Ginny. Still, Ginny would know where she was, and, whatever, she wouldn't let her down again. It was Saturday tomorrow; Ginny would be home when she got back. She'd have an opportunity to make things right.

* * * * *

For all she told herself, it was impossible to sleep, and in the morning she was almost as tired as she'd been the previous evening.

The day was bright and the forecast said, mild. There was a smattering of other guests in the breakfast room when they went down. As usual, Dov piled his plate with food: bacon, sausages, fried eggs, hash browns, mushrooms, tomatoes. Tammy couldn't help smiling as she helped herself to an orange juice and a black coffee.

Halfway through his meal, Dov put down his knife and fork. "What's it to be, Tammy? I have to know. I've told you about... You know all about her. She wants me to marry her. It's not fair on her and it's not fair on me, or Ginny either, come to think of it. We're all waiting for you to make up your mind."

He looked like a defenceless little boy, this man she'd known as a friend and lover these past years. She was carrying his child. A child he so desperately wanted.

She bowed her head. She couldn't tell him. At least not yet. She clasped her hands in her lap. 'What's it to be?' he'd said. It sounded so simple and harmless. A life's choice in four words. As easy as offering her a second cup of coffee. Warm tears ran down her cheeks. "Oh, Dov," she said. "What can I say?"

"You don't need to say anything, Tammy." He gently pushed his chair back and got to his feet. "I'm all packed, so I'll leave ahead of you." As he walked past her, he put a hand on Tammy's shoulder and squeezed it affectionately. "Goodbye, my love. Always and ever. Shalom."

One or two of the tables nearest to her had seen or heard the exchange and tried to look away discreetly. Not wanting to attract any more attention than she had, she sat for several minutes drinking her coffee, brushing away her tears with the heels of her hands. Less conspicuous than a handkerchief.

* * * * *

It was around 3.00 pm when the taxi dropped Tammy outside the flat in Queen's Park. She stood looking at the front door for a couple of moments, realising she was feeling a bit apprehensive.

Then, remembering she'd finally made her choice, she was awash with relief. Entering the modern block, she fished out her apartment keys, and experienced an overwhelming joy. It was Ginny. It was always going to be Ginny. She was so glad. There'd be an intimate dinner out this evening. Somewhere special. She'd get a booking at Zafferano in Belgravia. Michelin-starred Italian food.

For once the place looked tidy. Odd in itself, perhaps? There was none of the usual detritus of newspapers, clothes, or empty perfume bottles littering the place. For the most part, Ginny's housekeeping ran at odds with her office paperwork. The latter being immaculate, the former, chaotic. It was one of the few bones of contention between them. But then if Tammy ran an immaculate home, her paperwork was the bane of Ginny's life. Without Ginny to tidy up her desk in her absence, none of Tammy's paperwork would ever see the light of day.

But this was nice. Ginny had clearly made an effort. Why though, she wondered? Today of all days? She had a fleeting premonition, which disappeared as swiftly as it had crossed her mind. She was just intensely happy.

"I'm ho-ome," sang Tammy.

Then, "Ginny Gins? Where are you?"

The apartment echoed to Tammy's chant, but produced no response from Ginny. She was obviously out, and must have been for a while since Tammy's attempts to get through by phone on the train home had met with the unobtainable tone on Ginny's mobile. She tried to think where Ginny might have been for the past few hours where there was no mobile signal, but came up with a blank.

She'd checked the two bedrooms and the living room, before going into the kitchen and seeing it propped up by the Miele food mixer on the breakfast bar. It was a simple cream envelope, which Tammy tore open and read the note inside with increasing dismay.

My dearest, darling Tammy,

I hardly know how or where to begin. You've been a part of my world for so long. The past five years have been the most exciting of my life, and I don't regret a single moment of any of it. Given the chance and the choice, I'd do it all again.

But you must surely realise that we could not go on as we were. I see all the signs of your drug-taking and I know full well you're leading a double life. You're obviously expecting a child, although you've told me nothing about any affair, nor whether the father is a casual relationship or a prospective husband.

You spend nights away without telling me where you are or with whom. This is not what I want, darling, nor what I'd hoped, or planned for us both.

I know you've always wanted a family, but surely we could have worked something out.

You probably see me as inexperienced and immature, but I'm not a fool. It saddens me to think that I have in many respects been taken for granted.

I love you, darling Tammy. There will always be a special place in my heart for you. But you must know that anyway.

I hope your baby brings you much joy. But please think of the pregnancy now and give the child a chance. You must stop taking the drugs and cut out the smoking.

Best if you don't try to contact me. I'm going away for a while to get myself together again. I couldn't bear to hear your voice and then have to go through all this again.

Goodbye, my love. Goodbye.

Gins x

Ps. I've arranged a temp for Monday. The agency say Mrs Gilchrist is reliable. All new work is emailed to you and in a printout on your desk, which I've tidied. (Try not to lose it?) There's work enough promised right now to more than cover the rents at Bruton Street. Two diplomatic security jobs are requested. And there's been another of those warning emails that start, Read This Now. Do take care, my darling. Are those jobs worth the risks you take?

Tammy held the letter in her hands, hardly believing what she'd read, feeling as though she were gradually choking. Ginny gone? Truly? Five years of fun and laughter just a disappearing mirage? Impossible.

She blinked several times, and glanced at the letter again, as if to confirm what didn't need confirming. She was entirely on her own now.

Memories began crowding her like rising flood waters. Their chance meeting at Paddington Station. Meals shared. Holidays enjoyed. Dancing together, jogging in Queen's Park before sharing a delicious shower, poring over which TV shows to watch when time allowed. Umpteen episodes of *Game of Thrones* and *The Sopranos*. Peter Sellars comedies which had them giggling hysterically. Classic dramas, like *Casablanca* and *Brief Encounter*. The recollections kept bouncing around inside her head like a swarm of bees.

This place was their home. The colours and furnishings she'd chosen with such care, all with her beloved in mind. Ginny loved this flat. Now it was just a blur as Tammy frantically cast around searching for that which she'd squandered.

Tears pricked the back of her eyes and the wound at the side of her skull began to throb. Running her fingertips along the ridge of the scar, she sensed the tiny knots of flesh where the stitches had melted. It had been a close call, the fight. The pulsing in her head brought it all back vividly. Out there in the street in Lyme Regis in the cold dead of that night. She could have died. At this moment, it was as though a fist had been jammed down her throat. She was dying, right now. At least, that's how it felt.

A heavy vehicle rumbled past, sounding its horn, a dog barked in response. Overhead, a plane heading in to Heathrow roared. Then the place lapsed into black silence.

Again she told herself, it just couldn't be. The note was a mistake, a warning. Any second and Ginny would emerge. She must. She must.

Tammy continued to stand motionless in the centre of the living room, her hands on her hips, head to one side and listened, for anything. The slightest sound or hint of movement.

The apartment had a resonating hollowness about it. She'd run around the place going through cupboards and wardrobes. Everything was gone. Empty, empty, empty. All signs and trace of Ginny, vanished. Nothing left but a hint of her soft perfume, Rosabotanica by Balenciaga.

Tammy was shivering with cold now, her heart being gently shredded by jagged spears of cold as an inexpressible sadness crept over her. "Talk to me Ginny," she murmured. "Please, Ginny Gins."

She closed her eyes and breathed in deeply. She was a big girl. She'd had setbacks before. Everyone did. She'd survive. Of course, she would.

But it was going to be hard. Everywhere, she saw her lover. Ginny in red, looking like a pixie in those silly Paddington Bear slippers. Ginny pushing her owl spectacles up her tiny nose.

I mustn't cry, she thought, impatiently brushing a tear from her cheek with the back of her hand. "But, darling Ginny," she said out loud, "where are you right now, my own love? Will you come back to me soon?"

Tammy went and stood by the window looking out on to the street as though Ginny might suddenly materialise. Then casting her eyes up and down the road, she said, so very softly, "Will you come back ever?"

And then, finally accepting what could not be changed, she acknowledged, "I have to be strong. For myself. For my baby."

She thought about the man she'd just walked away from. Whom she might never see again. The father of her child. Would she ever tell him? Would she ever be able to tell him? Dear Dov. Big, masculine, kind. Her gentle Dov with whom she shared a love of Dickens. Joe Gargery, the simple blacksmith in Great Expectations, had told his beloved friend, 'Pip, dear old chap, life is made of ever so many partings welded together.'

There it was then, Ginny and Dov. Lost to her. Loneliness gripped Tammy like octopus tentacles.

On the occasional table, by the armchair, something had been left lying. She hadn't noticed it till now. It was a CD. Turning it over in her hands, she realised Ginny had left it behind for her. She slotted it into the portable CD player and listened again to Laura Pergolizzi singing, *Lost on You*, as she had the evening she'd come in to find Ginny dancing, and she'd joined in, laughing. Ginny with her vivacity and her all-embracing love.

Picking up her mobile, she dialed a number, and quickly got a response.

"Daddy?" she whispered. "Papa?"

"How you doin', dahlin'?"

"I'm fine, Papa. Just fine. A little setback today, but I'll be okay."

Then softly, smiling through the streaming tears, "Just have to get on with things. Can't sit around moping. Got a business to run."

A deep reassuring voice, "My own little girl. I know. Daddy always knows. I'll be waiting. Iced vodka in a chilled glass. Don't be long. We'll have a laugh together."

"Yes, Papa, we'll have a laugh, won't we."

EPILOGUE

ERIC GOLDCREST PLEADED GUILTY to the murders of his wife, Eleanor Goldcrest, and the autistic young man, William 'Billy' Anderson.

He was sentenced to two life terms to run concurrently, with a recommendation he serve not less than twenty-three years. Currently incarcerated in Her Majesty's Prison Wakefield in West Yorkshire, named the "Monster Mansion" because of the number of high-risk murderers and sex offenders there, he presently runs a book on who will get early parole.

DCI Downey was severely reprimanded by his superiors for his handling of the affair involving Billy Anderson. As senior investigating Officer, his performance left a great deal to be desired. Attempts are still being made to find the source of the leaked information regarding the DNA results thought to have indirectly led to Anderson's murder.

No-one else is being sought in the matter of the investigation into the deaths of the Goldcrest children, and the file is now closed.

* * * * *

Billy Anderson was buried in the graveyard of the local Anglican church. It was a cold, bleak autumn day. Brooding clouds threatened rain, of which a few spots had announced early notice.

Only three people attended, wrapped up against the weather. Apart from the vicar, they were Billy's mother, clutching a frayed and battered Eeyore to her chest with one hand and a handkerchief to her eyes with the other, together with Tammy, and Meg Copeland. A thin mist swirled about their legs.

The service was brief and sombre. The vicar, a man in his sixties, was tall and round-shouldered, his cheeks, ruddy from the wind, stark against his flowing white hair. "We therefore commit his body to the ground. Ashes to ashes, dust to dust."

As the coffin was lowered into the grave, Mavis, holding out the soft toy like an offering, looked at the vicar timidly, who nodded his assent and Mavis threw it into the grave. "He'd want it with him," she whispered. "My Billy."

"Of course, he would," said Tammy, her arm around Mavis's shoulder.

From the corner of her eye Tammy noticed a slight movement, then spotted a small and desolate figure, hunched inside too large an overcoat, partially obscured by a beech tree some twenty yards away. But DCI Downey had disappeared before the others broke up to leave.

* * * * *

Samuel Goldblatt closed the business of London International Investments Corporation. He is enjoying his retirement seeing much of his grandchildren and playing golf.

George Derby returned to the States with his family. He is presently employed by Goldman Sachs International Bank in New York.

Nigel Cudlipp is involved in London with a UK company dealing in foreign exchange. He spends most of his time speculating on the currency markets with his own money.

Leopold Kristof has disappeared. At Tammy's behest, her old boss Detective Chief Superintendent Bob Walker made enquiries of an FBI contact and found that Kristof is presently wanted in more than one State for questioning in connection with several cases of child assault and at least one case of murder.

Leonard Kristof has cleaned himself up. He still lives at the run-down home off the Woodberry Road. The local kids have got bored with his lack of response to their goading and leave him alone. His supervising officer remains on hand to help with things like the weekly food shop, so Leonard doesn't have to brave the stares of the locals who still regard him with caution.

A top London criminal lawyer, recommended by Tammy, has taken up the case of the possibly misinterpreted DNA results leading to his original conviction. There may be claims for compensation in due course. The case is high profile and the lawyer, hoping to raise his own standing still further, is working pro bono.

Meg's marriage chunters on. Whatever his shortcomings, she is fond of her husband, and he's gained some of his wife's respect for the way he dealt with their daughter's bullying issues. The girl, Jessica, is re-schooled, growing in confidence and doing well academically.

* * * * *

Dov lives and works in Dubai. He shares a flat with his girlfriend, Esther. His work is lucrative and satisfying. Esther is pressing Dov to marry her, but he is delaying. He longs to be with Tammy.

Ginny has gone back to Wales and is living with her parents for the time being. She has found employment with a small firm of chartered accountants and is planning to study for her professional exams. She misses Tammy and thinks of her all the time. She knows there is no going back.

Tammy lives alone.

She spends more time with her adored father whose Parkinson's disease continues to advance slowly and relentlessly. Against all odds, she is pregnant with Dov's baby and has at last relinquished the smoking, the drinking and the drugs. Nothing is going to harm her child.

Given the chance, she would have done nothing any differently. She loves Dov, but Ginny was always the one for her.

END

DISCUSSION GUIDE

WHETHER YOU'RE LEADING the discussion in your monthly book club, chatting with a friend over coffee or drinks, or musing to yourself about the story you've just finished, you may find some of the questions other readers have asked since *The Lyme Regis Murders* was originally published in 2021 helpful.

We've also left space after each one, so you can jot any thoughts or additional questions of your own, or from your group to keep the conversation going.

Please visit the author's website, or connect with him on social media, if you'd like to get a direct response. Or invite him to speak at an event or attend a book club meeting (most often virtually, unless you're in the London area or happen to catch him travelling to your vicinity).

www.AuthorAndrewSegal.com

https://www.instagram.com/authorandrewsegal/

https://www.facebook.com/authorandrewsegal/

https://www.linkedin.com/in/randrewsegal/

What did you make of the little poem that preceded the Prologue? Who do you think "R.A." is? How does the poet relate to the story?

What of the scene set in the Prologue? Did your initial image of the location and the four individuals match what you learned about them later? What were your impressions of the actions and thoughts of "the fourth" after the murders?

What were your reactions when the police met with the victims' mother? Did you find clues in Eleanor Goldcrest's statements or behavior?

What was your initial reaction to Eric Goldcrest when he called Tammy for help? Did your impression of him change as you learned more about him and his business partners?

What did you think about Tammy's behaviors toward Ginny? Toward Dov? Did you form ideas about how you'd advise her, it you were there as a friend or counsellor?

What did you think of the comparison between DI Copeland's daughter dealing with a bully and Tammy's bullying experience as a child? Did the input, or lack thereof, from a parent or school officials make a difference to how these events would shape the girls as adults?

What do you think of the author's style of "jump cuts" from one chapter to the next? For example, from Chapter 6, ending with Tammy receiving an unexpected call from Eleanor Goldcrest, to Chapter 7, where we find Dov reminiscing over his early encounters with Tammy in Israel, then to Chapter 8, opening with Ginny "moping around the flat" and eventually hooking up for a fling with a man, then to Chapter 9, where we get back to Tammy meeting up with Eleanor in response to that call in Chapter 6.

Can you think of other examples of such transitions that you found interesting or jarring? How so?

Which characters made it onto your list of suspects? Did your number one suspect change as new characters emerged?

Were you surprised when the killers of the various victims were revealed? By the outcomes with Tammy's relationships? What surpised you most?

Do you prefer mystery's where the villain is revealed early and you watch as the hero try's to figure it out, or where you are trying to figure it out along with the hero? How did this book fit with your preference?

If this is the first Tammy Pierre book you've read, were you surprised at the way she is introduced in the intial fight scene? Were you satisfied with the pace that her physical and behavioral characteristics are revealed in this story?

If you've read other(s) in the series before, what does this first book in the series add to or change about your impressions of Tammy?

If you could spend some time with the author, what would you like to ask him?

Reminder: Connect with him via —

www.AuthorAndrewSegal.com

https://www.instagram.com/authorandrewsegal/

https://www.facebook.com/authorandrewsegal/

https://www.linkedin.com/in/randrewsegal/

ABOUT THE AUTHOR

IN HIS "DAY JOB" PROFESSIONAL CAREER, handling bankrutpcy and corporate liquidation matters in London's business environment, Andrew Segal gained extensive experience with people and organizations pushed to the limits, including financial ruin and threats of violence.

In his personal life, he learned much about Caribbean culture from his ex-wife's mixed heritage.

He brings that knowledge to bear in creating his main character in this series, private detective Tammy Pierre. She's an ex-police detective, and before that, a "multi-lingual English, Spanish and French-speaking, Politics, Philosophy, and Economics, Oxford graduate with a postgrad MBA, and more than just a smattering of Hebrew."

Tammy's work now includes both criminal and forensic accounting cases. Skills and experience from both realms, combined with her imposing physical attributes and specialized martial arts training, helped her unravel devious schemes and deal with dangerous villains in *The Lyme Regis Murders.*

Now turn the page for a preview from the second book in the Tammy Pierre thriller series:

The Black Candle Killings

Come black candles, light the byre,
Illuminate the place with fire.
There's no joy here, a Christmas birth,
Just death for lives sans moral worth.

– R.A.

PROLOGUE

Yuh gonna die!

"Hmm? Watch you say, lady? Hear me now, hear me. Don't y'all cry. You muss up yuh face. Me ain't gonna hurt you none. Gonna be quick an' easy. All be over soon, soon. You understan'? De Lord, he am waitin' for yuh."

LILLIAN PERSAUD HADN'T HAD SEX with Tom for over a month.

As she made for the office at a brisk trot, she smiled to herself. Gorgeous fresh morning. Gentle breeze. A few spots of rain tapping at her brolly. Some wispy grey cloud. Might warm up later, though. Bound to really, she thought with her usual optimism.

Out of the corner of her eye she spotted something moving. A shadow; perhaps her own? Couldn't place it. Coming from behind a parked car? A moment of unease, but not one to break the glorious mood she was in.

The day ahead, filled with appointments, staff meetings and then, this weather forecast had said it would be a mixed day, so at least there'd be some sun to look forward to.

Business was getting busier by the week in her expanding company, Persaud IT Ltd. A hectic day ahead of her. Evening to think about.

Plans for sex, she mused. Lots of it. Asap. On the agenda. And about time too.

She smiled again at the prospect. Some soft music; modern jazz. The contemplative tones of Miles Davis's trumpet. Chic Corea on piano. Tom's favourite record, Peggy Lee singing, *Some Cats Know*', and she added mentally the following refrain, "How to go real slow." Tom knew how to go real slow. Lovely man.

What a wedding night they'd had. Not a real wedding, but an exchanging of vows and commitment before an Unofficial Officiant in a Humanist service. They both had their own reasons for preferring to avoid a religious ceremony. A couple of dozen close family and friends in a tiny hotel off the beaten track, near to Bourton-on-the-Water, in the Cotswolds.

Of course, it wasn't the first time they'd made love, but Tom made it feel that way. It was as if he'd saved something special for just that evening. Up till then, every night with him had been special. But, wow! she thought. Was that night extra special, or was it not?

Not too many nights like it since the baby. Gracie was a demanding tot, and now an even more demanding little girl. Still, she thought, their imp seemed to have got over her recent bout of sleeplessness.

Someone on the other side of the street, emerging from behind a tree this time, looking at her. Looking at her? A phantom silhouette. Following her. Dark tracksuit and trainers. Hoodie obscuring the face. Soundless steps. Were they smiling? She couldn't see.

Lillian frowned for a moment. No-one else around. Early morning. A few parked vehicles. An unexpected feeling of loneliness. Maybe they were scowling? She hurried on, getting nervous now, her heels clicking on the pavement, echoing in her ears.

Like being on the ghost train in a fairground. Never sure what was going to jump out at you. Nothing was going to attack her out here in the street. This was Bloomsbury where bad things didn't happen. She'd soon be at the office. Door locked behind her. Safe. Then, hot coffee. The world waking up. Staff arriving shortly.

Tom said she was a worrier. "Darling," he'd told her one day, "if you didn't have something to worry about, it'd almost certainly worry you." He was right of course. But worriers get things done, she'd protested. And, looking around, she found her imagined stalker had vanished. A heaved sigh of relief.

Baby Grace had been fractious and her sleepless nights had impacted Lillian and Tom. But there'd been six undisturbed nights when the parents had caught up with some desperately needed shut-eye, and now Lillian was beaming to herself as she mentally planned the evening in.

* * * * *

"Look! Look! See? It say in here in de Bible, Deuteronomy 23, verse 2, dat no-one born of a forbidden union may enter de kingdom of de Lord. Even to de ten generation, none of his descendants may enter de assembly of de Lord. Yuh gonna have to pay, lady."

* * * * *

Tom loved cooking, but he also liked to eat out. He'd probably booked somewhere for them already. It was their anniversary, that of the first time they'd met.

But tonight was going to be all Lillian's treat. And for a change there'd be no meat. Tom could eat lamb and beef for England, but he'd been told by his doctor to cut down as his cholesterol levels were too high. So tonight, would be fish. Cod, baked in fish stock, with chopped onions and tomato, and a handful of black olives to finish it off. Steamed new potatoes in their skins, dripping in butter, well, maybe not exactly dripping. A mixed salad, with her own dressing. A bottle of Pino Grigio. And for dessert, a blueberry pavlova coupled with vanilla ice cream by Marshfield Farm, an English make on a par with the best of Italian. Divine thoughts.

Tom hadn't seen the white thong yet. The one with the split crotch. The matching, barely there, white bra. The contrast with her ebony complexion would be stark. Heavens! she thought, I'll be stark, or as good as. She'd kept them for an occasion like she was going to make tonight's. Her legs went slightly wobbly at the thought. However would she make it through the day? she wondered.

The first thing she noticed upon opening up the office was that the alarm hadn't been set the night before. She frowned. Must have a word with the cleaners later today. But, just the same, she thought, worrying.

They'd kept all the original features of the beautiful Georgian building's interior, whilst managing to lay out desks with smart glass dividers to allow, if not privacy, at least the chance to concentrate on work without the immediate intrusion of others in the room overwhelming you.

There was a separate boardroom for client meetings, and it was to this she presently repaired. She needed to spread out paperwork in a manner more convenient than might be obtained, no matter how many screens she chose to work with. For all her IT skills, sometimes it was the old tried and tested routines that worked best.

Lillian was happy. Happier than she'd ever been in her life. After a ghastly childhood, from which she'd made a timely escape, things were coming together more satisfyingly than she had ever dared to hope.

* * * * *

"Dey all jagabat womans tink dey can fool me. Dey run away from me, but me have catch yuh. Me have seen you, lady, flahntin' y'all an' yer babby. Lady, de chile am barn of a forbidden union. Who you tink you is? Me ain't no dotish man. No mamaguy. Me am gonna bring y'all back to God."

*****

And yet, that shadow again, from the corner of her eye. And, here? In the office? Her mind playing tricks? Had to be. But why, all of a sudden? She wasn't normally given to random fears. She'd be seeing ghosts next. Shaking her head resolutely, she told herself not to be stupid.

Then the light pad of a muffled tread, a sharp pinprick in the back of her neck, the warmth of a thin stream of blood, her blood, running down her spine and a cultured voice warning her not to look round.

She felt as though she were being crushed with fear. She couldn't breathe properly. Her blood was freezing in her veins, as she shuddered, uncontrollably. She could see the papers spread around the boardroom table, but made no connection with them. It was as though she were marooned in a foreign country, where she could neither understand nor make herself understood.

She knew she mustn't panic, mustn't scream, because the shadow would want her to scream, would need her to scream in order to exercise power over her. She closed her eyes and breathed in deeply to try to calm her nerves. The voice was educated, could be spoken to. She might use reason. This was clearly a case of mistaken identity which she could quickly establish.

Then the voice changed. The tone dropped by a couple of octaves and to her consternation, the accent was now clearly patois.

Lillian heard a match flare, smelled burning tallow as smoke played around her head. She tried to think who it could possibly be. Racked her brains, uselessly. Didn't know who it was. No idea in the world. But they clearly knew all about her.

* * * * *

"De candle am burnin' dong. It have you name on de side, Lillian.

"When it reach de bottom yuh gonna die.

"Hmm? Ah! Now you screamin', Lillian? Dat's good. Show y'all repentin'. Keep screamin' now, Lillian, keep screamin'. Ain't no-one to hear you.

"Praise de Lord."

CHAPTER 1 DAY 1

THE DAY WAS OVERCAST and chill, heavy clouds scudding impatiently across a pewter sky as spots of rain started spattering the windows.

6.00 am and the central heating had just clicked on; the flat wouldn't be warm for at least another half hour. A sprinkling of goose bumps showed on her naked arms and legs, and she shivered with cold, the black shorty nightie quite inadequate to the task of covering, let alone warming, her six-feet frame.

She heard rather than felt the plop and splash of blood as it hit the marble-tiled floor of the bathroom. Then she felt it too. A wetness between the thighs, a drawing pain in her belly and a heaviness from the waist down that made her limbs feel like buckling. The blood smelled metallic, and as she watched, transfixed, more of it ran down the insides of her legs spreading in a pool at her feet.

"Merde!" she whispered softly. "Merde! Merde! Merde!" Propping her head against her fingertips, she watched helplessly as the life she was carrying, the life she'd so longed for, slipped away from her.

"I'm losing this baby," she whispered under her breath. "My baby. Dov's baby."

Then she thought of her father, with skin the texture of jet, the tall and distinguished, Matthew Pierre. This retired architect, originally from the island of Trinidad, now living close by in Queen's Park, was suffering from the advanced stages of Parkinson's Disease.

A normally taciturn man, Matthew had not been able to stop talking about the prospect of his grandfathering the child of his only daughter, Tamsin, when he'd been convinced that, at thirty-seven, she'd left it too late and it would never happen. So sad, he'd said, that Tamsin's mother, her maman, the irrepressible daughter of a French Jewish banking family who'd died of breast cancer ten years earlier, could not be alive to see her own daughter become a mother.

Her ribs still ached dully from the kicking she'd received in an assault some months previously by a man, apparently, called Bear. And the side of her head still throbbed whenever she was stressed, as she was now, from the blade that had all but ripped open the edge of her skull during the attack.

The tight curls had grown back where the hospital had shaved her to administer the railway track of black sutures, and she'd let her hair grow longer than the usual short cap of frizz she sported, to further mask the scarring. Andy, her hairdresser at Curligig in Westbourne Grove, had worked wonders, and some of her old confidence was returning.

It was now, more than ever, she felt the loss of her long-term partner. She ached when she thought about little Ginny and how she'd gone without warning, leaving only a farewell note and a CD of music they both loved. Ginny had guessed about her sometime Israeli lover and martial arts coach Dov, as Tammy'd started to show. And that, together with the cocaine habit she'd frequently warned Tammy about, had decided her to end the relationship.

Lifting the lid of the toilet, Tammy sat down on the seat, leaning forward, her head in her hands, and waited while the last of the blood carrying the baby she'd yearned for so fiercely escaped from her body like sand flooding through an hour glass. Then she stood over the toilet bowl and flushed it several times until the last traces of crimson and the promise it held were gone.

She tried to cry. She wanted to cry. Her temples ached and her throat felt tight, but no tears came. It was as though the baby had abandoned her. She was inadequate to the task of bearing a child. Lacking as a woman, and with no-one in her life to turn to for comfort. Heaven knows how she'd break the news to her father. Papa would be devastated. It would have to wait till later. Or maybe tomorrow.

She stood under the shower for fully fifteen minutes as though she could simply wash away the memory and thoughts of what might have been.

There was still some seeping residue of blood, so she used some of the standby sanitary wear she kept in the event a heavy period made the usual tampons insufficient in any given month. Then she wandered into the kitchen in her dressing gown and prepared a pot of strong coffee before forcing herself to consider the day ahead.

Life goes on, she thought sadly, with a feeling of the irony of it all.

Of course, she knew it was her own fault. Her GP, Doctor Aziz, had told her specifically not to engage in any undue physical effort. Her high testosterone levels meant it was mere chance she'd conceived at all, still less likely she would again if this pregnancy didn't go full term. But she'd obstinately ignored him, continuing to work out in the local Queen's Park gym, and at home whenever the time allowed.

Then there'd been that scuffle, a couple of days ago, when a visiting client from the States to whom she was giving close personal protection, had been approached, unannounced in a side street at the back of the Grosvenor Hotel, Park Lane where she was staying, by a member of the press, and jostled.

The reporter was an overweight individual, with a ruddy face and bulbous drinker's nose. The man had stuck a mobile phone microphone under the nose of the thoroughly alarmed client, a young, newly famous pop singer, dressed in a black mini skirt and black patent leather thigh-length boots, and demanded an interview. Tammy, discreetly turned out in a charcoal grey two-piece trouser suit, turned to the man and softly told him to get lost.

"Come on love," pleaded the reporter, clearly the worse for drink and, ignoring Tammy, addressed the young girl, "Giss a story darlin'. Is it true you're after Prince 'Arry? If you was yer too late now darlin'."

Then, apparently noticing Tammy for the first time as she loomed over him, "And 'oo are you mister when you're at 'ome?" A pause while he examined Tammy with slow deliberation. Then, "Blimey!" he intoned, shocked, as he got closer and looked up at her, "it's a bleedin' bird. An' a good lookin' one an' all. Always did like the black ones," and so saying, he dropped the phone, where it clattered to the pavement, and made a grab for Tammy's breasts.

The young charge looked as though she was about to make a run for it. But turning to her, Tammy said, "Don't worry. This is all perfectly in hand."

Then, quietly to the reporter as she straightened her rumpled jacket and blouse, "Now you really don't want to do that, do you, sir?"

"Oh, I think I do, dearie. You black birds all like a bit of 'ows yer father, dontcha?"

"Well, sir, this black bird doesn't, most certainly not in public, and very definitely not with a drunken oaf like you. Now, why don't you try to behave like a big boy and get out of our way."

"'Oo are you callin' a big boy, you patronisin' black bitch? You come to this country—"

"Do we steal all your women, sir?"

"What? Steal all our…? But you're a bleedin'…"

A small group of Japanese tourists had begun to gather, and Tammy realised the situation needed to be brought to a speedy conclusion. Turning to look over her shoulder at her now terrified charge, Tammy whispered hastily, "Hotel. Back entrance. You move. I'll deal with this and catch you up.

"Go on, my dear."

The man staggered slightly and lurched in Tammy's direction, alcohol on his breath, a hand outstretched as he reached again for her breasts.

Acknowledging the tourists with a broad smile and a shrug that said, Whatever do we do in this sort of situation? Tammy grabbed the man by the outstretched wrist and swiftly spun him around, twisting his arm up his back. He grunted in pain, and Tammy whispered in his ear, "Let's not make this any more embarrassing than it need be. Hmm? Sir?" and holding the man fast, she hailed a passing taxi with her free hand.

As the cab pulled up, the reporter staggered again, and Tammy caught him under the arms before he could fall. Then opening the taxi door, she heaved the man in and slammed it behind him. "Take him anywhere, cabby, as long as it's away from here," she said, grabbing a twenty-pound note from a pocket and thrusting at the driver.

"Okay, darlin'. Yer on," the young driver said with a cheery grin, and the taxi sped off.

The tourists gabbling animatedly began to melt away, and Tammy, acknowledging a worrying twinge in her lower abdomen, followed by a needlepoint of insistent pain, thought about the words of Doctor Aziz. A grey cloud of uncertainty settled around her. I'll be fine, she told herself. I'll be fine.

But she wasn't. She'd pressed her luck that day and now she'd paid the price.

* * * * *

7.00 am, time for work. She sighed as her mobile rang.

"Miss Pierre, I think you should come in right away. We've had the most unpleasant email arrive." Mrs Gilchrist sounded uncharacteristically perturbed.

"Thank you, Mrs Gilchrist, I'll check it out now on my mobile and be there in about twenty-five minutes."

* * * * *

A pinprick at the back of her neck startled her into wakefulness. She was in complete darkness, her wrists bound tightly behind her back. Her hands throbbed through the lack of blood, the fingers seemingly swelling under the pressure of the bindings till it felt as though they might explode.

The smell was familiar, but she couldn't place it. The seat, probably of wood, was hard against her thighs and buttocks. She made as though to stand, then realised her legs were bound to those of the seat. She was incapable of any sort of movement.

Sweat ran down her legs, her back and into her eyes. Her throat constricted with fear as though locked in an iron garrotte and she tried to scream, then realised she couldn't. She could barely breathe because her mouth was bound in tape.

The man, if it was a man, stood over her. She could sense his gentle breath over the top of her head as he leaned down to her and spoke.

CHAPTER 2 DAY 1

NOW READ THIS

You've been taking on some lucrative contracts, work by which we might have earned considerable fees. Our man, Bear, may have overstepped the mark, but he still couldn't dissuade you from muscling in on our patch. Believe me, we've got our eyes on you wherever you are. We'll tell you when you can take on a personal security job and when you don't.

Then there are people who shouldn't be allowed in this country, scum that shouldn't be protected. If we say leave it, you leave it. You were lucky with that Israeli mediator. Don't count on being so lucky next time. That scar on your head healed up nicely? How about us adding another to that pretty butch face of yours?

SHE WAS SEATED in an armchair opposite her PA, Mrs Gilchrist, in the reception area of her tiny suite of modern offices in Bruton Street.

The business name, Pierre Search and Security, was displayed by signwriting on the glass wall outside her offices, with the legend, 'Discreet investigations, Forensic accounting, Personal security', written in smaller lettering.

Tammy said, "It's just a lot of hot air. I can't believe we're dealing with another security firm, Mrs Gilchrist, it's just too unprofessional. Absurd, even. That, and being shadowed by a Lexus SUV like my own? Ginny might have mentioned it to you." She shook her head and smoothed the skirt of her business two-piece suit. "Bully boy tactics, Mrs Gilchrist, which neither threaten nor frighten me."

"If you say so, Miss Pierre." The efficient and redoubtable Mrs Gilchrist, Mrs Florence Gilchrist, whom Tammy's beloved Ginny had found to fill in as a temp following her departure, was now firmly ensconced as a permanent fixture.

* * * * *

The Black Candle Killings

Author's Edition

(COMING IN SUMMER 2025)

Printed in Great Britain
by Amazon

63051331R10221